Eyes
of the
Predator

Glenn Trust
The Hunters Series
Book 1

Dedication

For the victims.

Table of Contents
Eyes of the Predator

FREE Book Here!

The lightning waits for us all. When it calls, we will go.

Join us at Glenn Trust Books and receive a free download of *Lightning in the Clouds*

Download your Free copy today by following this link online
https://dl.bookfunnel.com/7046vhk5f9

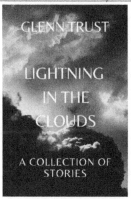

Click Here to get your Free Copy of *Lightning in the Clouds* today!

In addition to your Free copy of Lightning in the Clouds, you'll receive:

- Exclusive previews, insights and samples of New Releases

- Book Launch Giveaways and Promotions

- Advance Notice of Member Discounts and Sales

No Spam – No More than one email per Week – We never share your address... Ever.

1. Predator

The gray eyes blinked and moved in a head that remained motionless. Sweeping the area, scanning rhythmically, they were alert, intense, and searching. They were the eyes of a predator.

The only other movements were the slight turns and adjustments of the steering wheel as he guided the car through the parking lot to a space at the far edge. There was just the smallest of squeaks as the brakes brought the vehicle to a complete stop.

Not far away, an older, Japanese make car moved briskly between the rows and whipped into a space under a light pole. The eyes saw everything. People, vehicles, movement. They saw that the security camera mounted at the top of the pole would not be able to angle down enough to see her car, and that was good.

A pretty and petite brunette exited the car and began walking to the mall. She would not be picked up on the camera until she was at least five cars down the parking lot row. Anyone approaching her in that bit of space would be invisible to the watchers or the recording devices.

He watched, evaluating and assessing. She was right. Her hips swayed in a way that made his breath quicken. The familiar urge began to grow into a burning need. There was a momentary impulse to spring now, and for one instant, there was a small flicker in his fingers as his arm tensed, much like the twitch of the lion's tail when the prey is close but not quite close enough, and then the lion settles back into its stalking, crouching stillness.

A predator was in their midst and they were oblivious. It is always that way. The herd never wants to know the danger that surrounds it. It only wants to avoid it.

The car was nondescript and could have been one of any number of makes and models manufactured in the early nineties. They were all alike. Ford or Mercury. Chevrolet or Pontiac. This one was, in fact, a Chevrolet.

The vehicle was perfect for his purposes. Fading red paint on the hood and roof might have made it somewhat more distinguishable if not for the fact that virtually every other car made in the United States during the period had the same fading paint job. Manufacturers had been required to remove lead from paint formulas causing the exterior paint to fade away to the primer. It was a common sight on cars from that era. It still is on the ones that survive.

Sitting quietly in a space at the edge of a large parking lot, in a medium sized town on the outskirts of a very large city in northern Florida, the car was half a continent away from home.

The dark silhouette of the driver was barely visible behind the wheel. Completely still, he blended into the dark interior of the car. Had anyone noticed the car across the parking lot, they would have thought that the silhouette was just the high-backed headrest of the seat. Stillness was his camouflage.

But he was there and, like the car, he was nondescript and unremarkable in appearance. Of medium build, somewhat thin in the face, light brown hair neatly trimmed, no facial hair, there was nothing notable about him. Some might have found him attractive. Most would simply have found him - not ugly. Average. If he had attracted the gaze of others, they might have become aware of his uncanny stillness. But he attracted no one's gaze.

Human beings are always moving, even when they think they are not. They cough, fidget, turn their heads, eyes move to follow something of interest, yawn, scratch, take a deep breath, sigh, burp, fart, stretch. People do a thousand things when they think they are doing nothing, when they think they are quiet. It was instinctive, his stillness in the midst of constant movement. He was invisible.

Those others, the herd, would have been unnerved if they had been aware of his presence. They were not.

2. The Girl

The house was old, a small two bedroom frame house that had not seen paint in decades. Its weathered gray boards and panes of cracked glass gave it the air of a house much older. But a couple of windows with no glass at all, just a piece of plywood nailed over the openings to try and keep the cold and wet out, showed that its appearance was more from neglect than the number of years it had squatted beside the dirt road.

The girl's bedroom had a small window in it, with glass. The wood frame around the glass was old and dry-rotted, and the glazing was falling out from around the glass panes. As the wind blew, the glass rattled in the weathered wood frames. It was an empty, hollow sound echoing in the room and then out into the bleak night.

Headlights from her father's pickup cast a moving patch of light across the wall of her dark room. The lights went out, and she heard the door of the old truck squeak and slam. Like everything else around the place, it was worn out. The truck was tired. The land was tired. The old house was tired. She was tired.

The dog her father kept, it had no name, barked as her father walked towards the house. It yelped suddenly, and she knew that he had taken a kick in the side for the bark. He was a stupid dog. He always barked and Daddy always kicked him. You would think he would learn. Maybe he was just tired too, hoping in his old dog way that tonight might be different from every other night.

Stupid dog. Tonight *would be like* every other night.

There was silence and the girl, Lyn, knew that her father had stopped to take a piss on her mother's withered, scrawny rosebush beside the front porch. In her mind, she could see her father lean back, taking a long pull from a beer can, with his privates hanging out spattering pee on the poor rosebush and the porch.

There in her dark room, a look of weary disgust crossed her face. It wasn't the peeing outside that bothered her. This was rural farm country, and like as not, everyone did that. She had been known to squat behind a bush herself on occasion.

12

No, it wasn't his peeing outside that bothered her; it was the meanness of the act, the way her father did it, peeing on a rose that her Mama had dug the hole for and watered everyday throughout the summer, rinsing the spattered piss off every morning. It was his challenge to the universe and his mastery over them. He might be a nothing dirt farmer and day laborer, but when he was here, by God, he was the king—the boss—and they better not forget it.

Fuck the rosebush and what it represented; the wishful hope of something better, something pretty and soft, something different from the hardscrabble, mean life that he gave his wife and children. "Roses my ass," he would mutter as he shook off the last drops of piss. "I got your roses right here."

3. The Only Difference

He waited patiently, a lion in the grass at the edge of the herd. The herd grazed and moved around him and copulated and birthed and played and fought, and was completely unaware of his presence.

When the moment came, he would spring...relentless...merciless...brutal. He would be filled. For his prey, it would be terrible.

After a long time, his eyes moved again. She emerged from the bowels of the mall through the bank of double glass doors she had entered an hour earlier. Others passed her going in and coming out. They took no notice of the girl, nor she of them. He noticed them all.

Moving from one circle of light thrown off by the streetlights to the next, she was careful to stay out of the shadows, as a young girl alone should be. It would not help her.

Coming to the pole beneath which her car was parked, she opened the car door, threw the small bag she now carried into the back seat, and slid behind the steering wheel. A moment later, the car started and the headlights came on. It backed slowly from the space. He could see her twisting in the seat to peer around a truck parked beside her. Careful and attentive to her driving, she was oblivious to his presence.

Unknown and unseen by everyone but him, she was just one small part, an insignificant member, of the herd that was in constant motion. Her insignificance made her vulnerable.

They would not be there when she cried out. Eventually, they would become aware of her absence. There would be a search. The herd would ripple with fear, and at the same time, sigh deeply with relief that they had not been the ones taken.

Soon, the predator and the prey would be forgotten, and the herd would return to its random, frenetic movement, grateful that they had not been seen by the invisible predator.

But, they were seen. They had not been selected. That was the only difference.

4. The Hunter

George Mackey rolled his window down in the cool night air and shot a quick stream of tobacco juice between his teeth and out into the dark. The wind from the county sheriff's pickup rushing through the night air caused the mix of spittle and tobacco juice to spray back against the door of the truck. In the light of day, it showed as a brownish, dried stain covering the vehicle's side, and was a matter of some discussion and disgust by other deputies. They refused to retrieve any item from Mackey's truck by going through the driver's door.

The interior of the pickup's cab was a different matter. It was neat and organized. Deputy Mackey kept a small briefcase with reports, pens, flashlight, notepads, extra handcuffs, extra ammunition for his Beretta Model 92F military version nine millimeter pistol, and other essential items seat-belted in on the passenger side. These were his tools, and like any good tradesman, he kept his tools clean and in order.

Although some of his personal habits may have been the butt of jokes from his colleagues, Deputy Mackey's law enforcement instincts and abilities were not. By most, he was considered to be one of Pickham County's finest deputies.

In fact, his only real detractor was the person ultimately responsible for his continued presence with the sheriff's department. Pickham County Sheriff, Richard Klineman, himself, had taken a disliking to George Mackey.

Retired from a big-city police department, he had resettled in rural Georgia, feeling it his civic duty to run for sheriff so that he might bring enlightened law enforcement to his rustic and clearly unsophisticated neighbors.

Klineman had convinced a wealthy and politically connected county commission chairman to support him as a progressive who would usher the county sheriff's office into the twenty-first century. Old-timers and old money had bought into the idea, mostly because the sitting sheriff had been a non-political straight-arrow unwilling to grant favors to the good ole boys. Klineman, an outsider, but willing to play the game with them, won in a close election.

Not too much had changed under Sheriff Klineman. As it turned out, Mackey and the other Pickham County deputies were pretty good at their jobs and as dedicated as their seasoned, big-city detective cousins; maybe more so, since most of them had lived in Pickham County all of their lives. It was their county.

Sheriffs were elected. They came and they went. The deputies would bide their time until the political tides swept Klineman out of their lives and brought in the next candidate.

Frustrated at the slow progress, Sheriff Klineman's cleanup of the county was mostly aimed at George Mackey. The reason wasn't entirely clear to George. He worked hard, solved cases and helped out around the county. No one really complained about him...except Klineman.

And, in fact, that was the problem. He was like the rest of the community...cut from the same coarse cloth. Country. Redneck. Simple. In Sheriff Klineman's eyes, he was a hick...a tobacco-spitting, good ole boy in scuffed boots. Mackey could never be a true law enforcement professional.

But, he was a professional, recognized by his peers as one of the best in south Georgia. He also was not intimidated by the sheriff. Klineman was determined to change that.

On this clear autumn night, however, the world seemed right to George Mackey and worries about his sheriff were far from his mind as he whipped the county pickup into the gravel lot of a country store–gas station. The building was an old frame structure with faded white paint on the wood siding. It had been standing since the 1920's and had been operated by a succession of owners. Some had made a go of it, some had not.

It sat empty for a number of years before the current owners bought it as a family retirement business. They were making a go of it, sort of. The continued occupation of the old building by Elmore and Rosalee Cutchins was a doubtful thing on any given day of any given month.

The Cutchins place was one of a number of small isolated

establishments scattered around the county. George usually tried to stop by and check on the secluded businesses around closing time.

From his pickup, he could see short, white-haired Mrs. Cutchins standing behind the counter counting out a stack of bills. Two local boys, sixteen or seventeen years old, were standing outside beside a beat up old farm truck watching through the window. One nudged the other as they muttered back and forth.

George stepped out onto the gravel, closing the door loudly. The boys' heads snapped around in unison while their arms dropped to their sides in an effort to conceal the cans they were holding behind their legs.

"How you boys doin' tonight?" George's tone was firm, the look on his face a mixture of stern admonishment and curious amusement.

"P-pretty good Deputy," one stammered.

The other just nodded.

"Well, looks like they're closing up. You boys head out."

"Yes, sir. Guess so. See you later Deputy," The one who was the talker lead the way as they both climbed into the pickup, still trying to hide the cans.

"Boys," George said, "Pour out the beers before you crank up the truck."

"Oh...uh yes, sir." Talking boy looked over at the passenger side. "Better pour it out, Bobby."

Beer poured foaming into the gravel from the windows of the truck.

"All right now," George continued. "Head on out. I catch you drinking again tonight, and I'll be hauling you down to the county jail before I call your daddy. Right?"

Talking boy nodded solemnly, indicating his complete appreciation of the situation. "Yes, sir. We didn't mean any harm...I mean we'd appreciate you not calling our folks."

"That's up to you. Now ya'll head out." They both nodded. Talking boy cranked the old truck and pulled out onto the country road. He was careful not to spin his tires in the gravel, and accelerated on the road like a grandmother going to Wednesday night prayer meeting, causing a small smile to break across Deputy Mackey's stern face.

5. He Hated Them

It wasn't the beer either that bothered Lyn. Even in the backwoods Bible belt, everybody drank. It was a natural enough way to sooth the pain of poverty and ignorance. A beer, or even many beers, was one way to make the emptiness tolerable.

Her friends' fathers drank. They might hate their lives…the poverty…their failures…so they drank. Too simple and plain to put into words what they felt, they could be tender with their families in their own way. They were still good fathers and husbands. If hate was in their hearts, it was for themselves…not for their families.

Not Daddy though. It was not the poverty or the backbreaking labor. It was them. He hated them. She knew it.

He wanted nothing more than to torment his family. He was mean and ignorant and took pleasure in his own ignorance.

"I ain't never been more than fifty miles from Judges Creek in Pickham County, Georgia," he would say with pride.

"This here was good enough for my goddamned daddy, and I guess it'll be good enough for you," he would go on, the words spit out like a threat, warning her not to consider even the possibility of ever having more or wanting more out of life.

Her brother, Sam, had not been able to take it any longer than he had to. When he turned eighteen, he went to Savannah and joined the Army. He never said goodbye to his father, but he had taken Lyn aside one day and told her of his plan to leave. They cried and hugged each other, Lyn clinging to her brother for a long while. She had known he would leave one day, had dreaded that day, but knew that he had to. Staying, he would have killed Daddy, or been killed by him.

They sat for a long while that day, laughing a little about the plan they had when they were younger to run away to Canada, to get away from the meanness of their father and their lives. It was a child's dream, dreamt by children whose childhood bore the scars of abuse. Sam promised to come back and get her when he could. They would go to Canada. It had become her dream of dreams. Cool, green

Canada.

That was two years ago. Sam was buried now, behind the old Pentecostal church in Judges Creek. He came home a year ago, after a bomb alongside a dirt road in Afghanistan blew up the Humvee he was riding in. Lyn had no idea what a Humvee was, but she knew that the driver of the vehicle lost his legs. Sam lost his life.

The few letters he had written to his sister were hidden in a box under her bed. She kept them hidden from her father for fear that they would disappear during one of his drunken rages. She didn't blame Sam for leaving, but she missed him badly.

Mama missed him too. Lyn knew that she cried at night over the loss of her only boy. She also knew that Daddy thought it was because of his meanness that Mama cried, and took pleasure in that idea.

And there it was. Daddy was just hateful. He didn't want better for them, he just wanted to punish them. She didn't know why...had given up trying to understand.

To Lyn, he was just a mean, spiteful man who lived in the same house with them. Hating his own family and doing whatever he could to degrade them, he would condemn them to the misery that was his life. Right now that meant peeing on Mama's rosebush.

After a few minutes, she heard him thump up the three steps to the old porch. The warped floorboards creaked under his weight. The screen door screeched open and then clattered shut.

"Where you at?" he shouted.

Lyn heard the floor creak in the next bedroom.

"Right here, no need to shout." Mama's voice was tired.

"Get your ass out here. Where's my supper?"

"Didn't know when you'd be home. I'll make you some eggs," Mama replied softly.

Lyn winced at what she knew was coming. It was a nightly ritual. She could have repeated the dialogue before they said it in the next room.

"Eggs?" her father roared. "I want some goddamned food!"

"Well, that's all there is. And at that, it's more than Lyn and me had."

20

"I don't give a shit what you and that sneaking little bitch had!" He turned towards Lyn's bedroom door. "You hear me in there you sneaky bitch. I know you're listening. Afraid to show your face you little pissant! Always sneaking around. Get your scrawny ass out here!"

Mama was getting angry now. It was one thing to abuse her, but leave her baby out of it.

"You leave her be! She ain't done..." Mama's words were cut off by a sickening thud followed by a heavy thump, like the sound of a sack of potatoes hitting the floor.

6. He Just Was

Unaware, the girl drove her small car within fifty feet of the silhouette watching in stillness. It was a curiosity to him. Did she sense anything? Was there a twitch, a ripple of fear or nervousness sliding up her spine...the feeling that she had somehow come close to something very dangerous and menacing? Or, was she completely oblivious of her proximity to the danger and her fate?

Perhaps the tingling at the back of her neck faded as she navigated her car safely through the parking lot. Sitting in its secure, familiar interior doing a routine thing in a routine way, did the familiarity and the routine push the nervous, tingling fear away?

It was more likely that there was no tingling, no psychic connection warning her of the impending, nearness of extreme danger. He was good at that. She would not know of his presence until he wanted her to...until he needed her to.

As she turned to pull out onto the main road, he started his car. It moved quietly, not disturbing the flow of movement around it, but becoming part of that movement, using the flow around it to disguise its driver's focus on the small car a hundred yards ahead.

She was young. Her car was not expensive. No rich daddy or sugar daddy was taking care of her. Likely, she was on her own.

He absorbed the information unconsciously, unaware of the cunning and instinct within that noted these things. It just was. He just was. That was enough.

7. The Closest Bug Lost

George watched the two boys disappear down the road in their ragged pickup. They could have been him twenty years earlier; hanging out, under age, sneaking a beer. Things didn't change much. It was unlikely, he knew, that they would have ever done anything to hurt the Cutchinses. But a few beers might lead to some bad judgment, and then to a bad idea executed on an alcohol-tinged whim.

Watching until the truck's taillights turned off the road, he walked through the wooden screen door and into the small building. Mrs. Cutchins looked up from her counting. A smile crossed her face.

"Evening Deputy," she called across the room.

"Evening, Miz' Cutchins." George walked over to the small counter, crowded with racks of chewing tobacco, snuff, lighters, pocketknives, and gum. "Looks like you had a pretty good day." He nodded down at the stacks of bills she was counting out, separating them by denomination.

"Yep. We did good today. We were due." She smiled and continued her count, not missing a beat as she sorted bills from her hand into the stacks on the counter.

"Wonder if you could do something for me?"

A wisp of white hair moved around her forehead in the breeze from a small fan behind the cash register as she looked up questioningly. "What is it, George?" she said, laying the wad of bills on the counter.

"I would appreciate it if you could do your nightly count in the back room or somewhere but here, where everyone can look in and see what kind of day you had." He nodded down at the neat stacks of bills on the counter. "Quite a temptation to some young fella wanting to take his girl to Savannah for a big weekend."

"You think so?" The surprise was evident on her face. It had never occurred to her that someone might be tempted by what she and her old man had.

"Yep. I do," George said firmly. "Doesn't take much to tempt

23

some, especially these days. What you got there would be quite a lot to a lot of people; like maybe some young boys out having a few beers." George looked her in the eye, his face expressionless.

"You mean those Gantry boys. They were in here earlier," she said nodding, skepticism in her eyes. "They're harmless. Good boys just out passing some time."

"I mean them and lots of others," George said. "They may not mean any harm, and ordinarily it wouldn't even cross their minds, but...a few beers, a wad of cash, a hot night and a pretty girl waiting...it could happen. Probably good boys, but it'd be nice for them to stay that way. No need to put a temptation in front of them that would follow them the rest of their lives."

"Suppose you're right," she nodded. "I'll tell Mr. Cutchins, too."

"Yes, ma'am. Thanks." He added a question. "By the way, you wouldn't know where those Gantry boys got the beers I made them pour out in your gravel, would you? Seems like a waste of good beer. Besides, it's illegal, them being under age, you know."

The old woman started to smile, then realized George was serious. "Well Deputy, I make it a point never to lie, especially not to an officer of the law, so I guess it's best that I just didn't hear the question."

George nodded. "Well, I'm not much for lying myself, so I reckon it's best I don't hear an answer. Just remember, it's illegal...buying and selling in this case."

Reaching down into a barrel filled with icy water, George pulled out a can of Coke. He pulled some coins from his pocket and placed them neatly on the counter beside the stacks of bills.

"Thanks, Miz' Cutchins. See you tomorrow," he said pushing open the creaky screen door and walking out into the night.

"You too, George," she said as the screen banged shut. Brushing back the strand of white hair around her forehead, she reached down for the stack of bills and continued her nightly count.

Standing in the ring of gravel illuminated by the light from the store's window, George popped back the tab on the drink can and took a long pull. The night air was warm in this part of Georgia, even in the fall. The single light on a pole over the gas pump cast a cool fluorescent glow. A bat circled the swarm of moths and beetles that in turn circled the light. Flitting in what seemed an erratic way, it would dart here and there into the swarm. George knew that the bat's movements were not erratic at all.

Each swerve by the bat was the stalk of some unsuspecting insect selected by the bat from the hundreds in the swarming mass of insects. Selection seemed random, or it might be based on some rudimentary judgment by the bat. Size, type of insect, or taste perhaps played a part in the selection of the bat's victims. Or, maybe it was just proximity to the bat. The closest bug lost.

There was no way of knowing. One thing was certain though. Each darting attack into the swarm was a kill.

The light blinked off as Mrs. Cutchins threw the breaker and closed the store. In an instant, the bat and insects scattered into the night, but the hunt continued.

8. She Didn't Go Home

She didn't go home. She never would now. The little car traveled several miles. The four-lane highway turned into a two-lane road. The area was more suburban now, on the verge of rural. After another mile or two, she stopped at a discount supermarket. It was at the intersection of another larger highway. There were clusters of houses in small developments scattered around. Urban sprawl from the big city, but the area was far more country than city. The clusters of lit homes and buildings surrounded by the dark countryside made them seem more isolated.

It was an older store with an almost deserted parking lot. He drove by on the main road as the brunette cruised in and found a space midway down the parking row directly in front of the store's entrance. Turning at the next corner, he pulled into the parking lot from the side entrance and saw her walking across the asphalt and into the store.

"Yes." The word came out a slow hiss, guttural and low. It was an expression of aching hunger, like the deep-throated sound, not quite a growl, that the great cat makes before springing. He wanted her. He would have her.

Scanning the lot and exterior of the building with practiced eyes, he quickly saw that there were no cameras. This far out in the country, security was a minor concern. The only predators people knew here were gators along the banks of canals and ponds, and the occasional panther deep in the swamps. That would change.

Waiting until she had entered the store, he moved the old Chevy beside her parked car, with the passenger door next to her driver's door. Then, exiting his vehicle and leaving the keys in the ignition, he adjusted the passenger door so that it was slightly ajar. The interior light of the car did not come on. Always prepared, he had removed the bulb.

He had just started this 'runaround'. That's what he called it. When people at work asked where he was going, it was a runaround. They thought it meant a vacation road trip. To him it was something very different.

It was early in the runaround to be seeking a kill. When he had stopped, it was just to gather some supplies, but the feeling had hit him as he pulled into the mall parking lot. It was early in the trip, but it felt right, safe. The instinct took over. Within an instant, he had become the predator, and now he was outside the grocery store waiting for the girl.

Crossing half the country on I-10 in a day and a half, he had only arrived in northern Florida that afternoon. Sometimes it worked that way. With a successful hunt here, he might have a chance for another project before his vacation runaround ended. Who knows, maybe even two more. That would be a record, three on one runaround.

He walked across the parking lot and stood behind a van parked thirty feet away from the two cars. Twenty minutes passed before he saw her walking from the store, pushing a grocery cart. She didn't have much, just a few plastic bags.

He readied himself as she pushed the cart to the passenger side of her vehicle and placed the bags on the front seat. For a moment, he thought he had made a tactical error. She looked as if she was going to push the cart to the return stand, off to his right and closer to the store. If she did, she might see him moving around the van to stay out of sight. Not likely, but still, he was careful. It was a detail that might cause him to call it off. If his senses felt that the moment was lost, he would let her go and immediately leave in a different direction.

But that hadn't happened. She hesitated as if she sensed there could be some danger in crossing the parking lot in the dark. She was smart and careful. She left the cart by her car, as he knew she would, and walked around the rear to the driver's door.

People usually did that. Even though going around to the front was normally closer, they almost always went around the rear of the vehicle to get to the driver's side. It was a small idiosyncrasy that he found curious in the way a house cat might curiously regard a mouse trapped in a corner trying to find a direction to run. Of course, the girl had no idea that the cat was so near or that she was trapped. But she was.

27

He sensed which direction she would take, like a leopard sensing which direction the gazelle would leap. As she crossed the rear of her car and turned towards the driver's door, he moved. He was quick and silent. The thirty feet to the car were covered in seconds, long before she had a chance to unlock the car door.

The hunting knife in his pocket was out in a smooth, practiced motion. He pressed against her, pushing her against his car, the knife at her throat. He was positioned so that anyone in the store looking out would only see his back and not the hand holding the knife. She had only time to give a short, startled gasp before his hand was on her throat. He was not an overly large man, but the grasp was powerful. There was terror in her eyes. He smiled.

Her mouth opened as if to scream. Shaking his head, he pressed the knife more firmly against her throat, until the blade drew the smallest trickle of blood. Her mouth closed, and her head nodded understanding. No sound.

With a fluid motion, he opened the passenger door of the car, pushing her in with his body. He forced her down on the seat, holding her there with his weight. Pulling a plastic tie wrap from his pocket, the kind electricians use to bundle wires and cables, he looped it around her wrists and pulled hard. He knew that police officers used similar tie wraps to secure prisoners when they ran out of hand cuffs. Smart boys, those cops were.

The girl gasped in pain as the narrow, hard plastic strip cut into her wrists. Taking another plastic tie wrap from his pocket, he looped it through the one on her wrists and then through the seat frame by the door. This had all taken only a few seconds. The small gasp she had made could not have been heard inside the store and probably would not have been audible more than a few feet away.

His actions were swift, decisive, and powerful. The young woman was thrown into a state of confusion fed by her fear.

It hadn't always been that way. His hunting skills had been acquired through trial and error. He had been lucky more than once, but that was also part of the thrill of the game.

Now, years of planning and practice made his movements reflexive. When to make his move…how fast to move…how hard to grip the throat...where to press the knife. There was no thought about what he was doing. He just did it.

It was almost a little disappointing to him. He was too good. The thrill of chance was missing.

But it couldn't be helped. Better to be safe than sorry, he reminded himself when he felt the urge to take an unnecessary chance. He would have to make up for the lost thrill in some other way.

This thought must have flashed across his face in some way because the girl's eyes widened, and she opened her mouth as if to scream. That was only for an instant though. He pushed the knife hard against her throat, and this time blood trickled down onto her shirt.

"No sound," he whispered through clenched teeth. "Do you understand? Do what I say, and you will be okay. If you don't..." The knife's point pressed harder against her throat again making a new, small cut.

She nodded. Through eyes dimmed by tears, she saw him smile.

He closed the door softly, but firmly, not bothering with duct tape over her mouth. That was dangerous in public, even at night. Duct tape was fine to prevent screams from attracting attention when they were out of sight. In public, duct tape over the girl's mouth would attract immediate attention. Even at night, a roaming police car might get close enough for the officer to observe the girl in the seat.

Besides, it wasn't necessary. He was in control. The girl's trembling silence was testament to his ability.

It took him only a second to scan the lot for anyone who might have seen as he moved to the driver's side of the car. No one had.

Sliding behind the wheel, he turned the key. The old car started quietly. It was in excellent running condition, despite the fading paint job. The car glided through the parking lot, not too fast and not slow; just the right speed for a person who had picked up a few groceries and was casually heading home for the evening.

From the corner of his eye, he saw her turn her head towards the store. Two cashiers and a couple of customers could be seen

29

through the brightly lit window. A teenage boy was bagging groceries for one of the customers. She could see them, but he knew that they could not see her trembling, tear stained face or hear the soft sobbing sounds she made, as she struggled to follow his command to remain silent.

Huddled against the door, she was just a silhouette, sobbing in the dark car. Regarding her with curiosity, he wondered what she was feeling.

How deep was her fear? What thoughts crashed through her mind?

Sympathy, nor guilt, did not exist for him...only an intense, hungry curiosity. He would know. She would reveal it all to him. The fear. The terror. The hope for survival...and then her terrible realization that there was no hope. He would know it all before the night ended. It would all come spilling, tumbling onto the floor. He would wash himself in it.

"Are you ready for our night on the town?" he asked, almost softly.

Her sobbing grew louder. Perfect. A small shudder of excitement coursed through his body.

"What do you want?" she whispered between sobs. "What did I do?"

"Do? Why, you didn't do anything. You were just there."

His words were intended to show her the random and hopeless nature of her circumstances. They succeeded. Her sobbing grew louder again, "Please, please don't hurt me."

"Hurt you? Why, I'm not going to hurt you. Have I hurt you yet?" He let the question linger in the air, letting her consider it. Maybe there was hope. He wanted her to believe that for now. It would make her later realization of the truth even sweeter.

It worked. She calmed and her sobbing became softer again.

"Then why are you doing this? Please let me go. I won't tell...just please let me go."

"Calm down, honey. I could have hurt you, but I didn't...I won't." He let the lie linger there in the quiet of the car knowing that it would deepen her hope. Squeezing every ounce of pleasure and

30

satisfaction out of this game was a practiced ability.

"You know why I won't hurt you?" He looked over at her and saw the glimmer of hope brighten in her eye. "Because I have...needs. You can help me with those. Then I'll let you go," he said softly and honestly.

It was honest because it was true. When he had taken what he wanted...what he needed...from her, he would send her on her way...into the darkness that he imagined death to be.

Of course, his honesty did not extend to telling her that, or in what condition she would be when he did let her go. That would come later. She would know.

For now, he wanted her to hope, to believe, that she could survive. When the time came, her disappointment and terror at the realization of what he really meant would be exquisite.

He could almost hear her thoughts. They were like electricity in the car. Rape? Okay rape. I can get through this. I can deal with rape. Just survive. Don't do anything to make him do more than rape me. Survive.

She was the rabbit surprised and caught in the talons of the owl, lying still in the cool night grass thinking that if it made no sudden movement, the owl might release. But eventually the owl would tear into the flesh, and the rabbit would scream its high-pitched, eerie scream, knowing that death was near.

She wanted to believe in her survival, and so she did.

Turning right onto the main road, they drove north. The state line was another twenty miles up the road....Georgia. Georgia was on his mind.

9. Just Away

Lyn jerked her bedroom door open and saw her mother lying on the floor in the middle of the room. Blood trickled from her head. The beer can that her father had thrown was on the floor beside her. He stood there, a wolfish grin on his face, proud of what he'd done.

"You son of a bitch!" Lyn screamed at him as she ran to her mother's side.

Trying to stand, her mother held a hand to the side of her face where blood seeped down under her fingers.

"What the hell did you call me?" her father said, a tone of incredulity in his voice. Then recovering he shouted, "You ain't gonna talk to me like that you little fucking bitch!"

Lurching across the room, he made a drunken grab for his daughter. Lyn dodged, but he followed up with a backhand that caught her across the face and sent her reeling against the wall. Beer soaked as he was, he was still a powerful man. He reached down, grabbed her arm pulling her up with his left hand and balled up his right fist to strike her.

"No!" Mama screamed.

An instant later, her father's grip relaxed and he tumbled forward to the floor on top of Lyn. She dragged herself out from under his dead weight and stood up, a look of revulsion, mingled with dread, on her face.

Mama stood there, shaking with anger. Tears, mixed with the blood from the gash, streaked her worn face. A heavy iron skillet was in her hand. It had been on the old stove on the other side of the room.

Lyn had been wrong. This was not like every other night. Somehow, tonight had just gotten worse...much worse. Or maybe, she had just become aware of how fucked up they all were. All of them. Her father's evil bullying, her mother's acceptance, and her own silence in the face of it all. Everything that had been bottled up for so long had just come out at once. She looked down at her father.

"Is he..."

"Dead? I doubt it, but no loss if he is." Mama replied and then knelt down to check him.

Lyn saw a nasty lump forming over his right temple.

"He ain't dead," Mama said standing. "Just drunker than usual. That thump in the head was what he needed to put him out."

Lyn started crying and then sobbing. Her mother took her by the shoulders and pulled her to the threadbare sofa. Sitting her down, she held her, rocking back and forth, keeping an eye on the unconscious man across the room and a washcloth over the gash on her head.

After a while, Lyn's sobbing eased. Her mother sat her up straight and held her wet face in her rough hands, looking her in the eye.

"You have to leave now, baby girl."

"But...no, Mama..."

"Quiet." Her mother's voice was calm and firm. She continued, "I know you been planning to go for a while...for a long time. Well, tonight's the night. You are leaving."

"But, no... What about you?"

Her mother cut her off again. "We ain't arguing about this baby. I'll be fine. At least he won't do any worse to me than he has before. But you...you're his conscience. You're what makes him feel guilty. If you stay, he'll hurt you, maybe hurt you really bad. I won't let that happen. No, you're leaving...tonight."

There was finality in Mama's voice. And she knew Mama was right. Daddy would never tolerate her in the same house again. But where? Where would she go? How could she go?

Mama's eye softened and tears welled up and followed the others that had streaked her face.

"I know baby. I know what you're thinking. You go somewhere...anywhere. I can't say, but it has to be to a better place than this. We ain't got no family and there is no one around here that you can stay with. Daddy would find you. You have to go far away. I hate that it has to be this way, but it has to be. You go on now."

With that, Mama pulled her close and held her tight against her breast for a long time. She felt her mother's soft sobs and hugged her back tightly. After a while, Mama pushed her back, turned her face and stood up quickly.

"Come now," her voice was firm again, "Let's get you packed and out of here."

Mama walked towards the bedroom. Lyn sat there for a minute in a haze, hearing the heavy breathing from the man on the floor. Could he really be her father? This big, mean, drunk man? Was there a time when he could have been a real father?

A small framed picture sat on the table beside Lyn. She picked it up and peered closely at it. A big man in overalls sat outside on a kitchen chair in the yard in front of the house holding a small baby in the crook of his arm. The baby was Lyn. The man was her Daddy. At least that's what Mama had told her. Was it really him? Was it really her? Lyn couldn't remember.

She sat there until the small room seemed to close in on her so that she had to stand up to escape. She moved numbly into the bedroom where her few things were already being neatly folded and stacked on the bed by her mother.

Ten minutes later, she stood by the front door, clutching the old woman by the neck. She could smell the plain soap she used, the detergent in her clothes, the musty, earthy fragrance of her gray, thin hair. She tried to soak in everything about her that she could.

Finally, the old woman pried the girl's fingers off her neck.

"You have to go. Go," she ordered through her sobs.

Opening the door, she pushed her daughter out into the night.

"Go...now," she choked the words out and slammed the door.

She stood on the front porch of the only home she had ever known. Mean and rough as it was, it was all she had known.

She didn't know how long it was before her feet started to move numbly. First one, then the other. Unconsciously, they carried her to the dirt road and out to the two lane highway about a mile away. Her small bag dragged in the dust as she walked.

A soft moan escaped the old woman's lips. She was slumped on the floor against the door she had closed behind her only daughter. Her breast heaved in pain at the thought, and she sobbed.

A muttered prayer came trembling from her lips and echoed softly in the room. But the house seemed a black hole. It sucked everything into it, allowing no escape. Words, thoughts, happiness, prayers. It seemed that nothing made its way out of the dark house.

But her daughter had made it out. And she would do whatever she could to make sure the young girl kept going. Anywhere. Just away.

10. He Was Hungry

Across the Georgia line, the countryside was dark. On a section of deserted highway, he spotted what he was looking for.

The old wooden church with a dirt parking lot looked perfect. Surrounded by trees on all sides but the road frontage, it was dark and secluded. Not likely that any churchgoers would be around this time of night. Churches were usually deserted when the flock wasn't there praying or singing, or doing whatever it is the flock does.

The area was transitional between the busy city and the remote backcountry of northern Florida and southern Georgia. The little wooden structure had probably been there for seventy-five years. It had no parking lot lights, and the rear could not be seen from the road. The car rolled to the rear of the old building with its lights off. Yes, just what he was looking for.

This project started so quickly, he had no time to scout around for the spot. But then, he had always been lucky this way. This spot felt safe, and he was hungry. It was time to feed.

The wheels of the car crunched the gravel as it came to a stop behind the church at the far end of the lot. He put the knife to her throat again.

"I'll be right with you, sweetheart," he said holding his face so close his lips touched her cheek as he spoke. She shivered at their movement against her soft skin. He knew she could feel it, smell his breath. Her trembling thrilled him.

Opening the driver's door, he walked around to the passenger side, chuckling a little as he walked to the rear and then around. Closer to go around the front, he thought to himself. He found the irony amusing, that he was like everyone else in this little eccentricity.

Stopping for a moment, he breathed deeply. The night air was thick, humid, and pungent with the smell of vegetation and life. The buzzing, chirping, and humming from a billion insects and frogs filled his ears. Life rustled in the trees and scurried and slithered along the ground. It was all around him, and he was part of it.

36

Glancing at the car, he could see that the trembling girl was not. He exulted in the life swarming around him and filling him. She only awaited the fate he had selected her for...and for her. She was no longer part of the life teeming and swirling around in the night.

It was a curious thing to see her through the spotted car glass, isolated and separated from the life. He was part of it, the life. She was...something else. Separate, different, alien. Her separateness and isolation and difference excited him. It made him powerful.

Jerking the passenger door open, he slit the plastic tie holding her wrists to the door's armrest with a quick motion. She almost fell out onto the ground as it released.

11. Rocking on the Porch

"You hear that?"

The old man hunched over in his rocking chair on the front porch of the old house and squinted, as if that would sharpen his hearing. Light filtered out through the curtains of the living room behind him. The window was open and moths fluttered against the screen.

"What?" The equally old woman was sitting a few feet to his left in an identical wooden porch chair. Focusing on the cross-stitch embroidery she was working on in her lap, her peripheral vision picked up the side-to-side movements of his head as he tried to pick up the sound again. It was distracting. She dropped her work in her lap, turned her head and asked more sharply, "What?"

"Nothin'," the old man said leaning back in his chair. "Thought I heard something through the woods, over by the A.M.E. Church. Must have been nothin'."

"Maybe you should walk over and check around," the old woman said. "You usually hear pretty good for an old man."

A wheezy soft laugh escaped the old man. "Right, maybe I should." He reached over and patted her thin knee. "Old man, huh. Where'd you learn to talk like that?"

"From you I reckon," she looked over at her husband whose hands were bracing on the arms of the chair to push himself up. "You thinkin' you're not old?"

He chuckled and shifted a little, trying to push his old bones up from the chair.

"Young buck would be more right," he said, rising stiffly and shuffling his feet in a little jig to show his wife how spry he still was.

Her response was a shake of the head and a short, "Go on now. See what's going on through those woods."

"Why, yes, ma'am. I'll do just that. Wouldn't want nothin' to happen over at the church. I ain't never been a church person and don't suppose I ever will be, but still, I don't need any more points against me with the old man upstairs if something was wrong over

38

there, and me just sittin' here passing time with an old woman."

"What makes you think you get any points at all out of this? It was my idea for you to check it out. You are forgetful, old man."

"Well, *old girl,* I guess you could say I identified the problem and organized the expedition. That ought to be worth somethin'," he drawled back with a smile.

The screen door banged as he walked into the house and through it to the kitchen. A minute later, the door banged again.

"Think you're makin' enough noise? Not likely you're gonna sneak up on anyone with all that door bangin' goin' on."

"What makes you think I'm trying to sneak up on *anyone*? I want them long gone by the time I get there. No need to be overly ambitious or under cautious about such things." He smiled at his wife, still seated in her chair.

He clicked on the flashlight and shined it across the yard toward the tree line. The batteries were old, the light dim and yellow.

"Better hurry," she encouraged him. "Not much light left in them batteries."

"Yep. I better get movin'."

When he was half way across the yard, an uneasiness bubbled slightly inside her and she called out from the porch, "You take the gun?"

He turned, and reaching behind, the old man pulled the .38 Smith and Wesson, two-inch barrel revolver from his back pocket. He held it up for her to see as he walked toward the trees.

12. Appetizer

He smiled again as he jerked the girl roughly to her feet. The knife was at her throat. His body pressed hard against her forcing her against the side of the car.

"Don't make a sound, honey. Do you understand?" The grin was still on his face.

She nodded slowly, trembling.

"We're gonna have a little fun. Then I'll take you somewhere and drop you off. You can find your way home. Right?"

Again, the slow, quaking nod.

He glanced around and saw no lights through the trees. Just the woods and dark. Reaching into the car, he retrieved a roll of duct tape he kept under the seat. No need to worry about being spotted now.

With a quick motion, he circled the girl's face with the tape sealing off her mouth and any possible sound she might make other than the soft, muted whimpers she was trying to control. Her fear and pathetic effort not to make any sound as he had instructed was an electrical charge, buzzing through his loins.

Roughly, he jerked her away from the door and pushed her towards the front of the car. With one hand, he grabbed the back of her neck and bent her over onto the hood, banging her face against the metal. He knew she could feel the heat of the engine radiating through the hood onto her face.

The knife went down the back of her pants slicing through them and the panties beneath. She gasped as the cold steel continued down between the cheeks of her buttocks and rested there for a moment. An excited shudder ran through the man as he leaned against her, and she sobbed more heavily.

Stepping back, he looked at her pale skin just visible in the dark. Her bare, quivering white buttocks gave off a ghostly luminescence. Opening his pants, he moved back to her. This time, she would have screamed had she been able.

It only took a couple of minutes—painful, terrifying minutes for the girl. After, he stood quietly in the dark, leaning against her still trembling body. The powerful heat and force of his attack on the girl faded into a satisfied warmth. Not the afterglow of a pleasant sexual encounter, it was the desperate relief of drinking after a trek through the desert without water. This was the appetizer for what was to come. Soon, he would experience the belt loosening feeling of feasting after a long fast.

He could feel her shivering in fear against him. He drank in that which he had missed for too long.

13. A Walk in the Woods

"Maybe we should just call the sheriff," she called after him. "You might be too old to go traipsing through the woods in the dark."

"I'll be all right old girl. Most likely just a raccoon pulling on the back screen door, or some youngsters looking for a place to park," he called back. And now he was determined to check things out and show his woman that after sixty odd years of marriage, he was still a man. Maybe an old shriveled up man, he chuckled to himself, but a man nonetheless.

At the tree line, he stopped for a moment looking for the small path that led about a hundred yards through the woods to the back of the old church. Finding the entrance, he threw one backward look at his wife, still sitting on the porch. She watched him, and then conscious of his glance, looked back down at her cross-stitch work.

He scanned the ground ahead with the flashlight. Most anything out would scurry away as he approached, and there wouldn't be any gators here. No water nearby.

Snakes...that was a different matter...there were lots of them, and they tended to lie on the paths at night in the cool air. They weren't very active at nighttime, even in this warm climate. But they could get downright mean if you stepped on one in the dark. He was careful as he walked. He didn't like snakes.

Emerging from the woods, he clicked the flashlight off and stood quietly at the edge, trying to blend in with the tree line. Without the light, he would be nearly invisible from a few feet away.

He could make out the church across the rear gravel lot. Nothing seemed out of sorts and he could see no one. Walking as softly as he could through the gravel, he went to the back of the church building. The crunching sound his shoes made in the rocks caused him to wince at every step. Clicking the light on for a few seconds, he could see no signs of prying on the back door.

He walked around to the front of the church, trying to stay in the narrow patch of grass surrounding the building so that his steps were muffled. The windows were intact.

At the large double wooden front doors, he checked again with the flashlight for any signs of a break-in. There were none. The two large, wooden doors revealed chipped and peeling white paint, but no signs of prying or other damage. He stepped from the church's front porch.

Crossing the gravel lot to the road, he could not make out anything unusual. No way to tell if anyone had pulled into the lot. The gravel didn't hold tracks, and he wouldn't know what to look for if it did.

Shining the light around from the driveway of the church, he could see nothing unusual. The light sparkled brightly back at him from the reflectors marking the centerline of the road in front. No traffic, but that was not unusual here. In fact, any traffic would have been unusual this time of night. Something scurried in the brush across the road. Probably a possum, or maybe an armadillo.

Okay, so much for his adventure. Time to get back to his porch and his chair. Turning, he circled around to the rear of the church and the path leading through the woods to the old house.

Stopping at the edge of the woods, the old man scanned the building and lot one more time. The air was becoming thicker and damper as the night came on. A mist began to rise from the ground enveloping the base of the church, like something from a spook movie, he thought. An involuntary shiver crawled up his back.

Silly old fool, his wife would say, and she would be right, he thought. Enough. Definitely time to get back to the front porch. He turned and clicked the flashlight on as he swung around and started to step gingerly back into the trees. The dim, yellow beam of light reflected off something about a hundred feet away, and he stopped in his tracks.

Squinting, he could make out that it was a car backed up against the woods, almost hidden by them at the back edge of the lot. It looked like an older car and dull in the beam of the flashlight...the type of car someone from around here would drive.

Peering intently at the ground for snakes, alert to anything that slithered, the old man thought for a moment about going back into the woods and the comfort of his porch chair. An old car left in a parking lot in these parts wasn't all that unusual. In fact, it was pretty common. Probably one of the church goers broke down on Sunday…or maybe some kids laid down in the seat waiting for him to leave so they could get back to doing what kids did in the backseat of cars. That thought tweaked his curiosity.

He stepped back onto the gravel and walked along the edge of the woods towards the car. The shadows of the trees made the corner of the lot where the car sat much darker so that he hadn't noticed it as he walked from the woods. He had been focused on the church building. He still wouldn't have noticed it if the flashlight hadn't reflected dimly off the car's glass.

14. Ambush

Somewhere a door banged shut. It was a muffled sound and seemed a long ways off. Swiveling his head, the gray eyes scanned methodically in all directions. No light. No movement. But the sound had been unmistakable.

Roughly but silently, he pulled the cut clothing up around her waist and pushed the terrified girl into the car, binding her once again to the seat frame. His fingers left purple bruises on her arms. Putting his finger to his lips, he leaned close.

"No sound," he whispered. "No movement."

He stared at her with his eyebrows raised expectantly until she nodded her understanding.

Soundlessly, he moved into the woods.

The dim shaft of light emerged from the trees. The shuffling gait of the person holding it caused it to waver, swinging widely back and forth, as if searching for danger, but not truly expecting any.

The faint beam detected no trace of the man in the woods. He was invisible to the person holding the flashlight, and would have been difficult to see, even in broad daylight.

He watched as the yellowish beam made its way around the church. The person holding it shuffled to the woods, and for a moment, it seemed it would disappear into the dark trees. But then it hesitated and swung in the direction of the car. After a few seconds, the light bounced slowly up and down moving deliberately towards the old car.

He avoided looking directly looking into the beam allowing his night vision to give him a picture of the intruder. The silhouette and shuffling gait were that of an old man. Inside his chest, his heart raced with anticipation...excited. Outside there was only deadly silence.

Approaching closer, the old man shined the light through the windshield. There was nothing visible. Stepping up to the old car, he bent over with the light to peer inside.

Reckon what the car's problem is, he thought, unconcerned. The danger so close raised no hackles on is neck, no psychic warning, or premonition from the Almighty. It was just an old, empty car in a parking lot.

A startled breath escaped him, and he almost jumped back.

The girl, bent over sideways so that her head was below the window, had her hands tied and bound with something he could not make out. There was duct tape around her mouth. It was like something from a movie, and in the few seconds it had taken to approach the car and see what was inside, the old man really and truly wished he had let the old woman call the sheriff. He very much wanted to be on the porch of his house waiting for a deputy to come shine his lights around and make things right with the bright spotlights and not this dim little flashlight. What had he gotten into? It was less than a second before he discovered the answer.

He raised the light slightly, and the girl's eyes widened. It wasn't the light that seemed to frighten her. The eyes were focused on something…behind him.

Instinctively the hand not holding the flashlight started to move backwards towards the pistol in his pocket. It was too late.

Searing pain burned through his right kidney. Piercing the old man's body to the hilt, the knife's eight-inch blade penetrated completely through his thin frame, nearly protruding from his abdomen.

With his arm around the old man's neck and mouth, he worked the blade back and forth, in and out. The frail old body quivered at the pain and the shock of the knife's movements through his flesh and organs. A high-pitched wheezing sound escaped from his lungs, followed by a gurgling, rattling noise from his throat.

The attack was too sudden for him to struggle, and the placement of the blade was expert enough to be a death blow. It was not a quick merciful death, but death nonetheless.

After a minute, the quivering and feeble struggle ended. The old man's body crumpled to the gravel. Blood oozing from the wound thickened in the sand and gravel.

The attacker stepped back and examined his work. Unexpected, he thought…unexpected, but not unpleasant. It was a bonus, and he smiled at that.

He retrieved the small pistol from the old man's back pocket. He had felt it as he leaned closely, almost intimately, into him during the attack.

The girl looking up from the seat of the car could see him, although she could no longer see the old man who had peered into the car a few moments ago. Their eyes met, and the terror reflected back at him from the girl brought another surge of fulfillment to him.

Tears fell from her eyes but did not touch her cheek. They dripped, slowly at first, and then more rapidly across the duct tape covering her mouth and face until they plopped onto the car's seat. It excited him.

She was helpless. The only thing she could produce now was tears, and she was denied the sensation of feeling them drop across her face...the wet, weeping release of crying. They rolled from her eyes to the duct tape to the seat, never touching her skin. She cried them but never felt her own tears. It was an exquisite torture and it made him more powerful.

Opening the car door, he plopped loosely into the driver's seat and let the door slam shut. The engine started smoothly, and he pulled slowly around the church with the headlights off. Stopping by the road for a moment, he made sure there was no car approaching from either direction and then pulled onto the black two lane, headed for the interstate.

****

The old woman on the porch lifted her head. The sound of the closing car door came muffled, but discernible through the hundred yards of black woods.

"Harry? That you?" She knew her frail voice would not carry through the trees.

Silently, hands folded in her lap she waited, peering into the dark woods at the edge of the lot of the home she had shared with her husband for sixty years. He would be back soon. The old fool, she thought.

****

She was bound again to the seat frame. Her eyes had the look. He had seen it many times before. The look pleaded with him to drop her off now, as he had promised. It was pathetic and stupid.

She had just witnessed the murder of the old man, someone who might have been able to help her. Could she truly believe that he would keep his word and release her? He wondered at it.

The need to survive, the longing desire for her life not to end, overpowered her reason. It made her hope for the absurd...her personal survival. Somewhere inside, the synapses of her brain fired electric impulses that shut down reason. The hope for...need for...life became her reality.

Pathetic and stupid...and it thrilled him...the terrified, begging look in her eyes. He had seen that look before in his victims' eyes.

It was the same look he had observed once, watching a documentary show on African wildlife. The gazelle, hanging from a leopard's jaws, stunned and crazed with fear, eyes wide open, had that same pleading look. The animal was still alive, legs trying to run, twitching in the cat's mouth. Not dead...yet.

****

In a supermarket parking lot, some miles away across the Florida state line, ice cream melted in a plastic bag on the seat of a small Japanese car.

48

15. Backup

A tunnel of dark green embraced the truck. The headlights cast a long beam of light down the passageway of trees so that leaves and grass swirled in kaleidoscope patterns where the light illuminated. Beyond the shoulders of the road, little could be seen The heavy, humid aromas of the vegetation blew rushing through the interior. He savored the smell, rich and pungent.

He loved this time of night. Mist rose from the creeks and depressions in the ground. Unseen life moved, chirped, and scurried everywhere. It could be heard even through the rushing noise of the pickup.

George turned his head and spat a stream of tobacco juice, some of which actually made it beyond the door of the truck to hit the road with a splat. Squatting on the centerline, a lizard dodged the brown liquid as the pickup rushed by with a muffled roar. Undeterred, the small green reptile darted to the shoulder and the safety of the brush.

The radio crackled and spoke in a tinny female voice.

"302. Meet a woman at 715 Power Line Road in reference to a missing person, her husband. Subject is a black male, five feet, eight inches, thin build, seventy-nine years of age."

"10-4 Dispatch," another tinny voice, this one male, responded.

Located in southeastern Georgia, the I-95 corridor cut across the eastern edge of Pickham County. Most of the businesses and developed areas were along the interstate's path. The remainder of the county was primarily agricultural. Farms and small settlements dotted the landscape, with the occasional country store or tractor supply business located at a crossroad to provide service to the locals.

During the day and evening shifts at the sheriff's department there were three or four units working the county. Those on the day shift were numbered 101 through 104. Evening shift units were 201 through 204, and so on. On third shift, George's shift, they called it morning watch; there were never more than two units working, and some nights, only one.

Morning watch deputies had to possess a high degree of self-reliance. Backup could be a long ways off, as much as an hour away. It depended on what the Georgia State Patrol troopers were doing, what section of the interstate they were working, and which truck stop diner they had gathered at for their coffee and breakfast.

The gathering was a ritual that took place at precisely two a.m. every morning. George reckoned that between two and three in the morning you could run a NASCAR race up the interstate through Pickham County. All the troopers from the surrounding fifty miles were gathered somewhere for pancakes.

Before his divorce, George had thought about taking the exam and moving to the Patrol. Thinking was all he had done though. Darlene had wanted him to make the change. The pay was better.

After a while, Darlene had tired of waiting for her husband to move his career ahead, although she had never considered policing much of a career anywhere, including the Patrol. Still, it was a step up from Pickham County, and she expected her husband to be as upwardly mobile as he could be…given his limitations.

George told her he was waiting for the right time to make the change. He told himself that he preferred doing something besides traffic enforcement and drug interdiction stops on the interstate.

In reality, it boiled down to the fact the he was home. He loved what he did and really did not want to be anywhere else.

It wasn't until Darlene left with the girls that he realized he had waited too long. He told her he would apply for the Patrol if she would stay. She told him he was too late. He was always too late.

"Dispatch, 301, I'll be enroute to back 302." George put the microphone back in its cradle.

"Ten-four, 301," the dispatcher responded pleasantly. George could hear the chatter of other operators talking in the background at the central dispatch center that was funded by various counties and public safety units in this part of rural Georgia. The cheerful background conversations indicated that not much was happening in the law enforcement world of south Georgia that night.

He guided his pickup to an intersection and turned right. It was a ten mile ride to Power Line Road. There was no hurry. Missing persons did not constitute emergency calls.

The hum of the car's tires increased in volume as he increased speed. The buzzing of the night creatures a few feet away in the brush along the road diminished as the noise of the pickup increased.

An old car moved smoothly through the night in the opposite direction. No police officer would find any reason to stop him, especially not the one that passed him moving southbound well above the speed limit. The driver with the girl bound beside him, made his way to the interstate and turned onto the northbound entrance ramp, disappearing into the stream of red taillights.

16. Goddammit

Goddammit. The grizzled, old farmer waved a bony hand at her as the girl climbed down out of the aging Ford pickup. There was a deep look of concern in his eyes. Goddammit, he thought again.

"Girl, you be careful now," he said out the window. The old man had girls too, and he could see that this one was mistreated. Someone had done bad things to her.

He was a simple man and wanted to help. All he could think to do was to give her a ride away from the trouble. Damn, he had trouble enough of his own.

Still, he wanted nothing worse to happen to her, and he knew that plenty worse could happen. He didn't want to think too much about that.

"I mean it, girl. You be careful...especially about men and such."

"Yes, sir, I will," she said softly, and smiled back at him. Her words sounded tired as if there wasn't anything this old farmer could tell her about men or trouble or how they could combine together to create misery.

"Thanks for the ride."

She walked slowly away from the truck into the I-95 Diner, located coincidentally, at the entrance ramp to I-95. The old farmer watched her in the mirror.

Goddammit, he thought again, reaching the limits of his ability to articulate his concern for the girl and his guilt at leaving her at the diner in the middle of the night. Shaking his head, he moved slowly out of the parking lot.

The load of tomatoes in the truck bed had to be to market in the morning. The truck engine was missing on two cylinders, and the transmission missed a gear as he accelerated onto the interstate. The girl faded in the mirror, and his mind moved back to his own problems, coaxing the old truck down the highway.

Lyn turned towards the diner. The trip from Judges Creek, Georgia, her home up to this night, had only taken a couple of hours, most of that walking until she had hitched the ride with the old man.

It seemed like much longer, and her body was bone tired.

A large moth flopped loudly against the lighted I-95 Diner window. It beat itself over and over against the window as she watched. A shiver crawled up her back.

It wasn't' that she was afraid of bugs. The moth was helpless and hopeless. It would never reach the light. The futility of its efforts made her shudder. Endlessly, flopping and beating its powdery wings against the glass until it died.

She walked through the door and was assaulted by the odors of coffee and steak and eggs, thick in the close air. She touched the two hundred and fifty-two dollars in her pocket. Her mother had shoved two hundred of it into her hand as she shoved Lyn out of the door. It had taken Lyn six months to save the balance.

She considered spending some of it on a meal, then thought better of it. Her journey had only begun. Hungry as she was, the money had to get her a long way. She would eat only when it was absolutely necessary.

She could go a long time without food. Been doing it most of her life as her slight frame and hollow cheeks bore testimony.

She had always been thought of by the local boys as a pretty girl, but they had nothing to compare her with except the other local girls, all from families that struggled to get by. She had taken their advances as nothing more than boys on the rut, aching to plant their thing somewhere. After a few beers on a Friday night, they weren't all that particular.

There were times when feeling the heat herself, she would go with one of them. But she saved it mostly. Making those few times as special as they could be in the bed of some beat up truck. She didn't blame the boys for being on the prowl for tail.

What else was there to do? It passed the time, and for a few moments, it could even make you feel that there was more. It could make you feel that you and this young, hard-bodied boy could make a life far away from the pain.

But then she knew that it could never be that way with any of the local boys. They were all like their daddies. They had all been born in Pickham County, and they would all die in Pickham County.

They couldn't see beyond it, or didn't want to. Maybe they didn't need to. Maybe they were happy.

She guessed they were. Why not? Poor as they were, they did not live in homes with fathers who hated them.

Still, she knew they thought she was pretty, and she knew how to be sweet. She was going to let that take her as far as it could.

A plump woman in an apron behind the counter smiled at her. Her long, graying hair was pulled up, and there were little beads of sweat along her hairline attesting to the closeness of the night, even inside the air-conditioned building.

"How ya doin'. Why don't you set right here at the counter."

"Thanks," Lyn sighed as she pulled herself up on the swivel stool dropping the small canvas bag she carried on the floor.

"What can I get you?" The smiling waitress looked closely at her, making Lyn uncomfortable.

"Just some water, ma'am, thanks."

While the waitress moved off, she looked around trying to be discreet, but wanting to see who there might be to give her the next ride up the road. It was two in the morning, but a twenty-four hour diner on the interstate like this would always have someone moving in her general direction. North.

She avoided eye contact with the few patrons. A couple of young men, rough looking, were huddled at a table next to the window. They looked at her occasionally, and their glances made her uncomfortable.

A lone man, probably a trucker, sat at a booth under the window. He was large and heavy, wearing a tee shirt, but his face didn't look unkind. It was even a little grandfatherly. She had never known either of her grandfathers, but this could have been one of them. He had the look of a family man.

Loud talking at the other end of the counter caught her attention. A middle-aged couple was arguing. It wasn't clear what about. It seemed plain that they were both drinking. Lyn gave them another glance. If she got a ride with them, having another woman there could be a help. The arguing got louder, and the man raised his fist as if to strike the woman who raised her hand in threatened retaliation.

"Just do it, you piece of shit. Just do it! I'll have you in jail!" The drunk woman's voice shrieked at the man, who lowered his fist.

The waitress walked over to them, two cups of coffee in her plump hands and a stern look on her face.

"That'll be enough of that, or you can get out. Y'all just sit here and drink your coffee and let things settle. You hear?" Her voice was firm, and there was no doubt that she had run more than a few drunks, out of the diner.

Lyn was startled at the touch of a hairy arm brushing up against her bare skin. The large truck driver man was sitting on the stool beside her. He leaned over close and smiled.

"How ya doin' tonight, sweet thing?" The man's voice was thick and deep, like the black oil that leaked up through the ground under Daddy's tractor in the shed. On a hot day, you could smell the oil, pungent and thick, wafting in the air. This man's voice reminded her of the black oil and thick smell.

Her mouth opened but she couldn't think what to say. It was clear that he was not the grandfatherly type she had thought him to be at first glance. Her confidence sagged, and she knew that she must have looked like a scared little girl. The look in the man's eye told her that was what he wanted, and it scared her even more.

"Hey, hon! Sorry I got distracted by them two drunks; had to take care of business ya know." The plump waitress was back in front of her with a coffeepot and cup. "I sure am glad you stopped by to see your 'Auntie Kathy'."

The waitress looked at the big man and said curtly, "Henry, I'm gonna visit with my niece here so you go on back over to your booth and eat your eggs and leave us be." She just looked at him with no expression on her face at all, and that said it all. The man stood up, shrugged, and ambled over to the booth and sat down. He didn't look in their direction again.

When he was gone, the waitress looked at her and said simply, "I'm Kathy. Guess you heard that. You need a ride, right?"

Lyn just looked at her and nodded. She was close to tears and trying hard not to show it. The journey, her escape, had just started. She wasn't even out of Pickham County. How could she be in trouble already? It was too much. She felt her lip start to tremble and her shoulders start to shake.

Kathy put her plump hand out and settled it gently and solidly on her arm. It felt cool and reassuring.

"There now," Kathy said softly. "You're alright now. You don't want to let all them see you cry. You'll be needing them tears later maybe, but not now.

"Trust me, you don't want no ride with that Henry," she continued. "He comes by here few times a month, and he gives me the creeps. He's not good."

Lyn managed to squeak out through her tight throat, "You didn't seem too worried by him."

"Me?" Kathy smiled. "I ain't never met the man yet that I'm gonna let have the satisfaction of knowin' he scared me. Just look 'em in the eye, and they usually back down. Them big tubs like Henry don't know what to do when you stand up to them. They ain't used to it."

She chuckled in a superior way at her own knowledge of men and their ways.

"Of course, the good ones ain't trying to scare you. Most of them are just tryin' to get over bein' scared themselves before they talk to you. Just have to learn the difference." Kathy chuckled again.

She continued, "Now, you're gonna set here a bit, and I'm gonna get you a ride. Which way you headed?"

"North, Savannah I guess. Then further. Canada if I can get there," she replied a little embarrassed at how silly it must have sounded.

"Canada, huh? Long ways from here." Kathy shook her head and put her hand on Lyn's.

"I know," Lyn looked her steadily in the eye. "That's why I'm going."

"Okay. Good. You see them two boys over there?" Kathy nodded towards the two rough looking young men seated at the window

56

table. They saw her nod in their direction and stared down at their plates, shoveling food into their mouths as fast as they could. Clearly, they were as intimidated by the plump waitress as was Henry.

"Those boys are headed to just outside of Savannah," she continued. "They can get you that far. Then you can take I-16 over to Atlanta and go north from there, or head north up the coast on I-95. Me, I'd take the Atlanta road. Goin' up 95 takes you through all them big cities. Philadelphia, Washington, New York, Boston. Different people up there. I'd stick to the smaller places. Go up through Tennessee and Kentucky, that-a-way. "

"But," Lyn started "they kind of scare me, they looked at me..."

Kathy laughed outright this time, "Them boys? That's Cy and Clay Purcell. Harmless as pups. They work construction in Savannah and come home for the weekends. They're headed back to the city this morning, back to work.

"If they looked at you it was 'cause they ain't seen a girl pretty as you. Trust me, they come from Pritchard, down on the Florida line. Prettiest girl there gets milked every morning before sunup." Kathy paused to give a deep-throated laugh at her own coarse joke. "No, they're good boys. They'll get you that far safe and sound."

Before Lyn could say anything else, Kathy called out, "Cy! Clay! Come over here for a minute."

The two stood up and walked over to the counter, flustered to be summoned by Kathy in the presence of a girl. Lyn didn't know why she had felt threatened by them a few minutes ago.

"Yes, ma'am," one of the young men said as they walked up.

Lyn could see that they were both dressed in jeans, blue work shirts, and brown work boots. Though they were a little threadbare and ragged, and their hair was a bit long and shaggy, they were clean.

Kathy took immediate control, "Boys, this is..." She looked at Lyn.

"I'm...uh, my name is Lyn". She thought of telling them she was from Judges Creek, but then thought better of it. No need to let out too much. Never knew what Daddy would do when he found her gone, and there was no sense in leaving a trail if she could avoid it.

Kathy continued, "This is Lyn. She needs a ride up I-95 to Savannah, and I want you to take her. When you get her there, you take her to the big truck stop on the west side of the city, and you help her find another good, safe ride in the direction of wherever she's going. North she says. Okay?"

The 'okay' wasn't really a question about whether they were going to take her. It was more a confirmation that they understood her instructions and would follow them to the letter.

The two young men muttered simultaneously, "Yes, ma'am." They were waiting, somewhat anxiously, to be dismissed back to their table.

"Thanks, boys. Say hey to your uncle for me when you see him," she said smiling flirtatiously and touching her pulled up hair a bit. "Now go back to your table and finish your coffee. Me and Lyn are gonna talk for a spell and then you go. Right?"

"Yes, ma'am."

They turned away, bumping into each other as they tried to escape as quickly as possible to their table. The younger one caught Lyn's eye and smiled. She couldn't help a small smile back, but took it off her face as soon as she realized it.

Kathy gave a short laugh, "That's Clay, the younger one. Good lookin' boy. Lot like his daddy was." She laughed again and walked away calling over her shoulder, "Set right there, hon. I'm gonna bring you some breakfast."

"Thank you, ma'am... 'Aunt Kathy'... but I'll just have some coffee," Lyn said timidly.

"You sure? It's on the house."

"Yes, ma'am. I couldn't eat right now."

'Aunt Kathy' nodded with understanding. "Ok, hon. Coffee it is."

Henry watched the exchange from the booth. He couldn't quite hear what was going on, but he knew he would get no further chance to get close to the pretty, little thing sitting at the counter. He snorted and walked to the door. As he pushed it open, he saw Kathy walking back towards the counter.

"Bitch," he muttered, aiming it at Kathy, but being very careful not to say it loud enough for her to hear.

Kathy brought coffee and some toast for Lyn. When Lyn had finished it, Kathy nodded to the two young men, Cy and Clay. They stood up and waited while Lyn gathered up her few things. Then all three went outside to an old pickup in the parking lot.

The younger brother, Clay, opened the door for Lyn. She climbed onto the bench seat in the old truck. The brothers sat on either side of her. Cy, the older, drove.

The lights of the I-95 Diner faded as they pulled onto the empty interstate. The truck steadily picked up speed, putting distance between Lyn and her past life. An uncertain future loomed ahead.

17. A Search

Turning off the pavement, George followed the dirt drive up to the house and pulled beside Deputy Sandy Davies' Ford Explorer. He waited for the dust to settle and then opened the door and walked to the front porch. Sandy looked up from the small notebook he was writing in.

"Hey, Mackey, glad you could make it."

"What's up, Sandy?" George asked, nodding politely to the elderly woman on the porch.

"Mrs. Sims here says her husband went through the woods to check out sounds at the A.M.E. Church on the other side. Never came back."

"Anything else on the description?" George asked.

"Nope. Nothing," Sandy said, and then added, as an afterthought, "Oh, Mr. Sims had a gun with him."

"What kind?"

"She's not sure. Just a small handgun. Revolver she thinks."

The old black woman stood, hands clenched nervously in front. The veins in her thin arms pulsed with each squeeze of one hand on the other. The look on her face was one of embarrassment, to have troubled the sheriff with her missing husband.

George smiled up at her from the bottom of the porch steps. "Don't worry, ma'am. We'll find your husband. What's his name, by the way?"

"Harry...his name is Harold Sims. We all just call him Harry. Told him to just call the sheriff and let ya'll check it out. The old fool, he just had to go his self."

Deputy Davies reached out and patted her arm. "Well, don't worry. We'll go see if we can find him. He couldn't have gone far. It's a dark night and in the woods, it's even darker. He probably got lost or confused a little. We'll bring him home."

"He's awful scared of snakes and gators. Not like him to stay out in the woods in the dark like this," Mrs. Sims, said, more to herself than to the deputies.

Sandy turned and walked down the steps, his brow furrowed in serious concentration. He wasn't all that fond of snakes and gators himself.

Before he could say anything, George spoke, "Guess, I'll head back out to the main road and come around the front of the church. Why don't you go through the woods and check it out from that direction. I'll pick you up at the church."

Grinning, George climbed into the F-150. Deputy Davies shot him a look that said, thanks a lot, asshole.

Pulling down the drive, he could see in the mirror of the truck that Mrs. Sims was pointing across the yard to a dark patch of woods where, presumably, there was a path leading to the church.

Sandy nodded and plodded across the yard towards the woods examining the ground before him with each step. Snakes, he thought. Mackey knew damned good and well he didn't like snakes.

George turned onto Power Line Road, unimaginatively named for the high voltage power transmission lines that ran alongside the road. Sandy stood at the entrance to the path as if he were trying to negotiate his entrance into the dark, closed world of the woods.

While Sandy took his first tentative step into the black woods, George raced down Power Line Road to the main highway about half a mile away. It was called the Jax Highway, short for Jacksonville Highway. It was a two lane country road here, but as it crossed the state line and neared the Florida urban areas, it increased to four lanes.

Turning right onto the Jax Highway, it was about another half mile to the A.M.E. Church. George slowed rapidly as he approached the entrance to the graveled parking lot. Pulling off the highway, he stopped the vehicle for a moment in the entrance and scanned the church and parking lot. There was no movement and no other vehicle was visible.

After getting the lay of the land, he turned on the spotlight mounted to the truck, pointed it at the church, and slowly made a pass from front to back, tires crunching softly in the gravel. The bright light glared harshly off the white painted wooden clapboard siding of the church.

Nothing. No old man. No sign of any disturbance at the church. All was quiet.

George turned the truck and pointed it at the woods directly behind the church, guessing where the path through the woods might come out. The bright illumination made the green canopy appear almost white.

A few minutes later, Sandy Davies stumbled into view, the light from his flashlight washed out by the bright lights of the truck. He brushed something off his shoulder and waved his arm around his head as if trying to clear a clinging spider web.

Looking into the lights of George's truck, he shaded his eyes and walked towards it.

"How's that workin' out for you there, Sandy?" he called from his seat in the truck.

Deputy Davies bent over, brushed at something on his pant leg, and then squinted into the bright light and flipped George the bird. He walked around to the passenger side of the truck and got in.

"Anything?" he asked George.

"Nope. All quiet here, and I didn't see anyone walking on the highway."

"Yeah, I was wondering about that about half way through the woods. He might have decided to go back along the road instead of fighting his way through the woods." Sandy added as a theory, "Maybe someone picked him up."

"Yeah," George replied, "or ran him over and knocked him into the ditch. I couldn't see that on the way over, but I wasn't looking too close."

"Well, I guess you better take me back to my car, and we can spotlight both sides of the road. Look for any signs of an impact...or a body."

"Yeah. Just tell Mrs. Sims we are going to look around some, and we will get back to her. Don't want to frighten her for no reason if old Harry turns up after being lost in the woods."

Sandy nodded. "Right."

The two deputies clearly did not relish the task before them. The possibility of finding old Harry Sims lying in a mangled, bloody heap in the roadside ditch was a distinctly unpleasant one.

George turned the truck to the right so that it was parallel to the tree line along the edge of the woods. The bright lights picked up a small dark hump in the gravel about a hundred feet away.

"What's that?"

"Don't know," Sandy replied squinting through the windshield. "Get closer."

The truck rolled slowly forward. The dark hump on the gravel slowly grew in size. Its shape shifted in the glaring light and moving shadows cast by the truck's high beams. It changed from a shadowy mound and took on an identifiable form.

"Shit," the two deputies muttered in unison.

18. Roydon

Roydon was considered a small town. Actually, it was no town at all and not much more than an interstate crossroad. It was a settlement, a clustering of people for convenience.

There was no elected mayor or town council, but it did have a hierarchy, its own system of governing. It was the unofficial center of criminal activity for fifty miles in every direction, and the leaders of this activity were the unelected leaders of the community. The only discernible reason for its current existence was the interstate and the community's various criminal enterprises.

In addition to a very busy bar, frequented predominantly by people seeking goods and services unobtainable elsewhere in rural Georgia, there were two run down gas stations pretending to be truck stops, a couple of dirty motels and a few scattered trailers and shacks where the locals resided. These made up the entire settlement.

At one time, it had been a center of commerce for the surrounding farming community, as many of these rural, small towns were at inception. But the farmers had long since moved away or found other markets and means of transport.

Pickham County was generally considered a moderately low crime area. Except for Roydon. In Roydon, big-time, major felony type criminal activity was the standard, and the settlement continued to exist mostly for the sake of the illegal activities that took place at and around the bar, 'Pete's Place'.

The new Sheriff of Pickham County had said he was going to clean the place up and had even briefly involved the Georgia Bureau of Investigation (GBI). But finding witnesses in Roydon was problematic. Talking in Roydon about Roydon or its business enterprises was a dangerous proposition.

The occasional small-time dope case that law enforcement was able to make had no effect on the extensive illegal trafficking that took place. And the locals knew it was better to do time quietly than to speak to sheriff's deputies or the state patrol. Besides, they didn't want to speak. People who lived in Roydon, liked things just the way they were.

Like the reason for the town, 'Pete' had long since disappeared. In fact, no one even knew who he had been or where he had gone. But his bar remained and thrived.

Roydon, and Pete's Place had evolved with the times. Fifty years earlier, it had been mostly moonshine liquor. That was still available, but the inventory of goods and services had grown. Drugs of every description and type were available. Homemade meth to prescription painkillers, amphetamines, marijuana, crack cocaine, heroin and every narcotic derivation known to man could be obtained from the several suppliers who called Roydon home.

Then there were the girls. Georgia was not Nevada. Prostitution was illegal, but in a place like Roydon, it was just another item on the menu of goods and services. Girls were available for the use of the truck drivers and bikers who frequented the area. You had to know who to ask, and especially, how to ask, but they were available.

Some were there by choice because they could find no other way to survive, if you could call their existence in Roydon survival. Abusive men, fathers, brothers, husbands, or boyfriends had forced others into the trade. The stories were all a little different. The result was the same.

They were invisible, hidden and forgotten. To the families on their way to Florida vacations, truckers, business people, and military convoys passing by Roydon on the interstate, they were nonexistent.

The faded, old car pulled from I-95 onto the exit ramp to Roydon. The brake lights flashed as the car stopped at the top of the ramp. He looked both ways and then turned left, crossing over the interstate.

On the other side, he pulled the car into the parking lot of one of the filthy motels. The lighted sign said StarLite Motel, but only the 'S' and 'r' were lit. The other letters sizzled electrically, but their neon, phosphor glow had long since dissipated.

It occurred to the driver that he had probably seen a StarLite motel in every town he had ever visited, and he had visited quite a few on his runarounds. It must have been a popular name in the fifties and sixties, dawn of the space age and all.

He had been in places like Roydon before...had a knack for finding them. They dotted the American countryside, always filled with anonymous people and shady visitors. In such places, questions were not asked, and names were not recorded.

It was a comfortable place for him. Here he could move about without fear of prying eyes and ears. Averted gazes and deaf ears were the norm in a place like Roydon.

Reaching down, he checked the tie wraps holding the girl's wrists together and binding her to the frame under the seat. Her position was awkward and uncomfortable. She was forced to lean over on her side so that her head was not visible to passersby. Her pleading eyes peering at him above the duct taped mouth made him smile.

"Just checking us in to the honeymoon suite, dear."

The grin on his face made her tremble uncontrollably.

The lot of the motel was nearly deserted. Grass and weeds crowded the gravel at the edges and grew up the rear and sides of the old cinder block exterior. Two other cars were parked in front of rooms. One near the small office, and the other midway down the length of the motel. A fast food bag and several beer cans sat on the ground beside the nearest car's passenger door.

Pushing a plastic button on the metal frame of the office door, he heard an out of place doorbell chime. Through the glass, he could see someone stirring in the small room behind the desk.

After a minute, a bleary-eyed man with bedhead stumbled out to the desk pulling an overall strap over his shoulder. He bent slightly and peered through the dirty glass. It took several seconds of examination before he decided that it was safe enough and reached down to press a button under the desk. A loud buzz sounded and the office door unlocked.

There was no greeting from either.

"Need a room," the thin man said.

"How long?"

"For the night."

"All night?"

He nodded, and motel man clerk said, "Thirty-five."

He took cash from his front pocket and counted out the bills. Motel man reached behind him for a key on a peg board.

"At the other end of the building."

The man shrugged and replaced the key he had started to retrieve and handed over a different one.

Taking the key, he turned and walked through the door into the night. Motel man watched him through the glass. Sitting behind the wheel, he waited. After a minute, the man dimmed the lights and went back to the room behind the desk. It was not unusual for the StarLite's customers to want their privacy. Best to give the customers what they wanted.

When the motel desk clerk was out of sight, he cranked the engine and drove slowly through the lot to the other end of the building. He backed into the space in front of the room so that the car's license plate was not visible and so that the passenger door was away from the office and the possibly prying eyes of the night clerk. Parked in this position, he could easily and quickly move the girl from the car to the room.

Walking to the room door, he pulled the large plastic fob with the single key attached from his pocket. The door opened and he did a brief visual check. Taking the small trash can from beside the bed, he propped the door open. He did not turn on the light.

He walked outside to the car and glanced back at the office. The motel clerk was not visible.

With a quick motion, the passenger door was swung open, and he was leaning over the girl. She cringed and trembled but could make no sound. The knife was out and the tie wraps cut with a quick flick of his wrist, hands then feet. Another flick and the duct tape was cut and pulled roughly from her face, strands of her hair clinging to the tape where it had circled her head.

He probably could have carried her bound and gagged into the room and no one in Roydon would have noticed, or cared if they had noticed, but years of careful practice had taught him not to take chances. No need to arouse the curiosity of anyone who might have accidentally noticed them.

With strength deceptive for his size, he jerked her up and out of the car. The movements were so quick and the girl in such a state of shock, that there was no time or thought to escape. It would not have mattered anyway. She would not get away.

This was the moment of danger, moving his prey to the killing ground. If she cried out or struggled, they might be discovered.

But he had mastered the art of control, physical and psychological. Instinct, cunning, or skill, whatever the mechanism, he was in control and he knew it. More importantly, she knew it.

The girl stepped quietly as directed from the car. He was close, whispering in her ear. They might have been lovers, except for the knifepoint pressing deeply under her breast. The parking lot was dark, just the light from the neon sign casting a glow at the other end of the lot.

"Just get through this with me, honey. Help me. Then I will let you go."

Somehow, she was convinced. She wanted to be convinced. Deep inside, she needed to be convinced. She would survive. She had to believe it. Don't think of anything else, she told herself. Just believe it.

She nodded quietly. He saw the hope in her eyes and couldn't help a small smile. She smiled back a little. It thrilled and aroused him.

The whole process had taken less than thirty seconds. A final glance around the lot and at the office to see if anyone had observed, and he closed the door, bolting it.

He turned, his piercing gaze searching her pleading, terrified eyes. A long, deep sigh escaped his chest and hissed through his teeth. "Yes."

19. Driving Miss Lyn

Snug between the two brothers in the pick-up, she felt the fatigue set in. Not just the fatigue of the day, it was the bone weary numbness of a life of empty horizons and desperation.

Accepting the moment, and feeling warm and somewhat safe between the two young men, strangers though they were, she felt about as secure as she ever had. Her knees were close together, and she sat as upright as she could to avoid physical contact, but that was impossible in the closeness of the truck cab.

The breeze rushing by reminded her of the wind rattling against her bedroom window the night before. She shook her head trying to drive away the memory of the hulking man who filled their lives with misery and the image of her tearful mother firmly pushing her out of the house.

"You warm enough?"

She turned her head slightly. The young man's voice brought her back to the here and now. It was the one called Clay.

"What?" she said softly.

"You warm enough? You shuddered. Thought maybe you were getting cold. We can turn the heat up some if you want."

"No, I'm fine," she replied staring out the window into the pre-sunrise dark. Headlights approached and passed on the southbound side of the interstate in a streaming blur. It was hypnotic.

Lyn closed her eyes. She was tired.

The two brothers exchanged looks over her head as Lyn leaned unknowingly, on Clay's shoulder. Small breathing sounds escaped her partially open mouth as she drifted off.

"She sleeping?" Cy, the older brother and driver whispered.

"Reckon so," Clay whispered back with an eyebrow shrug.

"Gonna be a long day for her."

"Yeah. Looks like it's been a long night too."

The pickup rushed on in the dark. The brothers sat quietly, staring up the highway and listening to the girl's soft snores.

20. Crime Scene

Pungent diesel fumes from the generator on the county's fire department light truck hung heavily in the damp night air. The garish white light turned all color into shades of gray. Even the blood pooled around the shriveled, lifeless form of Harold Sims was just a darker charcoal gray seeping into the gravel.

The generator's noisy hum drowned out the night sounds. The light and droning white noise gave the little churchyard an isolated, surreal feel.

Two firefighters stood by the light truck drinking coffee and talking, watching what was going on. Every now and then, one would adjust the throttle on the light generator.

George Mackey stood beside his pickup 'preserving the crime scene'. The assignment left him little to do in reality. Sandy Davies was the primary on the call and would handle all county follow-up.

Of course, there were the Georgia State Patrol troopers who had gathered at the scene when the call went out. Standing, huddled around one of their high-speed pursuit cars, they talked quietly. A couple of them smoked. Their voices were hushed, almost reverent as if they were in church, or at a funeral. They also had no real function here, but what the hell, you didn't find an old man dead in a churchyard every night, at least not in this part of Georgia, not in Pickham County.

Mr. Sims' lonely, painful demise in the dark parking lot would be a remembered thing in these parts. Deputies and troopers on duty would spend a lot of time talking about the crime scene and their presence that night, even if they had no part in the subsequent investigation. They weren't happy about Harold Sims' death, but he was dead and being there was definitely something to talk about.

A deputy or state trooper in Pickham County might go years, even his whole career, without handling one murder. Accidental hunting shootings, sawmill accidents, traffic deaths, bar fights, yes, but a for real, stabbed through the kidney, bled to death in the dust, whodunit murder? Those didn't come around often, maybe never again. The death of Mr. Harold Sims, black male, five feet-eight, thin build, seventy-nine years of age would be remembered.

An investigator from the Georgia Bureau of Investigation stood with Sandy asking him questions. Occasionally, he would gesture at the body, the crime scene, or the woods, and Sandy would respond in short, direct sentences. It was clear that Sandy didn't care for the intervention from the GBI, but it was policy with the sheriff's department in Pickham County that all homicides were referred to the GBI. It was that way in many rural counties, and it made sense. They handled these cases routinely.

The GBI man gave a nod at something Sandy said and walked towards George.

"How you doing, deputy?"

"Had better nights," George replied, still leaning against his pickup. "Don't get many of these out here." He nodded towards Mr. Sims' form still lying in the dust.

The GBI man turned his head slightly and followed George's gaze. "Yeah, me too." He turned back to George and put his hand out.

"Bob Shaklee, GBI."

"George Mackey." George returned the quick handshake.

"This one's a puzzle. No apparent reason for someone to take out Mr. Sims. He and his wife heard noises, he comes through the woods to check it out, and then he's dead. She never sees or hears anything from him again. No scream, no shouts, nothing. The church is locked up tight, and there's no sign of forced entry anywhere. But he stumbled on something out here in the dark. Something bad, but no sign of what. No damage to the building. No way to make out tire tracks in the gravel. Nothing."

"Except Mr. Sims," George said nodding again toward the body.

Shaklee looked over at the body. "Yeah, that's going to be a tough situation. Mr. Sims, what's left of him, is the only evidence we have. Family's not gonna get the body back for a while. We'll have to take it to Savannah and have the medical examiner do the autopsy. There may be some evidence on the body. Fibers, hairs, something. The wound will tell us something about the weapon at least."

"It was a knife, a big one. Not too hard to figure that one out, and

71

tough as this might be for you, it's a hell of a lot tougher for old man Sims, I'd say." George looked at the ground and spit a stream of tobacco juice to the side.

Shaklee stood quietly, letting the acid in George's comment fade away into the night.

"Sorry," George said looking up. "A little edgy I guess. Like I said, don't get many of these around here. Shit, we don't get *any* of these around here."

"I understand," Shaklee said, nodding somberly. "Guess we have our work cut out for us."

"George. Call me George."

"Okay, George. I'm Bob. Let's get to it then. Deputy Davies said you know the county as well as anyone."

"Probably true. Been here all my life."

"Any ideas? Who might do something like this? Got some bad folks in the area? Drug dealers? Bad kids? Anything or anyplace we can start looking."

George thought of the Gantry boys out and about that night, but no, they weren't this mean. Whoever did this was just mean. Really bad, not just teenage drinkers.

"We have our share of bad folks, and there are some druggies in the county. Same as everywhere I expect. This doesn't seem to fit them though."

"Why's that?" Shaklee asked letting George think it through until he was ready to say his piece.

"Seems too professional," George continued slowly pondering the scene. "If they'd beat him, hit him with a tire iron, even shot him, might make more sense. But that knife wound, from the back, through the kidney. Seems like he was ambushed and then executed. Just one wound, least that's all I saw. If it was a local knifing, I'd expect it to be real sloppy, multiple wounds, a lot of them, some defensive wounds too, but non-lethal. Maybe one final death wound once he had weakened. But messy. Know what I mean?" George looked over at Shaklee.

The GBI man examined George with a bit more respect.

""That's pretty observant, George. Yeah, one well-placed knife

72

thrust. Seems pretty professional."

"One more thing," George added.

"What's that?"

"Professional but not military. I think the perp intended to cause maximum pain under the circumstances," George let that sink in for a moment. "Large knife, through the kidney. He didn't cut the throat and trachea to kill and prevent Mr. Sims from making noise at the same time. One thrust, right through the kidney, back to front. The shock and the pain must have been terrible. I think that's what he wanted. He's a mean asshole."

"Maybe they struggled and that was the only angle he had. Maybe he panicked and took the first opening he had with the knife."

"Maybe," George said slowly, "but I don't think so. Seems to me this was an ambush. Mr. Sims never saw his killer until the attack, maybe never saw him then. The knife was big. The single wound was large, extremely painful and deadly, but not immediately. The perp would have been able to watch Sims die, see his pain. I think he enjoyed it."

"Really," Shaklee said, looking thoughtfully back over at the body. "That's a pretty advanced theory from just one body with a knife wound."

George shrugged. "Maybe."

Gravel crunched behind them and a large white SUV with 'GBI Crime Scene Unit' stenciled on the side pulled up. Two crime scene techs got out and gathered up large briefcases that resembled a salesman's sample cases and a couple of camera bags. They walked up to Bob Shaklee.

"Hey, Bob," one said. "Sorry it took so long." He nodded over at George and George nodded back. "What you got?"

"I'll walk you through it," Shaklee replied, and then turned to George pulling a small plastic case from his pocket. "Here's my card, George. Give me a call if you think of anything else. I appreciate your insight on this," he said indicating Mr. Sims' body with a tilt of his head. "Anything at all, give me a call."

"Sure. If I think of something."

"Thanks," Shaklee said, leading the crime scene techs away. "Can

I get hold of you through the sheriff's office?"

"Yeah, they can find me pretty much any time."

Shaklee lifted a hand in acknowledgement and walked away with the techs, pointing at the area and indicating where he wanted them to start processing the scene. Unlike the crime scene tech television shows where the techs run the investigation, in real life they work for the investigator, not the other way around. Agent Shaklee would lead them through the scene, explaining what was necessary and the kinds of evidence they should look for in order to build a prosecutable case in the event that the investigators should find the perpetrator.

More gravel crunched and another county car, this one a large, new SUV, ground into the church lot, braking hard and spraying gravel. Sheriff Klineman stepped out in the midst of the dust cloud he had created.

Seeing George, he walked briskly to him. The aroma of aftershave filled the night air as the sheriff approached. He looked freshly showered and groomed.

Clearly, the sheriff had considered the possibility that there might be some cameras or reporters at the scene and wanted to put on his best face for the voters who would catch this on the morning news out of Savannah. This was a big deal in Pickham County. Unfortunately, the media had not yet had time to arrive, and the sheriff was all gussied up for nothing.

"What happened Deputy?" The sheriff's tone was short and curt, his distaste at having to interact with his least favorite deputy evident. It was a mutual feeling, and they both knew it.

"Came in as a missing person call. Husband went through the woods to check out sounds at the church here. He never came back. Sandy and I checked the area and found Mr. Sims there." George nodded over at the body on the ground by the woods. "He was stabbed from behind. Large knife."

"That it?"

"Yep. Right now that's all we have."

"Where's he live?"

"Other side of the woods. Have to go around to Power Line

Road. It's an old farm house."

"His wife know what happened?"

George nodded.

"Okay. I'll go visit with his wife after I see to things here."

The reality was that the sheriff was *only* there to visit with Mrs. Sims, and hopefully get his picture in the paper consoling the old woman. The crime scene was secure, the GBI would be handling the investigation from this point on and there was nothing for the sheriff to 'see to'.

Eventually, there would be television cameras and radio microphones. Sheriff Klineman would make sure the voters knew how involved he was and how much he felt for the plight of the little old black woman who had lost her husband in a brutal murder. There would be a television appearance showing him standing beside the victim's frail wife, maybe with a hand on her shoulder, or even an arm around her. That would be worth some votes for sure.

"Deputy Davies the primary on this?"

"Yep."

"And you?"

"Crime scene preservation."

The sheriff looked around. "Looks like it is pretty well preserved. You can go."

With that, Sheriff Klineman turned and walked towards the GBI man.

21. Way to Go George

George drove slowly from the A.M.E. church parking lot. In the mirror, he saw Bob Shaklee kneeling at the edge of the gravel beside the woods peering hard at the ground and shining a flashlight. Sheriff Klineman appeared to be talking to him, and Shaklee appeared to be ignoring him. George smiled.

Driving around to the front of the church, George shined the pickup's spotlight moving it in a slow arc around the churchyard looking for anything that might reflect the powerful spotlight beam. Anything, like maybe a murder weapon. There was nothing.

Pulling out onto the Jax Highway, he backtracked to Power Line Road, slowly moving the beam in arcs back and forth and along the roadside ditches hoping to catch something in the light that might be of use. The only thing the light picked up was an armadillo grubbing in the dirt on the side of the road, too blinded by the glare to waddle back into the woods.

At the Sims' place, he pulled into the yard, drove up to the porch and parked in the grass. Another GBI investigator, this one female, was standing on the porch talking to Mrs. Sims. The agent's gender immediately attracted George's attention. There were not many female law enforcement officers in that part of Georgia and one with the GBI was a rarity on a crime scene.

A man in his mid-thirties sat beside Mrs. Sims in a rocking chair holding her hand. George realized that this was probably her son or another relative. It occurred to him that the chair was the one Mr. Sims must have been sitting in when they heard the noises at the church. The man looked up as George approached the porch. He stopped at the steps.

The GBI agent was making notes on a small pad. Mrs. Sims sat staring straight ahead, gripping her son's hand. George could see that the veins in her wrist and hand were standing out from the force of the grip she had on the man's hand.

"You see my, Harry?"

The old woman's voice wavered and cracked, partly from age,

mostly from the pain and the loss of her husband. George realized after a moment that despite her gaze fixed on the tree line at the edge of the yard, she was speaking to him.

"Yes, ma'am."

"How's he look? Is he gonna be okay?"

The GBI agent looked around and down the steps at George. The expression on her face said, *'Okay, so now what are going to say? Oh yes, and why are you here...dumbass?'* George was wondering the same thing.

"Well...," he opened his mouth trying to think of the right thing to say, but there was no right thing.

"Mama," her son said. "You know what happened. Someone hurt Papa. Hurt him real bad, and he ain't coming back. You know that." He said it firmly but gently trying to help her through the moment.

She lowered her head. "Yes, yes, I know." Wet streaks glistened on her weathered cheeks. Her son leaned forward and put his head beside hers, his arm around her shoulders. They sat sobbing together on the front porch.

The GBI agent gave George another withering look that said this time, *'Gee, thanks for coming deputy. You really helped out and made things much better.'*

George understood and turned back towards his pickup.

"Deputy!"

George turned towards the old woman. She looked him firmly in the eye, lifted one weathered, brown hand and pointed at him.

"Yes, ma'am?"

"You catch this person, who did this to my Harry."

"Yes, ma'am. I'll try"

"You don't try, son. You catch him." It was final, nothing more to be said.

George nodded and walked to his vehicle. Glancing up at the investigator's face, he saw the smirk and the look that now said, *'Way to go...asshole'.* That was precisely what George was thinking.

The noise of the engine cranking made him cringe. It seemed loud and irreverent. He backed slowly away from the house, conscious of the old woman's eyes following him as he moved out on the road.

He drove deliberately, not in any particular direction, just away from the old woman's gaze and pointing hand. Her words echoing in his head. *'You catch him.'*

The GBI agent was right. Way to go asshole. Way to fucking go.

22. Blank Eyes

The room was perfect, small and dingy but with cinder block walls and a heavy steel door. The closest occupied room was about ten doors away, at least that's where the closest car was parked. No one would hear anything that was about to happen within the small space. Probably no one would have heard anyway but attention to detail was ingrained in his methods.

First things, first. As the door clicked quietly shut behind them, he motioned her to sit in a chair beside a small table. He did not push or touch her in any way. He simply looked at her for several minutes.

She avoided his stare. Her trembling increased as his gaze lengthened into minutes and she was shivering as if she had just stepped from icy water into an freezer.

Finally, he stepped behind her. She started to turn her head, but he reached out and roughly jerked it around straight, causing her to whimper in pain.

He pulled a piece of duct tape from his pocket and slapped it quickly over her mouth. This startled the girl, and she started to move but the knife was out and at her throat this time, pressing firmly into the groove between the trachea and neck muscle, at the point where the carotid artery would be.

Reaching down, he took a roll of the tape from the duffel bag he had thrown on the floor and looped a piece around her mouth, all the way around her head, and around her mouth again. No need to worry about anyone seeing now, and it was handy stuff, duct tape. It was used so much in movies and on television for just this sort of thing that you didn't really think it would work, but it did. It worked perfectly.

He stepped back in front of her. The hope was gone from her eyes. The fear was back. Her shivering was uncontrollable now. A shudder of excitement ran through his body.

"Now, honey. Let's start."

He saw the muscles of her neck and jaw contract. She was trying to scream. There was no sound. Her agony at not being able to make even a sound made something roar inside him. The animal in him had been raging. Now it was released to immerse itself in the kill, lapping up her pain and fear.

Over the next hours, her terror grew to a roaring crescendo, but no sound escaped. Her clothes had been cut away. A plastic tarp had been placed around and under the chair to catch what blood there was, but there wasn't much. He was careful. The knife was only there to cause pain.

The cuts he made were many but small. None bled very much. But each tiny cut was placed to cause the most pain and to inflict the most fear.

Lightly across her breasts. The corners of her nose. The soles of her feet. None would cause death, but all would cause pain and increase the greatest pain of all...her fear. He relished it like a great cat burying its head into a still warm carcass, withdrawing with fur bloodstained and gory.

The girl closed her eyes. It was an escape...an attempt to wash the horror of what was happening out of her mind.

"Open your eyes," he hissed.

She trembled, eyes closed. He lifted his right hand in a fist and struck her hard in the forehead. The blow left a bruise on her. She opened her eyes.

"Good," he said. The grin was back on his face. It was the grin she had closed her eyes to avoid.

He stood in front of her naked, his clothes folded neatly on the bed, hers severed and in tatters on the floor. Placing his hands around her throat, his grip tightened until her eyes bulged and she made an attempt at struggling for her life. It was futile. He had not spared the duct tape this time, safe in their little room at the StarLite Motel.

It was awkward standing in front of her straddling the chair, and it required a great deal of strength and time to kill in this way. That was good. He wanted it to take a long time, and the exertion now at the climax was part of his fulfillment.

Their eyes locked. Reality seemed to register in the girl's hopeless stare. It had finally become clear to her that there would be no escape. Devoid of hope, she was left only with the terror. It sat cold and heavy on her chest. Nothing could ward off what was coming.

Squinting in macabre concentration, he focused on his work, sucking out all of the fear and pain and hopelessness she was feeling. It was the marrow in the bone—the best part.

It washed over him bringing a shudder to his frame, and he relished it. Releasing the tension in his muscular hands occasionally so as not to hurry things, he gazed into the girl's eyes. They were moist and wet. He lost himself in the eyes until, after a time, they dimmed. No longer deep, liquid pools of life seeing the world around them, they were blank, empty and barren. That too, pleased him.

Sweating and trembling, he stood over the lifeless form bound to the chair. His chest heaved from the exertion…and something else. Waves of ecstasy coursed through his muscles and flesh. He stood in front of the dead girl until the trembling subsided and his breath calmed.

Turning, he fell onto the bed and slept.

23. Canada, Really

The old, banged-up pickup rattled some from age, but the engine hummed deeply. It was well maintained. Lyn sat between the two young men to whom 'Aunt Kathy' had entrusted her. She had offered to sit in the back, but the boys wouldn't hear of it. Besides, the bed was full of tools, ladders, and equipment.

Lyn's eyes fluttered open as they passed a large truck. Out of the side window, she could see the large tires of the trailer as they moved around it. Awakening fully, she realized that her head had dropped onto the shoulder of the young man beside her, Clay. With a jerk, she sat up straight in the seat.

"Nice nap?' Clay looked over at her with a chuckling smile.

"Sorry. I couldn't help it." She fidgeted and straightened her clothes out a bit in embarrassment.

"Don't be sorry. No problem."

"How long was I asleep?"

"Not long. Half hour maybe."

"Didn't mean to. I just got so tired." She yawned and stretched her arms out in front, fingers interlocked.

"No problem. Really."

A bump in the road caused some of the gear in the truck bed to bang loudly. Lyn looked over her shoulder through the rear cab window.

"What do you do? In Savannah, I mean."

"Construction," Clay answered staring out the side window at the passing landscape, still colorless and dark in the predawn light. "Working on framing up a new shopping center on the west side."

"You're building a shopping center?" Her voice made it sound like something big and important.

Clay smiled. "Well, we're one of the subs...subcontractors, working on it. Takes a lot of people, job like that."

Lyn nodded not knowing what else to say, not sure if she should say anything. These were just two strangers, and she was just a hitchhiker. Silence filled the truck's cab, emphasized by the hum of the tires and throb of the engine.

Minutes went by. "So, where you from?" It was Cy, the older brother and driver of the truck.

"Down south," she replied, not comfortable with giving out too much information.

Cy and Clay glanced at each other over her head.

"Yeah. Us too. We live down with our mama in Pritchard, just north of the Florida line a ways."

"Just your mama?" she asked. She wondered what that would have been like. Living with just a mother and no father. She wondered if she would be out here on the interstate with these two young men if there had been only Mama at home.

"Yeah. Just Mama," Cy replied. "Daddy died in a tractor accident when we were little. Turned over on him in a ditch and broke his neck."

Glancing down at her out of the corner of his eye so that she wouldn't see him looking, Clay could see that she was pretty. A little thin, but pretty. Auburn hair and long-legged. Her knees were pushed up as her feet were on the transmission hump in the center of the cab. It made her look more like a little girl, childlike. He liked that.

She may be a little thin, but so were a lot of girls who came up hard out in the Georgia countryside. He and Cy knew about that. Neither of them had ever exactly been overfed, but Mama had done her best to take care of them. They had grown up having to work hard, but it was never something they dreaded, just a fact of life. Might as well be mad at the sun rising.

Still, he and Cy had always had each other. That was something. That was a lot sometimes when things were tough. And Mama had been there for them.

What had put this girl on the road? She was young, not much more than a child it seemed to Clay. He couldn't really relate to a life so bad that you just had to walk away...run away...from everything. How did that work? He thought about it, trying to puzzle it out. He had no reference for it though. He and Cy always had Mama. Who did she have?

He felt compelled to say something. "We had Mama's brother, Uncle Thomas, to teach us some things about building, but mostly we came up without a daddy. How about you?"

Clay saw her discomfort. She sat stiffly, staring straight ahead out of the windshield, trying to avoid contact with the brothers on either side of her. After a time, she lowered her head and spoke. "I got Mama and a brother. He died in the Marines. We buried him at the church in..." She hesitated, almost naming Judges Creek and then said, "Back home." Another pause and then, "Got a daddy, too."

The boys listened quietly, sensing that there was more, knowing that any word from them would silence her, like stepping on a branch in the woods and spooking a deer you were watching.

Besides, they both knew it was none of their business. Bad things happened sometimes. Tractors turned over in ditches killing fathers. Things happened to young girls that made them leave home. There were lots of bad things in the world. That was all.

After a few minutes with only the highway hum filling the cab of the pickup, Cy decided it was his turn. "So, where you headed?"

Lyn shifted uncomfortably in the narrow confines of the cab. "North."

"North? That's pretty big area. Can't pin it down any more than that, just north?"

Lyn made no reply and continued staring straight ahead. Cy shrugged and focused on his driving.

"So, things must be pretty bad at home?" It was Clay, who spoke this time. "For you to be out on the road and all," he said, obviously waiting for an answer.

Cy cut him a sharp look over her head. He could tell that the thought of putting the girl out at the truck stop was beginning to worry his brother. They had no time for such concerns. When they next saw the waitress at the diner, Cy just wanted to be able to report 'mission accomplished'. The girl had been safely delivered to the truck stop and pointed north.

Lyn pulled the cuff of her pink pullover shirt down a bit and shifted her stare to her lap. The boy, Clay, was waiting. After several seconds, she reckoned that they deserved more of an answer for what they were doing for her, or doing for 'Aunt Kathy', at least.

"Yeah. Things are pretty bad I guess," she ventured as an opening.

Clay waited.

"Things are bad enough," she continued. "Me and my daddy had a fight. I guess we always have a fight goin'."

"You hurt?" Clay asked. He looked at her hand holding the cuff of her shirt tight.

"Not bad," she replied softly.

"Can I see?" Clay asked. "You might need a doctor."

"No, it's just a bruise," she replied, never looking up.

He reached over and slid the arm of her shirt up a ways. Lyn continued to look down at her lap. When she didn't resist, he pulled the sleeve up to her elbow.

The purple bruise on her forearm looked as if she had put it up to fend off a blow from someone much larger. He gently slid the shirt back down.

Cy missed nothing, but kept his peace. Clay knew it bothered him that he was showing an interest in the girl.

Cy was sympathetic and would never stand for anyone hurting a girl, but he was focused on the business. Drop the girl off and get to work. Anything else was a distraction they didn't need right now, and he could tell that this was turning into a distraction for his brother.

"Your daddy gave you that bruise?" Clay asked.

"I guess he did...he swung at me and...well, I got the bruise." She shrugged. "It ain't nothin'."

"That ain't right you know. What your daddy did ain't right." Clay looked down at Lyn who continued to avoid eye contact by staring at her lap or out of the window.

"It ain't nothin'," she repeated. "He just been drinkin'. Drinks a lot. He don't mean no harm, it just happens sometimes."

"Well, he ought to think of you and your mama some." Clay felt a small, growing pit of anger inside at the man who had abused this girl.

"I know, but he tries. He does," Lyn said, puzzled as to why she

85

felt the need to defend her father. "He just gets so angry sometimes. I don't think he even knows why. He just gets to drinkin'. It's like he's lost, and the drinkin' is the only way to find his way out. I don't know." She shook her head. "He don't like me, and I knew I couldn't stay no more. Mama wouldn't let me stay, was afraid for me. So I left."

She stopped speaking, wondering at all she had just said, letting things out. It was the most she had ever said to anyone about her troubled family.

The brothers soaked it all in. Hard as life had been without their father, it had never been abusive. It was hard to get their minds around the concept of beating a young girl.

"So where you goin'?" Clay decided to return to Cy's question.

Lyn said nothing and tugged at her cuff.

"C'mon," Clay urged. "Where you headed to?"

She looked up at him for the first time. "You promise not to laugh?"

Clay nodded and waited.

"I'm goin' to Canada."

"Canada? You got family there?

Lyn shook her head. "No. No family," she replied a little embarrassed.

"Well, then why go there? Why not someplace you know about?"

Lyn shrugged and gave a little laugh. "I don't know. It's a place my brother, Sam, and me always talked about goin' to get away. You know, kind of a place to start over. Different." She ended with another shrug. She knew it must sound crazy to him. At this thought, she looked up at him and added, "I'm not crazy you know. I know what I'm doin'."

Clay was quick to reply, "Never said you were crazy. Just tryin' to get it in my head. Canada, really?"

"Canada, really," she replied firmly with a touch of defiance in her voice. Maybe it *was* crazy, but she didn't have to put up with questions from this boy, who probably wasn't any older than she was.

He thought for a minute then asked, "So have you thought of

goin' anywhere else? Some place closer."

She shrugged again, looked down and said, "Don't have nowhere else to go. Canada seems right."

What exploded from him next surprised him as much as his brother.

"You could stay with us." He saw Cy looking hard at him and added, "Us and Mama."

The pickup swerved onto the shoulder and then back onto the road as Cy turned in his seat. He wanted to ask Clay what the hell he thought he was doing, but Clay returned his brother's angry look with a face that was hard and determined.

It was a look he knew all too well. Cy shook his head and leaned forward gripping the truck's steering wheel tightly. He focused on his driving, not wanting to hear anything else his brother might say to the girl.

Lyn, unaware of the silent interaction between the brothers, sat there in shock. No one had ever said such a thing to her or ever made such an offer. Why would this stranger make it?

"Now who's crazy? You don't even know me." The words blurted from her the way Clay's offer had exploded from him. It was unreal. Too much. The look on his face made her temper them a bit. "No," she went on. "That wouldn't be right. Besides, it was always Canada. It's always been in my head. It was the place. The place for Sam and me. I have to do it. Go there."

Having opened the door, Clay couldn't let it just slam shut. "But what are you gonna do? How will you live?"

"I got a little money to get there. Then I'll get a job. I can work," she answered.

"How much money?"

"Enough." Lyn was wondering just how far she would get on her two hundred fifty-two dollars, and suspected that it would not be nearly enough, although she would not admit that to this young man. Doing so would call into doubt her judgment in the matter, and the last thing she could tolerate right now was another man interfering in her life and her dream.

"It might not be so easy. You might not find work right off. They might not let you work up there. You won't have anyone there. Besides you need a passport if you're gonna go legal. You got a passport?"

Having no idea what a passport was she simply replied, "I'll get one, " and then added "I have to try." Her voice broke in a choking sob. "It's the place we were gonna go to be safe." A tear rolled slowly down her cheek.

Not knowing what else to do and feeling like a jackass, Clay moved as far away from her in the seat as he could, trying to give her what little privacy he could. The brothers exchanged glances again over the girl's head. This time the older brother's face was resigned. What the hell, he shook his head.

24. A Heavy Thud

The faded, old car pulled slowly from in front of the motel room door. The baggage had been loaded in the trunk, and the driver sipped a cup of made-in-the-room coffee. It was still dark, maybe an hour before sunrise. He noticed that the parking lot of the StarLite Motel was now empty. Apparently, the owners of the cars he had seen earlier did not require a room for the entire night.

Across the road, Pete's Place was lit brightly and glowed in the early morning mist. Business seemed to be thriving although it was well past the mandatory two a.m. last call and closing. Such minor details did not seem to apply in Roydon, at least not when the entire sheriff's department and all the state troopers within fifty miles were tied up at the scene of a murder.

Some old black guy in a church lot off the Jax Highway got knifed, the bartender advised his customers after hearing the news from one of his contacts with connections to the sheriff's department. The staff of Pete's Place kept tabs on the movement of the law around Pickham County. Such information was important in Roydon.

The patrons of Pete's Place were duly grateful for the information and contributed generously to the bartender's tip jar. No one at the bar paid any attention to the old car pulling away from the StarLite across the road.

Turning west away from the dusty, old motel, Roydon faded in the car's rearview mirror. Ahead, a quiet, empty two lane highway stretched into the darkness. He followed it a few miles, able to see only a couple hundred feet in front and the shoulder of the road. The rest was black.

The dark, predawn hour suited him. He knew he was surrounded by farmland and woods, and he knew what he was looking for. It was just a matter of finding it before the daylight exposed him.

The car proceeded at a steady pace, not so slow as to attract attention or so fast that he would outdrive the headlight

89

beams…searching. Five miles down the two lane road, he spotted a smaller country road and turned right, north. Then he saw another road, this time an unpaved dirt road leading off to the west again.

It looked right. He made the turn, cut the headlights, and crept slowly forward for about half a mile. Pulling as far to the right as the gravel shoulder of the road would allow, he put the car in park and left the engine running.

Opening the door silently, he stood and scanned in all directions for lights or other signs of houses and people. There weren't any.

He heard only the sounds of the night, insects humming, and the rustling of small animals in the brush along the road. Somewhere a rooster crowed.

There was no remote button on the old car, but he was practiced and had no problem inserting the key into the trunk lock in the dark and opening the lid. It took a little more effort to get his arms under the heavy, wrapped bundle so that he could lift it out.

The early morning predawn glow could now be seen off to the east, although he still stood in blackness on the small, dirt road. The night was waning.

Moving more quickly now, he hefted the bundle over his shoulder and walked about ten paces into the roadside brush. Beyond that, the vegetation was much thicker, and it would have been difficult to push through with his load. Besides, he could hear live things scurrying in the brush near him. There was no need to take a chance and possibly step on a snake.

He let the bundle fall from his shoulder. It hit the ground with a heavy thud.

Walking quickly back to his car, he gently closed the trunk lid with a barely audible click. He gave a final look around, got into the driver's seat and pulled across the road, reversed, pulled forward again, successfully turning the car on the narrow road, heading back the way he had come.

Fifteen minutes later, the car was passing through Roydon. The eastern sky ahead was lit with a cherry glow. In the soft, early morning light, Roydon was almost a pretty little hamlet. Almost.

The screen door of Pete's Place slammed as the old car passed by heading towards the interstate. Two large bikers stood outside blinking in the dim morning light after pulling an all-nighter. They talked animatedly for a few seconds, fist bumped, and climbed on their Harleys.

His gray eyes snapped up to the rearview mirror as he passed by, watching the bikers cross the road with a roar into the parking lot of the StarLite Motel. Smiling, he wondered if they wanted a room for the whole day, and if it would be the one he had occupied so recently. He was pretty sure the StarLite didn't promise patrons clean sheets.

25. A Sense of Well-being

A quarter mile farther up the dirt road from where the old car had stopped, Tom Ridley, who had lived in his small, frame house all of his life, was up for the day.

He had just walked outside to pee in the yard. His wife hated it when he did that, but early in the morning like this, she wasn't up and about yet. This was his private time, and that included peeing in the yard if he wanted. That's how they had done it when he was growing up, and it suited him fine. Besides, there was a sense of well-being and freedom, standing in the fresh morning air doing what nature called him to do with no one around.

As Tom was finishing his morning ritual, he thought he heard a small click. At first, he thought it was just the last few drops hitting the ground. A moment later though, he could clearly hear in the quiet morning air the sound of tires moving and turning and what sounded like a car backing up and then going forward, changing from drive to reverse and back to drive.

Probably Deputy Mackey sleeping out his night shift on the deserted dirt road and now heading home, he thought. He didn't blame him much. All them sheriff's boys had two or three part-time jobs. If they needed to catch a little shut-eye on his dirt road before going home, he was fine with that. He did the same himself sometimes out behind the chicken barns where he worked. A little nap in the middle of the workday made things seem right. They got it right down south of the border. *Siesta.* The older he got, the more he appreciated the concept.

Tom stretched, scratched, and pulled one strap of his overalls up over his shoulder. The night was beginning to fade. A light breeze came up, thick with the smells of the earth. He watched as the sky lightened.

To the east, down the little dirt road, Tom Ridley's road, the sun cast a reddish glow up over the horizon. The red glow lit the side of their small frame house in a way he never tired of seeing. It seemed that of all the houses in the world, the sun had chosen to spotlight his little house. The one where they had raised their boy, lived their lives, and most likely, where they would die. But not today, Tom smiled inwardly.

"Margaret, you up?" he hollered at the house.

A moment later, the rusty screen creaked and then clattered shut as his wife shuffled in her slippers onto the back porch.

"I'm up. I'm up. What you hollerin' about."

The plump woman in a worn robe and slippers lifted her eyes to the sunrise as she lifted a coffee cup to her lips. She smiled.

"That's a nice one, Tom. Real nice."

They stood quietly watching the world wake up for a few minutes.

"Here," she said. "Come get your coffee... and have you been peeing in the yard again?"

She shook her head and went back through the screen door. Tom Ridley thumped up the old porch steps and grabbed the screen door before it closed, casting one last rearward glance down the road towards the rising sun. The rightness of the scene made him smile.

26. The Crack

The whine of the car's tires hitting the rumble strip on the edge of the asphalt forced his eyes open. George Mackey was fatigued.

By this point in the night, the adrenaline had faded, and although Mrs. Sims' admonition to catch the person who had murdered her husband still echoed in his ears, he found his head nodding and eyes closing as he drove. The radio chatter from the units, state and local, responding to the murder scene at the church had faded into the early morning silence so familiar on this shift.

Directed by the sheriff that he had no further duties at the crime scene, he had made a wandering patrol of the county. When he nearly put the truck into a roadside ditch, George decided it was time to head for one of his 'cracks'.

A crack was a place where others usually did not go, and a deputy could fairly safely pull over and sit undetected and watch, or doze as was the case this night. All deputies had their favorite crack. George headed to his now.

It was an old rest area on a state highway. Not one of the big, fancy rest areas on the interstate, it was just a dirt pull-off from the two lane highway with a couple of picnic tables surrounded by large trees. The state maintained it, such as it was, because it was on a stretch of state highway that crossed southern Georgia from east to west, skirting the Okefenokee Swamp.

Backing his vehicle as far as possible to the rear of the rest area, George stopped amidst the trees and brush, and cut the engine. The brown sheriff's pickup was invisible in the dark and shadows.

Rolling the window down, he gave a knob on the radio a quick twist to turn the volume up and pulled his jacket tight around him. A minute later, his eyes fluttered closed.

It wasn't long before the tire and engine sounds of the approaching car had roused him. The noise increased in pitch as the car approached.

George sat motionless, head back against the headrest, bundled in his jacket, arms folded across his chest. His eyes were slit open and peering over the steering wheel as the car passed, the Doppler effect causing the engine noise to decrease in pitch as it moved away from the deputy's position. From habit, George noted the car, registering it in his subconscious.

Older model car, maybe a Chevrolet or Pontiac or some other GM model. Color was uncertain, maybe gray or faded brown. Very plain looking.

It was a little early for traffic to be out, but not unheard of. Probably a car traveling from the west across the state, headed to one of the coastal towns or barrier islands. George was not aware that the car had already passed this way heading west, not more than fifteen minutes before George had pulled into the rest area.

No big deal anyway, farmers around here all drove old cars. Normally, they rose and slept with the sun. While this was a bit early for them to be out, sometimes the old ones couldn't sleep like normal people and would be up and fidgety at ungodly hours for no apparent reason, checking on livestock or a vegetable garden or the chicken barns or some such farm stuff.

They couldn't wait until daylight. It was just their nature. He knew it because he had come up on a farm not far from here, and he had made up his mind not to live that life.

George Mackey shifted in his seat a bit, pulled his jacket tighter around his neck and waited for daybreak so that he could call the dispatcher and tell her he was going off duty. The old car's taillights faded out of sight. Dumb farmer, he thought.

27. Lylee

Leyland Torkman...he actually went by the nickname Lylee...was completely unaware of Tom's morning ritual or George's secret napping spot. Having retraced his route in the old Chevy back to the StarLite Motel and onto I-95, he relaxed a bit and scanned the interstate for danger...and opportunities.

The sobriquet of Lylee was one used by those who knew him, not because they were friends and on intimate terms. It would have been difficult, perhaps impossible, to find someone who actually called him 'friend'. People who knew him just learned to call him by the name his mother had used when he was a child because it was the name he used for himself.

He had not adopted the name through any attachment to his mother. The innocent, childlike sound of it suited his purpose. It was another form of camouflage. Others might have snickered at the childish name, but that was between them, and not within the hearing of Leyland Torkman.

The nickname from his mother had come possibly because she thought it a cute name for her cute little boy. She had told him in his younger years that *'Lylee'* was how he had pronounced his own name as a toddler, and so she had started calling him that. It was hard to believe that there had ever been any motherly affection in the life of this quiet, sullen man but, in fact, he had had a mother who thought he was the center of the universe. While they had lived on the edge of poverty, she worked hard to make sure he had the nice things that other children had.

That was a bone of contention between his mother and father, a man who worked at menial jobs trying to support his family and who felt that they shouldn't put on airs to be like others. The dead-end work and endless poverty had led his father to drink, and eventually an early grave.

The departure of his father from their life was hardly felt by Lylee. His mother had kept him isolated from the only man who could have been a part of his life. He belonged to her and no one else.

He was her little Lylee.

It hadn't always been so. The pride of fatherhood had brought them together as a family, at first. Although Lylee had no memory of it, and his mother would never have shared it with him, Bud Torkman had been as devoted to his son as the boy's mother was. But tension had grown between them as it became clear that she considered Lylee hers, not their son...hers.

Eventually, the tension with his wife and the burden of barely being able to provide for his family had worn him down. The alcohol and the emotional distance he put between himself and wife and child were a barrier. It kept them out and him in. In the end, the old man just came and went to work and barely spoke to his son or acknowledged his existence.

The loss of his father was not tragic. In fact, it didn't register at all to Lylee. The event had no significance and meant nothing to him. The boy continued in school as an average student. He had no extracurricular school activities, but did have an after school job at an early age. He was considered a good worker by a succession of employers, but none ever asked him to stay when he left. An air of inapproachability surrounded the young man. He moved through the world invisibly.

The only relationship in Lylee's life was with his mother, who became increasingly possessive with age and the barrenness of her own life. Relationship was, in reality, a stretch in describing the interaction between mother and son.

She doted on him and demanded a level of affection in return that he was not able to provide, nor inclined to return. For his part, he tolerated the woman who had given him birth, but just barely.

Eventually, he left for good. Some said that it was his mother's possessive clinging that had driven him away. Most people just knew that Lylee was destined to leave, and if he never came back, so much the better. He was a creepy kid anyway.

It was, perhaps, self-preservation and not an actual awareness that pushed him finally out of the front door and as far away from his mother's presence as he could get. The solitary young man put himself through technical school, studying computer programming.

It was a vocation ideally suited to him, requiring minimal interaction with other persons, and then only about the technical aspects of programming.

Hovering over a keyboard inputting code, required no unwanted contact or office bullshitting with co-workers. As long as he did his job, his employer was happy. The fact that he was an almost anonymous employee to even his closest supervisor was actually a benefit from a management perspective. He required little of their administrative time, never complained, and worked well without requiring much supervision. They cared not at all about his activities outside of work.

Visits to his mother became exceedingly rare, and when he did visit, there was nothing to say. She chattered as always about her little Lylee who had come to visit. It was a fantasy.

He knew that he had never been the cute, bubbly boy she babbled on about, and they had never been the happy family she portrayed them to be in her rambling monologues while he sat with a glass of cold lemonade dripping in the humid air over his fingers and onto his lap. He made the visits because it seemed that was what he was expected to do, although not sure who it was that expected it of him or why he cared.

Why did he care? That thought became the moment of awakening for him. Why should he care? He didn't care.

Somewhere deep in his psyche, awareness grew that he need only do what *he* wanted. It was a liberating concept for Lylee, and eventually the visits home ended.

From that moment. he was liberated by the isolation in his life and separation from the shreds of family memory that only barely existed at best. It was freedom to him, and the power he felt within grew as his separation and distance from the rest of the world increased.

At the age of fifty-six, his mother followed her husband to an early grave, probably feeling much the same isolation and desperation he had felt. The loss of her Lylee had been too much. She died alone and unremembered by her only son, her Lylee.

Now, he lived invisibly and alone within the isolation that

brought him security and freedom. And with that freedom, came great power. And the power brought him...everything.

Invisible and solitary, it grew within, the power. It raged and roared to be unleashed. And then one day, he opened the door. Instinctively, he became the predator.

The truth is that his family life probably had little causative effect on what he had become. It was coded deep in his genes. The sad and pathetic childhood he had endured, the absence of a strong fatherly influence, and the cloying possessive nature of the relationship with his mother only made it easier to transform into his true nature. It would have happened, sooner or later.

With the transformation, the world jumped into focus for him. A different light shone around him. Invisible to others, it illuminated the world around him differently than the normal light that others used to discern their surroundings.

Becoming the predator, his view of his environment and perception of others evolved into something not human. He learned the techniques of preying, carefully selecting the weak and the unaware. His runarounds were training exercises that honed his predatory skills. His power increased with each hunt.

The pain he inflicted on his victims was important only because it brought him greater power. He felt no more for them than a coyote does for the jackrabbit in its jaws. A true sociopath, it was right because it was good for him. That was enough.

28. Too Complicated

George Mackey dropped his Sam Brown belt with its gear on the weathered boards and plopped his ass down into a porch chair. Flipping up the lid of the scuffed and ever-present cooler, he grabbed a beer, popped the seal on the can, and held it to his lips for a long pull with his head tilted back.

"Little early, ain't it?" The old man came walking around the side of the house and deliberately took the three steps up to the porch, holding the handrail. The morning was turning hot, and on reaching the porch, he stopped and wiped the inside of his hat with a dirty handkerchief, then set the straw, wide brimmed hat back on his head.

"Had a long night," George replied taking another sip from the can.

The old man nodded and eased himself slowly into the other porch chair. They were really kitchen chairs that had become porch chairs when they had been dragged outside sometime in the past, long before George had taken up residence at Fel Tobin's place.

"Believe I'll join you." Tobin reached into the cooler and pulled out a beer for himself. By mutual, unspoken agreement, the cooler was always between the two porch chairs and was absolutely never empty. Both men threw the beer contributions in when it got low and added ice periodically.

George had come across the old man while looking for a place to stay during a drawn out and messy divorce. His friends all told him that divorce was an occupational hazard in law enforcement, even for deputies in a rural Georgia county. He had a different theory. His ex-wife, Darlene, hated him. It was a theory, elegant in its simplicity that seemed reasonably sound.

He admitted that she probably had good reasons. The list included her husband's good old boy, country ways, always worrying about the next paycheck and which bills to pay, the small, plain house they would probably spend the rest of their lives in, and the

100

fact that Pickham County was what it was. Darlene wanted more, and after the new had worn off their marriage, she had filed for divorce.

To her credit, it had taken ten years and two daughters to bring her to that point. In the end, it all boiled down to the same thing. She hated the life they had led while they were married, which meant that by default she hated him. At least, that's how George saw it.

He had asked her once during the fighting why she hated him so much. The question had made her catch her breath.

After a few seconds of silence, she had looked him in the eye and said, "Because you're late, George. You are always late. Late to pay the bills. Late to come home. Late to make sergeant at the Sheriff's Department. Late to apply for the Patrol. You were even late for the births of our daughters, busy with something or other in the county, but late just the same." She had taken a breath and ended with finality, "Late, George. You are always late and always will be."

For his part, George had quietly signed the papers and given her everything she wanted, which was everything. It didn't matter. It was the price of peace, and it was worth it.

He understood. It was true. He was always late. Late to be what she needed and to give her what she wanted. Darlene had remarried a year later to a man who was a supervisor at a paper mill plant out on the Georgia coast, and who was never late. George had found old Fel Tobin. It was a good trade to his way of thinking.

The day he had moved out of the house, he had gone to the grocery store bulletin board in Everett, the county seat. Everything was advertised there, free of charge.

A card with a telephone number had the words 'Room to Rent' printed in pencil in large block letters. As it turned out, it was two rooms and a small bathroom over an old barn. He went to the location and found an old man riding randomly around on a lawn mower, not really mowing anything in particular. It was a quick deal. George looked around and handed old Fel Tobin some cash, and it was done.

"So. You gonna say anything about it?"

"What? Oh, the night." George sipped his beer. "Had a stabbing last night. Old man was stabbed in the A.M.E. church parking lot out on Jax Highway. He's dead."

"The hell you say. Stabbed dead in a church parking lot? The hell you say."

"Yep. He's dead, and we don't know who did it, but it was a real bad person."

"Well, it would have to be a bad person to stab someone to death in a churchyard."

"It's more than that. Person who did this, did it to cause a lot of pain."

"Oh," Fel thought this over a bit, sipping his beer. "Who was it?"

"Don't know. We're looking for him now, but not much to go on."

"I mean the person that got stabbed. Who was it?"

"Oh," George said trying to shake out the memory of Mrs. Sims' pointing finger. "Harold Sims. He and his wife live over on Power Line Road."

"The hell you say. I know Harry. Bought a hog from him once. Damn, stabbed in a churchyard." He sipped his beer again and then repeated for emphasis, "Damn. You sure he's dead?"

"He's dead."

"Damn. Harry Sims stabbed dead in a churchyard. Damn."

"Yeah," George nodded in agreement and sipped his beer.

Minutes ticked quietly by, broken only by the sound of George retrieving another beer and popping the top. Although still morning, the day was heating up, and the heat filled the air with the rich aroma of green living things.

Grasshoppers buzzed around in the scalped grass that Fel never stopped mowing. A bluebird swooped to the ground from its concealment in a forsythia and impaled a grasshopper, darting quickly back to its perch.

The two spent a lot of time on the porch. Cold, sweating beer cans in hand, they might not say much, just sitting there in the humid evening, watching the twilight and then full night coming on.

To say that they sat there contemplating the meaning of life would have been too grand a description. Usually, they just sat watching drops of water slide down the cold cans and drip onto the

102

dusty planks of the porch, considering the puzzle of life. Sometimes it seemed that the puzzle pieces were pushed around and forced together, causing the picture to warp and buckle.

George stood up and tossed the empty can into the old wooden crate by the front door. It clanked against the fifty or so others that had been deposited inside. He picked the Sam Brown belt up off the porch and slung it over his shoulder, the handcuffs and keys jingling, and the pistol thumping him in the side.

"Well, guess I'll turn in," he said starting down the creaking steps. "You mowin' today?" He threw the question back over his shoulder, knowing the answer.

"Yep. Just like always."

George nodded and walked around the side of the house and across the yard towards the barn where his apartment was. An acorn thumped onto the hood of his county pickup parked under an old oak. As he climbed the steps outside to the second floor of the barn, the sound of Fel's lawn mower sputtering and then roaring to life filled the air. George knew he would spend the morning mowing before the day got too hot.

It all seemed so natural. The acorn dropping, the grasshoppers in the grass, the bluebird in the forsythia, the smell of the vegetation, the noise of the mower. How could those things exist in the same world as the dark stain in the gravel and dust of the church parking lot, and the old woman's brown, weathered hand pointing at him. "You catch him Deputy. You catch the person who did this to my Harold."

It was too complicated for George, and he was too tired to think about it. He hoped he would sleep.

29. Things Less Clear

The glow of the Savannah city lights ahead had been slowly overpowered by the sun rising to the east over the Atlantic. Cy wondered how breakfast at the I-95 Diner had led to this. Dropping the girl off at the truck stop seemed a simple task, but it had the feel of something different, and he wasn't sure what. It was something just beyond his ability to discern and understand.

It was clear that Clay felt it too, and was being taken in; maybe sucked into a situation they were happily ignorant of just a couple of hours earlier. As the light coming in from the east was changing the way things looked over the Georgia countryside, things for the brothers looked different than they had just a few hours before. Cy was not happy about it.

Up ahead a large sign lit in red, white, and blue letters said 'AcrossAmerica'. Cy took the exit, turned right and then left across the road into the lot. The old pick up bumped over potholes and gravel at the entrance torn up by the heavy truck traffic.

The truck stop located on the outskirts of Savannah, Georgia was a hive of activity. To one side there were big rigs fueling at the wide lanes around the diesel pumps. On the other side of the main building were gas pumps for cars and smaller trucks. The smell of diesel fuel and exhaust hovered in the air. Air brakes hissed, engines rumbled to life, and transmissions shifted quickly through the lower gears as trucks flowed back towards the interstate and the river of traffic that passed north and south along I-95 and to the west on I-16 towards Atlanta.

This was a full service truck stop, which meant that truckers could have their rigs serviced, take a shower, relax in the lounge, or play video games or pool while they waited for their next load. A small, attached motel offered cheap rooms for those who had had enough of the cab sleepers in their trucks or for those whose cabs did not have sleepers.

Services included a diner, general store, and a gift shop. A few older couples who had stopped for a meal or to gas their motor homes wandered uncertainly across the lot from the pumps to the store. They looked out of place in the midst of the truckers.

Cy guided the pickup to the few lined parking spaces for cars in front of the main building and parked at the entrance to the 'diner-cafe-restaurant'. It seemed like a good place to look for a ride for the girl. Lyn, he thought, Lyn, although he didn't want to attach a name to her. The more anonymous she was the better for them, at least as he saw it.

Clay pushed the creaky truck door open and held it while Lyn climbed out. He pulled her small bag out of the bed and walked inside with her. Cy followed. The plan was to get some coffee, scout things out, and see if they could hook her up with a ride. Someone they could trust.

Kathy's instructions, orders really, from the diner still rang in their ears. She had entrusted Lyn to them, and they knew they had better make a good faith effort to find her a ride, a safe ride, or at least as safe as they could reasonably ensure.

Finding a table in the restaurant, they ordered coffee, and the boys began looking around. Cy could tell that Clay was having a hard time letting go of the idea that the girl could stay with them, or maybe just letting go of the girl.

He had never seen his brother like this. Clay was always the stud with girls lined up, none of them serious, and he moving through them unattached, enjoying whatever they were willing to offer, but oblivious to their attempts to hold him to something more.

This girl...the name Lyn crept into his brain although he tried to force it out...was different. Best to find her a ride quickly then. Let her climb into one of the rigs headed north, and let the brothers get back to business.

The dining room was a busy clatter of dishes and cups punctuated by the scent of eggs and bacon. Truckers were downing coffee and huge platters of eggs in various forms and with assorted other food items in the eggs or on the side. Oatmeal and bran muffins were apparently not on the menu, or at least were not being consumed. A few read newspapers, others sat in the smoking lounge and chatted with other truckers.

Interspersed among them were tradesman like Cy and Clay. A few family travelers, usually older people driving big land yachts or the ones who had been fueling their motor homes at the pumps, made up the remainder of the clientele.

The Purcell boys and Lyn waited for their coffee and looked around. Cy was beginning to realize that the task they had been given, while simple enough on the surface, might be a bit more tricky than they had thought. He wasn't sure where to start or exactly who to talk to about getting a ride for Lyn.

He glanced over at Clay who was intently focused on Lyn. She was going through her purse carefully. It made her look small and vulnerable. She was counting money to herself. Cy felt something briefly tug in his chest, but then forced it away. He saw it coming but was powerless to stop it. Clay spoke to Lyn.

"You want some breakfast? I'm buying."

"Oh, no. It's okay. I've got some money."

"Well, you best save your money. Long ways to Canada, you know."

The waitress arrived with their coffee, and Clay began ordering breakfast for the girl. Cy gave up and stirred some sugar into his cup. How in the world did they end up here?

A reddish beam of light pierced the dirty café window as the sun broke suddenly above the window sill. The bright rays lit everything up from the side, making things stand out clearly in the contrast with the dark shadows.

Cy squinted at the window as a waitress moved over to close the blinds. The higher the sun rose, the less direct the light, and as the shadows faded, the less clear and defined things would be.

The world always appeared washed out and bland in the day sun. Without the side lit shadows, things were less clear. And that was how it felt. The longer they dawdled around with the girl, the less clear things were becoming for the brothers.

30. Gassing Up

The northbound traffic was light this time of day. Mostly trucks trying to make some miles before the heavy traffic crowded I-95. The old Chevy proceeded northbound keeping pace with the trucks.

His little bit of business done, Lylee settled back and began looking for a gas station and convenience store where he could fill the tank up in the old car and get some coffee. Just a guy on the road making miles. He could have been anyone.

The early morning hour made him feel alive after the night's activity. For much the same reason that Tom Ridley liked relieving himself in the yard in the darkness just before sunrise, it was his time. Quiet and solitary time. It gave him a sense of freedom.

The lights of a gas station lit up the horizon a couple of miles up the interstate. Pulling off at the exit, he drove up to the regular pump and started filling the tank. There were no other cars around. The digital numbers on the pump whirred by quickly.

Walking inside the little convenience store, he could smell coffee brewing. He found the pot and poured himself a cup. He was looking around for the clerk when she startled him coming out of the drink and beer cooler. A small laugh escaped from her when she saw him start.

"Sorry," the little blond said. She couldn't have been more than eighteen or nineteen. "I could see you through the glass door on the cooler. Just stocking the shelves for the day."

His 'charming' smile spread across his face. It was one of the many faces he could present to the world.

"No problem. Just thought there might be something wrong."

She smiled back, her 'be nice to the customers smile'.

"Nope. No problem."

She was still smiling. Lylee stood there in a casual way, staying away from the cash register and sipping his coffee, taking everything in.

"It would make me nervous working here at night on my own," he offered as an opener.

107

"Naw," she said matter-of-factly. "I guess I was a little nervous at first, but I been here seven months now and never had a problem. The deputies and state patrol usually stop by a couple times a night. Didn't see them last night though. They must have been busy.

Lylee nodded. Yep, they were busy. Definitely busy. They would be busier still, soon.

"And there's always a trucker or someone like you comin' in," she continued, "So I'm not alone here much."

"Besides," she added, "we got a camera". She nodded her head in the direction of the wall.

Lylee looked up with mild interest in the direction she indicated. It wasn't necessary. He had seen the camera right off. He had also seen that it was focused on the cash register and that if he didn't get within three feet…say five feet to be safe…it would never see him. He would just be someone off to the left talking to the pretty blond.

This was not a sign of a superior intellect. It was just a part of his instinctive cunning.

The predator in him never ceased calculating, figuring the odds, the probability of success or failure, and assessing danger. He was good at it. He had the knack of self-preservation, and of course, there was that luck that seemed to follow him and watch over him on his runarounds.

He told his few acquaintances at work that he just went for driving tours to some national park or historic site or city on his excursions. He made sure that he actually researched the places he was supposed to visit and always had a few travel brochures so that he could answer questions for the few people who would give a shit about what he'd been up to. It wasn't a very large group.

The excursions kept him sane, like a good vacation for most people. Of course, in Lylee's case, sane was a very relative term. If the details of the runarounds had been known to those who were acquainted with him, it is unlikely that sane would have been an adjective that anyone used in connection with Leyland Torkman.

At the moment his brain whirred on automatic behind the gray eyes, calculating the odds of having the pretty little blond join him on this runaround as project number two. He casually scanned the surroundings, outside and around the store.

He wondered how she would react if she knew about the bundle he had dropped off not ten miles from here. Would she still have that cute little smile on her face? Maybe not, but it made *him* smile to think of it.

"What? Did I say something silly?" the blond asked, seeing the smile.

"Huh? Oh, no, not at all. I was just enjoying your company and sipping my coffee, thinking what an unexpected pleasure to be able to spend a few minutes with a girl as pretty as you on a long trip."

This time he smiled for real. He really could be quite charming when he wanted. It was part of the disguise; high grass to hide what lurked below, blending in so that they wouldn't see the claws and fangs until it was too late.

Now she was smiling, and said softly, "That's nice. Men around here don't talk like you do."

Her Georgia drawl was a little softer and more syrupy than it was a minute ago. A few more minutes, he thought. She was still unsure, but soon he could invite her to breakfast or find some other pretext to get her from behind the counter and away from the camera.

"So where are you headed?"

"Oh, just taking a little road trip," he said sipping his coffee. "Thought I would go up to Maine. There's a place where the sun rises first in the entire United States."

"Really? That would be fun to see." The customer smile was gone, replaced by her 'I might want to know you better' smile. She leaned forward on the counter a bit. "I never really go anywhere."

"No?"

"Nope. Born and raised in Pickham County. Been to Savannah a few times. Boyfriend took me to Atlanta one weekend to see the Braves play."

"That must have been fun," he offered, still sipping thoughtfully at his coffee while evaluating the blond and waiting for an opening.

"Naw, not really. I'm not much into baseball. That was a while ago anyway. He's not my boyfriend anymore anyway." She dangled the statement there like an angler waiting for a bite, completely unaware of the extreme danger in baiting this particular fish.

Lylee smiled. "So, no boyfriend and you like to travel. And here I am, no girlfriend and I *am* traveling. Quite a pair, aren't we?"

The moment was close, so close.

"I guess we are," she said with a flirtatious giggle.

Air brakes screeched and hissed from outside. The focus on his prey had distracted him momentarily. Awareness of his surroundings came crashing in upon him.

He had been uncommonly careless, and he realized that maybe she was just a little too cute. It was only a short ten miles from this gas station to his dumpsite. He hadn't even left the county, not far enough for safety. Wouldn't be good for a stranger to be remembered talking to a pretty, young girl when his dumpsite was discovered.

Snatching a bill from his pocket, he reached out and threw a twenty on the counter. The girl started to make change.

"Don't bother. Keep it," he said, already opening the door.

The two men who climbed down out of the truck never really noticed him drive quickly, but carefully out of the parking lot. The little blond watched him leave, astonished at his sudden departure. She was off in an hour and was thinking they might have spent some time together before he had to move on.

Maybe, the thought had crossed her mind, she might have gotten to see the sunrise from the spot in the United States where it rose first before anywhere else. That would have been fun, or at least different. Something different from being stuck in Pickham surrounded by truckers and farmers and horny young boys. He was different. She liked that.

"Probably queer," she said to herself as the door opened and the two truckers came in.

"Hey, Beth, how you doin'?" one of the men said.

"Doin' good, Pete. Tommy. How y'all been. Haven't seen you here in a few weeks." The customer smile was back on her face.

"Yep. Just making a run down to Fort Lauderdale. What you lookin' at?"

110

Gazing over their shoulders, she was surprised to see no car out by the pumps. The strange man was gone.

"Oh. Nothing," she said and smiled her best at the two truckers. They didn't have the way about them that the stranger did. They were just customers.

Lylee was a mile up the interstate heading north. Reaching for the sunglasses in the car's glove box, he squinted his right eye in the bright sunlight that had just exploded above the horizon.

31. Plenty of time.

She ate with determination. Steadily forking it up and chewing it down without looking up. Other than the toast at the I-95 Diner, it was the first food she had had since early yesterday, long before the trouble started with her father. The Purcell boys just watched and sipped their coffee.

Cy eyed the truckers in the cafe, looking for one that might be trusted with the young girl. Clay eyed the young girl.

Lyn looked up at him and smiled.

"Sorry," she said. "I was hungry, I guess." She mopped up some egg yolk with a piece of toast.

"What you gonna do now?" Clay asked, looking down at his coffee. "Offer still stands. Come stay with Mama and us. At least until you get things sorted out."

Cy heard but continued to eye the truckers in the cafe. Let Clay do what he had to. He was going to make sure he fulfilled Kathy's instructions, while this little drama between Lyn and Clay played itself out.

Lyn looked at the young man and knew he was trying to say something to her and wasn't quite sure what. The fuller her stomach became the more worthy of consideration Clay's offer became. Almost, she could see herself saying yes and going off with him to stay with his mother. Almost.

But the boys were from Pritchard, not all that far from Judge's Creek. Daddy would find her, and when he did...what? She wasn't sure, but whatever it was, she couldn't drag these boys into it and make them a target for her father's anger.

"I don't know. It don't seem right. I just got this picture in my head of Canada, and I can't get it out." She paused and took a breath as if to try to understand for herself, "Sam and me. It was our way to get away from it all; from the fighting. I guess now it's just burned in me. I can't seem to let it go."

She glanced over at Cy, noticing the way he was studying the truckers.

"Besides, your brother is right, it's not really a good idea."

Clay shot Cy a sharp look, and he quickly looked down at his coffee. "It's not that," he said. "It just took me by surprise. 'Bout the same as you, I expect." He looked over at his brother, "Clay always was quicker to decide on things. Takes me longer to figure them out. That's all. You'd be welcome if you wanted to come back to stay with us and Mama."

Clay nodded and turned towards Lyn. "So, now you see we both want you to come home. No strings attached. It just ain't right for you to be out here on your own. I don't feel right leaving you here."

Cy looked up and added, "He's right about that, you know. I been looking around here, and I wouldn't know where to start or who to trust." He shrugged and then looked her in the eye for the first time. "It really is chancy to just get in a truck with someone." He looked away again and added, "Wouldn't want anything to happen to you."

She wasn't used to people treating her this way and didn't know what to say. They were good boys. The older one wasn't as taken with her as Clay, but they were both good.

She looked back at the younger brother.

"I don't know," she said shaking her head slowly. "Like I said, it's just burned in me, Canada. Crazy, I know." She shook her head at the irrationality of the dream and her situation.

"So, what are you gonna do then?" Clay asked. "You heard Cy. He's right. How you gonna know who to trust?"

"I don't know. I don't know. I'll just sit here and try to figure it out. I'll find someone to trust," her voice quavered, "or sit here until I do. I have to give it a try."

Damn. Clay realized that running into this girl at the diner was changing a lot of things for them. Before, there had just been the business and getting to Savannah. Work all day and a few beers, then a bed in a cheap hotel outside of town. Do the same all week, and then drive home with his brother Friday night.

Now there was...something else. The girl...Lyn...had stumbled into their lives. None of them had asked for it, especially her, but there it was...and whatever it was, leaving her there alone seemed wrong beyond all reality.

He took a deep breath and then took a napkin from the holder. "Here," he said scrawling on the napkin with a flat carpenter's pencil he had taken from his pocket. "This is my cell phone number."

Clay saw the question in her eye.

"Cell phone, one of these," he pulled the battered phone from a weathered leather case on his hip. "You know about cell phones, don't you?"

She smiled a little, "Yeah. Seen 'em before. Never had one. Never called one before."

"Well, this is the number to mine. You take it and keep it. We have to go check in at the job, but we'll be off around five this afternoon. Okay?"

She reached out and took the napkin from him. Their hands touched briefly, and they withdrew quickly, embarrassed.

"We'll be back this afternoon. You don't have to go anywhere. We'll pick you up after work."

She was stunned. Things were completely out of balance as she tried to process this new development. "I'll try. I can't promise. I don't know," was all she could say.

"You know, you got to trust someone sometime. We're not gonna hurt you. Your choice."

She nodded and looked away. Doubt was creeping in and clouding her plan.

"Okay, we'll pick you up. It's settled."

At that, she stiffened and looked Clay firmly in the eye. "Nothing's settled. I said I'd try, but I'm not promising anything."

Chastised, Clay looked away this time. More softly, he said, "Okay. Sorry, you're right. No promise, but even if you get a ride, call this number and let us know you're okay. Just so we won't worry. Fair enough?"

Lyn nodded.

Awkwardly, Cy stood up. There wasn't much else to say. She was old enough to be on her own if she chose.

He looked down at Lyn. "You take care girl. Call us if you need something, anything." He started to walk away and then turned and said, "See you tonight when we come by, if you're here." A few seconds later, he was across the room and by the door paying the bill at the cash register.

Clay stood, slowly. "I hope you're here this afternoon." It was a last plea.

Unable to commit to the end, she could only mutter, "I'll try." Her hand quickly flicked away a tear as Clay turned towards the door.

The two brothers clumped out of the cafe in their work boots. No one paid any attention to the little drama playing out in the cafe. No one except a heavyset truck driver sitting in a booth in the far corner.

Henry, the trucker, had watched with keen interest. He was in Savannah waiting for a load, and the AcrossAmerica Truck Stop was a gathering place for drivers with time on their hands. He couldn't hear what was being said, but it was clear that there was a lot going on at the table where the girl sat with the two boys.

Two punks, he thought. And the girl, Kathy's niece, my ass. That girl was just some straggler on the road, and Kathy had them two boys bring her down the road. Didn't trust him to do it. Well, he'd see about that.

Henry motioned the waitress over and ordered some more coffee. He didn't have a load until tonight. Plenty of time.

32. Runaround

An hour north of Pickham County, a police cruiser, lights flashing and siren wailing, roared south on the interstate passing the old Chevy in the opposite direction. Every nerve ending and sense twitched, testing the air for danger. They controlled his every movement. His face had the alertly concerned look of an alley cat caught with its head in a garbage can when the porch light comes on.

Somewhere in a buried place in his brain, everything was evaluated to determine what his next reflexive action should be. Remain motionless? Fight? Flee? Hide? His muscles were taught. Every sinew strained, waiting for the signal. The instinct for survival controlled him completely.

The police car did not jump the median and turn to follow him, but continued south. Gradually, his body relaxed. The animal alertness, still active, retired to some sublevel of his brain.

As the alert faded, he pulled into a gap between two northbound trucks in the right lane, immediately becoming inconspicuous, blending in...a moving particle in the stream of moving particles...vehicles rolling up the interstate. Camouflaged amongst the herd, he was anonymous, and anonymity made him safe.

After a few miles, he relaxed. The adrenaline rush from the possible danger gave him an almost narcotic high. A sense of well-being overtook him completely. It was an almost sexual release. He lived for these moments. It was all part of the runaround. The game. The hunt. The kill. The escape. All of it. He savored it.

The steamy miles up the Georgia coast passed as his mind slipped into a dream-like reverie. Like the drowsy sleep of the lion basking in the sun after a kill, he soaked in the sun's rays. The others on the highway with him were herd animals, unaware of his presence, and silently unaware of the danger nearby. They moved quietly around him, the killer, the predator.

Warm air blew in from the open window. Lylee puffed a cigarette contentedly. The smoke from the generic "no-name" cigarettes that he always bought from different convenience stores whisked out the window so that the car would not smell of it. He would not want to inhibit some health conscious, young lady from joining him for a ride. Another small detail.

The close call that morning with the young blond and the two truckers who had surprised him with their arrival was careless. Stupid, he told himself. No excuse. He would have to be more careful; get his head back in the game. The thrill of the night's kill had still been with him. Intoxicated by it, his judgment had lagged. He knew the danger from past runarounds.

Sometimes the bloodlust overcame all reason, not that anything he was doing was in anyway reasonable to a normal person. But for him, that lust for blood had a way of controlling his actions in the way that alcohol controls a drunkard or drugs an addict. The taste of the kill created the need for more.

If there was not a sufficient cooling down period after the kill, the animal in him would go on killing, and the risk of detection from his recklessness would rise accordingly. He was aware of this and tried to guard against it by giving himself a cooling down period before seeking the next kill.

It had been too soon with the girl at the gas station that morning. The rush from the kill had still roared drunkenly through him. Kills, he reminded himself. First the old man at the church, an unexpected but welcome appetizer, and then the girl, the main course. If the truckers had not arrived, the blond might be seated next to him in the old Chevy at this moment. He smiled at that thought.

The I-95 traffic was mostly trucks with a few cars interspersed. He liked running with the trucks. They knew what they were doing, usually. They knew how to go fast and how to avoid the police.

The old Chevy looked run-down with its faded red and primer gray paint job, but it was in good driving shape. He was careful to keep it that way. Car trouble with a load in the trunk to dispose of, or with one of his projects sitting beside him in the front seat, could be more than a bit inconvenient. It could mean survival. Never get careless. Never get caught.

Sometimes it came down to pure luck. At times in the past when his judgment had been overpowered by the blood, his survival had depended on luck. He had always been lucky, if not in birth and family, then in deceiving others about his true persona and in his ability to escape danger.

He believed himself to be a predator at the top of the food chain and knew that successful predators must be skilled in the stalk, powerful in the kill, and cunning in the escape. When cunning failed, they had to be lucky.

Sometimes, as on this runaround, he got lucky in finding his prey. He had run across the young girl within a day after his arrival in Florida.

He had driven straight through from Texas. He never conducted a runaround near home. They were always in another state and at least two states away from home. Staying on the wonderful interstate highway system that Dwight Eisenhower had given to the country, his Texas plates did not draw much attention and he could roam freely.

Taking I-10 across the Florida panhandle, he had ended up at the Atlantic Ocean. A few brief hours in a cheap hotel near Jacksonville, and the runaround had officially begun.

Thinking back twenty-four hours, it surprised him how quickly he had found the girl. Some runarounds it took days to find the right situation, the right prey. His early success meant that there might well be another opportunity before he had to return to Texas.

Here on the interstate, in the bright light of day, the memory of the previous night's encounter caused a smile to twitch across his narrow face. The eyes of the girl, terrified, then hopeless, then fading into a blank nothingness, danced in his mind.

A pleasant shiver ran through him. There would be another. He would make sure of it.

Lighting another cigarette, his eyes followed the smoke drifting out the window, gazing across the landscape.

The stretch of highway between the small towns dotting the Georgia coast appeared barren. The green coastal plains looked empty, but he knew better. There was prey out there. He would find it. It was his runaround. This was his time.

33. "Son of a bitch and Goddammit"

Tom Ridley stopped in the bare dirt of his yard and put his foot up on the bumper of his truck to tie the lace of a dusty, scuffed boot. He leaned back, hands on his hips stretching his back in a long arch then gave out a long burp. Margaret's breakfast of ham, eggs, grits and biscuits with gravy sat heavily, but pleasantly in his gut.

Climbing into the truck, he cranked it up to drive the two miles to the Holsen's chicken barns for a day of cleaning up dead chickens and shoveling chicken shit. Most people complained of the chicken shit in their lives. For him, chicken shit was his life. It was a recurring joke and one he didn't mind. He liked his life. He and Margaret had simple needs and enjoyed the quiet of life in the Georgia backcountry.

The bare siding planks of their wood frame house were gray and weathered in the morning sun, not as pretty as in the glow of the sunrise. He didn't mind though. The bareness now made him appreciate the sunrise even more. It was all part of the cycle of things, the rosy, early morning glow, a shadowless noon sun, and the fiery orange glow over the pines when the sunset came. It was all just fine with him.

Giving a last glance at the old house in the rear view mirror, he pulled from the yard onto the dirt road. Margaret walked out onto the porch as he left in a small cloud of dust and gave him a wave. He raised his hand in the mirror and headed down the road. He did not go far.

Tom Ridley drove slowly. The engine sounds and spinning tires earlier in the predawn dark came to mind, and he thought he might see something to identify who had been on his road in the night. He did see something.

A few hundred yards down the road, there were tire tracks that showed where the dirt had been dug up by a turning front tire as the driver had turned and backed and turned again in the soft dirt on the shoulder trying to reverse direction on the narrow road.

Glancing off to his left, he saw something that pissed him off.

119

Dammit. It hadn't been George Mackey after all. Trash dumping along the dirt road had become a problem, and someone had done it again while he stood peeing in his yard that morning.

There was a pile of something in the brush about ten feet off the road. "Sonsabitches," he muttered. Dumping their garbage right here on his road. Ridley stopped his truck and walked into ankle high grass on the side of the road to retrieve the trash and toss it into the truck.

"Sonsabitches", he said again, for emphasis.

The grass was still bent down where someone had walked carrying their damned garbage into the weeds. When he got to it, he saw that it was a blanket. Some kind of beige looking bed cover, like the one he and his wife had on their bed.

He was about to pick it up and throw it in the back of the truck, but thought better. No telling what they dumped, and there could be a snake hiding under there. Good place for a snake. Snakes were overly common around here, and no one liked them. Tom was no exception. He lifted the edge of the blanket with the toe of his boot then quickly pulled his foot away.

"Son of a bitch," he said, kneeling down, letting the words come singly and distinctly this time.

Gently, he lifted the blanket again. It was loosely wrapped around the bundle, but he raised it and saw…. Squatting beside the bundle, he couldn't help falling back into the weeds and grass as he reflexively backed away.

Recovering himself, he gingerly picked up the edge of the bed covering once more. A ghostly, pale foot with red painted toenails was visible. Beyond the foot was a girl's body. She was nude with bruises around her head and neck. The ones around her neck were deep purple with darker pinprick spots in them.

Tom Ridley was no sheriff's deputy, but he knew enough to know that the girl had been strangled. He was not a timid man and life on a farm had accustomed him to blood and dead things. Death was part of life…but this. This was different.

Damn! He let the blanket fall and ran to the truck. Backing at full speed, kicking up dirt and rocks, he made it back to his house in a few seconds. When he got there, his wife was on the porch, she'd heard the truck racing down the road.

"Tom, what is it?" she said as he rushed into the house. "Tom!"

He ran to the old red dial phone hanging on the wall and grabbed the receiver off the hook.

"Son of a bitch," was all he could say. "Son of a bitch and Goddammit."

34. Crime Wave

"So what the hell's going on in my county?" Sheriff Richard Klineman looked around the small circular table in his office at the two men and lone woman seated with him.

"We were hoping you might shed some light on that for us Sheriff." Bob Shaklee was calm. The GBI frequently dealt with local law enforcement officials, each with their own issues. Sheriffs were particularly noted for their agendas, and with all of them, the number one agenda item was reelection.

Shaklee's partner, Sharon Price, amplified Shaklee's curt response to the sheriff's bluster. "This is pretty unusual for Pickham County Sheriff. A murder like this might have local implications, you might say. It's possible that you and your people might have better insight into that than we would."

"What do you mean? Local implications? What are you saying...the Klan? Is that what you think?" The sheriff's face was red. "The Klan in Pickham County? Ridiculous, at least nowadays."

"We don't think anything. We're just asking, for the record. Black man brutally murdered outside a black A.M.E. Church. The question has to be asked."

Klineman turned his head incredulously towards the fourth person at the table, Chief Deputy Ronnie Kupman. He knew that Kupman was not necessarily his ally in any confrontation. In fact, he was only appointed the Chief Deputy in order to avoid a mutiny from the rest of the department. They revered him for his courage and forthrightness during a career spanning over thirty years. But ally or not, the sheriff knew that Kupman was an honest man and would respond truthfully to such a ridiculous question.

Kupman returned the Sheriff's gaze knowing that the Sheriff was waiting for him to speak to the situation. He sat quietly for a moment, appearing to be considering the possibility of Klan involvement, which made Klineman even more agitated. Finally he spoke.

"I would say," he began deliberately, "that Klan involvement is very unlikely. That's not to say that there might not be a few old throwbacks still living in the last century. But we would know about their activities. Pickham has a pretty small population and something like that would be hard to keep quiet."

Klineman turned back towards the two GBI investigators with a look of vindication on his face. The GBI knew, of course, that Klan involvement was a very remote possibility. They, along with the FBI and a number of other agencies from other states worked very hard to track the activities of all terrorist organizations, and the Ku Klux Klan was still ranked near the top of the list of organizations under scrutiny, even in the age of Homeland Security, and the threat of terrorism from offshore.

It would have been difficult indeed for a cell to be operating in Pickham County without their knowledge. As Price had pointed out, the question had to be asked because of the circumstances. Judging by his red-faced indignation, the only one at the table who wasn't really sure of the answer was the sheriff.

"Okay," Shaklee continued quietly. "Klan involvement is unlikely."

"Nonexistent," Klineman interrupted abruptly.

"We'll go with extremely unlikely," Shaklee said and continued before the sheriff could interrupt again. "So here in Pickham County, we have a real whodunit murder. I assume you want us to handle the lead in the investigation Sheriff?"

"Of course. Not that our boys can't do it..."

"No need to explain. We don't claim turf Sheriff. Your deputies are well trained and professional; we know that. The GBI has access to resources that many local jurisdictions lack, along with a certain expertise in these matters. Happy to support your department with the additional resources available to us." He paused to allow the sheriff an opportunity to comment on the expertise of his deputies. Klineman merely shifted uncomfortably in his seat staring at his hands clasped together on the table surface. Shaklee continued, "Happy to do it, and of course, your department can take as much of the credit as you like. Let's just solve the murder."

"That's what I need...we need. The citizens of Pickham County should know that we are diligently pursuing the investigation in this tragic murder of an innocent black man. I want all of the additional resources you can gather set loose on this case. And I would appreciate no further mention of the Klan."

Klineman made no mention that the citizens needed to know about their diligent investigation because next year was an election year. He didn't have to.

Shaklee couldn't help the small smile that flitted across his face. It always came down to that. Like many Georgia counties, Pickham had a significant black voting population. It was bad enough for the Sheriff that an elderly black man had been murdered, but if it was discovered that there had been Klan involvement or even rumored, Richard Klineman would be a one term sheriff.

Seeing the smile, Klineman turned to his Chief Deputy for support. "Right, Chief Deputy?"

Kupman took his time responding as usual to the sheriff's question and did so with his usual neutral, objectivity, merely stating the facts. "We must solve this murder, right."

Klineman stared at him as if he were from Mars. The two GBI agents were barely able to contain their laughter.

A beeping tone sounded on the desk phone. The Sheriff reached for it and a moment later, his face blanched. "What? Repeat that." Turning the phone to the side, he motioned at Kupman. "Turn your radio on."

Seeing the look on the sheriff's face, Kupman was already moving his hand to the radio on his belt. They heard the call being repeated to county and state trooper units in the area.

"...body of a white female on Ridley Road, half a mile off of Mason Road. Units responding advise."

The two day shift sheriff's units working immediately cleared on the call followed by a bevy of troopers from fifty miles around.

Chief Deputy Kupman was out the door running through the building to the lot where his county unit was parked. The two GBI agents were right behind.

Sheriff Klineman grabbed his sport jacket off the hook on the back of his office door and stumbled hurriedly through the outer office, checking his belt to make sure he was wearing a sidearm and shouting apoplectically, at no one in particular. "Do we have a fucking crime wave going on in this county? Someone tell me what the fuck is going on!"

The office staff clerks, secretaries, and jailers, mostly born-again Baptists, Methodists, and Pentecostals, outwardly professed shock at the sheriff's sudden and uncharacteristic blasphemy. Inwardly, they were laughing their asses off.

35. Awakening George

The insect buzz-humming in his ear was incessant and maddening. It seemed to fill his head from the inside out. He ignored it for a while, or tried to, but the insect was persistent, fading away in the distance for a moment and then swooping close around his head. The swooping hum grew louder and more annoying until it pried him from the beer-induced sleep he had sunk into after leaving the house porch.

He forced his eyes open, or at least one squinting eye. Even in the dim, heavily draped room, the morning light was too strong. Brow furrowed, he squinted harder and tried opening the other eye. It seemed that he could feel the iris cranking slowly shut around the pupil to keep the painful light out. Shit.

Lying on his back, waiting for consciousness, George stared through slitted lids at the spotted ceiling. He put his arm over his face and waited for the pain to subside. The insect suddenly shouted at him. He reached over and swatted the cell phone vibrating loudly on the nightstand.

Below his apartment window a crazed maniac shouted, "Get the hell outta the way. I'll run your scrawny ass over!"

Felton Tobin accelerated the riding mower, bellowing at one of the scrawny, feral cats that hung around his yard. Old Fel hated the cats, but tolerated their existence, as they were adept at hunting the field mice and other varmints that found their way into his yard from the surrounding fields and woods. It was a great satisfaction for him to see one of the cats stalking some unseen prey in the mixture of grass and weeds that made up his yard. Even better, if there was some struggling little creature hanging from the feline's mouth as it trotted across the yard, he'd give a whoop.

"Got the little fucker!" he would shout triumphantly.

If he was sitting in one of the old kitchen chairs on the bare wood porch, he'd raise his beer can in salute to the cat. George knew this because he had sat there many an evening with his own beer raised in salute to one of the felines.

The insect buzzed at him again. This time he reached from the bed to the floor and retrieved it. Squinting at the number, he recognized Ronnie Kupman's personal cell phone.

"Hello."

"George? That you?"

"What's up, Ronnie?" George yawned loudly. Dragging himself from the bed, he walked into the front room of the apartment and stepped out onto the small second story porch in his underwear. The sun was high, but Fel was still mowing so it couldn't be too late. "What time is it, Ronnie?"

"Not quite ten, George."

"Ronnie, I've only been asleep a couple hours. Can't this wait?"

"You gotta come in, George."

"No way, Ronnie, I've been up all night," he said. "Who called in sick?" He yawned again.

George walked back inside squinting and scratching. The Sam Brown belt was draped over a kitchen chair. Dusty boots tumbled on their sides beside the chair, grayish white socks thrown over them.

The Chief Deputy took a deep breath. George could be a good deputy...sometimes. Other times he was, well, he was from another time, the epitome of the redneck deputy. George presented just the kind of image that Sheriff Klineman was trying to end. Still, he had a way of being around when things happened, in the right place, or maybe the wrong place, at the right time. In any event, it didn't matter now. This was some serious shit, and George was coming in.

"George, put your boots on and come in. Now."

"Aw, Ronnie," he rubbed one cold foot against the other.

"Now, George." He paused and added, "There was another killing."

George stopped in his tracks and closed his eyes as the image of Mrs. Sims pointed at him over the body of her dead husband.

"What? What happened?"

"We don't know."

"Where?"

"Out on Tom Ridley's road."

"What? Tom Ridley killed someone?" George sat down in the kitchen chair and reached down for his boots, the phone against his ear, crooked in his neck.

"No, no. Not Tom. Tom found the body. Some girl. Haven't ID'ed her yet, but you were working the beat last night, and the sheriff wants you in, immediately. You got it? Right now, George."

"I hear you, Ronnie. Be there soon."

"And George, start thinking about anything you might have seen last night. We don't have much on this one. Nothing really. Anything you have is gonna be more than we have now. Oh yeah, one more thing, the GBI is here. They're gonna take lead on this case too, so try to look like a sheriff's deputy, please." Ronnie hung up and George started pulling his boots off again so that he could put his pants on.

Ronnie Kupman knew, and George knew, that Ronnie had saved his job a couple of times when the sheriff would have let George go as a throwaway to the past. Ronnie Kupman also knew that, while George might be a throwback to a different era in police work, he was not a throwaway.

He was a natural hunter. He knew where to be when the bad guy showed up. He was sloppy in his personal demeanor, some thought slovenly and lazy, but he was a good deputy. Who knows, in a big city like Atlanta, he might have been a great detective. Probably not though, George was one of those who did not fit in. Scruffy and unkempt, he didn't know how to fit in, and funny thing was, he didn't even know that he didn't fit in.

Still, they could use his help now. Ronnie looked across the small dirt road to the covered bundle in the brush. His face twitched at the grisly pictures that flashed across his mind. Bad. Real bad. He

128

wondered what the animal that had done this looked like.

With slightly shaky hands, he lit a cigarette and looked down at his boots in the dust. He was surprised to see a little smudge of blood from the girl's body on the side of his right boot. He scraped the boot in the dirt trying to scrub the blood off.

He inhaled deeply and looked across the road again. An animal did this. They needed a hunter. They needed George right now.

36. Other Plans

Henry watched the two young men tramp out of the truck stop cafe. One, the younger one, stopped as if he were going to come back, but the girl at the booth just looked down at the slip of paper he had given her. She wouldn't look up at him. After a moment, the young man followed his brother to their truck.

Such a tender scene. Henry gave a grunt of disgust. He sat at the booth watching the girl and playing with his coffee cup. Glancing down at his watch, he smiled. He didn't have to be in Chattanooga until tomorrow. Plenty of time. More than enough time. He held his coffee cup up and caught the waitress' attention, waving the cup at her.

The waitress got a hard look on her face and walked over with the coffee pot. She didn't like people waving cups at her. It was about as rude as pointing a finger or whispering. She sloshed coffee into Henry's cup, deliberately careless.

"Hey!" the big man said. "Try to get some in the cup, girl." Henry grabbed some napkins out of the dispenser on the table and sopped up the spilled coffee.

"Hey, yourself," the waitress replied, looking down at him, a hand on a hip and raised eye brows, like a mother eyeing a misbehaving child. "Where'd you learn your manners?"

"Same place you learned to pour coffee, I guess," Henry said looking up from the wet napkins on the table. He noticed the name tag on her chest, 'Marla'. He also noticed the full bosom underneath the tag. He could just make out the bra beneath the tight, white fabric of her synthetic waitress dress. At that point, he smiled up at her, but his eyes stayed on her breasts.

Marla shook her head and walked off. Truck drivers, she thought. What a bunch of pigs. Aware that Henry was staring at her ass as she walked, she threw a little more sway into her stride. Let the fat pig try to get that out of his mind tonight, jacking off in the cab of his truck.

Henry watched her go. In fact, he was looking at Marla's ass. A little plump, but he wouldn't kick her out of bed. She wasn't really his type though, mouthy with lots of attitude. He liked them more...subdued.

Henry turned his thoughts from the temporary distraction of Marla's tits and ass back to the young girl at the table across the room. Nope, Marla was definitely not his type. Henry had something else on his mind.

Unaware of Henry's attention, Lyn lifted her eyes from the napkin with Clay's cell number printed carefully on it. She looked around the truck stop cafe. How would she know who to ask for a ride? Who would be safe, if anyone?

Unable to focus on anything, the cafe and faces at the tables swirled around her in a kaleidoscope of movement and color, with no meaning and no point of reference. How would she find a ride? She had wanted to take Clay up on his offer, it was tempting, and she had almost found herself saying yes.

But the need to see this through, whatever it was, burned inside her. After eighteen years of living in the hell created by her father, she couldn't just take the first opportunity. It might be no better than what she had escaped. She had to do this or doubt herself the rest of her life. Besides, Daddy would be looking for her around Pickham County. She had to put more distance between them.

After a while, she stood up and walked from the cafe into the truck stop store. She did not notice the large man who stood up from the booth across the room and walked at a distance behind her. He watched her ass as she walked.

The big bosomed waitress, Marla, glanced up from her order pad. Just a fat pig, she thought. Looking at that young girl's ass like he had any chance with her, or like he would know what to do with it if he got his hands on it. And she was just a child. Besides, he didn't know what he was missing here, she thought, smoothing the tight dress over her thighs. His loss.

Conscious of the other truckers' eyes following her, waitress Marla put the coffee pot down and walked over to a customer who had just taken a seat at a table. The tight white skirt undulated over her round bottom as she walked. They were all watching. She knew it and her hips swayed more widely. The round bottom rolled wonderfully under the tight dress, to the delight of all the large men in the room.

Coming to the table, she caressingly smoothed the back of her skirt over her bottom and smiled at her customer. "What can I get you, hon?" she asked. The truck driver returned the smile appreciatively.

Henry was long gone and would have paid her no mind anyway. Henry had other plans.

37. "Jesus, Mary and all the Saints"

The gravel road to Tom Ridley's house was blocked. Deputy George Mackey had to park the dusty, pickup at the end of a long line of emergency vehicles. He made his way up the dirt road past four other county cars, two GBI investigative units, a crime scene processing unit also from the GBI, an ambulance and Timmy Farrin's van from the radio station in Everett. Timmy was probably providing a feed to the Savannah news channels, or hoping to.

The vehicles were all lined as far to the right as possible on the narrow dirt road. There were no flashing lights. That was all movie stuff. In real life, emergency lights were only used when necessary, as a warning to traffic, or to move people out of the way, or to alert the bad guy to stop. There was no traffic out here on this dusty road, just the humming of grasshoppers in the weeds along the side, and the bad guy, whoever he was, was long gone.

Up ahead, closest to the scene, he saw a black Cadillac hearse from Morton's Funeral Parlor. Two men, one short and one tall, in dark suits were leaning against it smoking. They seemed incongruously casual and unconcerned. They could have been waiting for the dinner bell at a Sunday church social after services.

Just beyond the hearse, yellow tape marked repetitively, "Crime Scene Do Not Cross" was stretched across the road. The tape extended into the woods several yards on both sides, but went further on the right a good fifty feet or so.

He came even with the two men leaning on the hearse.

"How you boys doin?" he said, walking by.

"Doin' good, George. Yourself?" the tall one said

"Had better days." He reached for the yellow tape to lift it.

"Yeah, well this one is bad. Pretty little girl. Bad." The tall mortician shook his head and took a drag on his cigarette, leaning his head towards his younger, shorter companion he said something inaudible.

George stepped under the tape and into the crime scene. The hearse driver's words fading behind him, he couldn't help but wonder what in the world would prompt a person to take up undertaking as a career. The men were harmless enough, but their casual manner was eerie. They gave him the creeps.

George was used to death and mayhem. Even out in the Georgia countryside, bad things happened—car wrecks, assaults, bar fights, and shootings. But when the police or ambulance or fire department arrived on the scene, they were busy trying to do something about it.

The undertakers just stood there, smoking and waiting. The image of vultures lining a roadside kill came to mind.

Timmy Farrin called to him as he walked over to where Sheriff Klineman and Ronnie Kupman were standing.

"George, they won't let me past the tape. How about letting me know what's happening. I got all the TV stations in Savannah waiting for some word. They got their people on the way, but right now, I'm it. Be something if we could scoop them and get the story out before they get here. Put Pickham County on the map."

George looked at him and shrugged, "Timmy, you know I can't do that," and then added more loudly for the sheriff's benefit, "All statements have to come from the sheriff's office or the GBI." It was a deliberately clumsy and blatantly insincere statement, intended more to annoy the sheriff than ingratiate himself with him.

He stepped over to the sheriff and Kupman.

"What's up, boss?"

The sheriff's gaze held a look of resigned displeasure. George Mackey's presence was a necessary inconvenience.

Ronnie was convinced that George could add something to the investigation. The GBI agent, Shaklee had echoed the sentiment, and for the moment, Sheriff Klineman would solicit assistance from any source. There was an election at stake.

To answer the question he had shouted rhetorically back at the office, two murders in one day in Pickham County *was* 'a fucking crime wave'. If they thought George could help, so be it.

George knew everyone. He had lived there all his life. Still, being sheriff and having George as a deputy was like fishing with worms. The fishing could be good, but every now and then, you had to reach in the can and grab another slimy worm to bait the hook. For the sheriff, dealing with George was like reaching into the worm can. He liked being sheriff, but he still had to touch the worms every now and then.

As George walked up, Klineman stated firmly, "*All* statements will come from the *sheriff's office*, not the GBI. Are you clear on that Deputy?"

"Sure. Absolutely, Sheriff." George thought about spitting tobacco juice near the sheriff's feet, but this was a crime scene, and he didn't want to contaminate it. Still...

Ronnie Kupman stepped in quickly. "Come on, George. Want you to take a look at things." He led George away.

Kupman was different. He genuinely liked George, although he wished the deputy would clean up his act and his boots some, and play the game with the sheriff and citizens a bit more politically.

Kupman saw no reason why the common sense of good old police work by good old boys couldn't be combined with an appreciation for advancements in police technology and procedure. He also acknowledged that times had changed, for permanent. The old days and ways were gone.

He accepted that as progress. He knew that George had a difficult time with the change. He also knew that that was why George would likely never be more than a road deputy. But, they needed road deputies, and George was a good one.

To Kupman's mind, George's common sense methods and modern law enforcement practice were not mutually exclusive, although he recognized that in George's case they were often mutually antagonistic.

"Follow me, George. Got a bad one here," Ronnie Kupman took a drag on his cigarette as if to take a bad taste out of his mouth. "Over here."

He led George across and off the right shoulder of the dirt road and into the brush. George followed exactly in Ronnie's footsteps. He didn't know what was there and didn't want to destroy any evidence that might be lying in the dusty weeds.

They walked beside a patch of grass and weeds that were beaten down as if something had been dragged over them. Ronnie stopped, knelt and pulled the sheet back that had been placed over the girl's body while the investigation continued. George came up even with him.

"Jesus."

"Yep. Jesus, Mary and all the saints. Not pretty."

Squatting a couple of feet from the nude body of the young girl, George eyed the scene from different perspectives. On the other side of the body, about ten feet away, a crime scene technician was bent over, methodically looking through the grass and weeds. A bedspread was on the ground next to him, and another technician was using a tweezers to pluck fibers and other minute items of interest and place them in plastic bags. Bob Shaklee, the GBI man from the night before, was standing beside the crime scene techs. He nodded at George who nodded back before returning his eyes to the body.

The girl appeared to be young, although the blood on her face and torso made it difficult to see. The blood seemed to come from slicing wounds on her face and upper body.

Ronnie squatted next to George taking a drag on his cigarette, exhaling slowly and deliberately as if the smoke would somehow change the scene before them as it cleared.

"Lot of surface blood," he said, inhaling deeply from the butt hanging from the side of his mouth.

"Yeah." George rocked back and forth with his forearms draped over his knees. "You shouldn't be smoking around the body, Ronnie," he added without taking his eyes off the girl.

"Yeah, I know. Couldn't help myself." He quickly stubbed the cigarette out on the pack of smokes and shoved the butt inside the pack.

"You're right. Lot of surface blood. Messy, but the wounds aren't deep enough to kill. The son of a bitch wanted to hurt her. Probably took his time with each cut. Cause the most pain." George looked down at the dirt between his boots and shook his head. "Fucking animal."

"Yep."

There was nothing more to say as they took it all in. Squatting

136

on their haunches in the Georgia dust and weeds alongside a dirt road, they contemplated what must have been the horror of the girl's last hours.

Sheriff Klineman came up behind them. There was something vaguely annoying about seeing them squatting in the dust like a couple of old dirt farmers talking about the rain and crops.

Of course, that was the life they had both come from. Backcountry, Georgia dirt farmers. The sheriff's department had been one of the few ways out of that life, although George still clung to his roots a lot more than Ronnie did. He shook his head at the site of the two squatting dirt farmers wearing the uniforms of deputies.

"So what do you think?"

George looked up. Ronnie stood up.

"Well," George said slowly rising, "she's dead."

The sheriff's face reddened. The look on Kupman's face was a warning to play nice, so George added nonchalantly, "Took her a long time to get that way. She was cut to cause pain, not to kill her."

"Yep, that's what the GBI said, too," Ronnie Kupman added to direct the sheriff further away from George's comment. He shot George a look that said, 'knock it the fuck off, Deputy'!

George smiled and shrugged as if to say okay, okay. Ronnie was always worried about what the sheriff was going to say or do.

"So, have they determined the cause of death?" George asked inclining his head towards the GBI looking for evidence on the other side of the body.

"Not yet, officially," the sheriff replied, eyeing George for some sign of insubordination.

"There are some ligature marks...bruises... on her neck," Ronnie added, again to distract the sheriff and lead George onto safer ground.

"I know what ligature marks are, Chief Deputy," the sheriff shot back impatiently.

"Right, probably strangulation. Won't know for sure until the autopsy is done."

"Yeah," George said softly, looking down at the girl's body. "He took his time with that too. Choked her slow."

137

"How in the world can you make that determination standing here?" The sheriff said with disdain.

George just looked at the girl. He was focused now. "He wanted to hurt her. Wouldn't have wanted her to die too quick."

Ignoring the scorn on the sheriff's face, he stepped carefully around to the other side of the body staying in areas where the crime scene techs and GBI had already searched for evidence.

"Hey, Bob."

Shaklee approached. "Hey, George. How you doin' today?" They stood side by side looking down at the body.

"Ok I guess. Better'n her, for sure."

"Yeah, for sure," Bob Shaklee replied somberly.

Shaklee had only met George the night before at the scene of the Sims murder, but he had already developed an appreciation for the deputy's commonsense abilities.

"Guess you'll be checking motels around for a missing bedspread like that one."

Bob smiled, "Yeah we're on it. That part is simple. Any ideas?"

George looked down at the girl and asked, "What's that? There on her head just under the hairline."

"Yeah, we saw that. Looks like he hit her with some object. Left a mark and broke the skin."

"Mind if I get a little closer?"

Shaklee nodded him forward. Good old boy or not, George knew his way around a crime scene.

George squatted again, this time near the girl's head. He took a pen from his shirt pocket and carefully, gently, separated some strands of bloody hair covering a mark on the girl's head. He studied the mark for a minute, and then took a small pad from the same frayed shirt pocket and began making notations on the pad.

Sheriff Klineman watched. He hated having George here. He resented the way the GBI treated George with a respectful familiarity, as if he were one of them.

George was a redneck, pure and simple. He was the perfect caricature of the country lawman. He was an embarrassment. The GBI were highly trained professionals, but they seemed actually to like George. He could not, for the life of him, understand why.

Therefore, Sheriff Richard Klineman resented George. He resented the GBI. He resented anything that might get in the way of his reelection. Most of all, he resented two murders in twelve hours in his county, casting doubts on his law enforcement leadership and possibly putting the election in jeopardy. Yes, he especially resented that.

Bob Shaklee and Ronnie watched George also. Ronnie stepped over next to Bob as George stood up and showed them his notepad.

"I know this isn't professional or even legal evidence, but I don't think she was hit with an object." George turned the pad towards the two lawmen.

"See this here, I kind of drew out the marks from that place on her head. There's kind of a rectangle with a sort of faint oval inside and these curved marks coming out of the oval. Wasn't an object. The asshole beat her with his fist. That's the imprint from a ring."

Bob and Ronnie studied the sketch on the rumpled notepad for a minute and looked at each other. George was right. It was definitely the imprint of a ring on the hand that had beaten and then killed the young woman.

"Kind of looks like a longhorn design doesn't it?" Ronnie looked over at Bob Shaklee. "You know, Texas Longhorn."

"Yep, it does," Bob said. "This is important, George."

Ronnie smiled at George, "Good job, Mackey."

"There's something else," George was focused and not interested in Ronnie's platitudes.

"What's that?"

"Bob, you remember at the scene last night? The knife wound?"

"Yes." Shaklee regarded the deputy through narrowed eyes. He thought he knew where this was going and knew the sheriff's reaction would be interesting.

"Well, that wound was designed to kill, but also to cause maximum pain."

"I agree." Shaklee let him speak.

"The wounds on the girl were not intended to kill."

"Right," Sheriff Klineman stated in firm agreement.

"But," George paused, "the wounds on the girl were designed to cause maximum pain, like the knife wound in Mr. Sims. That's the common denominator. Both murders were committed by the same sadistic bastard. At least that's how I would work it for now."

"What!" The sheriff's exclamation gurgled and sputtered out in disbelief. "You're saying we have a serial killer in Pickham County. My God, are you insane!" He looked at Ronnie Kupman, "And you said we needed him here. You must be insane as well. Do you know what would happen if people thought we had our own county slasher? Our own Ted Bundy right here in Pickham."

George shrugged. "That's how I see it. But don't worry; I doubt he's still in Pickham County."

"Sheriff, I have to say that we agree with the deputy's theory," GBI Agent Shaklee stated quietly, but firmly. "I assure you that the serial killer aspect will not be discussed in public, but it is an important part of our working theory in the investigation."

Klineman turned and strode briskly from the body, not being all that careful about where he stepped. "Jesus," he muttered pushing through the brush.

"Where do we go from here?" Ronnie asked Shaklee.

"I'll get a technician to get some good photographs of the ring imprint during the autopsy so we can use it as evidence when we find the bastard." He looked around the scene. "Be a couple of more hours here at least, then we'll start digging into it. I suggest we meet up with you and the sheriff say about six o'clock at his office.

"Sounds like a plan. If you don't mind, George and I are going to go down the road here and talk to Tom Ridley and his wife."

"That's fine. See you at six."

Ronnie and George started away.

"One other thing," Bob said.

The two stopped and turned.

"The person who did this may be looking for more victims. These cases go in different ways. Sometimes there are no more victims for years. Sometimes there are a lot in spurts. Don't know which this is gonna be, but we should hurry and see if we can catch up with him while there is some trail. If you have any ideas, don't sit

140

on them waiting for us to give the okay. We need to move quickly. If you need to interview someone, just do it."

George's eyes narrowed, "He tortured and killed this little girl and dumped her body like a bag of trash on a dirt road in my county. We'll be hurrying, Bob."

George spun and worked his way quickly back out to the dirt road.

Bob said nothing. He understood.

It was the second time that day that Shaklee had heard someone call Pickham 'their county', and he noted the look of displeasure on Klineman's face. The sheriff had overheard the remark.

Shaklee chuckled to himself as he turned to the crime scene tech. Poor George, there'd be hell to pay for that later. Right now, Klineman needed George. So did he, for that matter.

So did she, he thought, looking at the girl sprawled before him, but whatever they did for her now would be too late.

The girl on the ground stared open-eyed into the dusty weeds in agreement.

38. Ride This

She wandered around the truck stop store with no idea where to begin. Drivers, mostly men, were coming and going. A chubby clerk at the cash register was busily ringing up roller-heated hot dogs and sodas for customers, while pointing out the restrooms for others.

The few non-truckers seemed to be families on vacation or older couples. They all stood out, like her, she thought. It was a busy place.

It occurred to her to try speaking to one of the families or older couples. They were probably safer. But would they understand her need to get away, or just try to talk her into going home or even call the police to take her home?

They were regular people, family people, people with normal lives, whatever that was. She had no clue. Their normalness made it harder for her to try to speak to them. She was not part of their world. Trying to step into their world seemed as alien and impossible as stepping onto the surface of the moon.

Lyn moved over to the magazine rack in the store. She picked one up and stared blindly at the cover. Staring into the magazine, not seeing the page, she felt completely alone.

The brothers who had given her the ride to the truck stop had been told by Kathy to find her a safe ride. That was easier said than done, she now understood. They said they would check back on her after work. Probably just their conscience, guilty at leaving a girl alone here, but she was beginning to think that maybe she would just wait for them to come back.

She considered Clay's offer for her to go home with them. How could she do that? He seemed nice and normal, like the families wandering around the truck stop. Her life would be alien to him.

A young boy from one of the family groups came running down the aisle, chased by his older sister. The girl grabbed his arm as they brushed past Lyn.

"Mama said get over there, so get," she hissed at her brother through clenched teeth, dragging the struggling child to his mother.

She was lonely, surrounded by these strangers, the normal people doing normal things. How could she go up to one of them and ask for a ride north to Canada. Impossible.

More than that, it was ridiculous. Canada. They would laugh at it. The brothers had started to laugh at the idea earlier, until they realized she was serious. Her seriousness had surprised them and amused them, she knew.

But Clay had made his offer anyway, and now, her running away dream, the one she and Sam had sheltered under all those hard years, was beginning to seem less achievable than it had earlier. Worse, it seemed childish. In the cold light of day, she was frightened and unsure.

The deep voice beside her was startling.

"Well, hello again young lady." He spoke in his most grandfatherly tone. His deep voice and drawl made the words soft.

Lyn started and turned her head towards the voice. The large truck driver from the diner the night before, Kathy had called him Henry, was thumbing through a magazine a few feet away.

He smiled at her and put the magazine down.

"I thought I saw you in the cafe earlier. Did you eat?"

She nodded. Her throat was tight.

"Well good. I was a little worried about you last night when you went off with them two boys. They treat you all right?"

She nodded again, "Yes, they were fine. We had breakfast."

"Good, good. That's real fine." Henry looked out the window. "Looks like they got my rig fueled up and ready. Just wanted to make sure you was okay." He smiled and put the magazine back on the rack.

"Thanks, I'm fine," she said softly.

"Okay then, I'll be heading out," Henry said turning away, and then stopped and asked over his shoulder, "You looking for a ride? I'm headed north if you want to come along for a spell. I'm going as far north as Richmond, then headed back west."

"Oh, well...I, well I just..." Lyn was intimidated by the large man, but he seemed harmless now, just friendly. It was confusing.

Henry smiled again and in his deep syrupy voice said, "It's all

143

right. I understand. Look, I'm going to go pay for my fuel and check out the rig. Take about ten minutes. Then I'm gonna crank her up and head out up I-95. If you're going that way, you're welcome. Just come on out to the truck." Henry pointed out the window and added, "It's that big red Freightliner there at the pumps."

Henry turned around and walked away.

Lyn watched him, her head spinning. Two minutes ago, she was ready to take Clay Purcell up on his offer to go home with him and his brother. She had almost given up on Canada. Now, out of the blue, she had a ride to Richmond. It was a sign, maybe.

Richmond was north, she knew that. It was Virginia, and Virginia was closer to Canada than Georgia, although how much closer, she wasn't precisely sure. But from there another ride north would get her closer, maybe all the way. So why not go all the way, or at least try?

The uncertainty began to subside and her innate sense of determination began to take over again. She was poor, not well educated, but she was determined and that counted for something.

Lyn stood there for a few minutes looking out the store window and across the large lot. She could see Henry standing by the red truck. He was talking to the fuel attendant and seemed totally unaware of her. He had made no threatening statement. He had not tried to hurt her or intimidate her and he could have. He was big. No, he just walked away and said she could come if she wanted.

Again she thought, it was a sign...maybe...a chance. Maybe she should take it. Maybe she *had* to take it or never know.

She realized that she couldn't be overly picky. She was not going to get offers from church ladies. Leaving the store, she walked across the parking lot to the red truck and Henry.

The busy clerk at the cash register was not too busy to have noticed the pretty girl and the fat man at the magazine rack. He saw her walk to the truck and shook his head. Runaways, you saw them all the time at truck stops; usually young girls, alone and scared. They would fall for any line from these truckers.

The clerk didn't get it. Why, he would be happy to give the pretty little brunette a ride. Watching her slim form cross the lot, he felt the twitch in his balls and the start of a boner. Of course, no one would notice under his three hundred and twenty pounds.

"That'll be seven ninety-five," Todd the clerk said to the old couple with two hot dogs and two sodas at the counter.

Outside, Henry showed Lyn how to climb up into the tall Freightliner. The clerk watched over the heads of the old couple. He pushed his groin against the counter as he rang up the next customer. Little girl if you want a ride, he thought, ride this.

39. Confession

George Mackey and Chief Deputy Kupman walked away from the body of the girl, carefully retracing their steps through the grass back to the dirt road. George was quiet. Ronnie assumed he was thinking about the ring mark he had found on the girl's head where her murderer had apparently struck her. It was a good observation, the kind of thing that George was good at seeing...things that might be invisible to others.

Looking back, Ronnie saw that Sheriff Klineman was talking with Bob Shaklee, moving his hands animatedly. No doubt, he would be trying to put some spin on George's theory that the same person had committed both murders that had taken place in the county within the last twelve hours.

Bad enough to have two murders, but to have a serial killer going around killing old black men and young girls just weeks before his reelection campaign was scheduled to start was potentially devastating, at least for the sheriff. His reelection chances would be a toss-up at best. Klineman's actual concern for the devastation to the murder victims and their families was a matter of conjecture.

Knowing Klineman, Kupman realized he might just as easily be trying to find a way to spin it so that he could take credit for the potentially case breaking piece of evidence, the ring mark on the girl's head.

Something like, 'Yeah, I taught George everything he knows about law enforcement,' or 'Yeah, George is like a son to me. He discusses every case in detail with me to verify his theories' or at the very least, 'I always make sure my deputies have the very latest training in investigative procedures'...so on and so on.

Kupman shook his head. A smirk born of distaste for the sheriff plastered itself across his face.

They walked past the still waiting hearse drivers. Timmy Farrin from the local radio station had a portable tape recorder out and appeared to be interviewing the taller undertaker, for want of anyone better to question. The Savannah stations must be getting

146

close. Timmy was taking whoever and whatever he could get to fill the airwaves emanating from Everett. Not often a local story here got noticed by the big stations. Timmy had to make the most of it. Unfortunately for him, he didn't have the weight, meaning a sufficiently large audience, for the sheriff to grant him any special access to the scene or to interview the GBI or the sheriff himself.

Thanks to cable and satellite dishes, most people in the county got their news straight from the Savannah or Jacksonville stations. The AM station that Timmy worked for was mostly daytime religious programming for the folks out at the Pine Grove Retirement Home, with interludes of country music. Nighttime programming was mostly Braves baseball during the season, or local high school football and basketball call-in shows other times. The sheriff would make damn sure that the Savannah stations got the story first, and they in turn would make sure that he was prominently interviewed, in full uniform, stars on his collar and all, explaining how all the resources of his department were being allocated to finding the *killers* of the girl and Harold Sims.

It was going to be quite a spin job...making sure that all understood clearly that they were unrelated cases...oh yes, and that there was absolutely no Klan connection with Mr. Sims' death...oh yes, and that the killer, who was almost certainly not from Pickham County, would be caught and brought to justice swiftly. Oh, and did he mention that his vast resources were being completely dedicated to the two separate and distinct cases.

Quite the spin job, indeed, but Chief Deputy Ronnie Kupman had faith in his sheriff. Of course, Timmy would get his interview, after the sheriff had been seen by all the voters in the county on the evening news broadcasts from the major metropolitan areas.

George stopped by Ronnie's car looking at the ground for several seconds. Raising his head, he looked into Ronnie Kupman's puzzled face.

"Something I have to tell you."

Chief Deputy Kupman straightened up. It was unusual, but George seemed actually to have something serious and official on his mind.

147

"Speak up Deputy. What is it?"

"Last night...well," George hesitated then went on, "last night I saw, well I think I saw, the perp's car."

"You what?" Chief Deputy Kupman's eye narrowed.

"Well, I was parked in the old rest area out on Highway 28, backed up in the trees."

"When?"

"After I left the Sims' place. Before daylight but it was close to dawn, maybe couple of hours before shift change. It was still pretty dark."

"What you mean, George, is that you were sleeping in the old rest area, right?"

"Yeah, I was," George said, not flinching under Ronnie's gaze.

"What did you see, George?"

"Old model, maybe mid-nineties, GM make. Probably a Chevrolet, maybe a Pontiac. Wasn't shiny, more like it was covered with dust or dirt, or maybe primer paint. Couldn't really make out the color in the dark. It woke me up as it went by, so I got a pretty good look."

"You mean a good look for someone who just woke up and who didn't bother to check it out. I don't suppose you got a tag number did you, George?"

"No, sir. I didn't. But I could tell that it was not a Georgia plate. It was a lighter color and reflected, even in the dark. Sorry."

"Well, I suppose that young girl out there in the weeds might be sorry too, if she knew," Ronnie said harshly. The look on George's face made him immediately regret the remark.

George was taking this hard. He knew he had probably seen the killer, or at least his car, coming back from Ridley's Road and had done nothing but close his eyes and go back to sleep, while that poor girl lay in the weeds like a bag of garbage. No one would take that harder than George.

The fact was that after twelve years with the department, Deputy George Mackey made forty-two thousand five hundred dollars a year, plus overtime, which the sheriff routinely denied to everyone. He was never going to be promoted, at least not under

Sheriff Klineman. He would never have Ronnie's job as Chief Deputy, no matter who was sheriff. And, he would spend his entire career working every part-time job he could find to make ends meet and to pay his child support to Darlene, and to maybe put something away for the girls' college. Those were the facts.

George wouldn't complain because he loved what he did, and he was good at it, and he knew he was good. It was a hell of a thing, to find the thing you're good at. A lot of people never did. George was smart enough to recognize it, and he didn't want to lose it. And yet, he was telling Ronnie something that could cost him his job.

So George Mackey was tired last night, probably like most nights, and had seen a car go by that he didn't bother to check out. Standing morosely before Chief Deputy Kupman, guilt almost dripped from his pores into the sandy soil.

Kupman quietly considered the situation, staring hard at George and thinking it through. George waited, eyes fixed on the toes of his boots.

So sometime around four this morning, Deputy Mackey couldn't keep his eyes open and pulled into the rest area to 'rest his eyes'. While doing that, he caught sight of the possible perpetrator's car. Actually, it was the *probable* perpetrator's car since no one else would have been likely to be out on that stretch of highway that time of day. He had been at a murder scene a couple of hours earlier on the other side of the county, but at the time, no one knew about the second murder, the girl.

Kupman took all of this into account. He did this because if the sheriff ever found out, George would no longer be a deputy. And after taking all of the circumstances into account, he made his decision.

"Sorry, George. You didn't deserve that," Ronnie went on.

"Yes, I did Ronnie. You're right. She deserved better, whoever she was."

"No, I'm not. First of all, you shouldn't have been sleeping. That is my official opinion, and you are officially reprimanded for it. I mean it." Kupman paused letting the seriousness of his words sink in. "Having said that, let's consider the circumstances. At the time, we only knew of one murder. It was on the other side of the county and no one would have expected the killer to stay around and murder an unknown young girl. We all thought he was probably long gone up the interstate. You were pumped up on adrenaline. Once you had no other duties at the crime scene, fatigue set in. Understandable that you were tired and not your fault..."

"Not my fault? I could have stopped that car. Hell, on most nights, I would have stopped it just for not recognizing it and it being out and about on that road. I just..."

Ronnie interrupted sharply, "Not your fault that he committed the murder." He paused allowing George time to understand that he was not granting him blanket absolution. The murder may have been done but George should have stopped the car. They both knew it.

Fatigue or not, he should have followed through. It was his job. Their eyes locked and George gave a short nod to indicate that he understood.

Ronnie continued in an effort to rehabilitate one of his best deputies. "George, there was nothing you could have done anyway. She was already dead. The bastard just dumped her up Tom Ridley's road. You couldn't have known that. You shouldn't have been sleeping." He paused and looked George in the eye. "Cut back on the part-time jobs if you have to, work a different deal on the child support, but no more sleeping...ever."

"Okay, Ronnie."

"I mean it, George. This is a one-time pass. There will be consequences next time."

"I understand." He continued looking at the ground taking his medicine.

Putting it completely behind them, Kupman continued, "Good job on the vehicle description. We need to get this out and get all the jurisdictions around looking for the car," Ronnie gave George a light thump in the shoulder, "and a male driver with a longhorn ring on his hand."

"Ronnie, I feel sick about this. I could have stopped him. I should have."

"The way I see it, George, we have two real clues in this case, the

150

car and the ring, and they both came from you. Pretty damn good police work in my mind."

The look on George's face was doubtful.

"All right, George," Ronnie went on, "here's what we are going to do. You are going to go to your car, get on the radio and put out a BOLO on a mid-nineties GM make, probable Chevrolet sedan. Dirty, dusty or with primer paint. And a driver, probably male, wearing a ring with a longhorn head on it. Then you are going to go interview the Ridleys. I'll meet you afterwards."

George nodded quietly.

"I," Ronnie continued with a smile, "am going to advise Sheriff Klineman and Bob Shaklee that you reviewed your note pad from last night and found the description of the vehicle along with the approximate time you saw it. When the Sheriff asks why you didn't bring this up earlier, I will tell him that you wanted to check your notes and confirm the description and time before putting out potentially incorrect information. Just another example of excellent work by Deputy George Mackey." Ronnie's eyes crinkled in amusement, "He won't believe it of course, but as the Savannah stations will be here soon to interview him, he is damn sure going to make sure they know that the key pieces of evidence uncovered so far, were discovered by one of his deputies and not the GBI. He won't want to rock the boat with reports of any alleged sleeping in rest areas and such."

He chuckled outright. "Actually, George, thank you. This is going to be interesting."

"Ronnie, I can't...you don't have to..."

"Shut up, George. For once just do what I say. Oh, and make sure that that information about the car is duly recorded in your notepad...just in case someone wants to see it."

Chief Deputy Kupman walked off towards the crime scene and Sheriff Klineman. There was a wry smile on his face.

George Mackey turned to his truck, took the mike in his hand and inhaled deeply before sending the notice across the airwaves for officers to 'Be on the Lookout'.

"All units, BOLO..."

A minute later, the description of the suspect car and the ring was traveling at the speed of radio waves, which is the speed of light, throughout Georgia and northern Florida. It would make its way eventually through the Carolinas, Tennessee and Alabama by the end of the day, and then steadily across the country.

But George knew that if there was no follow-up information or additional evidence within the next day or so, the BOLO would be filed away and forgotten, along with a thousand others, in favor of newer more relevant notices coming through the law enforcement networks.

He finished giving the information over the radio and put the microphone back on its clip on the dashboard. Taking the notepad from his breast pocket, he wrote in it for a minute or two. When he was finished, he put his truck in gear. He had work to do.

40. Lions and Jackals

About the time the Purcell brothers were pulling their pickup out of the lot to go to their jobsite, Lylee Torkman had pulled the old, faded Chevrolet to the self-service gas pump furthest away from the truck stop store and cafe. He leaned forward as he pulled in scanning for CCTV cameras watching the pump. This was an old truck stop, and he did not see any that were obvious, but there were sure to be cameras at least to record tag numbers of vehicles that drove off without paying.

Reaching in the back, he plucked an old, white painters cap off the floorboard and pulled it over his head. It had a large bill that would obscure his face and made him look harmless...just a painter filling up before heading to the job.

He couldn't do anything about the car's plates, but some things couldn't be helped. He had taken the precaution of removing the tag off a similar make and model car in Texas and putting it on his own when he got to Florida. Stolen tag reports didn't make it across state lines unless they were associated with some other crime, and right now, he was not associated with any crime, at least that anyone knew about.

Stepping from the car he continued to scan around, ever cautious and alert to danger or, if he was lucky, his next project. Truck stops were busy places which made anonymity easy.

Lylee walked to the store to prepay cash for the gas he would buy. The windows of the store were plastered with signs advertising beer. It was a great combination, eighty thousand pound trucks and beer. The irony was not lost on him, and a thin smile flashed across his thin face.

Pulling the dirty glass door open, Lylee entered. There was movement everywhere. The herd was restless He would blend in without trouble, staying on the periphery and observing without being noticed.

A fat kid at the register was sweating and waiting on customers with an indifferent manner. Lylee noticed that he was a bit more

153

attentive to the rough looking truckers than he was to some of the other customers. The kid might have been an indifferent smartass, Lylee saw, but he was smart enough to know what line he best not cross with the truckers, roaming through the store looking for sundries or just killing time.

Avoiding contact with anyone, Lylee wandered and watched. He examined an item off a shelf now and then, but his attention was always peripherally taking in all that went on around him. In a sort of subconscious mental scan mode, he saw everything and everyone at once without really focusing on anyone specific, unless to examine and evaluate them.

The evaluation usually only took a second or two, and then Lylee was back to scan mode. But during the evaluation, Lylee's senses would soak in all that was possible to absorb. All of the data gathered was instantly used to classify the object of the examination as Threat, No-Threat or Project. Occasionally, not often, the classification might be, Interesting and Curious, and after a short diversion examining the curiosity, Lylee would move back to scan mode.

An old couple was standing in front of the drink cooler as Lylee walked by.

"Albert, they don't have Diet Pepsi, just Diet Coke," the old woman said to the frail looking man next to her.

"I don't like Diet Coke," he replied truculently.

"Well that's all they have."

"Well, I don't like it." The conversation was going nowhere.

The old woman threw up her hands, "Fine then, pick something you like and let's go."

Lylee squeezed behind the pair in front of the cooler saying, "Excuse me."

The tone was perfect, indifferent but polite, drawing no attention. Too friendly, and they would notice him, smile and possibly make eye contact. Eye contact might lead to identification. Too curt, and they might notice him for the opposite reason.

He moved by them in the narrow aisle. The couple remained unaware of the killer who had just brushed by, scanning them and taking in the old woman's thick perfume and the dark liver spots on Albert's hand, holding the cooler door open as he searched for the perfect soft drink.

Moving slowly from aisle to aisle, Lylee continued scanning. At the end of an aisle, he stopped in front of a rack of snack cakes. His peripheral vision caught sight of a pretty, dark-haired girl in front of the magazine rack. She was holding a magazine, but just looking down and not reading.

Instantly, his senses reacted, and he went from scan mode to detailed examination. Data was needed. Potential prey had been discovered. As he watched, a heavyset man, a trucker, took up station a couple of feet away from the girl and picked up a magazine. Lylee knew instantly that the large man was there for the girl, not for the magazine. The girl, however, was oblivious.

A short conversation started between the two. The girl was clearly uncomfortable. While Lylee couldn't hear everything, he could pick up that the man was offering her a ride. Lylee knew that the offer of a ride was just a pretext to get the girl into his truck.

The trucker was reasonably smooth though. Not expert like Lylee, but he knew enough to let her decide he was safe by not pressing the issue. She was desperate or she wouldn't be standing alone in the truck stop with that look of hopelessness on her face. The trucker knew, as did Lylee, that she would accept the offer.

She was frightened, alone, and intimidated by the business of the truck stop and the people around her. If he could win her trust, she would accept the ride, if only to escape the truck stop. She might not like the price she would have to pay for the ride, but that would not be collected until later, and she would have no choice at that point.

The large trucker gave her a smile and went outside. The girl stared after him.

Lylee walked down the aisle and passed behind the girl. She was unaware, still staring out the window at the trucker who was standing beside his truck. His senses drank in everything about her. Her height, the small mole on her neck, her scent, everything. That instant of close proximity to the prey aroused him profoundly. He felt the blood rise and the plan began forming in his mind.

Lylee walked up to the fat kid and put two snack cakes and a pint of milk on the counter.

"Three eighty-five," the kid said indifferently. Clearly, the slight man at the counter was not a trucker. No need to waste any politeness on him.

Lylee took two twenties from his wallet and tossed them on the counter. He kept his head down so that the hat's bill completely blocked his face from the camera behind the cashier.

"And twenty in gas. Pump seven," he said not looking up.

The kid gave a deep sigh of disgust, and turned to activate the pump.

"That all you got?" he said in annoyance, pointing at the extra twenty to pay for the milk and snack cakes.

"What did you say?" Lylee's voice was low, but the tone was hard and threatening. He raised his head just enough for the fat kid to see his eyes. The narrowed slits with only the pupils showing stared fiercely into the cashier's own eyes, which widened perceptibly at the intensity of the stare.

"Uh, nothing, just a little short of change. I'll make it work though, no problem." The kid swallowed, suddenly nervous. There was an air of danger about the man with the narrow, piercing eyes. No sense pissing him off. It was a judicious decision.

Lylee knew that he should have just paid the clerk and moved on without drawing any attention to himself, but his blood was up. There was prey near. His body twitched with excitement. He was the king, the predator, and whether this fat kid knew it or not, he would do well to show the king some goddamned respect.

"Would you like a sack for that, sir?"

"Yes, I would," Lylee replied. His threatening eyes staring at the cashier from under the bill of the painter's hat.

The kid quickly looked away, put the snack cakes and milk in a sack, and slid it over.

Giving him a last look, Lylee walked outside. The kid felt himself relax as the danger moved away. Nothing was said, and no one would have noticed the exchange between the two, but he sensed that he had just come close to some force that was dangerous in a way that was far beyond the normal tough guy trucker attitude...creepy.

The old couple was next in line and they placed their goods on the counter. Todd-the-clerk was intently watching the young girl who walked out in front of the creepy man and was talking to the fat truck driver. Annoyed at the distraction from the elderly couple, he began ringing up their items with his normal surliness, giving one last glance at the girl across the lot. Yea, a little skinny, but nice ass.

Outside, Lylee walked across the lot to his car and began pumping gas, showing no outward interest in her. She walked slowly and tentatively across the lot, unaware of his presence and of the gray eyes following her.

The girl spoke briefly with the trucker. He smiled broadly and showed her how to climb into the truck.

Lylee watched intently without appearing to. The prey was his. The fat trucker was nothing more than a scavenger, a jackal. Jackals didn't take prey from lions. This jackal just wasn't aware that there was a lion around. He would be, soon.

The anticipation beat rapidly in his chest, surging adrenaline through him. The predator would fight to protect its kill. A barely audible rumbling sound escaped the thin man at every smile the girl gave the big trucker. It would have been called a growl had it come from another species of mammal.

41. Orders

Tom Ridley stepped out on the bare wood porch of his house as George pulled the truck up the short gravel driveway.

"How ya doin', Tom," George said stepping out, hiking up his trousers at the waist as he walked to the porch.

"George," Ridley said nodding and standing with his hands shoved deep in his pockets. The screen door behind him creaked as his wife, Margaret, stepped out onto the porch.

"Want some coffee, George," she asked, nodding her hello.

"Sure. Worked last night. Looks like a long day."

"Yeah." Ridley looked up from the spot on the porch he had been staring at. "You see her?"

"Yeah, I did Tom. I need to ask you some questions."

"Okay, ask away." Tom looked back down at the porch.

"Tell me what happened, what you saw, heard, anything you remember."

Ridley continued looking at the porch and started speaking. "Early, before light, I was in the yard and I heard something. Like a car door or something. A minute or so later, I could hear the engine and the sound of the car moving on the gravel, like it was backing up and then moving forward, you know."

George nodded and waited, letting Tom continue at his own pace.

"Honestly, I figured it was you sleeping on the dirt road this morning in your car when I heard it turning around."

George's conscience twitched hard.

"No, Tom, wasn't me." Not on Ridley Road at least, he thought, feeling the knife prick at his heart. "What happened next?"

"Well...nothing. I just had breakfast and went about my chores here. Then I headed over to the chicken barns...but I never got there." He paused, and then continued. "I headed down the road and thought I saw some trash someone had dumped. I was gonna pick it up." He became quiet. The screen door squealed behind him and Margaret returned holding George's cup of coffee. Standing beside

158

Tom, she put her hand on his arm.

"Did you see anything else, Tom?"

"You mean besides that little girl out there? No not really."

"I know it's hard, Tom, but anything you saw or heard might be important. We don't have much right now."

Margaret reached down and handed the coffee to George. Taking a gulp, George shifted his focus to her. "Thanks, Margaret. How about you? See or hear anything?"

"No, George. I was still in bed. Just old Tom here peeing out in the yard, I could hear that pretty good."

Tom gave her a sideways glance, shook his head, then said, "George, all I heard was a click like a latch on a car door or something. After that, the sound of tires in the gravel. I could tell he was turning around in the road." He paused as if remembering the moment and then wishfully repeated his earlier statement. "Thought it was you, or someone dumping garbage."

Tom paused, head down. "I guess that's what it was. Someone dumped that poor little girl like garbage. How could someone do that, George?" He looked up. There were tears in the old chicken farmer's eyes.

George ran his hand through his hair and shook his head before responding. "I don't know, Tom. There's bad people. I don't know why."

"Most terrible thing I ever seen, for sure," Tom said softly staring back at the porch.

Margaret reached out, put her work worn hand on her husband's arm again and patted it this time. Looking George squarely in the eye, she said, "You catch whoever did this. You hear, George Mackey." It was a command not a question. "You just catch him."

George looked back at her solemnly and said, "Yes, ma'am, we will. We'll try."

"No trying, George." Her voice was firm. "You catch him."

It was an order, given in the same tone he had heard as a boy when he and the Ridley's boy, Robert, would get into mischief, and Mrs. Ridley would straighten them out. The order had been given, and she expected him to carry it out.

First Mrs. Sims, now Margaret Ridley. No pressure there.

George took a deep breath, nodded, and handed the coffee cup back to her. There was nothing more to say. He turned and walked across the bare yard to his pickup. Tom stepped off the porch following.

"George," he said.

"Yes, Tom." George stood with his hand on the half open truck door.

"I feel like maybe I should have caught the guy. I mean, I heard him down the road, just a little ways. He probably didn't even see the house. I could have sneaked up on him with my shotgun. At least maybe then…well maybe the girl would be alive."

George had to swallow down his own guilt as he tried to put Tom's mind at ease.

"Tom, there was nothing you could have done. She was already dead when he put her in the weeds."

"But I should have tried to do something. Instead I just stood there taking a leak." Tom swallowed hard. "George, that was someone's little girl, and now…they don't even know." His voice trailed off.

"Tom," George said taking firm hold of his arm in the way friends do. "You didn't do this, and you are not to blame. There is nothing you could have done, and besides, it's best you didn't catch up with him. This is a bad man, a really, bad man. Like an animal. You catch up to him, corner him, and he's likely to turn on you and hurt you, or worse, like a cornered bobcat. Shotgun or no shotgun, I'm glad you didn't go looking for him out there."

Tom just looked at the ground. Margaret stepped forward and took him by the arm, turning him back towards the house. The look she gave George over her shoulder said it all. Catch him!

George nodded his acknowledgement, accepting his orders quietly.

Pulling the pickup out of the Ridley's yard and onto the gravel road, he drove the quarter mile down to the crime scene and stayed far off the right side across the road from where the girl still lay in

160

the weeds. He drove through the grass and weeds until he was well clear of the crime scene and then pulled back onto the dirt road.

Sheriff Klineman and Ronnie Kupman stood behind the line of emergency vehicles talking. The sheriff looked hard at George as he drove by. George looked away and picked up speed leaving the scene. Fuck the sheriff.

Mrs. Sims and Margaret Ridley had given him his orders. There was nothing Klineman could add to that. For his conscience, and Tom Ridley's conscience, and the little girl still lying in the weeds, he hoped it would be enough.

Yeah, late again George, but you just get right out there and catch him. His foot pressed harder on the accelerator.

42. The Brothers

The whine of the circular saw drowned everything else out, echoing in the bare interior of the shopping center. Clay threw the freshly cut two by fours onto a pile beside the saw table. Oblivious to the sound and sawdust around him and in his hair, his mind was back at the truck stop with the young girl that he had met only hours before.

"Clay!" It was his brother Cy shouting over the noise.

He released the saw trigger and the screeching noise wound down as the blade slowed. The ensuing, sudden silence was heavy in the empty concrete space.

"What, Cy?" He spoke quietly but his voice seemed loud in the silence after the saw noise.

"That's enough," his brother replied.

"What? What's enough?"

"We don't need any more. That's enough. Let's start framing them up."

"Oh, right. Sorry. Yeah."

The brothers worked together in a quiet rhythm. Well practiced, the work went swiftly without talking. They made it look much easier than it was, the way a professional athlete makes hitting a fastball or catching a pass look like something we should all be able to do, although we all know that we cannot.

In a short time, they squared up the interior wall they were framing and started hanging plywood panels. The panels would be finished and covered with shelving to hold athletic shoes of the type and price they would never consider buying.

Dusting sawdust off, they walked over to an ice chest and each pulled out a drink can. Leaning against a nearby wall, they slid down until they were sitting side by side on the concrete.

"Pretty quiet today. What's up? Still thinking about the girl?" Cy asked after they sat for a minute sipping their drinks.

"Lyn," Clay said looking at his can of soda.

"Sorry," Cy said. "I mean Lyn. Still thinking about her?

162

"Yeah. I guess I am."

"So what are you going to do? Might sound crazy, but she seemed pretty serious about the Canada thing."

"I don't know." They were silent for a minute and then Clay continued, "It feels like I should do something. Go talk to her again. Something."

Cy sat leaning against the wall, knees up resting the drink can on them saying nothing. Clay was taken with the girl. She was pretty enough, for sure, but this was something different. He was distracted by her in a way he had not seen before.

"All right, brother," Cy said, breaking the silence, "Let's go back and see if we can find her when we get done."

"What then?" Clay said almost glumly. "She already said she was going on."

"Why, then you turn on the charm little brother. Make her smile, make her laugh, make her feel safe. Just be you, man. It'll work out if it's supposed to. Gotta give it a try though, so let's give it a try."

Clay studied the toes of his work boots. "Okay, you're right." He jumped up off the floor. Reaching back down to give his brother a hand up, he said, "Thanks."

"No problem. Now let's us get our asses back to work."

Five minutes later, they were working on another wall. Things he might say when they went back to the truck stop rolled around in Clay's head. He took his cell phone out and checked for calls. There were none. He didn't know if that was good or bad.

43. Clever Tommy

The images flowing by on the small TV monitor blurred. George shook his head to focus more clearly.

Leaving the Ridley's, George had gone to the interstate to check out places where the killer might have stopped. His gut told him that the murderer of Harold Sims and the girl would not remain in Pickham County and would move on quickly.

He picked the northbound side of I-95, mostly because there was more territory ahead for an escape. The southbound side went directly into Florida. Between Ridley's Road and the county line there were only a couple of exits on I-95 with gas stations. One was in Roydon. The other was several miles north, almost at the county line. He decided to check the one furthest north first and then come back through Roydon. It didn't seem likely that the killer would stop for gas so close to the site of body. Hell, he may not have needed gas at all, but it was worth a try.

The Minit Mart on I-95 had an antiquated video recording system. It didn't provide much. The one camera was pointed at the cashier, obviously intended to prevent pilferage by employees than to prevent robberies. Installed long before the advent of digital video recorders, the system had an old VCR that still recorded on VHS tapes. George wondered where you could even find VHS tapes anymore. Hell, even he had a DVR.

If the Minit Mart had had a digital system, he could have focused on a specific time frame and brought up only those images. With this old piece of junk, George was forced to rewind the tape from last night and watch it through, searching for...for what? It was a long shot. George shook his head again and pushed the fast forward button on the VCR.

He had bypassed for the time being the couple of country stores between Tom Ridley's road and the interstate as they were closed at night. But the Minit Mart was open twenty-four hours. The go-to-work crowd stopped there for coffee in the morning, and the after work crowd got their six-pack and lottery tickets on the way home.

The rest of the day, late at night, and during the early morning hours it was mostly cars and truckers off the interstate.

George had parked the pickup and gone in to have a talk with the manager. The overnight girl, Beth, was gone, off at seven.

Now, George was seated in a dusty old office chair at the manager's desk in the small room behind the cashier's counter. The tiny monitor and VCR sat on one side of the desk.

George held the fast forward button as the images flowed past. He had rewound the tape to about two in the morning to try to limit the search a little. Still, there was nothing to do but watch the tape grind by, minute by minute.

Even on fast forward, the minutes seemed to take forever. On top of that, there was nothing to see, just the cash register and small area behind the counter. Occasionally, the clerk, Beth, would enter the area, but she spent most of the time out of view of the camera. The manager said she stocked shelves and the coolers at night when there were no customers.

George looked around the cramped, dusty office and through a small, dirty, tinted window out into the store. This would be a lonely place to work at night. Too lonely, as the empty images on the tape attested. Too much could happen.

Then he saw Beth walk back into the frame. She was talking. She smiled. George thought it was the look of a girl who was flirting or being flirted with. He leaned forward, intent on the image. The person she was talking to was careful to stay away from the counter, just out of view of the camera.

The girl, Beth, smiled some more, tilting her head slightly and looking up at the person just out of view. It was definitely a flirtatious smile, pretending to be shy or flattered, but the unspoken message was, 'Yes, I am the cutest thing you've seen today. Keep talking. You might get lucky'.

George almost smiled himself at the young girl on the tape. Suddenly an arm was thrust into the picture from the spot just out of view. A bill dropped from the outstretched hand onto the counter. George stopped breathing and hit the pause button.

The arm was a man's arm, covered by a long sleeve shirt.

Nothing remarkable about it. Not too big, not too small. Just an average sized arm belonging, no doubt, to an average sized man. But the outstretched hand bore a ring.

He squinted hard at the screen. There was no zoom function on the system, but the more he looked, the more certain he became. George looked around for a minute and then called out.

"Tommy!"

"Yeah, George?" The manager poked his head through the door.

"Do you have something to make the picture bigger?"

Tommy thought for a second, wrinkling his brow in concentration. "Well nothing technical or anything like that, but..." he stepped into the cramped office behind George and rummaged around on a dusty shelf. Lifting a stack of yellowed papers, he pulled out an old magnifying glass. "Here try this. It might work."

"What the hell are you doing with that? Burning the wings off of flies?"

Looking slightly offended, Tommy replied, "No, we keep it to check out suspicious bills. You know, counterfeits."

"You know how to recognize counterfeits?" George was amazed.

"Well, not really," Tommy confessed, "but if we get a suspicious bill and bring out this big old glass, sometimes they get intimidated and leave. Actually works...sometimes."

George shook his head, even more amazed. He had no idea that Tommy was that clever. Probably no one else did either.

He took the glass from Tommy's pudgy hand and stared at the screen, adjusting the distance to magnify the image. It wasn't great. The GBI would have to clean it up, but it was unmistakable. A shiny, almost triangular shape with two curving prongs coming out of the top. There it was...a Texas Longhorn, or at least it could be.

George knew he was looking at the hand that had struck the poor girl in the weeds. The hand that had inflicted all of those painful cuts. The hand that had killed her, taking her life in the slowest most painful way he could. That hand was attached to a body and to a bad man. A very bad man who, except for his hand, could not be seen in the video.

George let the tape run forward and saw two men walk into the

166

frame. Truck drivers. They must have startled the man with the ring.

He rewound the tape and went through it one more time looking for anything he had missed. Cute little Beth did not know how fortunate she was. Probably lots of customers flirted with her, and she flirted back. Flirting with this one, the man with the ring, might have been her last if the two truck drivers hadn't showed up.

Well, now he had a witness. Beth had talked to the man with the ring. She might have noticed his vehicle, the vehicle George had seen the night before while he tried to doze in his county truck. He winced once more at the thought.

George felt the adrenalin surge. The hunt was on, but time was short. The word had to get out before there was another young girl in the weeds somewhere.

"Tommy!"

"Don't have to shout, George. I'm right here." Intrigued, Tommy was staring over George's shoulder at the screen. "What's up?"

"I'm taking this tape and get me Beth's address."

"Uh, okay, George. Something wrong?"

"Get the address, Tommy."

George ejected the tape from the old VHS machine, and leaving the cramped office, moved quickly outside to his pickup and the radio. Sitting behind the wheel, he reached for the microphone.

For a moment, he closed his eyes, and the image of the old car from last night floated in his mind. He imagined an average sized man's arm and a hand holding the steering wheel. On the hand was a ring, a ring that matched the mark on the forehead of a young girl. The average man with the ring had dumped the girl like garbage in the weeds alongside a dirt road...a dirt road that he had been responsible for patrolling.

George's eyes snapped open; soon there would be more than just an arm and ring in that picture. Beth would help with that.

Lifting the mike, he spoke.

"301 to car 2."

Ronnie Kupman's voice answered, "Go ahead, 301."

"We have a witness with a possible ID on the perp. Need you to meet me." George didn't elaborate on which perp. There was only

167

one right now. He read out the address Tommy had given him.

"On my way, 301," Ronnie responded and then added, "Good work, George."

Sheriff Klineman, listening on the radio in his car, winced. Great. George again. The hits just kept on coming.

44. "Don't do it son."

He watched the big red Freightliner leave the fuel pumps and pull through the parking lot of the truck stop. As it passed his car, he could just see the top of the girl's head in the passenger seat. He was prepared to follow, waiting for his opportunity. He did not have to wait long.

The truck did not pull onto the highway and head towards the interstate. Instead, the heavyset trucker steered around to the back of the truck stop where there was a large gravel lot full of parked rigs. Some of the drivers were there to catch up on sleep. Others were inside the truck stop relaxing for a while. Henry had his own plans.

The old Chevy followed carefully, the driver watching as the trucker pulled to the farthest end of the lot and parked along the edge where no other truck would be next to him. The big diesel engine clattered and shut off as the air brakes hissed. It was quiet.

Lyn looked at Henry questioningly.

"What are we doing?" Her voice quivered slightly.

Henry turned and stood up, bent over in the space between the two seats.

"Oh, I reckon you know, girl," he said grinning.

"But you were going to give me a ride north. You said as far as Richmond, then you go west."

"Yep. I did say that, and I will. But first you gotta pay the fare."

"Fare? What fare? You said..."

"Listen girl, don't play dumb. I know young girls like you have done it lots of times. This one more time ain't gonna hurt nothing. You might even like it. I know I will." Henry smiled.

"Now climb back there," Henry said jerking his head towards the sleeper behind the truck cab.

Lyn had tears in her eyes, "No...I just want to go away. You said Richmond. Just..."

Her words were broken off, and she let out a small shriek of pain at Henry's rough jerk on her arm. Lyn grabbed the seat armrests as the big man pulled.

Pulling his car alongside Henry's trailer, Lylee walked quietly in the hard packed gravel to the driver's side and stood outside the truck cab. He could hear the exchange inside. His hand rested on the door handle. At Lyn's shriek, he jerked it open.

Inside the truck, Henry whirled at the sound of the door opening. He was still standing bent over between the seats with a large hand around Lyn's upper left arm. As he spun, he nearly jerked her out of the seat. Looking down from the cab, he saw a slight man, his hand resting nonchalantly on the doorframe.

"What the fuck do you want?" He spoke in as threatening a manner as he could muster through his surprise.

Not even a jackal, Lylee thought, just a horny yard dog. "Let her go," he said simply and firmly.

"What?" Henry was rattled, unaccustomed to being challenged.

"Let the girl go, now," Lylee said, each word distinct and separate from the others.

Letting go of Lyn's arm, Henry slid into the driver's seat and then put his feet on the access step outside the open truck door.

He looked closer at the man holding the door. He was not a large man, but there was a hardness in him. There was something else too. The look on his face wasn't angry or determined. It was …dangerous.

The man's eyes were completely focused, on Henry, examining him in an uncomfortable way. The mouth held a barely perceptible grin. Henry sensed that the grin was a warning, telling him that he had already lost. Something in the look also said that he hoped Henry wouldn't take the warning.

He was dangerous and in control, and Henry knew better as he stood up on the truck step. He knew better, but pride required him to do something.

Looking down at the smaller man, there seemed to be no other choice. Twice now in a day, he was being challenged, first by that bitch, Kathy, at the diner and now by this jerk off. He didn't particularly want to, but he knew he had to do something or leave and never come back. The look on the smaller man's face made him

170

hesitate. Finally, he moved.

Stepping tentatively down to the next step, it was instantly apparent that he had made a mistake. The smaller man's eyes glinted, and the smile flickered and grew broader for just a fleeting moment, like a spark in the breeze.

His arm struck out with the quickness of a striking snake. Henry felt an iron grip take hold of his belt and then jerk with great force. There was nowhere for Henry to go but down.

The big man thudded heavily onto the hard gravel as Lylee stepped deftly to the side. Releasing the door, he took a step to where Henry lay. He was on his side, cradling his left arm. His face was scraped raw from the impact with the gravel and a cut on his forehead dripped blood onto the ground. Bits of sand and gravel clung to the raw scrapes on his face. He was a mess.

Lylee placed a heavy, work-booted foot on the side of Henry's face and pressed. Henry let out a moan. Lylee knew that with a little more pressure, he could snap the bones in Henry's cheek and jaw.

"Don't do it, son."

Lylee's head snapped around. Two truckers approached. One was about Henry's size and build wearing a camouflage ball cap. The other was smaller, shorter than Lylee but with massive forearms.

"What?" Lylee's tone was sharp and severe. His animal eyes narrowed and focused on the larger of the two.

It was the smaller of the two who replied.

"I said, don't do it. You made your point. He ain't gonna bother anyone now."

Lylee looked down at Henry. The animal rage boiled in his blood. He exhaled slowly, deliberately trying to calm the urges within.

He had made a mistake, and he wasn't used to making them. Normally thorough and careful, as evidenced by the string of tortured bodies scattered across a dozen states, he had been careless for the second time today.

His first easy success with the girl last night had made him overconfident. The bloodlust was in him, and he was not paying attention. He had been completely unaware of the approach of the two truckers.

He took his booted foot off Henry's face, turning his gaze to the smaller of the truckers. Lylee's fiercely intent animal stare was returned by a calm, unafraid look. This man was not intimidated.

Predator that he was, Lylee was able to recognize the confident strength in the other man. For a moment, he fingered the knife in his pocket and then withdrew his hand and forced a small, almost humble smile to his face.

"Sorry boys," he said. "Just got carried away. I saw this pig pick her up inside and figured she might need some help." He shrugged. "That's all. Got angry and carried away."

The trucker's gaze was intent and unblinking, weighing Lylee's words. He spoke to his companion.

"Leon, see if you can get her to come down."

The large trucker, Leon, called up into the truck cab.

"It's all right now. Come on down, young lady. No one's gonna hurt you. Come on now."

Lyn had watched all this transpire in trembling silence. It was too much. What was she thinking? Not thinking at all really, she realized. Head spinning, she moved across the cab to climb down. She placed one foot on the step and stood up. Everything went black.

Leon reached up with is burly arms and caught her as Lyn collapsed and tumbled off the step. He sat her down on the bottom step and let her head sink forward. With a look of concern, he looked at the other trucker.

"Bob, we might want to call an ambulance or something."

"Let her catch her breath for a minute," Bob replied calmly.

He turned his gaze back to Lylee. "We saw what you did. We were parked over there," he said, jerking his head to two trucks parked fifty yards away. "You did good, but it's enough now. Let's get this girl inside and find out what's going on." Bob looked closely at Lylee for any reaction...good or bad.

Lylee exerted all of his control to remain calm. The prey was so close. He could smell it, almost taste it. All of his senses twitched.

"Yeah. Sure. You're right. I just got carried away," he said again, his voice quiet and submissive.

Leon looked down at Henry, who remained prostrate on the gravel cradling his arm, hoping to be forgotten in all the talk. "What about him?"

"Well, as far as I can see, not much to do with him or for him," Bob said. Then leaning over, he spoke clearly to make sure Henry heard. "You took an ass whuppin' for sure, and as far as we can tell, you deserved it. You decide you want to press charges against this fella here, and we might have to say something about an attempted rape. You understand me?"

Henry looked up through his bloody face and nodded slowly.

"Say it," Bob said sternly.

"I understand. I won't press charges, just let me be now," Henry said through bruised and swollen lips.

Bob went over to Leon, and together they helped Lyn to her feet. She was coming around. Examining her, they could see no injuries.

Lucky for her, Bob thought. Another fifteen minutes and the fat trucker would have had his way with her, and like all bullies, he wouldn't have been too gentle.

What are these girls thinking, he wondered. It was common to find them on the road, hanging out at truck stops and bus stations. Could life at home be that bad?

He shook his head as he and Leon helped the girl across the parking lot, glad that his three daughters were safe at home in Tennessee. Fortunate for this girl, that thin fella had seen what was going on and decided to do something about it.

He looked around at Lylee who was still standing by the truck, tensed. Not tense like he was nervous or afraid, Bob noticed, but tense like every muscle in his body was coiled and ready to spring.

"You coming?" Bob asked.

"Yeah. Sure, I'm coming. I'll just pull my car around to the truck stop."

"All right then. See you inside" Bob said turning back and helping Leon guide Lyn.

Looking down at Henry, Lylee snarled in a low voice that only Henry could hear, "You're lucky. Not because of some attempted rape charges."

173

He paused, making sure that Henry was paying attention through the haze of pain. He was. Their eyes met...Lylee's fierce and piercing...Henry's wide and frightened. "One word to anyone, and I will gut you like the fat pig you are."

Henry's eyes widened even more. He nodded his understanding.

Lylee spit a tight stream of saliva that splattered on the gravel an inch from Henry's face, smiled, and turned towards his car. Cranking the engine, he put it in gear and gunned the gas, causing the tires to spit gravel over Henry's sprawled form.

A few minutes later, Henry managed to pick himself up. His arm was probably broken from the fall, and his face and head stung from the abrasions and cuts that the impact with the gravel had caused. He sat down on the step to the truck cab holding his arm. It was the same step that Lyn had sat on a few minutes earlier.

What the fuck? He rocked in pain on the step. One minute, he was about to get a tight little piece of ass, and the next he's beat all to hell.

It took several minutes of rocking back and forth in pain until he came up with the story for the emergency clinic he was going to have to visit. Slipped and fell off the truck steps. That was the best he could do. Nothing fancy, and he would take some ribbing from other truckers when they saw him, but that was better than another visit from that mean little bastard, the man with the fierce, dangerous eyes.

Henry was a bully and like most bullies, he was also a coward. He picked his battles carefully and always made sure he would win.

That little bastard was mean and scary. Henry had no doubt in his mind that he would keep the promise to come back if Henry ever said a word about it. He shuddered at that thought. Yeah, the little fuck was very scary.

Henry continued rocking and cradling his arm. Son of a bitch, it hurt!

45. Beth

George Mackey and Ronnie Kupman pulled up in front of the doublewide mobile home within a few seconds of each other. George stepped out of his pickup first and waited for the dust to settle while Ronnie shut his engine off and stepped out.

The adrenalin was pumping. They were so close. They needed an ID, a physical description to go with the arm and ring...something. He owed it to the girl in the weeds. The girl who, at some point, had been in the car he had seen last night. He owed it to Mrs. Sims and her poor husband Harold who took a walk in the woods.

As Ronnie came even with him, George turned and they walked to the house, leaving the county vehicles parked in the graveled drive behind a ten-year-old Ford Taurus. Following a bare dirt path, they walked towards the front stoop of the doublewide.

The yard wasn't much. Some weeds and dried up grass, but they were cut short and not overgrown. Not much money here, George thought, but they took care of what they had.

Extending his hand, George rapped sharply on the aluminum screen door. He waited fifteen seconds, and when there was no response, he looked at Ronnie and shrugged, opened the screen door and thumped hard on the doublewide's inner door.

They heard rustling and someone plodding heavily across the floor. The doublewide's walls visibly rattled and vibrated as the person moved to the front door.

A young man, about twenty or so, swung the door open wide and stood squinting in the sun. He was dressed in boxer shorts and a tee shirt. His sandy hair was rumpled. Surprise crossed his face as he looked at the two men in uniform on the front stoop.

"Mornin', deputies." He recognized the uniforms for what they were. "What can I do for you?"

"Mornin'. This your place?" George spoke. Ronnie stood to one side and looked on quietly.

"My parents'. I live with them. Something wrong?"

"No, nothing wrong, we just need to speak to Beth Hilts. She live here?"

"Yeah. She's my sister."

"Can we talk to her?"

"She's sleeping right now. Worked last night. So did I."

George stepped closer into the doorway. "We know. Sorry, but it's pretty important. Would you get her for us?" It was a question, but George's tone was a command.

The boy shrugged and stepped aside so the deputies could enter.

"Yeah, I'll go get her."

He walked down a narrow hall off the living room and stopped at a door on the left. He knocked lightly.

"Beth, you need to get up."

There was a muffled response from inside the room. The boy shook his head and knocked again louder, and pushed the door open slightly.

"Beth, come on. There's some deputies here to see you."

They heard her groggy, surprised, "What?"

In the midst of rustling and creaking of the bed, they could make out the questions mumbled to her brother.

"Deputies? What do they want? I just got off work a little while ago."

Her feet thumped audibly on the floor.

"Tell them I'll be there in a minute."

The boy turned and came back down the hall.

"She'll be right here." He stood there in his boxers and tee shirt looking back and forth from one deputy to the other. He was waking up more now and feeling a little more assertive and confident as the grogginess departed.

"Is Beth in some sort of trouble?"

George smiled and said, "No not at all, we just need to talk to her about someone she might have seen." He saw the protective and slightly aggressive look in the young man's eyes. That was his sister, and this was his house, or at least his parents' house. Deputies or not, they couldn't come in without some reason.

"You're welcome to sit in and listen too, if you want. I know she's your sister," George added in a tone showing respect to the young man. No reason to antagonize him. He had a right to question why they were there, and they weren't there to cause problems...just to get information. Very important information.

Chief Deputy Ronnie Kupman stood quietly beside George, hands hanging loosely by his side, a mild look on his face. He allowed his deputy to handle things. George may have been country and rough around the edges, but he knew how to deal with people.

He could be the toughest guy in the county when you needed him to be, but only when it was necessary. George wasn't afraid to kick an occasional ass when it was required, but 'ass kicking' was just a tool to him, to be used only when needed. He was not abusive or physical by nature, and preferred reason and respect as his tools, whenever possible.

Unfortunately, to a sheriff with no desire to offend any of his constituents, there was no ass worth kicking, only those worth kissing. And there lay one of the issues between George and his boss.

Ronnie watched with appreciation as George handled the situation, giving the young man no reason to take offense. His words had the desired effect. The hard edge in the young man's face softened somewhat.

"Okay. I will sit in. Ya'll can sit down there if you want." He motioned them to the sofa.

"Thanks," George said as they turned to sit. "Your parents can sit in too if they want."

"Naw, they're both at work. Won't be home till five."

"What's your name, if you don't mind us asking?"

"Brent. Brent Hilts."

"Well, I'm George Mackey and this is Chief Deputy Ronnie Kupman."

Ronnie nodded at Brent, and Brent nodded back.

"All right, well I'll throw some clothes on and be right back," Brent said, as if to make sure they didn't start without him. "Beth should be out in a minute. Takes her a bit of time to get up and about when she's been sleeping." He smiled and shook his head as if to say, 'Girls, what are you gonna do?'

177

The two deputies smiled and nodded back knowingly.

Brent Hilts padded down the narrow hall and went into the room across from Beth's.

"Good boy," George said, looking around at the walls.

"Yep, he is," Ronnie replied, squinting in the dim light at a family picture on the coffee table.

After 'throwing some clothes on' which consisted of a pair of jeans and flip-flops, Brent came back down the hall. Beth was nowhere to be seen.

Looking around and seeing that Beth had not made an appearance, Brent turned and shouted this time back down the hall.

"Beth! Come on out."

A second later, the bedroom door opened and a pretty little blonde girl walked out in a yellow flannel robe, buttoned up to the top. Her feet scraped along in white terry cloth slippers. Her hand patted and stroked her hair, trying to smooth and straighten it out. Her face showed confusion and anxiety at being called out of bed by the deputies.

As she came into the living room and focused on George and Ronnie, she was even more uncomfortable. The two deputies stood up.

"Is there...uh, something wrong?" Her voice was unsteady and nervous.

"They said they want to talk to you about someone you might've seen," Brent spoke up.

George smiled and added, "That's right, Beth. Nothing to worry about. We just want to ask you about someone you might have seen at work last night. Okay?"

Beth nodded. Still concerned, but they could see that her mind was working, probably going over everyone she had talked to last night.

"Should we sit back down so we can talk?" Ronnie said. They were the first words he had spoken, and he said them only to reinforce that there was no reason for concern, and so that she would not worry about the silent deputy looking at her and listening intently while she spoke with George.

178

Beth nodded and sat on a recliner positioned next to the sofa. The deputies sat back on the sofa and Brent, intently interested now, sat on a rocker across the room leaning forward and resting his elbows on his knees.

George smiled at Beth and began.

"Beth, do you remember last night, this morning really, about five a.m. maybe a little later, there was a man that came in? There was no one else in the store at the time. He left just before two truckers came in. Dropped a twenty on the counter and went out kind of quick."

Beth's eyes narrowed, looking back at George.

"Well, yes I do, but how do you..." She stopped and shook her head and went on. "Oh. The camera, right? The little TV thing?"

"Yes, that's right, the CCTV. I saw you on it, and I saw him. Well, I didn't really see him. Just his arm. That's why we're here. We need to know what he looked like."

"Why? What did he do?" Beth's voice was soft, her expression concerned.

She had reason to be concerned, but he didn't want to panic her. He needed her to remember calmly everything she could about the man with the longhorn ring on his finger.

"Well, we think he might have been involved in a crime," George said, and then added quickly before she could question him about that, "It would really help if you could tell us what color hair he had."

"Well it was kind of light brown."

"Good, light brown," George said making a note on a little pad he pulled out of his shirt pocket. "Now," he continued quickly, before she could ask him the questions evident on her face. "What about his eyes? Did you see what color they were?"

Beth thought for a moment, "No not really. We talked for a minute but I didn't really notice."

"Ok. That's fine. So how about his height? About how tall do you think he was?"

George stood up quickly and went on, "As tall as me? Taller or shorter?"

"Well it's hard to tell. I mean I was standing behind the counter

179

and he was a few feet away. He never got very close, even when he threw the twenty down. I thought that was kinda funny?" She looked at George. "I mean that was funny wasn't it? He kinda stayed away from me."

"Yes," George said, "that was funny. I think he didn't want to be seen on the camera. You know, he kind of kept out of view. That's why we need you to remember everything you can for us."

"Okay", she nodded. "Well, it's hard to tell how tall he was. I mean I'm not very good at judging."

"That's okay, Beth. Why don't you stand up and get about as far away from me as you were from him." George smiled again at the girl.

Beth stood up and moved back from George a few feet. She looked at George and then moved back another couple of feet.

"Ok. Right there. I think that's about how far away he was."

"Good," George said still smiling. "That's good. Now what do you think? Tall as me? Taller or shorter?"

Beth's brow furrowed for a second. "Shorter," she said. "Not much, but shorter than you."

"Good, Beth," George said then turned to Brent watching from the rocker. "Brent, can you help me here for a second."

Brent got up and walked over to George.

"Now, Beth," George continued, "I'm going to ask Brent to kind of squat down a little next to me and then rise up slowly. When he gets to about the height you think the man was, you say so. Okay?"

Beth nodded to George. George nodded to Brent who bent his knees and squatted down about a foot lower than George. George nodded at him again and Brent began rising up slowly. When he got to about three inches of George's full height Beth spoke.

"There, right there. That's just about how tall he was."

George looked at Brent beside him. "Good. That's good. So I'm six feet one in my shoes and he was about three inches shorter than me, so that would make him..."

"Five ten," Brent interjected.

"That's right, about five feet ten." George looked back at Beth. "Now Beth, how was he built? Kind of heavy set like me or thinner

180

like Brent?"

"Thinner," she said confidently. "Muscular, but thinner. More like Brent."

"Okay. Good." George looked at Brent, "Thanks for the help."

Brent nodded and went back to the rocker.

"All right, Beth, we're almost done. Was there anything else about him? Mustache, beard, scars, tattoos? Anything?"

"No, not really. His nose was kind of thin, and his chin too, but nothing really stands out."

"How about his voice? Did he talk to you?"

Beth's eyes narrowed for a second, and then she looked up at George. He could see the fear growing in her eyes. She nodded.

"Yes, he talked to me. I thought he was nice. I mean he was kind of good looking…and nice and…" Beth's chin quivered slightly, "Was he dangerous, I mean could he have…"

George broke in quickly, "Tell me about his voice, Beth. Was it deep or high pitched? Did he have an accent? Did he talk funny, or lisp or anything?"

She shook her head.

"It was just a normal voice not real low or high. He sounded like he was from the south, but different from around here. Not a Georgia accent, but not from up north, you know?"

"Good," George said with a smile. "Maybe someplace else in the south, Louisiana or Texas maybe?"

"I can't say. I'm not very good at that, accents and all. I know it was southern. I can't say from where though." Beth looked into George's eyes. "What did he do? Is he really bad?"

George put his pad back in his shirt pocket. "Sit down, Beth," he said.

George sat back on the sofa and continued. "Yes. We think he is really bad. He hurt a girl really bad, and we need to catch him. What you told us will help us catch him."

Beth's eyes were watering. She may have been from the country, but she was not stupid. From the deputies' questions and their seriousness, it was not difficult to understand that she had probably been very lucky in her encounter with the man.

181

"The girl, the one he hurt, did he…I mean is she…dead?"

George looked her in the eyes. "Yes, she is dead. And we are going to catch him before he can do it again." Then he added softly, "You might want to think about working another shift. I mean one where you aren't alone at night all the time."

Her face told them she was already thinking about that.

George and Ronnie stood and walked to the door. They turned and saw Brent standing with his arm around Beth. Her shoulders moved up and down as she sobbed.

"Thanks, Beth, for the help. This is important," George said, and Ronnie nodded simultaneously.

Beth and Brent nodded back.

There was nothing else for the deputies to say. There was information on George's pad that had to get out. They turned and walked through the front door.

The day outside the doublewide was clear and sunny. A small breeze stirred the dust in the driveway.

Ronnie turned to George and said, "Get it out, George. Be quick. Catch the son of a bitch."

46. No Place for the Girl

Lyn walked unsteadily into the truck stop between the two truck drivers, Bob and Leon. Bob looked around for a quiet place they could put the girl while they figured out what to do next. The breakfast crowd in the cafe had cleared out, and the lunch crowd was coming in.

"Leon, take her over there, that empty booth in the corner. Get some coffee or something. I'll be right there. Gotta do something first."

Leon, the big trucker, looked down at Bob and nodded. He didn't seem to say much. Lyn noticed that Big Leon was content to let Bob, who was clearly the more energetic, take the lead and direct things. Gently guided by Leon's large hand on her elbow, they walked towards the booth.

Bob walked through the store to the driver's lounge opposite the cafe and stood in the door for a moment wondering what to do about the girl. Drivers were sprawled in chairs watching a television high on a shelf in a corner, or sloshing down coffee from a pot on a table and talking.

The girl didn't belong here. The drivers weren't necessarily bad, or good for that matter. It was just not a place where the young girl should be. She didn't belong. He thought of his own daughters and took the cell phone from his belt.

Dialing 911, Bob waited a minute, spoke for a minute, and waited some more. Then, turning from the lounge, he put the phone back on his belt and walked through the store towards the cafe. Todd, the surly clerk, was mouthing off to an old woman who had asked where the restroom was.

For the fiftieth time in five minutes, Bob thought 'This is no place for the girl.' Spotting Leon and the girl at the booth in the cafe, he walked to them feeling better about the call he had just made.

47. A Visit to Roydon

It was turning into a long day. Working on less than four hours of sleep, George Mackey sipped his third large Diet Coke since he had arrived at the Minit Mart to review the video. Now his bladder was filling, but the pressure was keeping him awake as he made his way south on the interstate back to Roydon.

Bob Shaklee had radioed that he was checking the Roydon locations; two motels, two gas stations and Pete's Place, George was enroute to help. Shaklee and his partner, Sharon Price, had divided the two investigations with Price focusing on the Sims case, and Shaklee heading up the murder of the girl. George and Ronnie Kupman were assisting both as best they could.

Heading up the exit ramp into Roydon, George turned, towards Pete's Place, for two reasons. First, Shaklee's Crown Victoria was parked outside, and he didn't want to leave Bob there alone for long. Second, he had to take a leak, bad. The three Diet Cokes were ready to come out.

Parking the pickup at the end of the building, he exited, closing the door softly, listening for trouble. All seemed quiet. Like every deputy in Pickham County, George had answered a number of calls at Pete's Place. It could be…generally was…a rough crowd. He should have warned Shaklee.

He walked along the front of the building, peering through the dirty windows to spot any problem inside as he approached. Not much was visible from the outside. George was more familiar with the place at night, when the lights inside made it easier to see what was happening. Better to avoid any unpleasant surprise when you jerked open the door.

As he approached the door, he noted two Harleys and a beat up Dodge truck parked in front. It was quiet today at Pete's. At the other end of the building was a shiny Cadillac Escalade belonging to Roy Budroe, owner and daytime bartender.

All seemed quiet. George yanked the heavy steel door open and walked in.

It took a moment for his eyes to adjust to the dim lighting. A heavyset man with his fists balled and planted on the bar leaned close to Bob Shaklee, who was standing with his notepad in one hand, staring straight back into the big man's face. Two men in leather jackets stood close on either side of Shaklee, leaning against the bar.

George checked the Harleys off in his head accounting for their owners. In a far corner, two scruffy men in dirty blue jeans, torn tee shirts, and ball caps sat staring at the beers on their table, clearly not wanting any part of what was going on at the bar. The Dodge pickup was now checked off. The caddy was Roy's. All present and accounted for.

It was plain that Roy had been saying something to Shaklee when George jerked the door open.

"What's up, Roy? Have you met my friend, Agent Shaklee of the Georgia Bureau of Investigation?" George walked up to the bar, stopping about ten feet short. He looked at the two bikers who stood up straight and returned his gaze defiantly.

"You boys move away from the bar." George's tone was flat, even, and firm. The bikers looked at him now a bit uncertainly. "Now," George repeated with emphasis.

They looked briefly at Budroe, who gave a short nod, and then moved towards a table by the door. George turned his head following them.

"Uh, uh boys. Not there. Go grab a table over there near them other fellas so I can see you all at once." They hesitated for only a second and then moved to the corner where the pickup boys were seated. They picked a table and sat, turning their chairs so they both faced the bar.

George turned his head back to the bar. "Sorry, Roy. Were you saying something? Seemed like I kind of interrupted when I came in." He smiled pleasantly at Budroe.

"What do you want, George?" Budroe's gravelly voice filled the room.

"Well, didn't Agent Shaklee explain? Or did you give him time to explain? Are you being uncooperative with law enforcement again,

185

Roy? I know we've talked about that before." George shook his head in mock disappointment.

"Stop the horseshit, George. We know who he is, and he ain't got no jurisdiction here."

"Really?" George replied, his tone amused. "Roydon seceded from the state did it, and just forgot to get the word out?" He paused looking deep into Budroe's beefy face. "I don't think so, Roy. So, unless you want to be digging out from under the ton of shit that's about to land on your head, pay attention and answer Agent Shaklee's questions."

Shaklee, who had about enough of the local, good old boy bullshit, interrupted, "Listen up, *Mr. Budroe,* the GBI is working a case in support of the Pickham County Sheriff's Department. This is official business, and you are expected to cooperate."

Budroe's response was blunt and to the point "Bullshit."

That was it. In a move that surprised even George, Shaklee dropped the notepad and reached rapidly across the bar, gripping Budroe's wrists so that he could not take his balled fists from the bar top. George saw Budroe's arms flex and knew he tried to lift them, but they didn't budge under Shaklee's grasp.

Bob leaned into his face before he spoke. "Let's make sure you understand. I'm with the *Georgia* Bureau of Investigation. This shithole of a town is in *Georgia*. The GBI has jurisdiction. You have any questions about that?"

One of the bikers had started to rise when Shaklee grabbed Budroe. A cautioning shake of George's head in his direction, and he sat back down. George watched the little drama being played out on the bar top.

Budroe, not sure what to do, finally spoke. "What do you want?"

Shaklee released the big man's wrists and picked up his notepad. "We have a few questions to ask, and then we'll be on our way." He then went through the description of the suspect they were seeking, "White male, five feet ten or so, light brown hair, driving a faded or primer painted mid-nineties model GM car. Possibly a Chevrolet. Wearing a ring with a steer's head or Texas longhorn on it."

Budroe indicated that he hadn't seen anyone like that, at least not anyone that would draw attention.

Bob smiled. "Good, now we can go."

"Wait a minute for me, Bob. Something I need to do."

George walked by the bikers and into the restroom. A couple of minutes later, he walked out with a smile on his face.

Walking to the door with Shaklee, he called back over his shoulder, "Thanks, Roy. Never saw a better place for taking a piss."

Outside in the bright sun, they squinted across the road at the two motels, one on each corner. Shaklee glanced sideways at George.

"Thanks for the backup. Could have got ugly in there."

"No need for thanks. It's pretty much always ugly in there. Been trying to clean it up for years. You handle yourself pretty good."

Shaklee shrugged, "Old habits. Spent eight years policing the south side of Atlanta before going with the state."

"Shows," George replied with greater respect for the GBI man.

"Yeah, well," Shaklee nodded across the street. "It's getting late. I suggest that we split up. You take that motel across the street, and I'll take the one on the other corner."

"Sounds good. After that we can start checking up and down the interstate."

They got into their vehicles and drove across the street. Five minutes later, George was interviewing a very large, heavily tattooed woman wearing a short top with string straps that showed her large, bare, bulging midriff. The cellulite dimples and stretch marks made it difficult for George not to stare.

The woman claimed to be the manager of the Roydon Inn. The interview was going nowhere. She knew nothing, and no linen or bedspreads were missing. Then Bob Shaklee called him on the radio.

"Pickham County 301, this is State 115."

George reached for his radio. "Go ahead, 115."

"George, you need to come over here. The StarLite Motel, across the street."

"On my way." George walked out without another word to the large, manager woman.

For her part, manager woman just shrugged and flipped the

187

channel on the old nineteen inch television in the office to 'Judge Judy'. She was glad to see the law go. Wasn't good for business.

48. Coming of Age

Leon Tills stood quietly by the young girl. His large hands roamed restlessly in and out of his pockets while his partner, Bob Sully, talked to the Savannah PD officer. Lyn, standing next to Leon, was dwarfed by the huge man. She appeared even smaller and frailer, while Leon looked even larger.

Since encountering the young girl, they had been trying to decide what to do with her. Leon, for his part, was given the task of looking out for her, which meant standing watch over her. His hulking presence was sure to discourage any other potential problems like Henry from approaching Lyn. He accepted this task willingly.

Although he and Bob were partners, Bob was the thinker and talker, Leon was the doer. Leon was okay with that. He was a damned good truck driver, but Bob was the planner, always thinking ahead. He was better at talking to people, so Leon was comfortable letting him take care of that sort of thing.

Right now that meant that Bob talked to the police officer while Leon hovered protectively over Lyn. They stood alone about ten feet away from Bob and the officer.

The thin, hard looking man that had kicked Henry's ass hadn't come in with them, although he had said that he would. Nobody missed him though, and no one was going to talk about the little incident in the truck lot, especially Henry.

Leon thought about the man who had beaten old Henry. No doubt, Henry had deserved it. If he hadn't stepped in, there was no telling what Henry might have done to the young girl.

But there was something strange about him, Leon thought. Even though Henry was after the girl, they had felt that they needed to protect Henry from the man trying to save her. Leon didn't have words to explain it.

The man had a meanness about him. You could see it in the way he had attacked Henry. Leon was glad the man had been there to make sure the girl wasn't abused by Henry, but he figured that if he

189

and Bob hadn't come along, he might have killed Henry.

Leon shrugged to himself. Maybe that was what Henry deserved. Leon had a daughter of his own, and he didn't know what he would do if someone tried to abuse her the way Henry would have done the young girl. Still, he knew that he and Bob would have had their hands full stopping Henry's assailant if he had turned on them while he was kicking the dog shit out of Henry.

Leon looked over at Bob and the officer as Bob raised his voice.

"What!" Bob said, incredulously.

"Sorry, sir. That's how it is."

"But look at her," Bob said. "She's a child."

"Nope. She's eighteen. She's of age." the officer replied. "Not a thing I can do. She can go where she wants and do what she wants, 'long as it's legal. Hanging out in the truck stop isn't against the law."

"But she almost got raped."

"You know that for a fact?" the officer asked, eyes narrowing.

"Well no, not for a fact, but if this other fella hadn't come along and stopped it, there was this trucker that was gonna put her in his truck and I know it wasn't gonna be good for her."

"Look, I'm on your side. Where's this other fella? Where's the trucker that was going to rape her?"

"Well they're gone now, at least I haven't seen them around here for a while," Bob replied, knowing that it was over and done as far as Henry and his attacker were concerned.

"Well," the officer continued, "No suspects and no complaint from the girl equals no crime. Really, nothing I can do buddy."

Bob took a deep breath and looked down at the floor.

"Miss," the officer said to Lyn making his point "is there anything I can do for you? Get some help, call someone, get you a ride somewhere? Contact your parents? Family? Anything?"

Lyn looked up. She hadn't spoken since the officer had arrived and asked her name and what had happened. She had said that nothing was wrong anymore and that the two truckers were just trying to help her, but she was fine now.

"I'm fine, sir," she said. "Really, I'll be okay. I'm just waiting for a friend to pick me up. These men helped me, but I'm okay now."

The Savannah PD officer looked at Bob and Leon and shrugged. "Sorry guys. Wish there was something I could do. I know it's hard. There's hundreds like her out on the roads. Just not much we can do about it."

The officer turned and walked away. Bob looked at Leon and then looked at the floor. Leon, the stalwart, just looked back and stood protectively near Lyn.

"You know, we are going to have to leave in an hour or so. Have to get our loads down the road," Bob said to Lyn.

"I know. Thank you for helping me."

Bob shook his head fighting down his frustration.

"You don't understand. You'll be alone here again. Something could happen. There might not be anyone here to help." Bob looked around to demonstrate to Lyn that she really would be alone. "This is a big place," he said motioning with his hands, "and bad things can happen. I mean you saw that, right?"

Lyn looked down and shrugged.

"I have a friend. He is going to come pick me up. I'll be fine until then."

The two truck drivers looked at each other. Leon's face bore a look of supreme sadness; Bob's showed frustration.

Finally, Bob shrugged and said, "All right then. We'll be here for a little while anyway. If you need anything, come get us. We'll be getting our rigs weighed and serviced."

He turned and walked away, but then stopped and looked back at Lyn and said firmly, "You take care. Okay? Call that friend and have him come get you."

Lyn smiled slightly and nodded before looking back down at the floor.

Leon watched Bob's back retreat across the truck stop. He put a large, heavy hand on Lyn's shoulder for a moment, and they both stared at the floor. Then he withdrew his hand and walked slowly away following Bob. He didn't want to look back at her. Not knowing what to say or what to do, he could only walk away.

49. Evidence and Guilt

Gunning the pickup across the road, George spotted Shaklee's car and roared to a stop behind it, kicking up a cloud of dust. The car was parked at the end of the row of rooms away from the office. The door was open, and a man in overalls was standing outside. The door to the room next door was open also. Bob came out of that room as George walked up.

"Take a look, George. See anything familiar?"

Standing in the doorway of the room, George looked around briefly. It only took a second.

"The bedspread. It's the same."

"Yep," Shaklee affirmed. "The very same as the one the girl was wrapped in. Come next door."

Walking into the next room, the one at the end of the building, George saw what else had Bob Shaklee so excited.

"The bedspread is gone."

"Yes, it is George."

"That means that this could be the scene of the murder."

"I'd say that's exactly what it means. I have the crime scene techs on the way. Let's look around and keep everyone away until they get here. Then we're going to have a conversation with our friend here." He motioned to the man in overalls. "He says he doesn't remember anything from last night. Busy you know."

"Really?" George turned to the man. "Well, come have a seat in the back of my truck. Maybe you can think for a while and come up with something we might want to hear." George took him by the arm and led him to the pickup's rear, crew cab door behind the prisoner screen. Giving him a quick pat down, he opened the door, and the man climbed in. George slammed the door and turned away.

Let him stew for a while. There wouldn't be much business at the office as long as the lot was full of state and county vehicles, and there were more on the way.

George began looking around the parking lot in front of the room door. Bob worked inside, carefully noting every item in the

192

room, peering closely at objects, furnishings, and flooring, searching for any small bits of evidence. Unless the killer was a magician, chances are they would find something. Despite his precautions, there would be something he had missed in his efforts to leave no evidence behind.

It took George only a minute to spot the duct tape. It lay in the dusty gravel where a car would have been parked if someone were staying in the room.

Kneeling down, he turned it over with his pen. There were three layers, about the length to go around the mouth and head of a girl. It had been cut, not pulled off or unwrapped.

What appeared to be a small amount of dried blood stained the edge of the tape by the cut mark. The killer had probably cut the tape quickly and roughly without worrying about nicking the girl in the process. George had no doubt that the knife used was the same one that had plunged deep into Mr. Sims and had then inflicted the small tissue cuts on the girl's body.

Near the tape were two white plastic tie wraps of the type used by electricians to wrap wires and cables. They had also been cut.

Squatting in the dust, staring at the tie wraps and tape, George closed his eyes and saw the scene as it would have looked the night before. The girl bound, mouth taped, still alive, and not hurt much. She would have been forced to walk into the room.

Did she know she would never walk out? The thought must have been burning in her mind, desperately trying to find a way to stay alive. Hate for the animal that had done this boiled up inside. Every piece of evidence pointed to a person who caused pain willingly and with purpose. The pain was as much a reason for the murders as anything else.

He looked up and called to the room. "Bob, you have an evidence bag?'

"Yeah, George. What do you have?" Shaklee stopped in the doorway, looking at the spot where George knelt. "Good. Should be able to get the victim's DNA from the tape, probably the perp's too, or a print."

George didn't move. Shaklee walked to his car to retrieve the evidence bags and a camera to photograph the items in place before placing them in the bags.

"We've made some progress, George. We're a lot closer than we were this morning."

George looked up. "Lot of progress, but we still don't have a suspect. And even with his DNA, we won't know who it is unless he's got a record and it's in the data base. And the DNA test could take weeks. We don't have weeks, Bob."

"Yeah, but we also have a description of him, the ring, and the car. That's a lot. We'll find the bastard." He tried to sound more confident than he actually was.

At the mention of the car, Bob could see George's head drop slightly. "Want to tell me about the car, George?"

George stood up. "You talk to Ronnie?"

"No. I was there when he gave that bullshit story to the sheriff about you checking your notes to confirm the description. Haven't known you long, but information like that...well, I don't think you would have had to check any notepad about that."

"Well, you are correct, Agent Shaklee." George looked up at the sky and took a deep breath. "I was asleep."

"Okay. So how does that tie in?"

"The car woke me up as it passed, not too far from the Ridley's place. I saw it, but I didn't do anything. Didn't stop it, didn't get a tag number, nothing. Just pulled my jacket around me and dozed off again."

"Well, George, you wouldn't have known."

"Stop. Now you sound like Ronnie Kupman. We had a murder in the county. That doesn't happen often in Pickham. The car was on a road that really doesn't get traveled much at night. It was a car that I didn't recognize as a local. It had an out of state tag. I couldn't tell which state, but it wasn't a Georgia tag. You would think I would have at least followed the car to see where they went or how they were driving. I didn't. What I did do was nothing. I slept. Ronnie said I was checking the notes to cover me. He knows the sheriff would love to get rid of me on charges like that."

"I see. So now you're going to spend the rest of your career beating yourself up."

"What career? I'm working this case and then hanging it up. Turn myself in to the sheriff when we get this done."

"Really?" Shaklee said questioningly. "And give up Ronnie Kupman who covered for you. Seems a little unfair to him."

George had already thought about that. "I'm going to tell the sheriff that the story about checking my notes was my idea. Ronnie didn't know any better. He just stays quiet. It will work out."

Shaklee shook his head slowly. "George, I get it. Any of us would feel terrible about it. I also think your contribution to the case outweighs any error in judgment you might have made. We wouldn't be anywhere near as far along without you. Do what you want, there's nothing I can say to talk you out of it, I know, but it seems to me that it would be a pretty big shame to lose what you bring to the table. The way I see it, if your guilt stays with you, so be it. Maybe you *should* feel guilty every day the rest of your life. Maybe that's the price you pay to keep doing what you do best. I guess you could confess and cleanse your soul and be drummed out of the county. You might feel better, and the citizens of Pickham County might lose one of their best, maybe *the best*. Or, you could hold it in, take the pain and guilt, and keep doing what you are supposed to do. Maybe that's your penance. It's harder, that's for sure."

Gravel crunched and dust swirled as the crime scene SUV pulled into the lot. Shaklee turned towards the room.

"Let's get to work."

George followed him into the room that the girl never walked from.

50. Alone

On the front wall outside the truck stop cafe, there were a couple of old, beat up pay phones. Lyn stood in front of one. It was dirty. In the age of cell phones, they bore the signs of neglect. A brownish substance was hardened to the mouthpiece.

Only the poorest people used them anymore, Lyn knew. She knew that most people nowadays had cell phones, although she had never had one. She had seen many drivers walking around the truck stop with cell phones to their ears.

She wondered what that would be like. Just take a little thing out of your pocket and call someone on your own phone. She wondered who she would call. Clay Purcell, she thought. Today she would call Clay on one of those cell phones, if she had one. Clay had one. That was the number he had written on the napkin for her.

Lyn was accustomed to the frustration of seeing the modern world around her, a world filled with convenience and wonders, but never knowing what it was like to participate in that world. She saw it at a distance from the cage of her small life.

Lyn studied the folded napkin with Clay's number on it and took a deep breath. Reaching for the dirty pay phone, she shoved her hand in the pocket of her jeans searching for coins.

"Here, you might want to use this."

Lyn was startled by a deep voice behind her. It was Leon, the big truck driver. He held a cell phone in his hand and raised his arm, offering it to her.

"Oh…uh no, I couldn't," Lyn stammered, "I don't even know…"

"Here," the big man insisted, then showing her, he opened the phone, "Just press these buttons for the numbers, and then press this green one. That makes the call go through. Hold this up to your ear to talk and hear. Just close it up when you're done. I'll be in the store. You can bring it in to me."

Leon pushed the phone into her small hand and turned abruptly heading back into the store.

Lyn stood there with the thing in her hand. She was surprised at how light it was. Not like a regular phone, but then it was a lot smaller.

Tentatively, she opened the phone and then opened the napkin with Clay's number on it. It was awkward, but she managed to read the numbers and then press each one on the phone. She was surprised to see the numbers come up on a little screen.

She fumbled with holding the napkin and then pressing the numbers, but once they were all entered, she compared what was on the screen with the numbers that Clay had scrawled for her. They matched.

Taking a deep breath, she pressed the green button. It had a picture of a regular telephone receiver on it, which was not anything at all like the little device she held in her hand. Holding it up to her ear as Leon had instructed, Lyn heard ringing, just like on a regular phone.

The ringing went on for several seconds. Lyn thought no one was going to answer, but then she heard Clay's voice.

"Hi, this is Clay..."

"Hello, uh Clay, this is Lyn...," Lyn was cut off because Clay kept talking.

"...can't take your call right now, but leave a message and I'll call you back," Clay said and then there was a loud beep.

Lyn stood there with the phone at her ear not knowing what to do. After a few seconds, she closed it up the way Leon had said. Voice mail was something she had never encountered in the backcountry of south Georgia.

The phone hung loosely from the end of her arm as she looked at the ground. She was frustrated. She was alone. She fought back the tears that welled up in her eyes.

Opening the phone again, she carefully pressed the numbers and then the green button. Again, the phone rang. She counted six rings, then Clay's voice. This time she said nothing but waited a moment. Clay continued talking as he had before, telling her to leave a message. When he finished talking, Lyn spoke.

"Uh, hello, Clay. This is Lyn, the girl you gave a ride to. If you still want to come pick me up here, I'll be at the truck stop. I, uh..." she

197

didn't know what else to say, and for a few seconds, there was just silence until she realized she should just close the phone up.

What now, she thought. Just wait. What if Clay changed his mind? What if he didn't get the message? What if she was just left alone here? The tears began welling in her eyes again.

Maybe she should just go home, but then no, she thought, and then more emphatically, NO. Mama had risked everything last night, and there was no telling what Daddy would do if she came back. Actually, she knew exactly what he would do if she returned and he could get his hands on her. She felt the bruise on her arm.

Nothing to do but wait for Clay. If he didn't come, then Canada. The Canada running away dream was still an option...a distant one now, but there.

Dabbing her eyes on her sleeve, she turned and walked back into the store. Leon was standing quietly by the magazine rack. She walked over to him and held the phone out.

"Get hold of your friend?" his deep rumbling voice asked.

"Yes...yes I did," she answered.

"He coming for you?"

"Yes, he said he would be here in a while."

"You sure?"

"Yes, yes. I'll be all right. Just gonna wait here for him," Lyn answered not looking him in the eye.

Leon didn't know what else to do. He took the phone in his hand. For once, there was a soft look on his big, gruff face and he gave her a smile.

"Okay then. Well, we gotta be going soon. Here," Leon took a card from his shirt pocket and handed it to Lyn. "This is us, me and Bob. It's got our phone numbers on it if you need to call. Okay?"

Lyn took the battered, card bearing Leon's greasy thumbprint. It had big letters that said B&L Trucking and then some phone numbers.

She looked up and Leon's smile made her feel a little better.

"Thanks. I'm grateful."

Leon stood there for a few more seconds not knowing what else to do. Then he turned and walked to the end of the aisle where Bob

198

waited for him. They walked out the front door and across the lot to their rigs, parked side by side in the gravel.

Lyn was alone again.

51. Vernon's Dilemma

By Georgia standards, Pickham County was average in size. In a state with one hundred and fifty-nine counties, you were never more than twenty or thirty miles from the next county line. In some cases, the distance was much less.

Almost every county had their own sheriff and in the larger metropolitan counties, a separate police department. Throw in the various cities and state law enforcement agencies and there were a lot of cops in Georgia. Some thought too many...others too few. At this moment, there were a lot in Roydon, Georgia.

No less than eight law enforcement vehicles were gathered in the lot of the StarLite Motel, divided between Pickham County, GBI, crime scene technicians and the State Patrol.

More gravel crunched and spit from under the tires of two more vehicles, and there were now ten vehicles in the lot. George looked up and saw that it was Sheriff Klineman with Ronnie Kupman, followed by Timmy Farrin in the old radio station van. Time for Timmy's shot at an interview, George thought.

Sharon Price had arrived earlier and was going through the motel room with the crime scene techs while George and Bob Shaklee engaged in a heart-to-heart conversation with the StarLite's desk clerk, Vernon Taft. Mr. Taft was reluctant, at best, to remember any details about the guest who had rented the end room, and who had removed the bedspread upon his departure.

Cornered in the back of George's truck, he looked frequently at the small crowd that was growing outside of Pete's Place across the road. The larger the crowd grew, the more reluctant he became. George and Bob Shaklee stood in the open door on one side of the vehicle making sure the other side was clear and Taft's view of Pete's Place unobstructed.

It didn't take a rocket scientist to know why he was nervous. Conversing with the law in Roydon was an unhealthy practice, especially in broad daylight.

"You know, Vernon," George interjected during a break in the questioning. "You might as well tell us what we want to know, and tell us now so we can get you out of here." He nodded at the crowd across the street. "You think they're gonna believe you said nothing, no matter what you tell them later. Even if they do believe you, they won't be of a mind to take any chances in the future." He shook his head. "Maybe you talked, maybe you didn't, but why take chances? Yep, I can hear Roy Budroe saying it now, 'Why take chances?'" George let the words sink in for effect. "And somewhere tonight a gator out in the Okefenokee is going to have a fat supper."

"Bullshit. None of this has anything to do with anyone in Roydon or anyone at Pete's. Why should they care?" Vernon Taft's voice cracked in a plaintiff whine that did not have the bluster of his words. This was all so unfair.

"Great point, Vernon," George said nodding in agreement. "Go tell them that," he added, jerking his head toward the crowd.

Taft turned his head, looking out the side window. Roy Budroe stood there chewing a cigar, staring in his direction, his big meaty fists balled at his side.

Vernon raised a shaking hand to wipe the sweat from his greasy brow. The inside of the pickup reeked of the alcohol that was boiling out of his pores with the perspiration. George would air it out later and hoped that that would be the only stench he had to air out of the truck.

Vernon was powerfully scared, caught between the proverbial rock and hard place. No doubt, he would be changing underwear later, provided he was wearing any.

Shaklee leaned forward into the truck. "One more thing you might consider, Vernon. At this point, we know that this room is connected with a major felony. Your failure to cooperate and provide a description of the person who rented the room constitutes obstruction of an investigation, and I can assure you that the GBI takes that very seriously and will not hesitate to prosecute anyone who stands in the way of the investigation. And then there is the fact that your actions make you an accessory to..." Now Shaklee paused for effect. "An accessory to murder."

George and Bob watched the blood drain from Taft's already pale face.

"You didn't know that, did you Vernon?" Shaklee continued. "We're investigating a murder and that makes you, as it stands now, an accessory to murder. And I mean the big one. Capital murder. Murder in the first degree. And maybe you haven't forgotten that Georgia still kills murderers. Frankly, it's one of the things I love about the state...and my job."

Vernon finally managed to get something out. "You asshole."

Shaklee smiled, "Been told that before, Vernon. Hell, it's probably true." Then looking him hard in the eye, Shaklee added, "But don't doubt me. I will prosecute you as an accessory to murder without hesitation."

Shaklee moved back from the door. George's turn. Taft was almost at the breaking point; one more straw on his frail, alcoholic back, and he would crumble.

"Well, Vernon, I think Agent Shaklee has made it pretty clear where we stand. By the way, weren't you gone for a while doing time? I don't mean any soft time in the county jail, you did some drug time, didn't you?" George knew full well that he had, having already had dispatch run a GCIC criminal history check on Mr. Taft. "Keep in mind that you won't be a trustee washing cars this time. You'll be doing hard time, maybe waiting for the needle. Think it over, Vernon. You only have one play here."

Vernon Taft sat trembling in the back of Deputy George Mackey's county pickup. His chin fell onto his chest and a long sigh wheezed out of his bony chest.

"I don't know much, but what can I get if I talk? Can you get me away from here? I won't last long in Roydon if they think I cooperated with the law on anything." He looked out the window towards Pete's Place.

"You tell us everything you know, and I will see that you get to someplace safe."

"Sister in Valdosta. That's where I want to go."

"Okay, your sister's place in Valdosta. You can dry out and figure out what to do from there. Of course, we will want to know exactly where you are in case we need anything else." George left out the part about testifying in open court when they caught the killer.

202

Vernon Taft, alcoholic, former small-time drug runner, country boy gone bad turned shady old man, sagged in the seat and nodded his head. "I saw him, the man who rented the room."

"Right. Anyone with him?

"No, he was alone...least as far as I could tell."

"Talk, Vernon." And Vernon did. George pulled out his notepad.

Five minutes later, Vernon Taft, recently of Roydon, Georgia, had related everything he remembered about the thin, severe man who had rented the room at the far end of the StarLite Motel. True to his word, there wasn't much he could add to what the authorities already knew. White male, light brown hair, medium build, thin face. He paid in cash. Vernon hadn't paid attention to any rings that he might have been wearing. In fact, the man didn't go to his room until Vernon had gone back to the cot in the clerk's office.

One thing though, the man didn't know that as he backed and then pulled his car over to his room, Vernon had stood in the darkened office and watched, mostly because he was annoyed at the man's threatening attitude. Vernon was able to note that the car he drove was a 1992 Chevrolet with faded burgundy paint that showed gray primer through on the hood and roof.

Vernon knew this because he had owned the same make and model back in the nineties when they were new. He had run drugs up and down the interstate in his Chevy. Yes, it was a Chevy, old, but it ran good. Was that enough to get him protection from Roy Budroe?

The information only corroborated what they already knew, but George assured Vernon that he would be enroute to the Pickham County jail that very evening, and would stay there in protective custody until they could arrange transport for him to his sister's place in Valdosta. For the first time since the arrival of Bob Shaklee and George Mackey at the StarLite Motel, Vernon relaxed. In fact, he all but collapsed in the back of George's pickup. Peeking out of the side window, he could see that the crowd milling around outside of Pete's Place had grown.

"Hey, deputy," he called through the cracked window. "Got a smoke?"

"Sorry, Vernon. I got a chew. You can have some if you want, but

203

you can't spit in the truck."

At that moment, Ronnie Kupman stepped forward and pulled a smoke from his pack of Marlboros, opened the door, and handed it to Vernon, pulling out a lighter at the same time. Vernon leaned forward, sucked the flame into the cigarette, and then sank contentedly back into the seat.

"Damn, Ronnie. He's gonna smoke my truck up now," George commented on Ronnie's act of compassion.

Kupman looked unsympathetically at the tobacco juice streaks down the side of George's truck. Changing the subject, he said, "You've had a busy day George."

"Yeah, we had some luck."

"Luck maybe, but good police work."

Sheriff Klineman, who had watched the interview with Vernon Taft, and who had been restrained from interfering by Ronnie Kupman, walked up and spoke to Bob Shaklee, completely ignoring his deputy.

"Great work, Agent Shaklee. Seems our murderer is not from Pickham County or Georgia after all. What else do we know that can pin him down?"

"Well, by 'pin him down', do you mean apprehend the murderer, or make sure that he is not in any way associated with Pickham County?"

The sheriff reddened, something that was becoming a common occurrence. "I don't appreciate your tone or the implication that I may not have the best interests of the public at heart. I am deeply concerned about ensuring the safety of the public here in Pickham County. To think otherwise would be a slander to my office and, frankly, to me personally. Is that your intent?" It appeared that Sheriff Klineman was a bit testy and had had a long day as well.

"Not at all Sheriff. May I suggest that we go back to your office and review the cases? We have made progress, but there is work to do, and we need some rest. We've been working this since the Sims murder last night and everyone is tired."

"Agreed," Klineman replied and then turned to George. "Deputy Mackey, you are relieved. We have covered your shift tonight. Take tomorrow off."

"Excuse me Sheriff," Shaklee interjected. "Deputy Mackey has been instrumental in furthering the investigation today. It would be appropriate to have him assist in the debrief to you and Chief Deputy Kupman."

"Not necessary, not necessary at all, Shaklee. Deputy Mackey has been a big help, and we appreciate that, but we trust that you will be able to brief us fully on the investigation." He turned to George. "Mackey, you are relieved."

George shrugged and turned away, then seeing a nervous Vernon Taft in the back of his pickup said, "Sheriff, mind if I take Vernon here to the jail on the way home? We need to make arrangements to transport him to his sister's place in Valdosta."

Klineman turned, deeply annoyed. "Why would we do that deputy?

"Because we promised him we would," Shaklee interjected. "And because if we don't, you may well be working another murder here in Roydon." He jerked his head towards the crowd across the street.

Klineman turned, eyeing the crowd in the lot at Pete's Place. He would definitely have to clean that place up at some point, he thought. "Fine then. Mackey, transport your witness to the jail and place him in protective custody. After that, you are relieved. We will arrange transport tomorrow."

George turned towards his truck without a word of acknowledgement.

"Meet me at my office as soon as you are done here, Shaklee," Klineman said, turning towards Timmy Farrin who was waiting patiently by his van, recorder in hand.

"What a prick."

A look of mild surprise on his face, Ronnie Kupman turned towards Bob Shaklee. He nodded in understanding. "Yep."

Then he turned and followed his sheriff.

For his part, Shaklee wished he could recall the three words he had just spoken. Klineman's self-centered arrogance had managed to crack his professional veneer.

George Mackey neither heard, nor saw any of this. He simply

pulled his truck from the lot of the StarLite Motel heading back to I-95 and the jail in Everett. In the back seat, Vernon Taft laid down trying to make himself invisible to the crowd in front of Pete's Place. He felt as though they had x-ray vision, watching him through the sides of the truck.

52. Regrouping

Big Leon ambled across the lot to his rig and climbed up. Lylee Torkman watched from the side of the truck wash building at the other end of the fuel pumps. He leaned against the brick wall, puffing one of his generic cigarettes.

Even at a distance, it was clear that the big man was concerned for the girl. Well, he should be, Lylee thought. A momentary surge of adrenalin gave him a visceral thrill. He had watched as the girl used the cell phone that the big truck driver had handed to her.

Lylee stayed away from the truck stop's main building. He had already carelessly exposed himself too much on this runaround and had no intention of meeting the police officer that the truckers had summoned. It was time to regroup, to shake off the two careless mistakes he had made that day, and make sure there were no others.

He thought carefully, formulating his plan. The intervention of the two truckers had saved the girl, for the time being. But their meddling in his confrontation with Henry only made his appetite for the girl grow into a raging, undeniable need. He would have her.

When the officer left without the girl, another plan began coming together. The two truckers would leave, sooner or later, and the girl would be alone. He would be ready.

Lyn had watched quietly from inside the store as Leon and Bob walked to their rigs. The tractors rumbled to life and belched exhaust from their stacks and then slowly moved out of the lot, Bob first, then Leon.

Loneliness settled heavily on her narrow shoulders. Standing just inside the front door of the truck stop store, she looked out through the dirt specked glass. Her presence there was like one of the specks on the glass, invisible unless you focused on it. She was invisible.

There was bustling activity all around, but she was unseen and unnoticed. It seemed that the rest of the world looked through her and around her. She was a ghost...a flickering image to those others.

The call to Clay made her feel even lonelier. Would he get the message? Would he show up at the truck stop? She shook her head to clear the despair. Nothing was working out. Canada. What a stupid idea.

She turned and walked back towards the cafe to wait. There was nothing else to do. Taking a seat on a swiveling stool at the end of the counter, away from everyone else, she waited for the girl behind the counter to notice her, but she didn't. She was invisible.

But someone did see her. In fact, Lylee Torkman saw almost nothing else.

Making his way along the edge of the parking lot, Lylee found his car. He had left it in the gravel between two rows of parked trucks.

He started the car and rolled slowly up and down the rows, thinking and making his way closer to the main truck stop building. Coming to the end of the lines of trucks in the gravel lot, he drove past the back of the building.

The car rolled slowly, almost idling, past the garbage dumpster and rear loading door. Coming to the other side of the building, he turned left and was able to park in a spot along the building's side wall, just adjacent to the rear of the building.

There were no vehicles parked on that side of the building. Trucks parked out in the lot. Cars were all parked directly in front. This side of the building was a quiet, out-of-the-way spot. All of the activity was near the building's entrance. At the same time, it was not so secluded that someone might hesitate to walk to the car, but there…where the sidewall joined the rear…no one would be paying attention.

Lylee sat there for a few minutes. There was no traffic. Leaning forward to look up through the windshield, he scanned for cameras. He could see none. Finally, he stepped out of the Chevy.

Leaning back and stretching as he turned, he scanned three hundred and sixty degrees. Building corners, light poles, everywhere. No cameras. Phase one of the plan was completed.

Of course, 'plan' was really a misnomer. This was a stalk and a hunt. Like all hunts, there was a dynamic element. He could set the trap, but what would follow would be fluid and changing, depending upon the actions of the prey.

Each bounding spring of the gazelle caused the lion to change and adapt its attack. It was a part of the hunt that thrilled him. Confident in his skills, a tingle of anticipation went up his back at what was about to follow.

Walking quietly down the side to the front of the building, he moved quickly. Timing was important...swiftness while appearing unhurried.

Although the side of the building was secluded now, the dynamics of the hunt meant that could change. A passerby might pull in near his car looking for a blow job from some truck stop whore. An employee might go there to take a smoke break. Things could change. Right now, they were as near to perfect as he could get them, but that would not last. Phase two had to be executed without delay.

Lylee walked through the front door and scanned the store quickly. She was not there. Moving to the doorway that passed from the store into the cafe, he saw her instantly.

She was seated at the far end of the counter. There were three empty seats to her right and then a cluster of drivers, drinking coffee and talking loudly. The waitress was leaning against the counter laughing and talking with the drivers, coffee pot in hand. Lylee could see that she hadn't noticed the girl at the end. Without thinking about it, this was automatically factored into the plan.

Walking across the cafe to the counter, he took a seat. Leaving the one directly next to the girl open, he took the one beside it. Close enough, but not too close.

"Well, hello again." Lylee's face bore the broad, charming smile he could turn on and off at will.

Lyn looked up from her lap. She was startled to see the man who had saved her from Henry. The memory of the violence of his attack on the big man was slightly eerie. She had been almost as frightened of him as she had been of Henry.

"Hello." Her voice was timid and soft. She returned her gaze to her lap.

Lylee saw the apprehension in her eyes. He spoke softly, to

dispel her concerns. "Listen, I wanted to apologize. I know I got a little carried away out there earlier with…"

He took a deep breath as if he were struggling with his feelings and went on.

"Well, with that big truck driver. You know, I saw him…and he was going to, well it wasn't good what he wanted to do, and I just…well I just lost it, you know. I couldn't control myself."

Lylee lowered his head and looked down at his own lap as if struggling with what to say and how to explain it to her.

Out of the corner of her eye, Lyn saw him lower his head. She said, "That's okay. It just scared me." She raised her head and looked at him.

Lylee, kept his head lowered, not looking at her. He knew that she was now focused on him. "I just, well," he continued in a contrite way, "It's just that my sister was attacked once by some men. They did… things to her, and I…well, anyway…" He shrugged and looked up. "I just lost it when I saw that guy with you. I knew what would happen. I couldn't stand it, so I…well you know. You saw."

Lyn smiled just slightly at him. "It's okay. It scared me, but I'm glad. I mean, I'm glad you did what you did and helped me."

Lylee turned and looked her in the eye. This time he put a look of gratitude on his face, accented with a soft, caring smile.

"Those other two men were looking for you. You know the ones who stopped you from…well you know, those men who came by," Lyn said, not knowing what else to say.

"Yeah, I know," Lylee said. He shook his head again. "I just had to clear my head and walk around for a while. I was pretty pissed…sorry, I mean I was pretty mad, and I needed to calm down."

Lylee looked directly at Lyn. The charming smile was back. She smiled back at him for real this time.

"Look," he said lightly as if to change the subject. "Do you want something to drink or eat. My treat."

"No that's okay. I was going to get a Coke, but the waitress hasn't seen me yet." Lyn shrugged.

"Oh, she hasn't, has she?" Lylee said taking control like her big brother. He turned towards the waitress laughing with the truck drivers. "Miss," he said loudly, "we'd like to order."

The waitress looked up, turned, and placed the coffee pot on the hot plate behind her. Pulling an order pad out of her apron, she said indifferently, "What can I get you?"

53. "I'll call you later"

Clay released the trigger, and the circular saw whined down to silence once more. He carried the freshly cut lumber to where Cy was framing up the header on a door. In the dense, dead silence, he heard the beep from his cell phone.

Dropping the lumber next to Cy, he reached for the phone on his belt. He had a missed call, two actually, from the same number. It was not a number Clay knew. There was also a voice mail message.

Clay dialed in to retrieve the message. His heart pounded when he heard her timid voice.

"This is Lyn...I'll be at the truck stop," the voice said.

Cy looked up and saw the look on his brother's face.

"What's up?" he asked.

"Lyn. She left a message, said she would be waiting at the truck stop."

"Well that's great," Cy said smiling at his younger brother.

"Yeah," Clay replied, "but she sounded scared. Like something happened."

"Well, we can go pick her up when we get off. She said she'd be waiting, right? We can run her back down to home, drop her off with Mama and head back up here," Cy said and then added, "Won't get much sleep tonight you know. You can be a pain in the ass for a little brother."

Clay nodded back "Yeah, that sounds like a plan. She just didn't sound right though."

"Well, call her back. She probably called from the pay phone. She might still be around it waiting."

"Yea, good idea, but the number doesn't look like a Georgia number."

Clay used his thumb to redial the number Lyn had called from.

Even through the rumble of the big rig's tires, big Leon felt the vibration of the phone in his shirt pocket. He plunged two large fingers, all that would fit, into the pocket and retrieved the phone.

Glancing away from the road, Leon studied the number on the

screen. Not his wife or anyone else he knew. Probably someone with business, and they called him by mistake. They should have called Bob, who was a half mile ahead in his rig. As always, Leon would just as soon let Bob do the talking and arranging. He put it back in his pocket. Whoever it was would get his voice mail and would call Bob's number.

"This is Leon. Leave a message."

The deep, gruff voice on the phone startled Clay, who was expecting Lyn's soft, timid voice. Who the hell was Leon, he thought. Damn. This wasn't good.

Clay dialed the number again.

Leon was annoyed as the vibration started in his pocket again. He didn't like talking much, and didn't like talking on the phone even more. Still it might be something about one of his kids or his wife from a number he didn't know.

"Leon!"

Clay recognized the voice from the voicemail announcement. The voice sounded pissed off. Too bad.

"Hi Leon, this is Clay Purcell. I'm looking for a girl, Lyn. She called me from your number."

Oh, Leon thought. Forgot about that. Clay couldn't see it, but the big man's face softened.

"Yeah. She did. Are you the friend she called?"

Clay detected the softer tone in Leon's voice.

"Yes, I am. I mean I guess I am. Is she with you?"

"No, she was at the truck stop last I saw her. Waiting for you. Are you the friend that was gonna pick her up?"

Clay answered with more confidence now. "Yes. Yes I am. I told her to call, and I would come get her."

"Well, that's good son," Leon's deep voice resonated in Clay's phone. "She needs someone to get her away from there."

"Why?" Clay felt the anxiety rise in his chest. "Is something wrong?"

Big Leon remembered the little girl standing beside the pay phones at the truck stop when they left. She may have been eighteen and full grown in the eyes of the law, but that little girl didn't need to

213

be alone there.

Leon felt an ache inside. They should have done more. Something. But there wasn't anything they could do. She had called her friend, and they had to drop a load in Birmingham. Leon could never have put words to all of this. He said what he could.

"She had some trouble with a trucker. Another fella helped her out, and then we took her in to the truck stop. Bob wanted…"

"We? Bob? Who's Bob" Clay asked, his anxiety growing.

"Bob? Bob's my partner," Leon paused to get the story back on track. "Bob's my partner. We saw the trouble with the trucker, but this other fella stepped in first, then he left, so we took the little girl back in the truck stop. Bob called the police, but they said she was grown so she could do what she wanted. I let her use my phone to call a friend to come get her. She must have called you," Leon concluded. He was relieved to get it all out. He added, "Then you called me."

Clay was overwhelmed. There were too many questions.

"So you left her?" Clay asked.

Big Leon didn't sound or feel so intimidating now. His voice sounded contrite. "Yeah, we did. Sorry. I hope that's all right. Wouldn't want anything to happen to her. She seems like a nice girl. Someone should go get her and take her home. Is that you?"

"Yes," Clay said firmly. "Yes it is. Is she okay?"

"Last we saw she was standing by the pay phones outside the store waiting. For you, I reckon." Leon's conscience and concern made him add, "There wasn't anything else we could do. Least it seemed that way."

Clay took a breath. It was lucky for Lyn that Leon and his partner Bob had come along. Not their fault. They hadn't done anything different than he and Cy had done, leaving her at the truck stop. His conscience twinged painfully.

"Well, Leon thanks for helping her out. I'll get her at the truck stop. Thanks."

All Leon could say was, "Okay then. Thanks." The conversation ended. There wasn't anything else to say.

Clay looked at Cy and said, "I gotta go."

Cy looked up, nail gun in his hand, surprised. "What, now?"

"I gotta go," was all Clay said.

Cy wasn't happy. "Why do you have to go now? We got to get these walls framed. We have responsibilities, Clay."

Clay dialed his voice mail back and handed the phone to Cy. He listened intently. The look of annoyance on his face became one of resignation.

"Okay, okay. Take the truck," Cy said.

"Thanks." Clay hesitated, "You know I'll have to..."

Cy cut him off, "I know. You're gonna take her to Mama. No reason to come back here for me. I'll catch a ride to the motel with one of the guys. Grab dinner and a couple of beers and go to bed." Resignation plastered across his face. Cy reached in the pocket of his blue jeans, and tossed the truck keys to Clay. "Go on. Do what you gotta do."

Catching them in midair, Clay turned and walked away.

Opening the door, he shouted back to his brother, "I'll call you later."

Cy didn't hear. The circular saw was screeching through another piece of pine.

215

54. Delicious

"Sure you're not hungry?" Lylee asked between large bites of a cheeseburger.

"No, I'm fine," Lyn said, making wet circles on the counter with the ice filled glass of Coke. She looked up and smiled appreciatively. "Thanks for the drink." The Coke was the least of things he had done for her. "And for, what happened earlier," she added.

Lylee reached for some fries and shoved them in his mouth, then took a sip of his own Coke. His attitude was that of a hungry man focused on his food. Mouth full, he looked sideways at Lyn, smiled, and then swallowed.

Shaking his head modestly he said, "No need to thank me. I told you why. Just sorry I got so carried away. I know that must have scared you some." He lifted the cheeseburger to his mouth and then stopped and added, "You really do remind me of my little sister."

Lylee's words received the desired effect. Lyn smiled broadly at him. Good, he thought. Soon, very soon.

He turned back to his food. He really was hungry. And with what was to come, no telling when he would get a chance to eat next. Another big bite of the cheeseburger disappeared in his open mouth.

Lyn leaned forward over her drink, elbows on the counter. There was an empty seat still between them. After a moment, she looked at Lylee and said, "You know I do have a brother."

Lylee showed mild interest and said, "Really?" Inwardly, he was on fire. He tingled with anticipation. Outwardly, he was the stalking cat, moving ever so closer to the catch. A brother. He sensed, he knew, that he could use this. He awaited the opportunity.

"Yeah," Lyn said. "My brother Sam. My big brother."

"That's great," Lylee said, cleaning up some ketchup with a french fry. "Well, what does he think about you being here. I mean he must not like it, huh?"

"He doesn't know."

"No? How come?," Lylee asked, playing the interested friend, the protector.

216

"Sam was in Afghanistan, in the Army. He was killed. He's buried back at the church at home."

"So, why are you here? Because your brother was killed?" Lylee asked with the greatest sympathy and interest, and then added politely, "Sorry, I don't mean to pry into your business."

In reality, he couldn't have cared less *why* she was there. He was only interested that she *was* there.

Her story provided information that would bring her closer, ever closer to the trap...close enough for him to spring. Listening intently, he sought that one piece of information, the key that would open the door to what was to come next.

"I had some trouble at home." Lyn looked down again. She really didn't want to go into all that had happened last night.

And again, Lylee couldn't have cared less about her trouble at home, but he saw her withdraw on this topic. He had to keep her talking, bringing her closer.

He smiled broadly at Lyn, "Well let's not talk about the trouble. My name's Bruce, Bruce Starns."

Lylee made the name up on the spot. Initials BS, he thought seemed perfect for the occasion. He found the irony humorous. It was even more humorous that she was unaware of the bullshit he threw her way with every bit of information he provided and every answer to her questions. He stuck his hand out to shake her hand in the way new acquaintances do.

Lyn shook the ends of his fingers the way a young girl who never shook hands would and said, "I'm Lyn."

"So how come you are here in the big city in this delightful place?" he said letting go of her hand and waving his arm around at the truck stop, laughing. As he did so, he saw it happen. He saw the barrier come down. She got too close, and the best part was she didn't even know it, and when she did realize it, it would be too late.

Why not just tell him, she thought. "Me and Sam always had a dream of going to Canada." She shrugged and then added, "So I thought I would go to Canada." She paused self-consciously and then continued, "I know it sounds crazy."

The broad, charming smile was back. "Are you kidding?

217

Canada's great. Beautiful place. I think that's a perfect place to dream of going."

"Really?" Lyn asked. "You been there?"

"Sure. I was there just last year. I took a little runaround there on vacation." Lylee laughed inwardly again at the use of his special word for these trips. If she only knew...but she would know, soon enough.

"Really?" Lyn knew she was repeating herself. "I mean what's it like? In my dreams, our dreams, me and Sam thought it would be...beautiful."

"It is beautiful. Big and full of trees and mountains. And lakes, lot's of lakes." Lylee's only real knowledge of Canada was what you might gather watching television or looking at travel magazines, but Lyn didn't know that. Lylee knew that she didn't know, and her innocence only increased his desire and whetted his appetite for what would come. Soon now, very soon.

Lylee watched Lyn look at the wall behind the counter as if she were staring at some far away lake. She was imagining what Canada was like. Trees and mountains and fresh air.

Oh yes, he thought, and by the way, don't forget the grizzly bears and the mountain lions. Claws that would tear into her soft flesh. Teeth that would sink into her throat as she sat happily beside some mountain lake. The inward laughing was uncontainable, and it became a smile on his face.

Seeing the smile, Lyn was embarrassed. She didn't understand the smile. She had no clue that the smile was her cue to run for her life.

"Sorry," she said. "I know I sound silly."

"Nope. Not at all," Lylee said bringing the smile under control, pushing the laughter deep inside where she wouldn't see it and maybe realize that all was not right. "So, you're headed to Canada then. That's why you were with that truck driver, huh? Ride to Canada?"

Lyn's face changed slightly. The memory of what had happened, or almost happened if it hadn't been for this man, was a sharp pain.

Lylee saw the change. It was what he had intended. Remind her

218

of what he had done to help her, to protect her.

"Yeah. He was gonna give me a ride north. Not all the way, but closer. I guess I was pretty stupid."

"It's never stupid to follow your dreams," Lylee said smiling again, this time at the banality of what he had just said.

This was too good. Follow your dreams. Reach for the stars. Climb every mountain. And so on and so on. Her innocence was delicious, irresistible. He savored it. Soon he would feed on it.

"So are you still going to Canada?" he asked.

Lyn sighed and shook her head. "I don't know. I called a friend. He might come pick me up. I don't know if he got the message or if he's coming."

Lylee sensed it was time.

"Listen," he said, "Sorry I can't give you a ride to Canada, or north, I'm headed out west through Atlanta. Got to get where there's some wide-open spaces. I'm from Texas, you know, and I miss the plains after a while."

There was just the slightest bit of disappointment on Lyn's face. Perfect.

He continued, "Hey," he said as if the thought was a surprise to him. "I've got some travel brochures of where I visited in Canada if you want them. Might help you decide where you want to go. Canada's a big place you know. Anyway, the pictures are pretty."

"I'd like that. I've only seen some stuff on television and in a couple of school books," Lyn said.

"Okay, then," Lylee nodded his head smiling. He looked at the check the waitress had left on the counter, pulled some money out, and dropped it on top. Without looking at Lyn, he stood up and started walking away. "C'mon, I'll get them for you," he said almost indifferently over his shoulder.

Lylee didn't have to see to know that Lyn had hesitated only for the briefest of moments before standing up and following. He kept his head and eyes forward. His indifferent, matter-of-fact way enhanced his harmlessness.

He didn't have to look back as he pushed the door open, walked outside, and turned right towards the corner of the building. He

219

heard the door open right after him and knew that the girl was following.

Lyn's split second of hesitation had faded almost instantly. She walked after the man, Bruce.

Yes, she had met some bad men. Her daddy had hurt her and then Henry, but most of them had been good to her. The brothers Clay and Cy, big Leon and Bob the truck drivers, and now Bruce. He had even saved her from Henry. It seemed like there were more good ones than bad ones, and she began to get a little of her confidence back.

She watched him walk ahead of her, his hands pushed harmlessly down in his pockets. He was softly whistling. He seemed happy and at ease.

Lylee *was* happy. He was very happy. He looked down at his feet shuffling slightly as he walked to appear even more harmless.

Coming up to the car, he walked around to the passenger side, which was nearest the rear of the building. He had positioned the car so that it would provide cover from anyone who might be outside and look their way.

"They're just in the glove box here. I'll get them."

Lyn stopped at the rear of the car. Lylee continued walking and then stopping by the passenger door, he exclaimed in disbelief, "Damn! Look at that."

"What," Lyn asked surprised.

Lylee looked up at the sky in simulated frustration and anger. "I can't believe it. I go inside to grab a bite to eat, not gone more than thirty minutes, and look at this. Someone took a key or something and scratched up the side of my car."

He knelt down by the door shaking his head and said, "I'll bet it was that guy that tried to get you into his truck." Shaking his head he said, "Yeah, gotta be him, trying to get even, that jerk."

And then Lyn made the final mistake, the big one. She stepped too close to the un-caged animal that was Leyland Torkman.

Moving forward she looked at the side of the car, as Lylee stood up to show her. "Where?" she said. "I don't see…"

Lylee's movements were swift and fluid. His right hand pulled

220

open the passenger door. His left hand emerged from his pocket with the knife.

Lyn gasped as she was pushed hard against the car. Something sharp pressed against her chest.

Lylee pushed the knife hard against her ribs. Leaning against her with his body, anyone who saw would think he was just trying to knock off a piece there in the parking lot, something that had probably happened more than a few times back on this deserted side of the building. His face was next to hers. His lips almost touched hers.

Lyn looked into the fierce, sparkling eyes. A small, terrified shriek started to escape her throat.

"Not a sound," Lylee hissed at her through lips that barely moved. "Not one sound, or I will cut you deep and hard. I promise it will hurt. You understand?"

Lyn could only look at him with wide, panic-stricken eyes. The memory of his attack on Henry flooded into her consciousness, and she knew what he was capable of.

"Do you understand?" Lylee said each word slowly and deliberately. "Nod, if you do."

Lyn nodded her head once slowly. The sparkling eyes narrowed as they stared deep into hers.

Holding the point of the knife firmly against her, Lylee reached down with his right hand and pulled a plastic tie wrap from the car seat. It was exactly like the one found by Deputy George Mackey at the StarLite.

He quickly wrapped the tie around Lyn's right wrist, tightened it, and then used the knife point to push her into the seat. Pulling another tie out, he ran it through the one on Lyn's wrist and then around the frame at the bottom of the seat. Lyn's right arm was now secured to the car. The tie bit into her skin if she moved.

Leaning over her, Lylee hissed again, "No noise or I will hurt you and then I will kill you."

He pushed the knife harder into her ribs, hard enough to break the skin. He knew there would be a little blood but not much. Just enough to make her believe and remember. Then he kissed her hard

221

on the lips biting her lower lip on the inside as he did so. It drew blood.

He savored the salty taste. Anyone who might have seen the kiss would think that they were off to find a private place for some truck stop sex.

Lylee closed the door and walked quickly to the driver's side. With the door handle removed from the passenger door, Lyn could not have escaped even with both hands free. She didn't try.

Traumatized by this final betrayal, beaten, and alone, she sat trembling. A numbing emptiness crawled over her. Although the man had caused no serious injury to her yet, she felt as if life was leaving her. Her body was an empty shell. She was already going somewhere else.

Lylee sat down and started the car quickly. The engine purred powerfully. Pulling away from the building, he drove around to the front. The girl in the seat beside him was silent, dazed.

The fat clerk from the cash register, Todd, was outside puffing a cigarette as they drove by. Seeing Lylee, he averted his eyes. Watching the car drive out of the lot headed towards the entrance ramp of the interstate, the kid took a deep breath, glad that the creepy guy was gone. He was sorry to see the thin, pretty girl go. Probably wouldn't be much to look at the rest of the day.

The car was quiet inside. Lylee lit a cigarette. He looked over at the girl. She appeared to be catatonic.

He put his hand out and rested it on her thigh. The muscles in her leg quivered and trembled, and the tingling thrill inside him increased. This would be special. He would take his time with this one. This hunt and the capture had required all of his skill and cunning. He had been exceptional, and the kill would have to be special.

He would savor it. Drink it in. Drench himself in it. It would be delicious.

55. A Chance in Hell

The ride to the county jail in Everett was uneventful. After a couple of miles, Vernon Taft peeked his head above the door and looked around. Satisfied that none of the Roydon locals were following, he sat up.

In the rearview mirror, George could see that Vernon's face twitched nervously, his head bobbing and swiveling on his neck constantly, checking passing cars and trucks for any threat. George knew that this was not an overreaction and that the things he had told Vernon to coax him to cooperate were not an exaggeration.

He would be a marked man in Roydon, likely already was. It would not have mattered what Vernon had told them. Fuck off. Bite me. Eat my shorts. The result would have been the same. Suspicion would follow him, and suspicion in Roydon was as good as a conviction.

Eventually, old Vernon would turn up missing. It wouldn't be a big deal. Time would have passed so that there could be no immediate connection to today's encounter with the law, but he would be gone and no one would see him again, including his sister in Valdosta. The end of Vernon Taft, pure and simple.

After a few miles, he began to relax. The nervous twitches remained, but his constant turning and bobbing, surveilling the passing cars, and road slowed.

"So, was it the girl?"

"What?" George's eyes jerked abruptly to the mirror, peering intently at Vernon.

"The murder. Was it the girl?"

Pulling onto the shoulder of the highway, George jerked the car to a stop. "What are you saying, Vernon? You said you didn't see anyone with the guy in the Chevy."

"Did I? Well I was pretty nervous." Dammit. His own big mouth had just turned everything upside down. "I mighta seen more." Stopped on the shoulder of the road, Vernon's head started turning and bobbing again, and his scared shitless quotient rose by a factor of ten. "Do we have to stop? Can't you just keep driving?"

"Vernon, don't fuck with me. I've had just about all of your bullshit I can stand for one day. You got something to say, say it. Otherwise, I'll wheel this truck around and drop you at Pete's Place."

Vernon's face blanched. "You wouldn't do that, Deputy."

"I would and I will. You know something more...talk. Now."

"Okay, okay. Well, I did see that there was a girl. Couldn't see her when he was parked by the office. But I stood there in the dark in the office and watched. He pissed me off with his attitude, he was kind of...scary. But I knew he couldn't see me standing in the dark. I think he could do bad things."

"No shit, Vernon. What do you think we been talking about all afternoon?" George waited, looking at him expectantly in the rearview mirror.

"Well, like I said, I could see it was a girl. When he got to the room, he opened the door and bent in the car sort of. I thought he must have been waking her up. Maybe he was untying her or something." He paused momentarily, expecting some comment from George. All he received was a cold, hard stare. "So, anyway, I could see it was a girl he pulled out of the car."

"Did she walk or did he carry her?"

"She walked. She had her head down, and it was pretty far so I couldn't really tell what she looked like. Dark hair, brown maybe. He moved her into the room pretty quick and stayed real close. Kinda looked like he had his hand on her tit."

George let all of this sink in. Vernon Taft had been the last known person, other than her killer, to see the girl alive. It seemed to make it all worse somehow.

No memory, no farewell to family, no last words to be remembered, just Vernon standing in the dirty, dark motel office watching her being dragged into a dingy motel room. And then nothing.

His eyes jerked back to Vernon who looked more nervous than ever. "Did you hear anything? Any sounds or cries for help?'

"No, George. Honest, I didn't. Those block walls are pretty thick, and they were down at the other end of the place."

"And you didn't even think to call the sheriff's office or try to help her?"

"For what?" his voice had the tone of an unfairly persecuted saint. "Men take girls in that place all the time. We don't, uh...interfere." Vernon seemed pleased that he had thought of such a big word. "That's why they come to the StarLite. You know that Deputy."

George took a deep breath. "All right, Vernon. What else can you tell me?"

Vernon thought for a moment. "Well, that old Chevy...it had a Texas tag on it."

George was instantly attentive again. "You sure?"

"Yep. I know my tags."

"Did you get the plate number?"

Vernon's response was nervous. "Well, no. I didn't. We don't keep such records there at the StarLite." George's look of exasperation lasted only a second before Vernon added, "But there was a bumper sticker on the car, right rear." George was all ears. "One of those funny kind. It said, 'If you can read this bumper sticker, get off my ass'." A small chuckle escaped from star witness, Vernon Taft, until he noticed the look on George's face.

"Yeah, that's real fucking funny, Vernon."

George yanked the radio microphone off its cradle and within a few seconds had given the additional information out over the air. It would soon be broadcast around to the other police and state agencies. Texas tag and a bumper sticker. Now at least they had a chance, as opposed to no chance in hell, of finding the car. And the animal driving it, George thought.

"You still gonna take me to my sister's place?" Vernon was clearly terrified that the deal might be off. "I was gonna tell you all of it. That's why I started talking to you Deputy. I didn't want nothing bad to happen to the girl. Hell, it could have been my own sister. I was just scared there in front of Roy Budroe and his gang. I just needed to get away from there."

Realizing that there was probably some truth in Vernon's admission, George sat still for a moment calming himself. Then,

225

looking hard at Vernon in the mirror he said quietly, "Vernon, I will take you to jail and put you into protective custody tonight. Tomorrow you will be taken to Valdosta to your sister's place, but you better remember this. You are a material witness to a murder. You stay at your sister's where we can find you. If you leave…" George paused to make sure that Vernon was paying close attention. "If you leave, I will hunt you down, Vernon. And when I find you, you will wish to holy hell that Roy and his boys had found you first. You understand me, Vernon?"

Vernon Taft nodded. He understood.

56. Meeting of the Minds

The four tramped through the sheriff's outer office, past the desk deputy, receptionist, and office staff. Curious heads looked up and nodded politely as they passed.

There was no acknowledgement. The day had been long. The results of the two murder investigations, while making progress, had not provided any identification of the killer or any other definitive lead. Sheriff Klineman had become more agitated as the day progressed. Finding fault with nearly all of the actions taken by the GBI and his own deputies, he was not a happy sheriff.

Granite faces and eyes focused ahead, they passed without speaking. Ronnie Kupman, the last man through, closed the office door behind them as the others shuffled into the seats around the small circular conference table. There was quiet while everyone gathered their thoughts. The sheriff spoke first.

"Let me begin by saying that the lack of coordination and cooperation today has disappointed me. The citizens of Pickham County deserve better."

"Really?" Shaklee's tone was bemused, feigning real curiosity.

It was clear by the expressions on Sharon Price and Ronnie Kupman that they all knew what was coming, and they were all annoyed. Shaklee noticed that there was something else on Kupman's face. Disgust maybe.

"Would you like to elaborate on that comment Sheriff?" Shaklee asked mildly.

"Yes, I would. First, you begin the investigations by insinuating that there is a Klan problem in Pickham County...an insinuation that is an insult to all of the good people of the county."

Price, who was tired of the day's bullshit which had mostly emanated from the sheriff, nearly came out of her chair. Shaklee waved her down.

Klineman continued, "Do you have any idea the issues that such an accusation could raise in the county?"

He paused as if waiting for some acknowledgment from the

group. Stony expressions greeted him. Glancing over at Kupman, Shaklee noted that the look on his face was definitely one of disgust mixed with something else. Contempt.

Hearing no comment, Klineman continued, "Second, a body is found in our county with no proof that the murder was committed in our county, and you immediately postulate that we have a serial killer wandering the county. Such assumptions are not indicative of good investigative work and would certainly send the wrong message if they became public."

"What message would that be?" Price asked, her annoyance growing.

"That Pickham is not a safe place. A good place for people and families."

"Really? A safe, family place like Roydon?"

"We may have our problem spots. I'm sure every county in the state does, but in general..."

"Sheriff," Price could not contain herself any longer, "a place like Roydon does not exist unless someone turns a blind eye to it. What happened in Pete's Place today, overt threats to a GBI investigator, is indicative of just how much attention you've *not* paid to that particular *problem spot.*"

"Agent Price, I am not going to bandy words with you and I would remind you that I am still the chief law enforcement officer in this county. Now, getting back to the point, I've seen this before, when investigators *assume* that a certain theory of the crime is correct and eliminate all other possibilities, never exploring avenues of investigation that might be more productive and..." there was a pause while the sheriff considered the next word, "...and beneficial. Case files are replete with unsolved crimes because investigators would not look beyond their preconceived theories, or they prosecuted the wrong person, adding miscarriage of justice to their poor investigative skills."

At that comment, Sharon Price *was* out of her chair standing over the others at the small table. "Are you insane? Or are you living in another universe? We asked the questions that needed to be asked. No insinuations were made. If you are that sensitive about the issue of the Klan, maybe you should check around your county and clean up your own house if necessary."

She took a breath before speaking her next words, and she spoke them through gritted teeth, trying to control her anger. "Any fool would see that two murders in Pickham County on the same night might possibly be connected...especially since there are not more than a couple of murders a year in the entire county. Good investigators would ask the necessary questions and follow the necessary leads. That doesn't mean that there are no other possible scenarios, but as this one is the most likely, it must be eliminated or proven, and quickly, before moving on to other possible theories. That's what we're doing." Still seething, Price took a deep breath and sat down again.

The thought occurred to Ronnie Kupman that Klineman might be taping the conversation to edit later, ensuring that he was seen only in the best possible light by the voters of the county and removing himself from any connection with the possibly unfruitful murder investigation. It was the kind of thing that Klineman would do.

There was something in the tone and manner of his words that made them seem to be intended for someone beyond this room. He knew that, in reality, the sheriff was primarily concerned with the sheriff first and the department secondarily. Successfully finding the killer, would be the last on his list of priorities.

Kupman glanced discreetly around the room wondering, until his eyes found the sheriff whose face seemed to have taken on a serene quality with Price's outburst. Was that what he had wanted?

"Okay, okay," Kupman interjected. "Let's calm down. It's been a long day and night, for that matter. We're all on edge. It's understandable." Eyes still fixed on Klineman's face, Kupman saw that he was watching Price, his hands clasped together on the table like a Buddha in a brown uniform.

"Have you finished, Sheriff?" Shaklee asked, wanting to hear it all before making any comment.

"As a matter of fact, it is not." Six eyes focused intently on him as he gazed around at the group. "In addition to the lack of coordination

229

and taking the investigation in directions that I do not approve of or agree with, you have insisted on involving a member of this department in your investigation whom I consider to be a marginal law enforcement officer at best. You have acted against my wishes and against my better judgment. In the spirit of cooperation, I have said nothing throughout the day, but I feel it is time for this office to exert more control over the investigation."

Whom? Who the hell says 'whom'? Bob Shaklee's expression was bemused. Ronnie Kupman, used to the sheriff's frequent bombast and pomposity, showed no surprise. Sharon Price could do nothing but glare at the man, her loathing for him evident on her face. She couldn't have cared less what words he used. As far as she was concerned, they were all bullshit.

"Dick." Klineman's head spun around incredulously to face Kupman at the use of his first name with no title attached. The flush in his face indicated that he was not pleased with the familiarity in the midst of the ass chewing he was intent on delivering. Unperturbed, Ronnie Kupman continued. "I suggest that you finish stating your concerns and then allow Agents Shaklee and Price to respond."

"Chief Deputy, are you taking sides with them?" Klineman nodded to the two agents.

"I don't believe there are any sides to take. Just want to hear what everyone has to say," Kupman replied smiling. He seemed supremely at ease, while the sheriff's look of serenity had been replaced by a rosy flush.

"Fine. You and I will speak later."

"Whenever you like, Sheriff." Ronnie smiled pleasantly.

Turning back to the GBI agents, Klineman continued, "As I stated, George Mackey is a marginal deputy with marginal skills. In my opinion, the investigation is going down paths that are leading you away from apprehending the killer, partly because of his folksy, overly dramatic interpretation of the evidence. And frankly, relying on Mackey's interpretation of evidence calls into question your own judgment. Finally, none of this is serving the best interests of the citizens of Pickham County and that is my primary concern."

230

This last statement was enunciated in a clear, firm voice, slightly louder than the rest of the sheriff's remarks. Kupman and Shaklee couldn't help exchanging raised eyebrows and simultaneously looking around for the recording device that they were now certain was present.

Klineman, no doubt assuming that they were shocked at his firm control of the situation, continued. "As of this moment, I am going to take supervisory control of the investigation."

"Really?" Shaklee said coolly, looking directly into the eyes of the sheriff. "And if we continue on the investigative 'path' we are on, what will you do?"

"I will have you relieved."

Shaklee laughed and then let the smile fade from his face as he spoke. "Is that a fact? Perhaps I should enlighten you as to our roll here. We have been pulled into this investigation because we have the resources to support local, rural departments. Departments like yours, Sheriff."

He paused to let that sink in. "If you didn't need us, we wouldn't be here. Frankly, our superiors would love to get us off this case quickly. We have quite a substantial caseload as it is. But here's the rub. We are what you get. There is no bullpen for you to go to and request another team. On top of that, there is enough evidence to suggest that the perpetrator is not from Pickham County, which, in effect, makes it a GBI case. In fact, with the additional evidence that Deputy Mackey has provided, it appears that the killer may be passing through from Texas, or some other state. That being the case, we would expect him to travel through a number of Georgia counties and cities, and that definitely makes this our case."

The smile returned to Shaklee's face as he saw his words register somewhere in Klineman's brain. The sheriff's face reddened.

"Now let me speak *frankly* to you...Dick." Klineman's face turned a deeper, more purple shade of red, almost maroon, Shaklee thought. "I don't give a rat's ass about your reelection. An old man and young woman have been brutally murdered in *your* county. You might want to consider the effect on the good citizens of Pickham County and your political future if those crimes go unsolved."

"I won't tolerate…"

Shaklee cut him off. "You will tolerate it Sheriff." He smiled at the sheriff and spoke calmly as if reasoning with a petulant child. "You have no choice. We have the resources and you don't. We can make things very uncomfortable for you in the press should there be a lack of…shall we call it, mutual aid."

Klineman could do nothing more than blink. It was clear by the expression on his face that he was trying to absorb the fact that Shaklee had just threatened him.

"But I will give you this promise," Shaklee continued, looking around the room for the recording device he suspected was activated. He raised his voice a couple of decibels to make sure that what he said was picked up by any unseen microphone. "I give you my word Sheriff that when this case is solved, and I believe it will be, you will personally receive full credit. If the investigation is a dead end, the GBI, meaning I, will take the hit for it in the press. There will be no fallout for you."

"I don't understand." And the look on Klineman's face showed that he truly could not grasp the reality of what he had just heard. Honesty and accountability were foreign concepts to him.

"Understand this," Sharon Price threw at him. "We will give you full credit for solving the case. If we fail, we will take all of the blame. I know that's hard for you to comprehend, but there it is."

"One other thing," Shaklee continued smilingly. "In the spirit of *mutual aid*, we would like to have one of your staff assigned to work with us on the investigation. As you have pointed out, there are a number of investigative avenues to pursue. We could use the help."

Trying to recover some of his dignity, Klineman squared his shoulders and cleared his throat before speaking. "Well, I think having one of my staff assigned as part of our mutual aid agreement in this investigation is important."

The pomposity was back in his voice. It was amusingly clear to the others at the table that you just can't keep a good politician down for long.

Klineman continued, "In light of the seriousness of the matter, I am inclined to have my most seasoned and experienced deputy work with you." He turned towards Kupman continuing, "Chief Deputy please remove yourself from your normal responsibilities and begin working exclusively with Agents Shaklee and Price."

As the sheriff concluded and awaited acknowledgment from Kupman, Bob Shaklee clarified their request.

"Sorry Sheriff, I don't think I made myself clear. While we appreciate the offer of Chief Deputy Kupman's services, we would like to have George Mackey assigned to work with us."

"He's right. George has done some good work on the case and has the continuity with both crime scenes," Ronnie Kupman added. "It's the right move, Sheriff." Kupman refrained from using Klineman's first name again figuring that there was no reason to rub his nose in the dirt any more this day.

"Well, as I said earlier..."

"We know, we know," Sharon Price interrupted. Her temper was on a short fuse, getting shorter all the time. "Mackey is a 'marginal deputy with marginal skills'. That may be so, and if you are right, we will take the blame. If he works out, you get the credit. It's a win win for you, so for god's sake, let's just move on."

"Yes, well..."

This time Shaklee interrupted, tiring of the word games. "It's a done deal. We will take Mackey on the assignment." Then to help enlighten the sheriff and remove the puzzled look from his face he added, "This is not a negotiation Sheriff. We will take Mackey. My promise to you still holds, but taking Mackey is part of the deal."

"I see...I...uh..."

Ronnie Kupman stood up abruptly. "Good. It's a deal then." He looked at the GBI investigators. "We better get you checked into a hotel here in Everett. Pretty sure you're gonna have an early start tomorrow. Gotta let George know too. Want him bright eyed and bushy-tailed in the morning."

Kupman strode to the door followed by the GBI agents. Sheriff Richard Klineman sat looking at his hands still clasped on the table. The pinhole camera and microphone in the center of the plaque behind his desk whirred softly, recording nothing more than the sheriff's profile for several minutes.

57. Not The Smartest Decision

The old pickup came to a rocking halt in the gravel outside the truck stop store. Clay let the door bang shut loudly behind him as he walked briskly into the building. They had left Lyn in the cafe. He went there first.

It was a quick walk around, waving the waitress off when she wanted to seat him. Checking all the tables and counter with no results, he went back through the store and crossed to the driver's lounge.

The sign on the door said 'Professional Drivers Only'. Clay ignored it and walked in. It wasn't much of a lounge. There were doors to the restrooms on one wall, a large television with some padded chairs scattered around it and an old sofa directly in front. Tables and more chairs were scattered along the other walls and throughout the room.

A few drivers were at the tables, playing cards or eating snack foods from the store. There wasn't much of a crowd there this time of day. Mostly truckers waiting for a load to somewhere or letting some hours go by so that their driver's log wouldn't show too many road hours without down time if they were stopped by the troopers.

Clay recognized one of the room's occupants, sitting alone at a table in the corner. Henry had his left arm wrapped in a makeshift sling and a bandage covered his left temple. His face was swollen and lumpy, a mass of scratches and scrapes covered with dried blood. A large knot on his cheekbone was plainly visible even through the heavy flesh of his face.

Clay walked over to the table. Pulling a chair back with his booted foot, he sat down across from Henry.

"What the hell happened to you?"

Henry looked at Clay, cradling his left arm with his right.

"None of your goddamn business, I reckon. Who the hell are you?" he said after a few seconds of trying to stare Clay down.

The attempt at intimidation was not successful. Clay knew Henry for what he was, a bully.

Clay smiled thinly. "Fair enough," he said. "None of my business. I saw you at the diner this morning out on I-95. Remember? My brother and me were having breakfast. Seen you there a few times before too."

"Oh?" Henry said in mock surprise, and then added sharply, "So the fuck what? You can get your ass up and move on."

Clay regarded the big blowhard calmly.

"For a fella that seems to have gotten the shit kicked out of him, you have an awful surly attitude." He smiled, making it clear that he had no intention of moving.

"I didn't get no shit kicked out of me. I fell," Henry said.

"You fell? What the hell did you fall off of?"

"Slipped getting out of my truck and hit the ground. Now get the hell outta here."

"Slipped my ass!" a big woman at the next table laughed loudly. Her hair was pulled back in a long gray ponytail. She looked like she could have been an aging member of some seventies rock band who had lived a very hard life. She was playing cards with another woman. Both wore blue jeans, men's work shirts and heavy boots. They were drivers.

Clay turned towards the woman as she continued.

"Old Henry here got his ass whipped by some guy, about your size."

"Shut up!" Henry managed to hiss through clenched teeth and swollen lips. He would have gotten up to walk away, if he could.

"Shut up, yourself," the woman said. "If I was you, I'd rather say I got beat in a fight than say I fell outta my truck like some dumbass rookie."

Clay smiled and nodded. "Yep, that does sound more...manly." He turned towards the two women and continued, "What I was going to ask was if Henry, or you, have seen a girl. She's about eighteen or so, thin with dark brown hair. I come to pick her up. She called me."

The women's faces hardened, their eyes narrowed.

"Really," he continued, reading the suspicion on their faces. "If ya'll have seen her about, I'd appreciate you letting me know where she went. Left her here this morning and said I'd come back for her if

235

she wanted, but I can't seem to find her. Like I said, she called me."

They regarded him sternly for a few seconds more, the suspicion clearly lingering. They may have been drivers, but they were also women, and they knew what could happen to vulnerable young girls alone at a place where men like Henry loitered about.

The one that had been quiet to this point spoke. "You left her here, huh?" She had bright red hair and a cigarette hanging from her lower lip. Laying her cards on the table, she stared at Clay.

"Yeah. Told her we'd come back for her later."

"Well why would you do a thing like that? She working the truck stop for you?"

Clay realized suddenly that the women thought he might have been pimping Lyn and answered quickly. "No, no. Nothing like that. We gave her a ride here. She was leaving home and going north. We didn't like leaving her."

"We? Who is we?" Red asked, her suspicions not dispelled by his explanation.

"My brother and me. She hitched a ride with us. We dropped her off here cause that's what she wanted, but we were worried about her and told her we would come back and get her. Hell, we tried to get her to go with us and stay with our mama." He finished his explanation with a look of embarrassment.

The two women looked steadily at him for a moment, studying him and weighing his words. Finally, Red said, still looking him hard in the face. "I guess you might be all right."

Old Gray nodded at her companion. "Yeah, we've seen her wandering around some today. At least there was a little girl that looked like the one you describe. Saw her a while ago sitting at the counter in the cafe with another fella. They talked for a while, then he got up and she followed him out."

Clay felt his stomach sink.

Red saw the look on his face and added, "I don't know what they were doing. She didn't look threatened or anything."

Old Gray added, with a tinge of guilt, "She just kind of walked out behind him. Couldn't even tell if they were still together. Didn't see where they went."

"No, couldn't tell where they were headed," Red agreed.

Now that they had put away their initial suspicions about Clay's motives, they were feeling embarrassed about not having intervened for the girl.

Red gave a hard look in Henry's direction and leaned towards Clay. "But there is something you ought to know."

"You sure?" Old Gray leaned closer to her companion, speaking in low tones. "We don't need any trouble here."

"Yeah, I'm sure." She looked at Clay, "Henry's had his hands on my ass too many times for me not to know that if I was a little thing like that girl, he would have tried to have his way with me too."

Clay's face turned dark and threatening as his head swiveled towards Henry. The injured man just sat looking at the table, wishing this would all just go away. It was clear he did not want his ass kicked a second time that day.

Clay turned back to Red, thunder on his face. "What happened?" His voice was almost inaudible as he tried to control the rage he felt building inside.

"Well it seems he got the little girl to go out to his truck with him. Got her up in the cab, but then this other fella came along and dragged him out and whipped his ass." She paused, watching Clay's fist clench and unclench on the table. After a few seconds, she continued, "Might have been the guy she sat at the counter with. I don't know that. I never saw the guy who beat up Henry, but it might have been him at the counter. Bunch of us was sitting there talking just a couple of seats away, and we had the idea that he was the guy."

Clay looked at her, unclenched his fist and asked, "How'd you know all this? About Henry and the fight and all if you didn't see? Henry didn't tell you did he?"

She laughed, "No, no not Henry. It was Bob and Big Leon. That's a couple of truckers. They kind of took the girl under their wing. Leon told us what happened before he left ." With a pained look on her face she added, "We should have looked out for her when they left. Just didn't think to. There's always a lot of girls hanging around truck stops. After a while, you don't even think about it and why they might be here. It's a tough place. Anyway, sorry we didn't do

237

something for her."

Clay looked at her, "No need. You didn't know. I appreciate the information." He took a deep breath then asked, "So you don't know if she left or not?"

"No," Gray said. "Couldn't tell you. She kind of wandered around here all morning. Haven't seen her in a while though." She looked down at her cards. The two women clearly felt rotten about the situation.

"It's okay, I'll find her."

He stood up suddenly, pushing the table forward as he did so that it sank into Henry's fat belly. Leaning across the table, he moved in close to the big man's face. "If you weren't already crippled, you and me would step outside you piece of shit."

Clay turned and walked through the door that connected the driver's lounge to the store. Henry pushed the table away out of his stomach but did not look up. He definitely wanted this goddamned day to be over.

Entering the store, Clay looked around. There was no one at the counter, so he walked to the clerk. He noted the name tag that said 'Todd' pinned to a dirty white shirt covering Todd's huge gut.

Clay started talking without any preliminaries. "I'm looking for someone."

Todd started to give him his annoyed 'why the fuck are you bothering me' look, but saw the look in Clay's eyes and thought better of it.

"Yeah, who would that be?" Todd asked.

"A girl, about eighteen, thin, dark brown hair, pretty."

Who isn't looking for that, Todd thought, but only said, "Yeah, I saw a girl like that around here today. She was hanging around, going back and forth all day."

"Where is she now?"

"Don't know," Todd said simply and without interest.

Clay took a deep breath, "Look, did you see her leave?"

"Yeah, I did."

"When and who with?" Clay was losing patience. "Tell me everything you saw."

Todd realized he should just say it and get this guy away from him. "I went out front to take a smoke break. I saw her in a car. It was like an old Chevy or something, kind of beat up looking, but seemed to run pretty good."

"Who was driving?"

"I don't know. Some guy that had been in here earlier."

"Tell me. What did he look like?"

"Guy about your size. Thin. Light brown hair. I could see through the car pretty good. It looked like the girl on the passenger side."

"Was she all right?" Clay asked, desperate for some real information about her.

"Yeah, I guess. She didn't look happy, but she didn't look hurt. Had her head down. Maybe she was crying or something."

"Crying?" Clay's voice rose. "Didn't look hurt, but she was crying? You didn't do anything?"

"I said crying, maybe...I don't know...seemed that way. What was I supposed to do?"

"Yeah," Clay said walking away in disgust. Pushing through the door, he jogged across the lot to his pickup.

Cranking the engine, he sat for a minute pondering the situation before spinning the pickup's tires in the gravel as he turned through the lot to the exit. He would have to call Cy and let him know he probably wouldn't make it back for work tomorrow.

The pickup accelerated quickly down the ramp to the interstate. Seventy-five and then eighty miles an hour. Clay wasn't sure what to do, or where he was going. Things were spinning out of control, confused.

Cy would be pissed. Hell, *he* would be pissed if the shoe was on the other foot, and he couldn't even explain it in a way that made any sense in his own mind. He was going to try to find a girl he didn't even know, and he couldn't even say why. Not the smartest decision he had ever made...he knew that much, at least.

58. The Hunt Begins

The whining of tires on asphalt raised George Mackey's eyes
from the cold beer can slowly dripping condensed water onto his
knee. A cone of light from the approaching car's headlights lit up the
pine trees along the side of the road. A few seconds later, the lights
turned into Fel Tobin's driveway and the tire whine was replaced by
the crunch of gravel. George squinted into the glare as the car
approached the front porch where he was firmly seated in one of
Fel's old kitchen chairs.

From the other side of the cooler between them Fel asked, "Who
you reckon that is?"

"Don't know." George took a pull from the can and studied the
car making its way up the drive.

It rocked to a halt in front of the porch and the headlights
blinked off. It was Ronnie Kupman's county car.

"Hey, George." Ronnie called exiting the vehicle.

"Ronnie. What's up?" George noted Bob Shaklee and Sharon
Price coming out of the car's passenger side and nodded at them.
"Everybody. What's up?"

"Evenin', Mr. Tobin," Ronnie said walking up to the porch and
nodding to Fel.

"Evenin' Deputy," Fell nodded back. "Come on up and have a
beer."

"Sorry. Can't. Gotta get home. Thanks anyway."

Ronnie put one booted foot up on the first step and leaned
against the railing along the steps, lighting up a cigarette. Inhaling
deeply, he turned his head up looking into the early night sky. A tinge
of red still lingered dimly on the western horizon.

The two GBI agents came up to the porch and stood to his right
at the foot of the steps. The two on the porch watched patiently,
sipping their beer until Ronnie figured it was time to get to the point
of his visit.

"Hell of a day, George," Ronnie said. It was a statement of fact.

"Yep. Hell of a day." George nodded to the GBI agents. "Fel

Tobin, this is Agent Shaklee and Agent Price from the Georgia Bureau of Investigation. They're working the murders." George took another pull from his beer can.

"Sorry, George," Ronnie said looking to his right. "Should have made the introductions. Guess I'm distracted. Seems like a long time since yesterday."

"No problem."

Fel Tobin gave the obligatory head nod to the two agents, smiling with particular interest at Sharon Price. Now this was something different. Sheriff deputies, even the Chief Deputy, stopping by, that was one thing, but the GBI. Well, that was *something*.

"Workin' the murders, huh? Get 'em figured out yet?"

Fel was seriously interested. George never talked much about what was going on in the county. And this, well today he had been downright closemouthed about things. But by now, everyone in the county knew about the killings, except Fel Tobin.

"Not yet Mr. Tobin, but we're working on it. We'll figure it out." Sharon Price smiled an affectionate smile at him as if he were an old uncle.

A little embarrassed by her pleasant but steady gaze and not knowing what else to do in response to the pretty girl's smile, Fel smacked a weathered hand on his bony knee and gave a short laugh, managing to say, "Well, that's good. That's real good."

He raised the beer can to his lips never taking his eyes off Agent Price of the GBI. Yep, this was something. Two GBI agents, and one of them a girl. Really something.

George turned his head regarding Fel curiously. Since losing his wife, old Fel did not interact much with the ladies, and he was always taken with any female that showed him any attention. It didn't take much for him to start acting like a bashful teenager.

"So, Ronnie," George said getting back to the business that had interrupted their beer drinking. "You didn't come all the way out here to talk about what a shitty day it's been. What's up?" It was the third time he had asked the question, and it resulted in disappointing Fel when the pretty lady agent turned her attention to the deputies.

241

"Got an assignment for you, George."

"Really? What's that?"

"You've been assigned to assist the GBI," Ronnie Kupman shrugged towards the two agents at this side.

"Assist. What does that mean?"

"Means you're gonna work with them and find the killer."

"Really?" He turned the beer can on his knee and then looked thoughtfully for a few moments at the dark, wet ring on the denim. "I don't know, Ronnie…"

"This is not a request, George." Kupman cut him off. "Take it as an order if you need to, but we need you to focus on this case. You are relieved of all other duties for the duration." And with that, Ronnie released a cloud of cigarette smoke that hovered over his head as if to settle the matter.

George gazed at Ronnie wondering why he would shove him into the middle of things after his failures of the night before. He was about to speak when Bob Shaklee settled it for good.

"Look Deputy…George…we realize this must be tough for you. We know that maybe you feel somewhat responsible for some of what happened." George shot a look at Kupman who gazed back calmly from his wreath of cigarette smoke. The look was not missed by Shaklee who continued, "The bottom line is…and I don't say it as a compliment…it's fact…that most of the evidence and leads we have in the murders came through your efforts. We want this case solved. You want it solved. You should be part of this, George."

George listened, no emotion discernible on his face. Shaklee looked hard into his eyes and added one final thought. "If you've got sins to pay for George, this is how you do it. We're going to find this killer. You will be part of that."

A flicker of emotion darted across the deputy's face. Bob Shaklee had struck a nerve. Yes, there were sins to pay for. That was surely true.

"Okay. Meet at the office at seven in the morning." Ronnie Kupman pulled his boot off the porch step and turned towards the car.

There was nothing else to say. The two agents turned and

followed. A few seconds later, the sound of the tires receded as the county car returned to Everett.

"Got the fucker."

George looked up from his beer at Fel's exclamation. One of the feral yard cats that hung around the place was just visible in the dim pool of light cast across the yard from the living room window.

It had successfully stalked and hunted some small prey and was now pinning it to the ground with its paws as it tried to gain a grasp with its teeth. The cat shook its head forcefully, side to side, ending the struggle of the small animal in its jaws and trotted off across the yard, ignoring the two men on the porch.

Downing the last of his beer in salute to the cat, George tossed the can into the trash crate and headed across the dark yard to his place above the barn.

"'Night, Fel," he called over his shoulder.

Walking through the dewy grass, the image of the cat with the helpless creature dangling from its mouth remained. If the killer leaving bodies across Pickham County was the cat, what were George and the others? Hunters? Different though, he thought. Hunters don't think too much about the cat's prey, they just hunt the cat.

He stood at the bottom of the barn steps and took a deep breath, shaking his head as if that would clear things up for him. To catch this killer, he would have to focus on the cat...on the killer.

This was now a hunt, so hunt, George, he told himself. Find the son of a bitch and there won't be any more victims.

59. Pit Stop

The old Chevy pulled up the exit ramp and turned left, crossing the bridge over the interstate. Bouncing across some railroad tracks in the dark, it turned left again so that it was headed south, parallel to the interstate. The car moved smoothly over the dirt road. Ruts and bumps filled in by sand and ground shells made for a soft ride.

After a mile or so, he turned the car right onto another dirt road that ran up into a pinewoods. This was logging country, and large tracts of land were owned and planted by lumber companies that harvested the trees and then planted more in their place.

For Lylee, it was sufficient that the area was secluded. At this time of day, the loggers would all be throwing down beers at some honky-tonk.

The car stopped silently in the soft sand. His head turned towards her, and Lyn cringed as far away from him as she could in the confines of the car.

"Pit stop. I need to take a piss," Lylee said with a grin. "How about you?"

Eyes wide, Lyn made no sound, unsure if he was serious or if this was just a continuation of his mental manipulation…part of his plan, whatever that might be. Young and possessing a naiveté born of her humble, backcountry origins, she was not so inexperienced as to be unaware that she was in serious danger. This man, who could change so completely in a matter of seconds, was ominous and frightening, and she sensed that her fear pleased him in some way.

He studied her curiously, waiting for some response. After a minute, Lylee shrugged and pushed open the driver's door. From the front seat, she watched as he walked to the front of the car, unzipped his pants and began to urinate.

She could not see clearly in the moon light, diffused by the surrounding pines, but she could hear the stream splash loudly in the dirt. He arched his head back while the pee flowed.

The backlight of the moon caused his narrow, dark silhouette, pointing up to the evening sky, to take on an animal-like appearance.

244

Framed in the moonlight, head back, he reminded her of a picture she had seen of a wolf on a snowy night with its head back, howling at the moon. A shiver moved uncomfortably between her shoulders.

Finished peeing, he moved toward the passenger side of the car, zipping his pants as he walked. The door jerked open rapidly, and Lyn saw the knife in his hand. A gasp caught in her throat and her eyes widened. "No! No!" The words screamed through her brain, but before she could make a sound, he reached down and cut the plastic tie that held her to the frame of the seat.

"Get out and pee." His hand took her arm roughly and jerked her up and out of the car.

"I, uh I don't...," Lyn started, but was stopped by a short, hard open-handed slap across the face.

"Pee," Lylee said, still holding her arm with his other hand. "Squat down and pee. I'm not going to have you piss all over my car, so get to it." Sensing her continued resistance, he took hold of her throat and with one arm threw her to the ground.

Lyn's face stung from the slap, and she tasted salty blood on her lip. She rolled over on her stomach in the sand and pushed herself up. Squatting, she lowered her jeans and did as he had ordered, trying to be as discreet as possible.

The wet splash in the dirt embarrassed her, and she could not help but glance at him. Lylee stood watching her with interest, holding the knife in one hand and tapping the blade in the other.

As she finished, he jerked her upright and pushed her towards the car. Lyn fought for her balance and then squared her shoulders and stood up straight. She walked steadily to the car.

She had begun to sense that her continued survival would depend on her ability to walk a fine line between complete surrender to her terror, and her ability to maintain some sense of dignity and identity. She must resist in small ways, but not enough to seriously defy the man.

She felt certain that angering him could result in her immediate death. But completely submitting would result in the same end.

Her understanding of this was completely instinctive, in the same way that a person might instinctively react to a large barking dog by facing it and trying not to show fear or run away. You could not outrun the dog, and when he caught you, it would be worse.

Running was not the thing to do, at least not yet. She knew what the result would be if she ran and was caught. Her instinct for survival was not evident to her as even a complete thought. It was a subconscious response.

For his part, Lylee smiled and felt the thrill burning in him at her ever-so-discreet defiance. He would take his time with this one. Slowly turning that defiance into trembling, quivering terror would be sweet and delicious work.

Lylee guided the car through the pines, retracing their route back to the interstate. Picking up speed down the ramp, they merged anonymously back into the northbound traffic.

60. Limit to a Brother's Patience

Clay's arms and legs ached. He became conscious of the discomfort and realized that he had been hunched forward clenching the wheel of the truck as he tensely scanned ahead and around for any sign of an old Chevy.

A couple of times he had passed cars that might fit the description, but pulling up beside them, had not seen Lyn or anyone that looked like the man who might have taken her from the truck stop.

He forced himself to relax. Think. He had to think.

The first thought that came to him was, 'what the hell are you doing?' It was a legitimate question.

He had no better answer for himself than he had for his brother. Lyn might have gone willingly with the man in the Chevy. From what he had learned at the truck stop, it seemed that the man had rescued her from whatever old Henry had planned for her, so maybe he was just offering her a ride north. After all, that was why they had brought her to the truck stop, to find a ride to Canada.

Canada. It sounded silly, childish, but that thought made him feel guilty. Who was he to judge?

Clay remembered the look on Lyn's face when she had told them about her running away dream. The one she and her brother had constructed.

Their lives at home must have been hell. Living in hell might cause anyone to dream a dream that might seem crazy to others not living in hell. He couldn't really relate to that. Life had been full of hard work for the Purcells, but it was a long way from hell.

Was it unrealistic, maybe even farfetched? Yes, he had to admit, looking at it from the outside. But it was not childish. No, there was nothing childish about the pain and weariness he had seen in her face.

The girl's dream was a dream of escape. Clay did know a little about that. With the support of his mother and uncle, he and Cy had never suffered. But they knew what it was like to want something more than could be had just scraping by in the south Georgia backcountry.

Poverty and hard times were the life they had lived with their widowed mother. He and Cy were working on their dream now, building their business. There had been those who thought they were crazy for striking out on their own.

Canada was Lyn's dream of escape. In her way, she was trying to achieve that dream, without any help or guidance from anyone. He and Cy had the guidance of a mother and an uncle. She had none. That thought gave him a deeper respect for her and her Canada dream.

Respect. That was something. Was there anything else there? Some deeper feeling? Sure he felt sorry for her. Pity, but that seemed insulting and the thought made him feel guilty again.

The cell phone on the truck seat rang.

"Hello," Clay said, knowing who was on the other end.

"What are you doing?" Cy's voice was calm, without inflection and clearly annoyed that Clay had not called.

"Wish I knew." Clay had been expecting this call as the distance between himself and Savannah and his brother grew. Taking a deep breath he continued, "She wasn't there, at the truck stop."

"Oh. Sorry. I know you were counting on seeing her."

"No, it's not that, Cy...something's not right."

"Not right? What does that mean?"

"She got in a car with a stranger..."

"Clay, *we* were strangers this morning. She got in the truck with us. Might be a pattern here, you think?"

"Maybe, but it doesn't seem right. The voice mail she left was, well, she seemed scared, frightened like something had happened."

"Something did happen," Cy was trying to be patient with his brother, but it was a struggle. "She had a bad fight with her father, bad enough that she had to leave for her safety. Then two strangers...you and me...take her to a truck stop in a strange city and leave her."

"That was because..."

"I know, because she was going to Canada. I know. Sounds silly but I felt for her too, Clay. It was silly but kind of innocent. Couldn't laugh at something like that. I get it.

But now she is gone. Probably found her ride to Canada, or at least to some place closer than Savannah, Georgia. That's the way it is."

Clay was silent, allowing Cy's words to sink in. They made sense to a point.

"The voice mail, Cy. She was scared, and she trusted us and called. Can't let that go. She was counting on us because we offered her a place to stay."

"Clay," Cy's voice sounded tired. "We are strangers, and she is a stranger to us. I think you are carrying this too far."

"I know, Cy. One more thing though. At the truck stop, I talked to some people who said she got into some trouble with a trucker and another fella had to save her. She left with that guy, but no one knew if she left voluntarily."

"Sooo...?" Cy said, asking for the point his brother was making too slowly.

"So, she was scared. She got into trouble with a trucker who tried to force her into his rig. Another guy comes along and saves her from the trucker. She leaves with him later. But in between, she called us, Cy. She was counting on us being there. She trusted us. I don't think she has too many people to trust."

"No, I don't reckon she does." Clay could not see the look of complete resignation on his brother's face, but he heard it in his voice. "Well, I guess you need to do what you're doing brother. Seems right, I guess. I'll keep things going here. You keep in touch." As an afterthought, Cy added, "Be careful, Clay. We don't know what this is all about."

"I will. You too." The brothers disconnected simultaneously and the road noise filled the pickup's cab.

Despite the passion of his argument in explaining things to his brother, Clay's thoughts were a turmoil of emotion. The only thing he knew for sure was that he had to make sure Lyn was not in danger. For now, there were questions about that.

If she had made up her mind to take the brothers up on their offer, why had she left with the man in the Chevy?

She had had the trouble with Henry. Why would she get into a car with another stranger?

If he was the man that had saved her from Henry, maybe she trusted him, but why would she have called Clay to pick her up?

There were too many questions. The memory of her recorded voice, confused and frightened, settled it.

At the very least, he would have to make sure she was safe. Clay's head pounded at trying to sort it out any further than that.

An older model Chevrolet Impala got onto an exit ramp up ahead. It was only about ten years old, but Clay didn't have much to go on. He followed the car up the ramp and into a gas station. Pulling through the station, he watched the car.

The Chevrolet pulled up to the gas pumps and an older couple got out. The man went to the rear of the car to pump gas. The woman went inside the convenience store.

Clay pulled through the lot and back onto the road. Driving down the entrance ramp to the interstate, he accelerated quickly. No telling how many cars had gone by while he had gone up the exit. He had to move quickly to catch up, looking for old Chevys as he headed west on I-16 towards Atlanta. The largest city in the state seemed as good a direction as any.

Tools rattled in the bed of the truck. Cy was going to be really pissed if he didn't wrap this up soon. There was a limit to a brother's patience.

61. Day's End

Bob Shaklee kicked his shoes off and stretched out on a hard bed in the Colonial Hotel in the center of Everett. It was a hell of a lot nicer than the StarLite motel in Roydon, but a long ways from the Ritz in Atlanta.

He had worked a case involving threats to the governor once that had taken him to Atlanta. The governor's office had put him up at the Ritz Carlton in the upscale Buckhead neighborhood, instead of the usual mid-market, garden variety hotel the state generally provided. But today the hard bed and austere room provided by the Colonial were fine with him.

Pulling his cell phone from the case on his belt, he leaned back on the pillow and punched 'Home' on the speed dial. A smile that erased the weariness and unpleasant memories of the day spread across his face when his sixteen year old daughter answered.

"Whatcha doin', Punkin'?"

"Daddy! Hey, mom. Dad's on the phone." The background noises coming from his home melted the memories of the day.

****

In a room on the fourth floor of the Colonial, Sharon Price stood leaning on the window frame and staring out onto the quiet court square of Everett. The fourth floor was the highest floor in the hotel. That made it the smoking floor, which suited Price completely.

She inhaled deeply from the cigarette in her hand and let the smoke wisp away into the night air through the open window. Slowly the thoughts of the day faded. The images of the bodies of the old man and young girl receded from the front of her brain where they had been seared in place all day.

There was no phone call for her to make. She was alone. Sharon Price had grown up in a backwater part of Georgia, not much different from Pickham County. Change the names of the towns; you would hardly be able to distinguish one from the other.

Her mother had died of breast cancer at an early age. Her father had been there when she went away to the University of Georgia in

251

Athens. He was a good father who had done his best to raise a daughter on his own. She had come home for Christmas during her sophomore year and then never saw her father again.

Just after the New Year, he had been working late in the convenience store he owned on the outskirts of the small town where they lived. It was a town much like Everett.

Someone had come in while he was closing and shot her father in the chest. Robbing the till, the killer managed to make off with a grand total of three hundred seventy-four dollars. He was never caught.

Her father lay bleeding out on the floor. They said it probably took over an hour for him to die. He wasn't found until the next morning when a local farmer came in for coffee.

After the funeral, Sharon Price changed her major at the university from accounting to criminal justice. She landed a job with the GBI after graduation and worked her way into investigations.

The cigarette smoke drifted through the window into the night air letting the day's memories drift out with it until the room began to chill. Stubbing the butt in the small plastic ashtray that had not been cleaned after the previous tenant, she tugged the window shut and pulled the musty drapes. Time for bed. There was another long day ahead tomorrow.

****

Anxious frustration pushed Clay on his quest, and his foot pushed the accelerator of the pickup. Scanning side to side and ahead, he looked for any vehicle that might resemble an older Chevrolet sedan.

Having no idea where to go, he had been driving around east Georgia, searching the major highways and interstates for the old Chevy. Eventually he had decided to just head west from Savannah towards Atlanta, two hundred and fifty miles away.

It wasn't north, but it was a central hub for interstates and highways. Anyone traveling very far in any direction through the state might well pass through Atlanta. And there were several truck stops. He would search them all if necessary. Besides, it was still in Georgia, still home, or close to it.

Like Lyn, his backcountry Pickham County roots might make him seem naïve, but he was not stupid. He knew that trying to find the old Chevy...trying to find Lyn...was useless...the search for the proverbial needle in a haystack. Hours earlier, he had stopped trying to understand what compelled him to search and just accepted it.

The odds of finding the girl were...well, finding her wasn't very likely. He would give it another day, no more. Then, having fulfilled whatever sense of obligation it was that urged him on and, hopefully, shed of the guilt and sense of responsibility that had preyed on his mind all day, he would have to turn back to his brother and the job in Savannah.

A light rain had begun to fall, and the drops of rain on the sides of the windshield reflected the lights from the cars around him. Some of the drops reflected red and blue light, as if from a prism.

Clay glanced at the mirror while traffic around him slowed. The police car, emergency strobe lights flashing, roared up to his bumper.

Great. The perfect end to the day.

He guided the car through the slowing traffic and moved onto the shoulder of the interstate. The Georgia State Patrol cruiser followed. As they pulled off the road, the rest of the traffic picked up speed, resuming their trips. Clay waited impatiently in the truck, both hands on the wheel, as the Trooper approached carefully, flashlight shining into and around the truck's interior.

****

Spray from the semi rig he was passing covered the windshield, temporarily blinding Leyland Torkman. He turned the wipers on with a jerk and continued moving around the truck. Easing back into the right lane, he signaled carefully and put some distance between the Chevy and the big rig.

The bright pinkish lights of the I-95 and I-26 intersection glowed garishly ahead in the rainy mist. Knowing that police communications between states were notoriously unreliable, and that in the unlikely event anyone had reported his abduction of the girl, it would take hours for that information to make its way to local police, even in an adjacent state, Lylee had decided to leave Georgia.

He proceeded up the coast of South Carolina. The old car

253

whirred steadily along on the wet pavement. Contentment flowed in a loop from him into the car, to the wheels splashing on the pavement, back through the chassis and frame into the seat, and into him. It was a pleasant sensation.

Turning his head, he reached out and placed his hand on the thigh of the pretty brunette. After several hours in the car with him, she had overcome the initial shock and fear. She stiffened and looked at him with defiance.

A smile spread across his face at that. He moved his hand up and down her thigh as she straightened as much as she could in a symbolic effort to resist him.

Defiance. That would change, he thought, smiling more broadly at her. Before he was done, she would be whimpering at the realization that defiance was pointless.

There was to be no salvation. He would take his time. She was special. The end would be special. He would see to that.

Blue and red emergency lights ahead signaled an accident on I-95 that had traffic slowed at the giant interchange of the two major traffic corridors. There was no thought, just reaction as his planned direction changed in an instant.

Smoothly, Lylee guided the car onto the ramp from I-95 to I-26 towards Columbia. He would not be slowed, or possibly stopped, while the law muddled around him at a traffic accident. Merging into traffic, he settled again in the seat and the contentment returned.

****

Swallowing the scream down and pushing the fear deep inside, Lyn glared at the man touching her. She had been staring through the rain speckled glass, head resting against the window when his touch had startled her.

As she had earlier during their 'pit stop', she sensed that it was important for her immediate survival to show some resistance, to challenge him just enough to show that she was different, but not enough to anger him. It was a fine line to walk, and a mental effort that heightened the fatigue she felt, but she had no choice.

Hours ago she had forced out of her mind all of the 'what ifs'. What if she hadn't had a fight with her father? What if she hadn't taken the ride to the truck stop? What if she hadn't gotten into the truck with Henry, or into this car with...with whoever this was?

For now, she had to live with what was happening and survive. Most of all survive.

The thought of Clay and the call she had made to him on Big Leon's phone was a guilty memory to be pushed down inside for now. She was where she was. There had never been any dramatic rescues or heroes in her life. She expected none now.

****

Sitting on the edge of his bed, stripped to his underwear, George Mackey cradled a dirty tumbler holding three full fingers of bourbon in his hand. The thought of calling his ex-wife and asking to speak to the girls crossed his mind. He considered it for a moment and then pushed it aside. He had no desire to fight tonight, and a call to Darlene would inevitably lead to an argument. Besides, it was late and the girls were probably in bed.

Turning the glass of bourbon slowly in his hand, he wondered if the parents of the girl murdered and left on Ridley Road had been notified. He had made a few death notifications in his time with the sheriff's department.

Traffic accidents mostly. It was always unpleasant, but traffic accidents were something people knew about. They had some connection to everyday life. Not everyone died in traffic accidents, but it wasn't unheard of. It was something a parent could hate but understand.

How did you tell parents that their daughter had been brutally and sadistically murdered, for no apparent reason, other than some animal had picked her out of the crowd? What understanding could they have? What sense could they make of that? It was something he had not had to do, and he was glad of it.

Closing his eyes, George saw the old Chevy glide by in the dark, except this time, he followed in his sheriff's department pickup and stopped the car. He pictured himself walking up. The slender brown-haired man would be behind the wheel. The girl would be in the passenger seat, and he would stop anything from happening to her.

But that couldn't be. It would never be. The girl was already tortured, dead and in the weeds on Ridley Road.

She was dead. George was too late. Darlene was right. He was always too late.

But at least he could have looked the animal in the eye. And then what? Yes, then what? Arrest him? Kill him? Be killed by him? All possibilities. George was too tired to figure it out.

In one gulp, he downed the bourbon and laid back on the bed waiting for the alcohol to dim the day and allow him to drift into sleep.

****

Angel Sims...Mrs. Harold Sims...sat on the front porch of the house she and her husband had shared for sixty years. They had raised their family there. The chair he had been sitting in the night before rocked gently in the breeze blowing in with the rain.

Unconsciously, she reached out to touch the arm of the chair where his arm would have been resting. The wood was damp and cold, and her fingers recoiled quickly, settling in her lap.

A lone tear marked its way down her brown, weathered face. She watched the woods where the trail entered on the other side of the yard, where he had disappeared into the dark just about this time last night. Mist swirled across the yard, brought up by the rain and the cool night air. It was as if Harold had disappeared into the mist.

It was a melancholy fantasy. She knew he wasn't coming back, but her gaze was expectant, hopeful, as if he might appear from the mist at any moment. In her heart, she knew he never would.

62. Traffic Stop

"Driver's license and proof of insurance, please." The trooper's flashlight shone directly into Clay's eyes causing him to squint.

Clay took his hands from the steering wheel and reached into his back pocket to retrieve his wallet. Flipping it open, he handed the license and insurance card to the trooper who kept the light partially in his eyes and partially on the license so that he could read them in the dark.

"Guess I was speeding, officer," Clay said, uncomfortable with the trooper's scrutiny and light in his eyes.

"Yes. Yes, you were, Mr. Purcell." The trooper raised the light so that it was full in Clay's face again. "Is there some reason for that?"

"I'm looking for someone."

"Looking for someone? Who?"

"A girl. Her name is Lyn," Clay said impatiently. "Look, sorry I was speeding officer. I know I got a ticket coming, and I'm not trying to be smart, but I need to get moving again. Could you check me out and write the ticket, and I promise to hold the speed down from now on."

"A girl named Lyn," the trooper continued calmly and without acknowledging Clay's request. "Who is she? Girlfriend? Wife? Some sort of domestic problems between you?"

Clay's head dropped in exasperated resignation. "No. Nothing like that. She's a girl my brother and I met last night...this morning...at a diner on the interstate. She needed a ride so we took her to a truck stop outside Savannah."

"That was nice of you. So where's she headed?"

"Canada."

"Canada? Really? Where's she from?"

"Somewhere down in Pickham County. She wouldn't say where exactly."

The trooper's next question was spoken in a voice that had suddenly lost the neutral-toned modulation of a routine traffic stop. "Tell me exactly where you met this girl and where you left her. The whole story."

The trooper's tone startled Clay. The traffic stop had just taken a turn, and he wasn't sure if it was for good or bad. The one thing it did, for certain, was raise his concern for Lyn.

Clay quickly recounted the encounter at the I-95 Diner and the trip to the AcrossAmerica Truck Stop. He explained the phone message Lyn had left and his search for her at the truck stop. When he got to the part about Lyn leaving in a vehicle described as an older, faded Chevrolet in the company of a medium built white male with brown hair, the trooper stopped him.

"Mr. Purcell. I need you to come back to my vehicle with me." He opened the door of the pickup and backed up waiting for Clay to follow.

Clay's heart pounded in his chest. Stepping from the pickup, he moved past the trooper and towards the cruiser.

"You carrying any weapons?"

Clay turned at the trooper's question.

"No. Nothing."

"Show me your belt line and pockets."

The trooper watched closely as Clay pulled his pockets inside out and turned around.

"Good. Have a seat in the passenger side," the trooper said as he moved to the driver's door.

Clay did as he was instructed. Once in the cruiser, he told the story again. The trooper was particularly interested in the description of the Chevy and the man driving it, and of the girl.

When he was done, Clay sat quietly while the rain tapped on the cruiser's windows and ran in sparkling drops across the glass. The trooper picked up the radio microphone.

In a businesslike manner, he began speaking into the mike. He gave the information Clay had provided about the car and driver and added the description of the young girl going by the name of Lyn who may be accompanying the driver.

He added that the vehicle might be associated with the murders in Pickham County earlier that date, and the vehicle and driver should be approached with caution. Clay's heart raced, as if it might pound itself out of his chest.

When he was done, the trooper looked at Clay and said, "I need you to follow me to the state patrol post at Statesboro. There are some GBI investigators that will want to speak with you."

Clay nodded. Murders. In Pickham. The pounding of his heart moved to his throat and prevented him from saying anything more than a choked, "Yes."

A minute later, he was back in his truck following the state patrol cruiser. Their speed increased to ten miles an hour over the limit, but this time it was legal.

63. Another Wake Up

"George!"

The cell phone that had been annoying him a moment before rested on the pillow and leaned against his cheek. George Mackey lay with his eyes closed, hoping the voice in the phone would stop yelling at him soon so that he could go back to sleep.

"George! Dammit, George answer."

George pushed his eyes open and squinted at the light from the illuminated face of the phone. The voice was not going to stop yelling. Reluctantly, he spoke.

"What is it?" he asked through the fog in his brain.

"George, you need to get up."

"What? Why...who is this?"

"It's Bob...Bob Shaklee. Start waking yourself up, George. We're gonna need you."

"Bob? Why? It's the middle of the night, Bob...what time is it?"

His voice had the pleading, groggy whine of fatigue mixed with what, Shaklee knew, was alcohol. It was apparent that George had self-medicated before going to sleep.

"It's just after two in the morning, George. Now get moving."

"Bob, can't this wait until daylight?" George's voice was pleading with fatigue.

"No, George, it can't. The Chevy was seen at a truck stop outside Savannah. We have a witness at the state patrol post in Statesboro, and we need to get moving. Meet us there."

The fog began evaporating from his brain, and George sat upright in the bed.

"Right. I'm moving now. Won't take long."

"One more thing, George. There may be another victim. Young girl from the truck stop. She was last seen alive, and he may not have had time to hurt her yet."

George's mind whirled as he shook himself fully awake.

"Girl. Another one?"

"Yes, George. Another girl. Last seen alive. We may be able to

260

find the killer and maybe save the girl...if we hurry. It's a long shot, but..."

George cut him off. "On my way."

He ended the call, tossing the phone onto the nightstand with his wallet, badge, and the off-duty nine millimeter Glock he carried when not in uniform. Grabbing a pair of semi-clean blue jeans from a chair by the bed, he tugged them on as he hopped into the bathroom where he washed his face in cold water and ran a comb through his hair.

Squinting into the mirror in the dim, yellow light, he shook his head wryly acknowledging to himself that he looked exactly like what he was, a boozed-up, middle-aged man trying to mask his condition and pull himself together enough to take care of the business at hand.

Turning from the mirror, he went back to the bedroom chair and grabbed a faded, short sleeved, plaid shirt that had been under the jeans he was now wearing and hurriedly buttoned the bottom two buttons and then shoved his feet into the boots beside the chair. Grabbing the wallet and badge from the nightstand, he shoved them in his back pockets and pushed the belt clip of the Glock's holster down over the waistband of the jeans.

The coffee he craved would have to wait until he was on the road. George lifted the pickup keys and an old khaki windbreaker from a hook by the front door. Thirty seconds later the tires of the county truck were spitting gravel as it pulled from Fel Tobin's driveway.

Redemption for his sins was not something George Mackey expected, but he would not be late again.

64. Uncertain Status

A gust of wind caused the rain to rattle against the window behind Clay Purcell. The room's fluorescent lights reflected off the glass and aluminum window frame. Outside there was only black. The storm blocked any moonlight or starlight that might have made its way to the window.

He had been in the room for over an hour. The trooper who had brought him in sat at a desk across from him completing paperwork of some sort.

Not long after arriving at the state patrol post, Clay had impatiently asked the trooper, "Am I arrested?"

The trooper had looked up from his paperwork and said simply, "No."

"Well what then? Can I go?"

"No." The trooper's tone was even and firm.

"I'm not under arrest, and I can't go. What if I just decide to leave?"

"Don't." The trooper, the little silver nametag on his shirt said 'Collins', looked up from his paperwork and stared into Clay's eyes. The look said it all. Clay was not leaving, and Trooper Collins would make sure of it.

Clay just nodded and resumed looking around the small office from his chair. What Trooper Collins did not say was that Clay's status at this point was unclear. At the least, he was a possible material witness to two homicides, and they needed all the witnesses they could find right now. At the most, well that was to be determined.

The young man seemed to know quite a bit about the old Chevy and its driver. Criminal files were full of suspects who had tried to appear helpful and to be on the side of law enforcement in order to evade detection or capture. In Clay's case, maybe he was telling the truth, maybe not. But Trooper Collins knew that he was not the one to make that determination, and until the GBI investigators arrived, he would make damn sure that Clay Purcell kept his ass in that chair.

The room that the non-arrested Clay sat in was painted government tan over cinder blocks. The furniture was institutional metal gray. A hallway on one side led to several small rooms. They had to be small, Clay knew, because of the dimensions of the building he had noted as he entered.

A door on the other side of the room was closed. Clay wondered where it led. He had heard that the patrol had barracks for troopers who were posted away from home and wondered if there were more troopers, off-duty, on the other side of the door. There had been a couple of other cruisers in the lot as they had entered the building.

As he pondered the possibility of additional troopers sleeping in the building somewhere, a radio on a shelf behind the desk crackled.

"Post 12, from State 115."

Trooper Collins turned and pulled the mike from the clip on the side of the radio."

"Go ahead, 115."

"Post 12, we're thirty miles out, ETA twenty. Is the subject standing by?"

Realizing that he was the 'subject', Clay looked up and into Trooper Collins' eyes. Yep, he was still standing by. No doubt about that.

Collins returned Clay's look and nodded as he spoke. "Ten-four, subject standing by."

Clay was a little concerned about being the 'subject', but he was more concerned about Lyn. It was clear the patrol and GBI were working on something big, and it seemed that Clay had stumbled into the middle of it. And if he was in the middle, what did that mean for Lyn?

Trooper Collins shuffled his papers, but he remained focused on Clay. He would have to cooperate with them. Hell, why wouldn't he cooperate with them? They were the Georgia Patrol and the GBI. If there were something wrong, they would be the ones to take care of it. They would be the ones to help Lyn.

Those would be Cy's words for sure. They made sense but somewhere inside, Clay wanted to hurry back to his hunt.

Hunt. Things had changed for him. This had started as a search.

263

But now? Yes, that's what this was feeling like now, a hunt. He wasn't sure who the hunter was, but there was an uneasy feeling that Lyn had somehow become the prey.

65. California or Bust

The rain slackened as they approached Columbia, South Carolina. The cool night air caused the mist to rise eerily from the wet pavement. But eerie was not a word that troubled Lylee Torkman. In the eyes of most others, he was normally the eeriest person around.

On the outskirts of the city, he pulled the Chevy off the interstate and into the parking lot of a small, deserted convenience store in a shabby part of town. He could see an older, heavyset woman reading a magazine behind the counter. She squinted out the window at the headlights that pulled up. He knew that in the glare of the lights, she could make out no details in the car from inside the store.

Lylee glanced around. The lot was empty. The street was empty. The rushing of traffic on the interstate was the only sound. He looked at the girl beside him.

"We need food. I'm going to get us something to eat. You stay still and quiet. You hear? No sound. Nothing. Any noise and I will kill that old lady, and then I will kill you." He lifted the knife that was never far away and let the tip rest under the girl's left breast. After a moment, he lifted the breast with the tip of the knife and smiled as she winced. He added as an afterthought, as if she might not understand, "I'll make it hurt. Hurt bad. So don't move and no sound. Got it?"

He expected an answer, and Lyn struggled to give a nod that demonstrated her understanding while still maintaining her resistance. The best she could do was to look him briefly in the eyes while giving one quick up and down jerk of her head. It was enough to plaster one of the sick smiles on his face. She was becoming accustomed to those smiles, and more frightened by each one.

Moving suddenly, he was out of the car and through the door of the store. She could see him inside rapidly gathering up bags of chips, candy bars and sodas. He dropped them on the counter, paid the clerk, and was back in the car. He could not have been gone more than two minutes.

Lyn had watched him frantically trying to decide what to do and if she should attempt to escape. It was useless. Her right hand was still strapped to the frame of the seat. The door was locked and could not be opened from the inside; there was no one around, except for the old woman in the store who probably couldn't even see if there was someone else in the car.

As it was, he was back, and she was still there. He pulled open a bag of chips and popped a can of Coke, munching a handful of chips as he backed away from the store.

A minute later, they were back on the interstate. With one hand, he held the bag of chips in front of her as he drove. When she made no move, he looked at her and shook the bag. "Eat. Don't know when we'll be stopping again."

Lyn reached up and took a chip from the bag. She had forgotten how long it had been since she had eaten and how hungry she was. Quickly, she reached up and grabbed another chip before the bag moved away.

Lyn could see that they were circling a city on a large highway, an interstate. The signs said Columbia, and she knew this meant she was in another state. She had never been in another state, not even Florida which was not many miles from her home in Pickham County.

After a while, she saw a sign that said Augusta. She knew that Augusta was in Georgia.

Lylee watched her, and the grin was back. It seemed always to be there when he hurt her or she was confused or frightened.

"Figure out that we're not headed to Canada, did you?"

Lyn stared out the window at the interstate signs that said I-20 Augusta, Georgia.

"Well, I figured we could take a little detour. Did you know that if you get on I-20 here and drive west, you can go all the way to west Texas and hit I-10 east of El Paso? From there just keep heading west and you end up at the Santa Monica pier in California. What's that the old pioneers used to say? California or bust." He made the little snickering sound that caused her flesh to crawl.

Lyn made no reply. In her heart, she knew that she had no more chance of seeing California than Canada. All she could do was stay alive as long as possible and hope for some chance of escape.

66. Waiting

Sharon Price wheeled the unmarked, silver-gray Ford into the lot of the state patrol post, splashed through a puddle, and came to rest beside an old pickup parked by the front door. The GBI car rocked from her braking.

They had taken one vehicle so that they could more easily discuss the case and developments with the young man who had been stopped by the patrol. George would be bringing his county pickup.

"Nice landing." Bob Shaklee was unbuckling the seatbelt he had snugged down when they left Everett. Bob was a better driver than he was a passenger, but they both knew that Sharon was the better driver when it came to getting somewhere quickly, and they had gotten to Statesboro very quickly. He couldn't deny that.

Walking briskly to the building, they peered into the bed and interior of Clay Purcell's pickup as they passed. There was nothing remarkable inside.

"Looks innocent enough," Price commented.

"Yeah. He seems to know a lot about this though," Shaklee replied, referring to Clay's knowledge of the old Chevy and the physical description of the driver, details he claimed to have picked up at the truck stop. "We'll see."

The door squeaked open and then clattered shut. Clay looked up from his seat across from Trooper Collins and eyed the two persons who stood there for a moment taking in the surroundings.

One of them, the male, looked over at the desk across from Clay. "Trooper Collins?"

"Yep." Collins stood. "You Shaklee?"

Bob nodded affirmatively.

"Come this way and I'll fill you in."

Bob Shaklee followed him into the hallway to Clay's right and then into the first small room where they closed the door. Clay was left alone in the office area with Sharon Price.

She regarded him intently, as if waiting for him to say or do something. Her silent gaze continued for what seemed like a much longer time to the young man, but was probably no more than thirty seconds.

The intensity of her look mixed with the silence and absence of any conversation made Clay uncomfortable in the extreme. Just as he was about to speak and at least fill the room with something besides her silent stare, the woman smiled and took a step towards him.

"My name is Sharon Price." She held her hand out. Without thinking, he shook it as she continued her introduction. "My partner and I are with the Georgia Bureau of Investigation...GBI." She pulled the leather badge and identification case from her waist and held it up for inspection.

Clay nodded. "I know. The officer told me you were coming to ask me some questions."

"Did he tell you what we wanted to ask you about?"

"Not much. He stopped me for speeding."

"Were you?"

"Yeah, I guess I was," Clay nodded and gave a slight, boyish grin. In the land of NASCAR, a speeding ticket was almost a badge of honor for young men, and Clay was no exception. But the reason why he had been cruising the interstate returned to him, and the grin evaporated.

"So you were speeding and the trooper stopped you, and you told him why you were speeding."

Clay nodded.

"Tell me."

Bob Shaklee and Trooper Collins watched on the video monitor in the small room they had entered as Clay recounted the day from giving Lyn a ride at the diner, to the phone message she had left him, to his search for her at the truck stop.

Sharon Price waited until he had finished before speaking. "Do you still have the voice message?"

"Yes, ma'am. On the phone." Clay nodded towards the desk where Trooper Collins had been seated.

"Do you mind if I check the voice mail on the phone?" The words were spoken very clearly and louder than she had been speaking, which put a look of surprise on Clay's face.

"No. Go ahead," he replied, nodding slightly.

"I'm sorry, Mr. Purcell. Are you saying that you are giving me permission to check the voice mail on your cellular phone? If you are, please speak clearly for me."

The look of surprise faded. Clay realized he was being recorded. "Yes," he said, raising his voice and speaking self-consciously in clear, separate syllables. "I give you my permission to check the voice mail."

Price smiled and spoke more softly as she walked to the desk to retrieve the phone. "Thanks, Clay." Flipping the phone open, she found the voice mail button quickly. "Password?"

Clay told her, and Price punched the keys with familiarity. She held the phone to her ear and then asked, "Who's Cy?"

"That's my brother," Clay said with a sigh.

"He doesn't sound happy."

"No, he's not."

"Does he know about all this?"

"Yeah. Everything except getting stopped for speeding and..." Clay looked around the small state patrol office, "And being here."

"So Cy was with you all day."

"Yes, until I left to go back to the truck stop. He's pretty pissed off right about now."

Price smiled at him, "Yes he is. Where's he at now?"

"Motel in Savannah. Where we stay during the week while we're on the job."

Price noted the name of the motel that Clay gave her. It was a budget place; the kind that tradesmen and truck drivers stay in on the road. Then she punched up the next voice mail.

Her eyebrows furrowed as she listened intently to the young girl's voice. When it was done, she replayed it, turning the volume up, and putting the phone on speaker so that Clay could hear, along with the video recording device.

The sound of Lyn's timid, frightened voice filled the room, and the look of anguished concern that came across Clay's face was unmistakable. When the playback ended, Price saved the voice mails

270

and ended the call. She looked up at the camera in the corner of the room by the ceiling. A moment later Trooper Collins came into the room.

As Price walked towards the small room where Bob Shaklee waited, she spoke over her shoulder to Clay.

"Be back in a few minutes, Mr. Purcell. Please wait here with Trooper Collins."

Clay glanced at Collins who had retaken his seat behind the small desk. Collins nodded at him, and he nodded back. Yep, he would just wait here with Trooper Collins. It seemed like a good idea.

Collins picked up the radio microphone and repeated the BOLO that he had given earlier, adding a few details and directing that the information be passed to surrounding states and jurisdictions. Listening intently to the entire description broadcast by Trooper Collins, Clay made mental notes. In addition to what Clay had told them, he learned that the man with Lyn was wearing a Texas longhorn ring. He wondered how they had come upon that bit of information.

When Collins was done, Clay asked, "Can I go now? I really want to get out and see if I can find her. I won't speed and I'll be careful. I promise."

Trooper Collins' face had lost the hardness that had been there earlier, but it was still firm. "No son. You need to sit here for a while. There may be some more questions. We have units out looking all over the state. You can do more good helping us here."

It was all Clay could do not to go through the door and to his truck. He had cooperated, and he didn't think they could hold him legally. But where would he go? It seemed like they had a plan at least. He had nothing. He would sit and wait, for now.

67. Someplace, Away

An hour and a half after turning west on I-20, Lylee's senses told him there was enough distance between him and Pickham County. It was time to get off the interstate system and onto roads where the old Chevy would blend in and where he could make a quick change of direction if necessary.

Taking U.S. 441 north from the interstate, the old Chevy proceeded quietly through the dark, empty streets of Madison, Georgia. The old antebellum mansions spared by Sherman on his march to the sea stood elegantly silent as the Chevy passed by. Lyn had never seen homes like that. They reminded her of the movie 'Gone With the Wind' she had seen on television once.

An hour later he had skirted the city of Athens, home of the University of Georgia, on side roads and then picked up 441 again as it headed to the north Georgia mountains.

As the distance from the busy interstate increased, Lylee's senses relaxed. He knew that on the old country roads the old car would not draw attention. If someone had seen him abduct the girl at the truck stop, and had been interested enough to take the time to report the act, the local authorities would likely have only given the information to the state patrol.

He was familiar enough with the workings of law enforcement in its various forms to know that the likelihood of the description of the Chevy, the girl, and himself making it to some rural, north Georgia deputy this quickly was remote. He leaned back and stretched contentedly as he drove. It was time to start looking for some place to stay. Unlikely as it was that they would be identified, he wanted to be off the road come daylight with the car parked somewhere out of sight.

Then, as the daylight hours passed, he would see how thick the young girl's shell was. He knew she was putting on a show of strength, preserving her identity, and exercising what little control she had in order to make it harder for him to kill her.

He smiled at that. She knew very little about her captor. Her resistance only made his hunger for her deeper. The end would be the same. He would feed and be satisfied, and she would pay the price for her attempts to resist.

But she was right about one thing. He needed to break her first, to crush the hope from her chest and to feel her trembling terror vibrate from her body electrifyingly into his. That would be the moment. The end would come for her then.

Looking over at the girl turned from him, and huddled as far away as possible, he marveled that she sensed how to prolong what little was left of her short life. He had thought, momentarily, to squeeze it from her when they had taken their pit stop earlier.

Normally, he would have and left the fragile shell of her body in the pinewoods for the loggers to find or the raccoons, or both. But her feeble effort at resistance had caused him to pause and think of the pleasure it would bring to break her shell away piece by piece and watch it fall as her fear rose. The girl the night before had been good, but this one would be extraordinary. He would savor her in every way.

Reaching out his hand, Lylee felt the muscles in her thigh tense. The grin plastered itself across his face.

Although she saw only her own dim reflection in the window glass of the passenger door, Lyn knew that the sick grin was there. She fought to control the quivering muscles in her leg.

The miles riding in the dark had been numbing. She was aware that they had left the interstate, although she had no idea in what direction they were traveling. The car had passed through some small towns and around one larger one, and then they had entered a world that was black on the other side of the window. The light from a farmhouse or country store would flicker by occasionally, and then the darkness would wrap itself around the car again.

She was relieved that he had not touched her or spoken to her since leaving the convenience store in Columbia. In the silence, she had drifted away. She did not know where she had drifted to, just somewhere away from here. Away from the car, away from her father, away from Pickham. Somewhere away, that was all.

It was dark there and quiet. There was no sensation and no

awareness. Maybe she had slept. She didn't know. But as she fought back the revulsion at his touch, she tried to force herself back to that someplace, away.

68. Taste of the Kill

The door clattered open again and Clay looked up from his chair to the newcomer entering the room. Thickly built but lean, he appeared to be in his early forties. He wore a short jacket, jeans, and boots. He looked like a tradesman or trucker. There was a vague familiarity about him that Clay could not quite place.

Trooper Collins looked up curiously and the newcomer spoke.

"George Mackey, deputy from down in Pickham County. Supposed to meet Shaklee and Price here."

"Oh. Right. First door to the right down that hall," Collins said, motioning with his head towards the door that Sharon Price had entered a few minutes before.

George looked down and exchanged a mutually curious glance with Clay as he walked by. He noted that the look from the young man was not nervous or anxious.

As the door closed behind, Shaklee and Price looked up from the table.

"Glad you could make it, George," Shaklee said with a slight smile.

"Got here as quick as I could." He looked at Price, knowing that she would have been the one to do the initial interview. "So what do you think?"

"I think he's telling the truth," Price replied with a shrug. "Held out his hand and shook. Hand was dry and the grip was normal. Gentle like most men shake hands with a girl. But not nervous."

"That it?"

"No. He is anxious about the girl. Met her earlier in the day and offered her a ride, but she was hitchhiking, so they dropped her at the AcrossAmerica Truck Stop outside Savannah. Not sure if they have a relationship, but there's something there."

For the next several minutes, Sharon Price recounted Clay's story of the day, including the voice mail and the information Clay had obtained at the truck stop.

Playing the voice mail for them, she was stunned by a look that

275

could only be described as pain that played across George Mackey's face. After replaying the voice mail for them three times, she flipped the phone shut.

Shaklee and Price watched George closely as he struggled visibly to compose himself.

Finally, Sharon Price spoke. "You okay, George?"

"Yeah. I'm okay," the deputy managed softly. "Just didn't expect that. I didn't expect to hear that voice. She sounded young. She could have been the girl..."

"She wasn't, George," Price interjected abruptly. "That was not the girl found in the weeds on Ridley Road. You understand that, right?"

"Yeah, I know. But maybe if I had done something last night she wouldn't be..."

"There are no maybe's, George. You know that." Bob Shaklee leaned forward and looked in the deputy's eyes. "No maybe's. Understand. What matters is now, what happens now. We need you on this case with us and you need to get past whatever baggage you are carrying around. Push it down, George. You want to help her? Then focus!"

The sharpness of Shaklee's words had a sobering effect. George visibly squared his shoulders.

"You're right." And the deep breath he took seemed to clear away the guilt, at least for the moment. "So what now? The boy isn't involved, so where do we go from here?"

They sat quietly, each staring at the table thinking until Bob Shaklee spoke.

"All right. We have a bit more in the way of a description of the perp. And we know that he has another possible victim with him."

Mackey and Price both started to speak, but Price was first.

"Not a possible victim, Bob. That girl will be the next victim, if she isn't already. You know it as well as we do."

"Okay, right, he has another definite victim." He thought for a moment before continuing. "So what will he do? How long do we have before he kills the girl? Where will he go?"

There was silence again for several seconds as they considered

276

those three important questions. This time George spoke first.

"I think she is probably still alive...for now."

"Why is that, George?" Price asked.

"Well, I'm not sure he intended to kill the old man, Mr. Sims. He had the girl with him, and Sims just happened to come along. He enjoyed it, killing him. Took pleasure in making it as painful as possible, but it was a fluke, a chance thing. He was there in the dark at the church with the girl to do to her whatever it was he was going to do."

"Right. So...?"

"Well, then he takes her to the StarLite and during the night, he does kill her."

"We know all of this, George. What are you getting at?" Shaklee said trying to urge him on and hoping he would hurry.

George sensed the impatience and looked up. "Let me walk this through my head as we go here, Bob." He looked towards the dark window, took a breath, and continued. "So he leaves the StarLite, and now he is leaving two bodies behind in Pickham County. That would concern him. Any animal will try to avoid danger, and that's what he did. We know he headed north on the interstate, putting distance quickly between him and Pickham County. But then he got sidetracked..."

George paused to think through this part of the scenario. Price picked up the thread and spoke.

"So he stops at the truck stop, fuels up, gets into a fight with a trucker..."

"Over the girl," George added. "He fought over the girl...his girl. He saw her there, and she became his. His prey."

"Okay. He gets into a fight over the girl and then leaves with the girl," Shaklee interjected. "Seems a little rash doesn't it? Considering what he had done just a few hours earlier?"

"He's arrogant. Confident and thinks he's smarter than the rest of us," Price contributed to the picture they were sketching.

George nodded slowly and then continued, speaking deliberately as if he were explaining the puzzle to himself. "Yes, and something else. He's got the taste." The others looked at him questioningly and he continued, "The taste of the kill. Like a cougar that leaves the swamp and kills one dog in the backyard, and then kills the others just because he has the taste and they are there, and he is pumped up on the rush of the kill. He can't control himself. He needs it. Yes, he is arrogant and confident, but most of all he needs it. The taste of the kill."

They sat contemplating this for a moment before Shaklee spoke.

"So, this other girl, Lyn, is probably dead. That what you are thinking, George?"

George shook his head. "No. Not yet. He has her. That keeps the rush and the hunt alive for him, but he knows he can't expect to leave a third body this close and get away. I think he wants to put some distance between us and him," George said with certainty, and then added a little less certainly, "And the girl is with him until he feels safe enough to dump another body."

Price spoke up with urgency. "Okay, so the girl is alive with this asshole. How do we find her? We do not have a lot of time."

"Well, he's trying to put distance between himself and Pickham County. That means north or west, and the fastest way is on the interstate."

"Right, north or west," George agreed. "And I think he will get off of the interstate when he can."

"Why?" Price asked.

"I don't know really." George shrugged. "It's what I would do. More options if I have to run. Small towns, country roads, dirt trails. Not as confined as the lanes of the interstate heading in one direction. Just seems like what I would do if I had to get away."

"Okay," Shaklee spoke, summing up. "The asshole is trying to put some distance between himself and us. He is probably heading north or west. We don't know which direction, however. And he probably still has his latest victim, the girl named Lyn, with him, but there is no telling how long she will be alive. That about it?"

Price and Mackey nodded their agreement with Shaklee's summation.

"Okay. I propose that we split up and position ourselves in the general direction of his probable routes of escape. We may not be

278

close, but we'll be closer than we are now. And if we catch a break, we can be on him a lot quicker than just sitting here."

The others nodded agreement.

"All right. I'll go west along I-20 and hold up at the Alabama line. Sharon, you and George head north." He turned towards George. "Any particular route you want to take since you think he might be off of the interstate system?"

George stood up and crossed the room to a map of Georgia and surrounding states covering one wall. He traced his finger along the map for a minute and poked it.

"Right about here, I'd say."

Price walked over to the map peering at the highway and area where George's finger lay. He had traced a route north along U.S. 80 and the adjoining state highways leading from Statesboro and then into the network of interstates and country roads spread across northeast Georgia and the South Carolina state line. His finger came to rest at Toccoa, not too far west of I-85 before it crossed from Georgia into South Carolina.

"Looks about right to me," Price agreed.

"Good," Shaklee said. "We have a plan...sort of."

"We have a plan," Price said. "What we need now is a break. We need some trooper or deputy to get lucky and spot the car."

"A break is definitely what we need and what the girl needs." Bob looked at the others before continuing. "We can only stay on the hunt for another day or so unless we catch that break and someone spots him. After that, the trail will be too cold, and the girl..." He stopped in midsentence, not wanting to say what they all knew. "Well after that, we will have to assume that we will probably not be able to save the girl and will have to get back to following up on all of the leads we have. Go to Texas. Check sex offender files. Cases in adjacent states. All the usual paths of investigation. It won't be a hunt and rescue anymore, just plain plodding investigative work."

He stopped speaking and looked at the others to make sure they understood his meaning. They had another day to save the girl, no more.

Sharon Price nodded solemnly in understanding as she offered a silent prayer for that break.

George was quiet. The hunter in him knew that patience was far more important than luck in bringing down big game, and this was the biggest game there was. A beast in the form of a man.

He pushed the memory of the girl's voice deep down inside. He had to have control. Patience. It was likely they would only get one chance to save the girl, if that.

69. Cy Would be Pissed

Clay looked up from his seat when the big deputy and two GBI agents walked from the office. They crossed the room to the front door with purpose and Clay started to rise. The female agent, Price, stopped and faced him.

"I want to thank you for your help, Clay," she said with the forced but patient smile of someone with something else to do. "Trooper Collins there will give you a receipt for your phone. Not sure when you can have it back, but we'll do our best to get it to you." She paused clearly not knowing what else to say but knowing what he wanted to hear. "I have to be honest with you; we don't know what is going to happen. You know this isn't good."

Clay nodded.

"Well, we have every trooper and deputy in the state looking for her, for Lyn. You know I won't lie to you and promise anything. You know I can't do that."

He could only nod again.

"Well then..." she paused not knowing what else to say to the young man, but wishing there was something she *could* say, something positive.

"You did good, son." George Mackey spoke up in his slow, south Georgia drawl. "You're from down in Pickham aren't you?"

"Yes."

"Well near as I can tell, this girl is lucky she ran into you."

"My brother, Cy, too. He was there."

"Right, you and your brother. Best thing you can do now is head home and wait. We'll let you know what happens. We have your number."

"You have my phone."

"I'm from down in Pickham, I'll find you. Besides, the trooper has your home contact information in the report. Right?" George looked over at Trooper Collins who nodded. "So go home now." George paused. Like Price, he had no idea what to say next, so he said what he could. "We'll do what we can."

281

With that, the three walked out of the door and into the dark early morning. Clay stood looking at the door for a few seconds, then Trooper Collins spoke.

"Here's the receipt for your phone." He held up a slip of paper. "Do what the deputy said, Clay. Go home. Go find your brother."

Taking the slip of paper, Clay mumbled a thanks and stepped through the door. The early morning air was dark and damp from the earlier rain. The tires of the two vehicles hissed on the wet pavement as they pulled from the lot onto the highway.

He watched the taillights of the state car and the deputy's pickup disappear in the mist. When they were gone, he climbed into his truck, turned the engine over, and backed carefully away from the state patrol building.

Pulling onto the highway, he turned north and increased speed until the taillights of the Pickham County deputy's pickup were just visible through the mist. Matching speed with the vehicle, he settled in. He didn't know where they were going, but he was going there too. As he drove, the seeds of a plan started to form in his brain.

He would follow them until daylight when he would have to back off. They would know his truck immediately, and he knew if they looked in the mirror and saw him, they would send him packing, with an escort if necessary. But they would be getting to Augusta about daylight and once they got there, he would see if he could make his plan work.

Doubt started to settle in, but he shook it off. He didn't have his phone, but he had a very clear memory of the girl's confused and lonely voice in the message. He was committed now. He would follow until he knew what had happened to her. He owed that to her.

For the hundredth time that day he thought, 'Cy will be really pissed'. He pushed that one away for now.

70. Soon

The settlement of Crichton was in the Appalachian foothills. It had taken the old Chevy less than a minute to pass from one end of the village to the other and then back out into the predawn gloom of the forest canopy, split narrowly by the two lane road. The north Georgia mountains were dotted with little crossroads settlements hidden among the forests and hills.

Lylee knew that it was time to get off the road for a while. With the bloodlust rising in him, he had taken chances that he would normally have avoided after a kill. He had been lucky so far.

Now it was time to rest. Once again, his hand reached out for the girl's thigh. Stroking it, he felt the hunger rise in him.

Practiced eyes scanned the roadside in the dark. A few miles north of Crichton, he found what he was looking for.

The sign made from rough cut logs said "Creek Side Cabins". Lylee slowed at the entrance and peered down the gravel drive into the dark. At the end of the drive, a small building surrounded by pines was visible in the headlight beams. The creek side cabins were not in view.

Good. They would, no doubt and as the name suggested, be nestled cozily beside some small mountain creek surrounded by the thick mountain trees. A picture postcard scene that would be lost on the two in the Chevy. One had plans that would turn the rustic setting into a very unpleasant place. The other just wanted to stay alive.

The car bumped heavily as it turned sharply onto the rough drive. Lyn could not suppress a gasp of surprise. Headlight beams illuminated a narrow tunnel of green through the trees. She fought down the fear and the urge to scream. It was an overwhelming urge that nearly boiled the scream from her. But that was what he wanted, she knew.

She also knew that the turn down this dark road meant that there would be more reasons to scream. Soon. She did not think she would be able to stop those screams.

71. Getting Lucky

Arriving in Augusta, George guided the Pickham County sheriff's pickup through unfamiliar territory until they were on Washington Road. Passing Augusta National Country Club, home of the Masters Golf Tournament, George slowed a little as they both turned their heads and tried to peek up Magnolia Lane. Not much was visible in the early dawn light.

"Humph," George said increasing speed again. "Lived in Georgia all my life, and this is the first time I've been here."

"Yeah. Me too," Price said studying the map on her. "Been to Augusta a few times passing through. Never to visit and sure never to go to any golf tournament."

George nodded his concurrence with a smile.

"Yeah. Golf isn't real big in the part of Georgia I come from. Bankers and lawyers play, and the sheriff. That's about it." George bumped the speed up again. Washington Road was taking them north, out of the city. "Which way we headed?"

Sharon Price looked up from the map. "About like we are now. We can take the state highways to the northwest. Little slower than the interstate, but a lot more direct. We'll cross back and forth across the state line into South Carolina a few times following the Savannah River, but we'll end up where we said, around I-85 in north Georgia, the Toccoa area. Who knows...," her voice trailed off in uncertainty.

George looked over at the GBI agent. "I know it's a long shot. We don't have any idea where the son of a bitch is headed."

Price cut him off. "No need to explain, George. It may be a long shot, but it's the only shot we have. And something else." George's head turned with interest towards her before she continued. "He's due to make a mistake, and we're due to get lucky."

He nodded slowly. The hunter in him knew that this last was true. You could plan, arm yourself, stalk, and make all necessary preparations for the hunt, but in the end, after patience, it helped to have a little good luck.

He had known plenty of experienced hunters, himself included,

284

who spent days in the field without a kill, while the rookie stumbles noisily upon a trophy buck standing in the trail and is able to get off a shot. He would take that, he thought. A lucky shot would be just fine, and they could end this now. End it before he was too late...again.

The speed limit increased to sixty-five as they distanced themselves from the environs of Augusta. George pushed the accelerator until the speedometer read seventy. Plowed fields and stands of woods flashed by in the graying dawn. There was little traffic at this hour but they examined every vehicle that came into sight, hoping to get lucky.

72. "Honey, we're home."

Lyn watched him climb the steps made from logs cut flat on one side. The building was a small cabin also made of logs. It looked like something from an old western movie to her, only nicer.

A dim light was visible through a window that had red plaid curtains hanging and pulled back at the bottoms. There were flowers planted in barrels on each side of the door. It was like one of those garden magazines. Pretty and picturesque, a far cry from the bare, gray walls of her room in the shack she had called home.

The sound of running water splashing on rocks made its way into the car from somewhere not too distant. Lyn looked around as far as she could turn with her hand bound to the frame of the seat. They seemed to be in the middle of the woods. The surrounding country that was visible in the early morning light was hilly and rose up sharply all around.

Sounds from the porch caused her to turn her head. An old man in a flannel shirt opened the door with a smile.

"Mornin'. You're out pretty early, even for us old-timers."

Lylee smiled back his 'charming' smile and added a bit of 'good ole boy' to win over the old man's trust.

"Sorry about that, sir. My wife and I are headed up to Sliwell, Kentucky. Driving all night, thought we might could stop and spend a day or two in one of your cabins."

The old man regarded the stranger quietly for a moment. Craning his head to one side he looked past the thin man to the old Chevrolet parked at the end of the walk. He was unable to make out more than just a silhouette of someone in the car.

"Well, we do most of our business by reservation, but just so happens we haven't started our busy season yet, and we do have a few cabins open. In fact, they're all open." He pulled the door wider and stepped aside as an invitation for the stranger to enter. "If you're only staying for a couple of days, that is. Got most of the cabins rented out this weekend to leaf watchers wanting to see the colors turn on the trees. They come up from Atlanta on Friday and leave

286

Sunday afternoon."

"Not a problem," Lylee said, smiling more broadly. "We'll be gone by then. Just want to rest up and enjoy the scenery for a day or two. Then we'll be out of your hair."

"Gannet, step out of the way and let the boy in." An old woman who had clearly heard their conversation came from a room off to the right, pinning her gray hair back as she walked. "Let's get you signed up and settled in." She motioned with her head to the door. "Gannet, go outside and ask the young lady to come in. I'll fix up some breakfast for us. Not much going on now, until the weekend. You'd be welcome company."

Lylee held his place in the doorway and said, still smiling, 'No, ma'am. Can't do that." He smiled again at the old woman's raised eyebrow and added, "Sarah, that's my wife, is sleeping. She's pretty exhausted. We got some food in the car. What we are really needing right now is some sleep in a good bed instead of the front seat of that old beater." He jerked his head towards the car outside. "Besides, she's not very presentable, traveling and all. She'd be annoyed that I didn't let her get herself tidied up a bit. You know how you ladies are." He smiled in his appreciation of the ways of her gender.

The old woman smiled back, nodding her understanding. "Well, let's get you settled in then. You want a creek side or tree side view?"

"Creek side," Lylee said without having to think. The noise of the flowing water would dampen any sounds that might come from the cabin. He followed her to the desk and signed a card, entering a false Texas home address to go with the stolen Texas plates on the car.

"We'll put you someplace quiet, all the way in the back at the end of the property. You should be able to get some sleep there without being troubled by traffic on the highway."

"That'd be perfect, ma'am."

The woman picked up the card, peering at it through the bottoms of the her glasses. "Texas, huh? Thought that accent didn't sound like Kentucky."

"No, ma'am. I'm from Texas. All my life. My wife's from Kentucky. We're going to visit her family."

"Must not be in any hurry to get there," the old man chimed in.

287

"Is anyone ever in a hurry to visit the in-laws?" Lylee said, grinning like an experienced married man.

"You got that right, boy. You got that right," Gannet said, avoiding the sharp look the old woman gave him. "So, let me show you in and help you with the bags." He added changing the subject quickly.

"No need. Just point me in the right direction, and we'll find it. Besides, Sarah would be upset if I let anyone see her right now. I'd never hear the end of it."

Old Gannet nodded with a smile—the way men do who are experienced with their women. He held the key out for Lylee. "Just take the drive all the way to the end, then right along the creek. Your cabin's the last one on the end."

"Thanks a lot. Really appreciate it," Lylee said, taking the key that was chained to a small stick carved to look like a log from a cabin. Looking over at the old woman he added, "I'll bring Sarah around to say hello when she's had some rest and a chance to clean up."

"You do that," the old woman said politely.

There was something in her eye that caught Lylee's attention for just a second. It was a look that said, 'Something's not quite right. I can't say what, but something's not just the way this young man is telling it.' Lylee marked the look in his brain without a comment, filing it away for future reference that might require some action on his part before he departed the Creek Side Cabins.

The cabin key clutched firmly in his hand, Lylee went out onto the wooden porch and down the log steps to the car. Lyn watched him walk quickly to the driver's door.

Peering from the lighted window of the office, the old woman could not make out anything inside the car. The morning was still dark and only a hint of dawn light streaked the sky above the mountains. In the shadows below, the night lingered.

Turning her head, Lyn could see the old woman watching and squinting through the window glass. She knew that she was invisible to the woman.

They pulled away from the small log cabin office making the

turn down the drive. The sound of rushing water grew louder. Pulling to the end of the drive, the car stopped in front of a small cabin at the end of a line of cabins along the creek. All looked deserted. There were no lights, no cars. Beyond this last cabin, there were only trees. Lyn's eyes closed as she fought back a shudder. His hand was back on her thigh.

"Honey, we're home," he said, softly.

73. A Plan Materializes

As daylight came on and the Pickham County pickup disappeared up the road, Clay had pulled into a strip shopping center on Washington Road in Augusta, Georgia, knowing that if he continued following the deputy and GBI agent in the daylight, they would become aware of his presence. They had made it clear that he was to head back to Pickham County.

The shopping center had a national chain electronics store, and Clay's plan began to materialize. Sleeping fitfully in his truck in the shopping center parking lot, he had waited until eight o'clock when the sign on the store said it would open. It was eight-fifteen when a young man walked across the parking lot, put a key in the door, and then walked in, turning on lights as he went.

Clay waited a few more minutes and then went into the store.

"Morning. What can I do for you?" The young store manager seemed a bit surprised to have a customer so early.

"Well, I'm looking for one of those radios that pick up the police and all." Clay wasn't sure exactly what he was looking for, but figured the manager would know.

"A scanner?" The manager asked with a puzzled look on his face.

"Yeah. That's it," Clay said with some relief that the man knew what he was talking about. "A scanner that can pick up police frequencies...state patrol frequencies."

"Why do you want a scanner?" the man asked with a puzzled look.

Clay was afraid that he had stepped into some forbidden territory with his request and was wondering where this would lead. "They're legal, aren't they? I mean I thought anyone could own a scanner." He tried to conceal the nervousness in his voice.

"Oh sure, they're legal as hell. Just not much use around here anymore." The store manager saw that Clay did not understand and added, "Everyone went digital encryption. Got away from analogue radios. I can sell you a scanner, but you won't pick up much around here."

Clay's face showed that he was trying to soak this information in and extract its meaning. His reply was a simple, "Oh."

"What's up, man? What do you need a scanner for? Fill me in, and I'll see what I can come up with." The store manager spoke with a 'one young man to another' familiarity.

Why not, Clay thought. The more people who knew, the better the chance that someone might spot the car...and Lyn.

He went through the basics of the story. When he got to being stopped by the state patrol on I-16 the night before, the manager interrupted.

"Wait. Are you the guy they stopped last night? The one that gave the information about the man in the car and a girl named Lyn? You got a voice mail from her, right?"

The rapidity of the questions, and the fact that this young man seemed to know an awful lot about Clay's situation, caused his mind to whirl. "How...who...told you?"

"You did man. You did." Laughing, the manager turned and walked towards the back room of the store. "Follow me," he called over his shoulder.

The back room was a maze of shelving stuffed with various electronic parts and components. In one corner was a low workbench with a light on a flexible neck bent over some electronic equipment on the bench that was a mystery to Clay.

"Here," the manager said reaching out and pressing a button on the equipment on the bench. Immediately the device was illuminated and an LED display indicated a number. "Listen," the young manager directed.

Clay stood quietly listening to nothing for a few seconds and was about to speak when a voice came from the device. "One seven Alpha, ten - eight." A different voice responded, "Ten - four, one seven Alpha, ten - eight."

The perplexed look on Clay's face drew a boyish laugh from the manager who explained, "It's a radio from a local Augusta police vehicle. I work on them."

"You work on them?"

291

"That's right. Have a contract with the county. They bring me their problem radios, and I fix them. Good chunk of our business here. Reason I come in at eight in the morning."

"Sooo..." Clay said, absorbing the information and trying to sort it out.

"So, I was working last night late," the manager said, adding, "Real late. I heard the trooper stop you, and then later heard them take you to the Statesboro post. And then the information you gave them about the old Chevy, the man, and the girl he has with him." He paused and then asked, "She's the girl you dropped at the truck stop, right?"

"Yeah, she is," Clay said slowly. "You sure picked up a lot on that radio." He was beginning to feel somehow that his privacy had been invaded.

"Oh, that's not all. They briefed the GBI and some deputy from Pickham County over the radio, so I pretty much heard the whole story. That's how I knew about the voice mail and the truck stop." He paused to let this all sink in.

There was a delay before Clay extended his hand to the manager. "Clay Purcell. From Pickham County."

"Don Potter," the manager said, taking Clay's hand. "So what's your plan?"

"Well, it's kind of sketchy. Actually, I don't really know, except that I thought I would follow the deputy from Pickham."

"That would be Pickham County 301. That's how they identified him on the radio last night. What are you going to do after you follow him?"

"That's the sketchy part. I don't really know. Just want to be around if...*when*, they find the girl. When they find Lyn."

Don Potter nodded in solemn understanding and said, "All right. Fair enough. Let's get you fixed up."

Half an hour later, Clay pulled out from the shopping center parking lot. The portable radio leant to him by Don Potter, the electronics store manager and police radio repairman, sat on the seat beside him. He had been hesitant to take it, but Potter had assured him that it was a loaner. He used it to swap out with the

292

police department when they brought him one for repair. It would not be missed.

He made him make just one promise. He could listen, but no talking on the radio. It was for law enforcement, and Potter assured him they would both be in a world of shit if he got caught broadcasting on it.

What had been a hazy plan was materializing, thanks mostly to Potter and the loan of the radio. Proceeding north out of Augusta, he followed the route he had last seen the deputy and GBI agent taking.

Listening intently for any transmission to or from Pickham County 301 that might give him a location to head to, he drove steadily northwest along the Savannah River crossing back and forth from Georgia to South Carolina as the highway led him.

Somewhere ahead of him, the deputy's pickup was doing the same. And somewhere ahead of them? The question in his mind sent a chill down his spine.

74. Away In the Pines

He had chosen well. No lights in the parking lot, only what little light escaped the frilly curtains of the cabin windows. These would be empty until the weekenders came up from Atlanta to take photos of the leaves beginning to turn colors on the centuries old hardwoods that covered the mountains. Even if they had been occupied, the cabins were not connected, making any noise transference unlikely, not that Lylee would have allowed that to happen.

In the gray morning mist drifting up from the creek, he cut the bands holding her to the seat frame and pulled Lyn roughly from the car. The hours of driving without the ability to stretch or move had left her weak and shaky. She nearly toppled over as she tried to stand, but the powerful grip on her upper arm steadied her while it caused her to wince with pain.

With a practiced hand, Lylee kept the point of the knife blade in her back as he walked Lyn to the cabin door. There was no one there to see, but had anyone been watching the couple, walking so closely and intimately, they might have been taken for newlyweds.

Entering the room, Lylee put the chain on the door and without saying a word pushed Lyn into the bathroom.

"Stay here and stay quiet," he said with a small smile, putting his index finger to his lips.

Then he closed the bathroom door. He had work to do, preparations to make.

In the main room, the curtains over the window that looked out over the rushing creek waved in the breeze from the air conditioner. The room was frigid. Lylee had turned the air conditioner up to high, even though the early autumn mountain air was cool. The loud hum from the fan covered any other sound in the room.

Although clean, the cabin smelled slightly musty from years of guests. The air was scented with overtones of wood smoke that had drifted for years from the fireplace in one corner and permeated the furnishings. Such details were lost on Lylee who was oblivious to everything except his preparations.

Leaning with her back against the wall of the bathroom, Lyn looked around and saw that the only window was a six-inch wide glass slit running horizontally over the tub near the ceiling. Slowly, she sank down the wall until she was seated on the floor, her head resting forward on her raised knees and her hands over her ears. She tried not to hear the sounds coming faintly through the door.

A cricket hummed and chirped from a corner behind the small trash can. She listened to the sound lilting and rising and then quiet for a few seconds.

When it stopped, she would count the seconds until the cricket took up its song again. She forced herself to focus on the cricket's chirps until she drifted away…away from this place to a place where time had no meaning anymore. She just was.

There was no connection to anything in the room…no connection to the man in the next room. She was in an empty place, alone with the hum of the cricket.

She stayed in that empty, distant place until, after a time, she became aware that she was no longer in the bathroom. Raising her head, she saw that she was seated on a chair in the main room of the cabin. The curtains over the window fluttered in the breeze.

It was cold. She wanted to move to fold her arms together to warm up and realized that she was bound again, this time to a steel tubular chair with a hard plastic seat.

Metal rivets and brackets holding the chair together cut into the bare flesh of her thighs and back. She became aware that she was nude. An uncontrollable shiver overtook her thin frame, partly from the cold and partly from the fear of what would happen next.

She stared hypnotically at the swaying curtains in the window. Her eyes, fixed on the them moving in the breeze from the air conditioner, saw nothing else. She had no idea how long she had been sitting on the cold, hard chair. Tie wraps, like the ones that had bound her in the car, now held her wrists securely to the steel tubular frame. A piece of duct tape covered her mouth.

Someone was with her, but she stared past the form standing in front of her to the fluttering curtains. She let them take her mind to a different place. The curtains became tall pine trees swaying in a Canadian breeze. There were mountains in the distance. Not like the Georgia mountains, these were tall and snow covered.

She shivered in the cool air blowing from the mountains. It was cold but refreshing. It was as she had dreamt—cool, crisp and clean.

She had finally made her escape. It was a quick trip, faster than the jets she had seen flying high overhead on clear days in south Georgia.

One moment she was in the small cabin room staring at the swaying curtains, hearing the loud hum of the air conditioner fan...the next, she was in the midst of the swaying pines and cool, Canadian breezes.

Tatters of memories, far past and recent, flashed by in a confusing blur. The misery of her life at home in Judges Creek...the pain and abuse inflicted by her father...the poverty and hopelessness...the emptiness at the loss of her brother.

There were more recent ones too. The betrayal by Henry at the truck stop...the man in the room with her now. The memories chased her mind to the faraway place.

Somewhere deep inside she knew she was safe there, in the swaying pines. It was dangerous and frightening in the cabin. She did not want to be there, could not be there. In the pines, surrounded by the cool breezes, there was no pain, no betrayal, and no fear. It was her running away dream. It had come true.

The faces of the brothers, the ones who had dropped her at the truck stop, flashed by in the whirlwind of scattered thoughts. The face of the young one came into focus for a moment.

Clay. That was his name. He looked concerned. She thought from the midst of the pines that it was a good face. She wondered why he had not come to get her, why he was not with her in the pines. But then she pushed the thought of the young man away, because thinking of him threatened to bring her back to the cabin room, a terrible place.

No, she would stay away in the cool pines. No one would find her, not the young man, or her father, or the other man. She was safe in the pines.

A hand reached out to her, and one of the horns of the man's ring circled the nipple of Lyn's right breast, scraping it lightly. When there was no response, Lylee dragged the back of his hand and the sharp horn of the ring across the breast leaving a red, bleeding scratch.

Lyn's head moved from side to side, as if trying to escape from something. Lylee pushed the sharp ring hard into her breast, and her head came up. Her eyes opened and focused on him for just a second, and then she tried to flee to that faraway place, but Lylee would have none of it now. He grabbed her by the hair at the back of her head and pulled her head back so that she was looking into his eyes.

"Time to wake up, hon," he said gently.

The softness of his voice and the artificial tenderness were more frightening than if he had screamed at her. The incongruity of his tone now, with the harsh grasping pull on her hair and the sting on her breast from the ring, was confusing. Bringing her eyes up to meet his, they widened with fear. And this was, of course, what the man had intended.

The man's glistening, nude body stood in front of the girl. Despite the chill in the room, he was covered from head to foot in a sheen of sweat and excitement. The dim light from the bathroom behind the girl cast a yellowish glow across the room.

In his right hand, Lylee held a large hunting knife. The blade rested on the top of the girl's shoulder. Without putting any pressure on the knife, he slowly dragged the heavy knife across the shoulder and the flesh separated into a small cut, dripping blood. The girl's eyes widened and focused on him through the stinging pain.

Good, he thought. Good.

The man moved his left hand down to his groin and held himself. In a brief swirling moment of lucidity, Lyn realized that her struggle for life now depended on her ability to maintain her distance from what was happening in the room, and from what was happening to her.

Giving in to the terror and pain would give him what he wanted and take her to a place she would not survive. Desperately, her wide, frightened eyes focused on the fluttering curtains. She searched frantically in her mind for the pines swaying in the cool breeze. They were lost. She was lost.

Her eyes clamped shut so that she would not see what was happening in the room. Somewhere a cricket chirped distantly. She focused on it, following the chirping hum until she dared peek out through half closed lids.

Her eyes opened wider, and she was there again in the cool pines where the breezes blew. She was safe in the pines, and she would stay there as long as she could.

75. The Plan Worked

"Pickham 301, out at state patrol post, Toccoa."

Clay's head jerked violently at the words from the portable radio beside him on the seat.

"Ten - four, Pickham 301, out at Toccoa."

Amazed that his plan had worked, at least a little bit, Clay pulled over to the shoulder of the two lane highway to scan the map he had been driving with in his lap. Since leaving Augusta, he had meandered his way through the northeast Georgia countryside to the area of I-85 and the South Carolina line. Finding the highway he was on, he placed a large finger on the dot that said Toccoa on the map. Maybe an hour he thought, maybe less.

Then what? Good question. Somewhere in his brain, Clay knew that this whole excursion was now more obsession than anything else. He had to know that the girl was safe. Had it not been for the traffic stop by the state patrol last night and the subsequent information he was able to gain from his time at the patrol post, he probably would have turned back by now. He would be listening silently to Cy's justifiable anger at his desertion from their job and business.

But knowing that the girl, that Lyn, was in a car with a killer had changed all that. He would go on. He had stopped wondering why. The question no longer troubled Clay. He was committed to seeing this through to the end. That was that. Figuring it all out could wait until later. For now, he would follow the trail and see where it took him.

Pulling back onto the road, he steered the truck to the northwest. Somewhere up there ahead was an old Chevy with a young girl in it and a man who had left two bodies behind in Pickham County and was capable of who knew what. The thought caused Clay's foot to press slightly harder on the truck's accelerator.

76. Lunch Break

Rye County Deputy, Grover Parsons, had been on the sheriff's department for just a little over two years. It had been his dream as a young boy to go into law enforcement. The local department was just his starting point. He had bigger plans.

He was building his skills and gaining experience so that his application to the State Patrol would be well received. In the meantime, he enjoyed patrolling the woods and farmlands of north Georgia.

He was young and single, and like most of the young men in the area, he had grown up hunting in the mountains and fishing the cold streams. These had remained his primary off-duty activities and had developed in him a self-confidence and independence that served him well as a deputy.

His dad liked to brag about the time his boy, Grover, had been fishing a creek alone up on Taylor Mountain when a black bear had come out of the woods not fifteen feet from where Grover stood knee-deep in the cold water. Telling the story, his dad made it sound like his boy, Grover, was a modern day Davy Crockett, wrestling the bear and subduing him with a pocketknife.

The truth was that the bear and the young man had stared at each other for several seconds, both equally startled by the other's presence. Eventually, Grover turned, pointed his fishing rod at the bear, and waving the rod tip in the bear's face shouted, "Go!"

The bear did, and Grover went back to his search for trout in the mountain stream. Still, Grover was known around the county as a calm, independent, and robust young man who would not easily back down and who was very resourceful.

Wheeling his county car into the parking lot of the small country store and cafe that sat at the crossroads in Crichton, he advised the radio dispatcher that he would be out having lunch. Walking through the front door, he nodded at the old man behind the register who was reading the Atlanta paper spread on the counter in front of him. The old man gave him a quick lift of his head in return and went back to studying the paper.

Seating himself at one of the four small tables on the cafe side of the building, he greeted the man at the next table.

"Hey, Gannet. How's it goin'?"

The man smiled back over his cheeseburger and gave a muffled reply through a mouthful. "Good, Grover. Pretty good."

"Afternoon, Fran," Deputy Parsons said to the heavy woman who walked up, wiping her hands on a white apron.

"Afternoon, Grover," she said with a smile and then looked quickly over at the counter where the old man, her husband, still had his head bent over the newspaper. The smile turned to an exasperated scowl for a moment before she looked back at Grover and asked, "Usual?"

"Yep. Cheeseburger, fries and a coke."

"Right," she nodded, and waddled to the small kitchen in the back.

The deputy looked over at the man at the next table and spoke to pass the time until his food arrived.

"Wonder what she would do if I ordered a tuna sandwich?" he said grinning.

Gannet stifled a low laugh through a mouthful of fries. Everyone knew that you could get two meals at Fran's cafe. Fried eggs and bacon for breakfast, and cheeseburger and fries for lunch. That was it. No reason to order anything else, but she always came out to ask.

"So anything goin' on at your place, Gannet?"

"No, not really," the owner of the Creek Side Cabins replied. He munched a bite of burger and added as an afterthought. "Had a young couple check in this morning. Early, just after five."

"Really? That's a little strange, isn't it?" Grover looked towards the kitchen where the sounds of metallic scraping on the old griddle signaled that lunch would be ready soon. He was hungry and his stomach growled.

"Yeah, but they'd been traveling all night. Needed a place to rest for a couple of days, they said. Told them we had a full house this weekend, but they could stay until then."

The kitchen noises were now accompanied by the aroma of the

301

sizzling burger wafting through the area. Grover's stomach gurgled in anticipation.

"Kind of unusual, isn't it? Someone checking in so early and in the middle of the week this time of year?"

"Yeah. Bit out of the ordinary. They seem like nice folks though. Man's from Texas."

Deputy Parsons' eyes squinted slightly. "From Texas?" he asked reaching into the breast pocket of his shirt.

"That's what he said. Had Texas plates on the car."

Parsons opened the small notebook he retrieved from his pocket and scanned down the page. "Gannet, you remember what kind of car?"

"Chevrolet, I think. Older one, but seemed in pretty good shape."

"And the man? What did he look like?"

"Not real big. Kind of average. Thin, brown hair. Not much else." Gannet looked at the deputy with concern. The cheeseburger was forgotten. "What's wrong, Grover? My wife is still there. Is she in some kind of danger?"

"No, probably not, Gannet. Tell me about the girl. What did she look like?"

"Can't."

"Why? You said it was a couple."

"Well, that's what the fella said. He and his wife. He called her Sarah. But she stayed in the car and never came in."

Deputy Parsons stood up quickly, stuffing the notebook back in his pocket. He called to the kitchen. "Gotta go, Fran. Box it up, and I'll come back later."

"It'll be cold, Grover!" she shouted after him. "And that's no fault of mine." Fran poked her head out from the kitchen to see Grover Parsons move quickly through the door followed by Gannet trying to keep up with the deputy. She gave another scowl at the old man at the counter, who never looked up from his paper, and then disappeared back into the kitchen where agitated banging and clanging could be heard for some time.

Outside, Parsons turned to Gannet. "Follow me. When we get there, you go in the office and stay there with your wife. Don't come

302

out."

"What is it, Grover? What's going on?"

"Probably nothing, and then we can go back and finish our burgers. Just need to check it out. That's all." With that, the deputy cranked the car and pulled onto the two lane road that would lead back to the Creek Side Cabins and an old Chevrolet.

Deputy Grover Parsons picked up the mike as he increased speed. All of north Georgia law enforcement heard the transmission or had it relayed to them within seconds.

77. The Break

The break came in the early afternoon. George Mackey and Sharon Price had only spent a brief time at the state patrol post outside Toccoa. Nervous energy and knowing that there was only a limited amount of time before a third murder, in as many days, would be committed by the man in the Chevrolet, made the anxious waiting unbearable.

They had checked in with Bob Shaklee, who was doing the same in west Georgia near the Alabama line. Waiting. It was all they could do.

They were all in position as best they could be without knowing where the Chevy had been headed. They all knew that the clock was ticking for the young girl. They hoped the break would come before time expired. They were also aware that the break might never come.

Investigative success usually involves a combination of detailed, professional retrieval and analysis of evidence, deductive skill, and artful intuition that leads investigators on the right path. The two GBI agents and the deputy from Pickham County knew that many investigations took wrong turns and headed down false paths only to be later recognized as such.

Successful investigations often turned on the slightest of chances...a single misspoken word, a chance witness, an escape vehicle breaking down, or some other random, fortuitous act. These and a thousand other items *might* lead an investigation to a successful conclusion. Unfortunately, there were a million things that could steer it wrong.

The fact that the description of the vehicle, perpetrator, and possible next victim had been broadcast across Georgia and the southeastern States might bring them the break they needed. Or, it might not.

Scores of BOLO's are broadcast across the law enforcement frequencies daily in Georgia in addition to the thousands across the entire country. The sad reality is that most never turn up a lead, at least not a timely one.

In a nation of three hundred and fifty million, and twice as many vehicles, the odds were against them. One older model Chevy with a white male and white female occupants, riding in plain view on the public road system were as hidden as a cockroach under a rock. They were all but invisible.

If the driver was a bit more cautious and made efforts to conceal his movements, spotting them would be highly improbable, if not virtually impossible. Unless the gods smiled soon and they got their break, the clock would expire for the young girl in the Chevy.

It was Price who finally spoke in the midst of her nervous pacing.

"Let's go, George."

He looked up from a metal chair in the Toccoa Post's break room.

"Where to?"

"I don't know. Anywhere. We can do our own search grid for the car."

"There's troopers and deputies all over Georgia looking, Sharon. Not likely we're going to be much help. We need to stay in the north Georgia area and Bob in the west so we can respond if the car or the man and girl turn up."

"I know, but that doesn't mean we have to sit here." She paused, thinking. "Let's start our own grid and start checking every little road."

"That's a lot of roads."

"Yeah, but not as many as down in the flat lands. The hills and mountains up here limit the number of roads." She paused again, conscious of how ridiculous she must sound, and then shrugged and said, "It's a shot, George. That's all, just a shot. Besides, I can't stand just sitting here waiting, doing nothing."

George thought of the young girl's voice on the cell phone message. Like Sharon, he knew that her time was limited, if she still lived at all. He shook his head to shake that thought away. He could not be late again. And with that fear burning in his brain, he looked up.

305

"All right. Let's do it. I can't stand the waiting either."

After grabbing some triangularly cut sandwiches and drinks from the break room machines, they loaded into George's pickup and headed out from Toccoa. Sharon outlined a fifty square mile grid to the north and west, crisscrossed by small winding county roads and state highways. She navigated and George followed her directions as they munched the cardboard sandwiches and gulped their drinks.

Both knew that their small search was almost certainly futile, but they didn't speak about it. Sharon studied the map, George drove and both scrutinized every vehicle they saw.

George would slow whenever they came to some small store or gas station or crossroads so that they could examine the vehicles and any people they might see. After the brief inspection, he would pick up speed again, eyes scanning alertly for an older Chevy with Texas tags. It felt better to be moving, doing something, doing anything, futility be damned.

They were miles from Toccoa in the rising foothill and mountain country when the radio chattered to life.

"All units, all units, be advised, Rye County deputy reports the possible suspect vehicle associated with the homicides in Pickham County, older model Chevrolet bearing Texas plates, now possibly located at the Creek Side Cabins, ten miles north of Crichton on the state highway. Units responding advise."

The radio crackled and a trooper on a traffic stop on I-85 advised he was enroute to Crichton. Some lucky motorist was about to be sent on their way with a warning. Another trooper in Toccoa responded, and then George picked up the mike.

"Pickham County 301 responding with State 155," he said firmly and then added, "Advise the Rye County unit and all responding units that the male suspect is armed and extremely dangerous. If possible and there are no signs of immediate threat to the female, stand by for this unit."

"10-4, Pickham 301." The pickup grew quiet while the dispatcher switched to other frequencies to relay the information to other law enforcement agencies in the area responding.

"Which way?"

Sharon looked up, squinting from the map. Her finger pointed to an almost invisible dot. "That's where we're headed. Take a right on the next county road. It winds around that mountain there, but looks like the shortest route."

"How long?"

Sharon studied the map for a second. "Thirty minutes…maybe. We're closer than we would have been back in Toccoa, but the way the roads wind, it's hard to say."

George's foot pressed harder on the accelerator, trying to shave some minutes off their arrival time. Lucky break, maybe. They were certainly due for some luck.

The hunter in George knew that he had to capitalize on the luck, or it meant nothing. If you stumbled upon your prey but didn't get the shot off, or missed or just stood there in surprise, your luck would change.

To this point, the man in the Chevy had had it all his way. Luck, predatory skill, or a combination of both, he had been invisible to them. But now, they had their break.

The pickup truck fishtailed slightly as he made the turn onto the county road and increased speed again. George leaned forward into the wheel. They did not speak.

He and Sharon Price stared ahead, willing the pickup to the Creek Side Cabins outside Crichton, Georgia, determined not to miss their shot. It was time to end the hunt.

78. No Need to Complicate it

The jerk of his legs at the radio's blaring alert almost spilled the large drink cup Clay had nestled between his knees as he drove. Arriving in Toccoa, he had passed the state patrol post and seen the Pickham County pickup parked by the front door. He had no idea what to do, but knew that he had better not be seen staking out the deputy from Pickham County.

After an endless thirty minutes in the parking lot of a nearby convenience store, Clay had decided to explore the area, listening carefully to the radio on the seat. The deputy and GBI must be here for a reason, although that reason was not altogether clear to Clay.

The radio broke squelch with a burst of static.

"Pickham 301, 10-8 from Toccoa post. Circulating in the area."

"10-4, Pickham 301."

Jerking the truck into gear, Clay raced back to the state patrol post. Keeping the Pickham County deputy close was the key to finding the girl, or at least, was his best chance. But as he passed the post, he saw that the deputy's pickup was gone.

Hitting the steering wheel with his fist, he could not suppress a shouted, "SHIT!" and cursed himself for not staying closer and watching. He took a deep breath and tried to think. Now what? Which way?

Reaching for the radio on the seat, he turned the little knob for volume up a bit. There had been no radio traffic about the Chevy, just Pickham 301 saying he was circulating in the area, whatever that meant.

Despair settled down on him. Having come so far, the thought of turning back did not occur to him, but now he had no plan. He had no idea which way the deputy had gone. He could only listen to the radio and hope for some information.

Driving in aimless circles through the back roads of north Georgia, Clay wound his way out of the Toccoa area. The heavy darkness of the lost cause settled in on him. What was he doing? What was he going to do?

The thought of the girl's voice and the message on his cell phone, which was now in the custody of the GBI, rang in his ears. It was a moment of clarity. That was the reason he was here. No need to complicate it more than that.

It was the one wild, unpredictable thing he had ever done, and he would pay the price when he got home. Cy would see to that. But for now, it was the voice on the phone that vibrated in his ears. That was enough.

The radio crackled, and a state trooper advised the dispatcher that he was on a traffic stop on I-85 near the Toccoa exit.

Another burst of static, and a trooper advised he was out at the Toccoa post.

Silence. Wooded hills and back roads flowed by.

And then another crackle, "All units, all units, be advised, Rye County deputy reports the possible suspect vehicle ..." Clay struggled to steady the drink cup between his knees while reaching for the radio. He guided the truck to the shoulder as the dispatcher gave the lookout.

Grabbing the tattered, unfolded map from the passenger side floor, he laid it across the steering wheel. Crichton. His finger swirled over the map searching for the small dot indicating the town's location.

"Pickham County 301 responding," Clay's head jerked up, recognizing the deep voice of the deputy from Pickham County. Reflexively, he wrinkled the map in his fists as the deputy's voice calmly and firmly added, "Advise the Rye County unit and all responding units that the male suspect is armed and extremely dangerous. If possible and there are no signs of immediate threat to the female, stand by for this unit."

Scanning the map frantically, Clay searched for the dot that was Crichton. After a minute of tracing various routes on the map, it was there. It seemed to loom suddenly at him off the page. A blunt finger drew a course to it from what he thought his present location was on the map.

Seconds later the dirt clods spun out from under the truck's tires as Clay made a U-turn across the road, engine roaring.

79. Not Yet

Dragging the knife blade across the girl's flesh, he stroked himself. He moved the blade to a spot that had previously been cut and had dried. He let it drop heavily onto the cut and opened the wound again so that it started bleeding. The cuts were shallow, made only by the weight of the knife, but the knife was sharp and the cuts were painful, bleeding wounds that widened and gaped with every touch of the knife.

For a brief moment, he saw the flicker of awareness and pain cross the girl's face and then it vanished. He knew that she had run to some faraway place, trying to hide from him.

He smiled, that was fine, little girl. He would bring her back little by little, cut by cut. He would show her there was no escape, and then her desperation and fear would overwhelm her. And as her fear overwhelmed her, Lylee would have what he wanted...what he needed.

His body quivered at the thought. He let the blade drop heavily to the top of her left breast where the point made a little hole that started bleeding. His arousal grew.

He stared at the girl's tormented body. Blood trickled from her shoulders and over her breasts. His hand moved to his groin again.

He could see the goose bumps on her flesh. She quivered and shook slightly in the cold. Her eyes were fixed somewhere behind him. He lifted the big knife blade and let it fall again on her shoulder, sawing it slightly back and forth to open the small cut further.

Still holding the knife, he turned the back of his hand to the girl and rubbed it in the flow of blood. Something flickered in the girl's eyes, and then she fled away again. He smiled. Soon, he thought. Soon you will not be able to hide.

His hand moved faster, stroking himself to a climax. Lylee's body tensed for a moment.

Drained, he threw himself backwards onto the bed. He put his hand behind his head and lay there looking at her. Yes, this one was special. He could not bring himself to end it.

Normally, he would have been long finished with the girl, the duct tape over her mouth muffling her screams and cries. His hands would already have closed around her throat as he looked into her panicked eyes. The realization would have already come into those eyes that there would be no deliverance, no escape.

The fear would be so strong that he would smell it in her sweat and the urine that escaped her bladder. Slowly, painfully, her life would be choked away. It would be his.

Normally...but not this time. Not yet. Lylee wanted to bring her back from that place her escape had taken her. He wanted the complete victory that came with the perfect kill. Her awareness of her own death and impotence to prevent it would bring Lylee the awareness of his own power, and the force within him.

Somewhere deep inside, the predator's voice called to him. Beware. Caution.

For a moment, he thought that maybe he should listen. End it now and move on. But the nude girl sitting there, her underwear cut off in tatters around the chair, blood dripping over her breasts, her eyes gazing into some far distant place, pulled him away from the warning voice.

Lylee lifted his hand to his face. He could smell her blood on it. He put it to his mouth and tasted it with his tongue. No not yet. Just a little longer, and he would bring her back. He would taste her fear along with her blood.

A shiver of excitement coursed through his body as he drifted to sleep.

80. What the Hell

Clods of red clay and gravel spun in arcs from under the brown sheriff's car as it bumped roughly down the dirt drive to the Creek Side Cabins, jarring Deputy Grover Parsons' teeth in the process. Roots of the large trees lining the drive had caused the surface to buckle and swell in places, and the car was almost airborne as it took some of the bigger bumps in the drive, which had definitely not been graded for such high speed.

Gannet Carlson, proprietor of the 'Cabins', as they were known locally, struggled to keep up. When he got to the office, which was also the home he and his wife Margaret shared, he found Grover standing outside his vehicle in a cloud of dust.

The front door to the office creaked open, and the old woman who had checked in the young man from Texas bustled out onto the porch in none too good a humor.

"Grover Parsons! What on God's green earth..." She stopped in mid-sentence as more swirling dust from her husband's sliding pickup billowed up onto and over the porch.

"Gannet! You tell me what is going on and do it right now."

Her husband stood beside his truck waving the dust away from his face as he answered, "Don't really know, Marge. Grover here said he had to check something out. Something about that young fella that came in this morning. One from Texas."

Marge Carlson looked Deputy Parsons in the eye. "Tell me what's going on, Grover."

"Don't know for sure, Mrs. Carlson. The man you checked in and the car match the description of a man we're after...the whole state's after."

"What did he do, Grover?"

"Don't know that he did anything. Just matches the description is all. I need to check it out. That's all."

"Well then, why all the commotion, coming in here like you was after Billy the Kid."

"Sorry, Mrs. Carlson. Can you tell me which cabin they're in?"

312

"Of course I can, Grover. I checked them in, didn't I?" The old woman slapped her hands down the front of her shirt in an effort to beat some of the dust off. "They're in twenty-three, creek side. Around the bend and last cabin. They wanted some place quiet where they could rest up. Been driving all night."

"All right then. You and Gannet stay here in the office. I'll check things out. There may be some other folks coming. More deputies, state patrol maybe too."

"More?" Marge Carlson's voice rose in a small crescendo of concern.

"Yes, ma'am. If they do, just point them in my direction, please."

"Right, Grover. We'll do that." Gannet moved onto the porch beside his wife and took her hand. It was clear that there was more to this than just checking something out. "You be careful now, Grover, you hear."

"Yes, sir, I will. You two stay here now. No matter what. Okay?"

The couple nodded solemnly at the young deputy who climbed back into his car and moved forward down the drive. The car disappeared into the surrounding trees, and Gannet Carlson led his wife into their small home.

A hundred yards down the drive, Deputy Parsons passed the turn off to the left to the forest view cabins. Another fifty yards further, and he came to the turn to the right that led to the creek side cabins.

The car coasted to a gentle stop at the turn with just the slightest squeak of the breaks. Ahead the creek rushed noisily, full from the previous night's rain. To the right, the drive continued in front of the cabins that lined the creek.

Peering down the line of cabins, Deputy Parsons saw the old Chevrolet. It did appear to match the description of the one they had been giving in the BOLO from the state for the last two days. Of course, there were a million other old cars on the road that would also match.

Exiting his car, Deputy Parsons reached down and turned the volume down on his portable radio. The air was crisp and cool by the creek, full of the aroma of the lush vegetation lining its banks. With an eye on the cabin, alert to any movement, Parsons crossed the drive to the creek and went down the short bank to the edge of the water. Crouching low, he then moved along the creek towards the cabin until he could make out the tag on the rear of the Chevy.

Peering up over the bank through the trees and vegetation, there was not much chance that he would be seen, even if someone were watching for him. Still, cautious hunter that he was, he took his time and slowly moved his head up until his eyes could see the cabin and the car.

Curtains fluttered in the window by the door, and he became motionless, watching. After a few seconds, he determined that the window was closed. No one was visible. His eyes shifted to the car. The license plate of the Lone Star State was impossible to mistake. He had confirmed two critical pieces of information, the car and the tag.

Moving slowly, he made his way back down the bank to the spot where the drive came down from the office. His car was there, parked on the drive beside the first creek side cabin and invisible to anyone looking out from the end cabin.

Crouching by the side of the car, Parsons spoke into his portable radio mike and advised the dispatcher and responding units that the vehicle was an older model Chevrolet bearing a Texas license plate. He had seen no one and could not confirm who the occupants were or if the female was in danger.

"10-4 Rye County. Be advised, instructions remain to standby unless there is imminent threat to the female."

"10-4," he acknowledged.

Imminent threat. How the hell was he supposed to know what was happening in the cabin. The girl could be imminently threatened right now, and he would never know it.

Still crouching beside his car, he leaned back against it. Wondering what to do. Standby. Those were the instructions.

If the man in the cabin was the suspect they were looking for, he was definitely armed and dangerous and had killed at least two people in the last couple of days. That thought definitely made standing by seem like the best course of action.

314

But there was the girl, if she was there. The Carlsons never actually saw her, after all. If this was the right car and the right suspect, the girl might be in no immediate danger. Or, she might already be dead. He pushed that thought away.

Watching the cabin, he contemplated the best way to approach and maintain the element of surprise. They would need to have a plan when the other officers arrived. He could at least help with that.

Crouching beside his car, Deputy Parsons considered the best ways to approach the cabin and maintain the element of surprise. Surprise would be critical.

Minutes ticked by. Parsons had come up with a plan of approach. It was really pretty simple. Start from here on foot. Stay close to the fronts of the line cabins so that you were invisible to anyone looking out the front window of the cabin at the far end, until you went up on the porch that is. Surprise would be gone then. Still it was the best you could do.

A few more minutes ticked by as Deputy Grover Parsons watched the cabin. A woodpecker rapped a staccato beat on a nearby tree. It was the only sound audible above the rushing of the creek.

He looked up into the cool, clear autumn sky. Dappled sunlight filtered down through the trees, most of which still had their leaves. Mid-afternoon, he thought, taking a deep breath of the cool air.

The sound of a vehicle approaching slowly on the dirt drive turned his head, and he stood up. About time, he thought, and then added in a mixture of surprise and consternation, "What the hell?"

81. Confronting the Beast

The sign to the Creek Side Cabins caught Clay by surprise, and he slid the truck's tires trying to slow enough to make the turn. Not knowing what to expect, and expecting to be in some trouble with the GBI and the big Pickham County deputy if they saw him, he proceeded down the drive cautiously and much less recklessly than Deputy Parsons had before him.

As he approached the small cabin-like office, an elderly man and woman came onto the porch. He started to stop and speak to them, but they motioned him around, pointing down the drive. It was clear they were signaling him to go further.

Shrugging, he thought, okay. Clay continued down the long dirt drive, figuring he was committed now. In the mirror, he saw the couple, arms around each other, watching him and speaking into each other's ears as if they were whispering. Very strange.

Approaching the bottom of the drive, he could see the creek and the first of the line of cabins that stretched along the creek. Parked on the drive beside the first cabin was a brown sheriff's car, and beside it was a deputy whose crouching form rose as Clay came to a stop twenty feet behind the deputy. The look on the deputy's face was primarily one of annoyance, with just the slightest trace of relief mixed in.

The deputy approached as Clay climbed out of his pickup. "Who are you?"

Clay tossed the portable radio he had been holding onto the truck seat and turned to the deputy. "Clay Purcell," he responded, offering nothing more.

"Mr. Purcell, I'm going to have to ask that you back up the drive and stay at the office for a while. The Carlsons shouldn't have sent you down this way."

"They didn't. At least I don't think they meant to. They motioned me on like they thought I was with you."

"Oh, right," Deputy Parsons nodded remembering the instructions he had given them. "Well, you're still going to have to go back and wait at the office."

"What's going on?" Clay ignored the deputy's instructions, not feeling too intimidated by this young deputy after his dealings with law enforcement over the past couple of days. Grover Parsons was not Trooper Collins of the Georgia Patrol after all.

"An investigation, Mr. Purcell. Sheriff's business, and you are going to have to turn around right now and go..."

"Is it the old Chevy with Texas plates?"

The reaction on the deputy's face told Clay his question had the desired effect. The deputy took a step back, so that he could see Clay's entire body. The look on his face turned from its initial surprise to stone.

"What do you know about that?"

"Quite a bit."

"I assume you have a good explanation for that, so start talking."

Two minutes later, Clay had explained how he came to be at the Creek Side Cabins on that sunny, fall afternoon.

"So you're the one the patrol stopped last night. I'll be damned. Well, you're a hardheaded son of a bitch. I'll say that for you." Grover Parsons shook his head before continuing. "So what is the girl to you?"

"I don't know. Maybe nothing, maybe something." Clay looked down at the ground trying to come up with a good answer, and finding none he said simply, "Conscience I guess. Guilt." He shrugged not able to give a better response.

He changed the subject and asked, "So, what's the plan. Have you spotted them."

"The plan is to stand by for the other units. You heard that on the radio you...borrowed."

"They said stand by if there was no threat to the girl. Is there a threat?"

"Well, not that I can tell," Parsons responded, clearly not comfortable with his answer.

"Not that you can tell? What does that mean?"

"Means...I don't know," said the deputy honestly, looking Clay in the eye. "I've been squatting here trying to decide what to do and come up with a plan. Truth is, I have no idea what is going on in that cabin."

"So, the girl could be in danger. There could be a threat."

"Could be," Parsons agreed, looking down and avoiding the look on Clay's face.

That look was a reflection of what Parsons was feeling inside, and the realization stung enough that he looked up and said, "You're right. I don't know if there's an *imminent* threat or not, but I know that if this is the suspect, the man has killed. If the girl is with him, nothing good is going to come from it. That would seem to be a pretty clear threat."

Parsons turned and walked towards his car.

"What are you gonna do?" Clay asked the young deputy, realizing for the first time that they were about the same age, and that the deputy must be about as scared as Clay suddenly was.

"Gonna check it out. Backup might be thirty minutes away, and I've been here fifteen already. As far as I'm concerned, there's a threat."

"I'll go with you."

"No," Parsons replied without looking as he reached in his car and pulled the shotgun from the rack between the front seats. "Go back to the office and wait. I'll let you know when things are in hand."

"I'm going with you." Clay's tone was firm.

The deputy regarded him thoughtfully for a moment. "Okay. You have a weapon?"

Clay shook his head.

"Take this," Parsons held out the Remington twelve gauge shotgun. "You've got five rounds. Use it to protect yourself only. You know how to use it?"

Clay replied by pumping a round into the chamber.

"Good. Now be careful, and let's hope nothing is going to happen. Sheriff finds out I handed you my shotgun, I'll get a bunch of time off...that is if I don't lose my job."

"I'll be careful," Clay assured him, holding the shotgun with a familiarity that put Parsons' mind slightly at ease. "Just for

318

protection. I got it. 'Course if it comes to that, I guess we're both gonna be in the middle of a shit storm," They exchanged a quick grin and a nod as they turned towards the cabin.

"You go to the rear. Stay in the tree line. There's a small back deck on each cabin. Watch that area. If he comes out, try and keep an eye on him, but don't let him see you if possible. Let the backup units know which way he went." Parsons paused and looked at Clay one last time. "That shotgun is for protection only. Remember."

With a final nod, the young men moved forward to confront the beast, slightly less confident than when they had been considering their plan, but committed just the same. They were not aware that this same beast had been the object of manhunts in a dozen other states. None had come so close before, or in such proximity to its fangs before, other than its victims.

82. To Hurt or Not to Hurt

The softness of his voice and the false tenderness were more frightening than if he had screamed at her. Awake and energized by his nap, Lylee was ready for the final feast.

He would use the girl up completely now. He would not stop until he had consumed everything. He would gorge himself until the pleading terror in her fear-widened eyes dimmed, and the eyes became empty.

Kneeling beside her, he whispered in her ear.

"Time to wake up."

Slowly, the girl's eyes opened, and she returned to the room. To the present. To him.

He stood up taking a grasping pull on her hair. His hand moved in a wide arc leaving a stinging slap on her face. Lyn was wrenched out of the faraway, safe place she had found until she brought her eyes up to meet his. When they did, they widened with fear.

Drifting back to reality, to the cabin, Lyn's eyes darted around the room trying to understand. Trying to remember where she was, why she was there. Wide, fear filled eyes swayed back and forth while her head was held stationary by his grip on her hair.

Slowly, she realized that they were still in the cabin, and the memory flooded back, unwanted, into her mind. She had to find a way back to the safe place, to the swaying pines and cool breezes, away from the man standing nude in front of her, tearing at her hair.

The curtains over the air conditioner hung limp. The air conditioner was off. Her arms were still secured to the chair. No cricket hummed and chirped. There was no escape.

"Let me explain how this is going to work," the man whispered into her ear, so close that she felt his breath on her neck. "We're going to spend some time together until you give me what I want. And you will give it to me. Understand?"

Lyn tried to nod her head, but his grip prevented her from moving. He could feel her try though.

"Good," Lylee said. "Now, I'm going to take the tape off of your mouth. We're going to talk."

Still holding her hair, he moved his left hand up to her throat until Lyn felt the knife press firmly against her trachea.

"If you make one sound, except to answer me or to talk when I say, anything at all, I am going to hurt you." He looked fiercely into her eyes. "I will hurt you bad. You believe me, don't you?"

She tried to nod again, and this time he let her hair go enough that she could move her head up and down a little.

"Good," he said while reaching down with the knife, cutting the plastic tie wraps that had held her in place since he had strapped her to the chair.

Lylee jerked her roughly out of the chair. She stood uncertainly. Her legs were numb. They tingled painfully as the blood began to flow through them. Lyn became conscious of the plastic she was standing on. Looking down, she saw dried red spots and smears on the plastic. She knew it was blood...her blood.

With the knife still at her throat, Lylee pushed her towards the bathroom. The door was partially closed, and he thrust her in bumping her hard into the door.

"Clean up. Five minutes. Pee or shit if you need to, but get clean," was all he said.

He turned away leaving the door open. Lyn looked into the mirror and saw the dried blood and cuts that covered her shoulders and chest. She stared at herself. The image staring back at her brought her back farther from the faraway safe place and closer to reality than she had been in hours. Was this image really her? Was this really happening?

"Clean up! And be quick!" Lylee said sharply from just outside the door.

Lyn picked up a washcloth, wet it, and began to wipe her face, arms, and chest. Tears fell across her cheeks. She was alone. What was going to happen, would happen.

She may be alive for the moment, as long as the man needed her, but she knew that her life was already slowly draining away, washed down the sink with the reddish brown drops rinsed from the washcloth in her hand. The image in the mirror was a shell. Soon

321

there would be nothing of substance left.

In the bedroom, Lylee busied himself with straightening the plastic under the chair and making sure there were no telltale signs of what had been taking place in the room. This was not the first time he had toyed with his prey before the kill, but it was definitely the longest period of time he had allowed himself to do so.

Again, the cautious predator came into his mind warning him. End this. Quickly, before they come, end it!

He pushed the cautious voice out of his brain. The need to extract what he wanted, what he needed, burned in him. In his mind, he shouted back at the cautious voice. I will end it when I have her...all of her!

He looked into the bathroom. The girl stood in front of the sink, robotically wiping her body. The washrag was streaked with dried blood. Remember the rag, he thought. Have to take the rag and towel with what was left of the girl. But not just yet.

Lyn's right wrist stung as the man reached into the bathroom and jerked her roughly. The skin where the plastic tie had secured her to the car and then to the chair in the cabin, was a raw, red, bleeding sore spot that burned at his touch.

Pulling her to the spot on the plastic in front of the chair, he stood close in front of her. His hand moved up between her legs. Her body stiffened.

"You ignoring me? Don't." The word was a warning.

Lyn tried hard to focus on the curtains. Tried hard to find a way to the safe place, as she had done before. It was gone, and she could not find her way there.

"Do – not – ignore – me," he said, each word a separate and distinct threat.

His hand moved to the inside of her thigh. He grabbed the skin and pinched hard.

Lyn gasped at the sudden pain. She tried to push his hand away with her left hand, despite the knife that rested point first against her abdomen, as they stood close. He pinched harder.

"I warned you. I'm afraid that's gonna leave a mark." Under the fierce eyes, the grin was back.

Lyn forced her eyes to find his and looked into the gray eyes of the beast. They were full of life. They observed her, considered her every action and reaction with an inhuman, animal curiosity, like the cat toying with a captured mouse.

Her gaze into his eyes was what he wanted. He released his grip, and the sharp pain from the pinch subsided.

"Don't you want to look at me?" he asked, again taunting.

Lyn said nothing.

"You know you should talk and be nice. After all, I'm the one who's taking you to Canada." His words mocked her.

Lyn blinked and said nothing. Canada was gone.

She became aware that the man was stroking himself with the hand that had pinched her thigh. She stared blankly into the gray eyes, not wanting to see or know what he was doing. The trauma and fear were suffocating her. Any reason she had left was rapidly departing, leaving an empty shell behind. She welcomed the emptiness.

He grinned at her. "Did it really hurt?'

Lyn said nothing. She just looked at him through tear clouded eyes.

Lylee took her wrist and twisted. Lyn gasped as he bent the wrist backwards.

"I said, did it hurt?'

"Yes, it hurt," Lyn gasped.

"Did it hurt bad?" Lylee twisted harder on her wrist.

The pain moved up her arm to her elbow, and Lyn could only whisper through clenched teeth, "Yes. It hurt really bad." The pain in her wrist and elbow was blinding. "Please, stop....please," she whispered.

Lylee released his grip, and her limp arm fell to the side of her trembling body.

"Good. So which would you rather be? Hurt or dead?" He looked at her, and the animal was back in his eyes staring hard into her. "I can make dead hurt a lot more than that."

Lyn said nothing. He couldn't really mean for her to answer.

But Lylee did mean for her to answer and choose. It was part of

323

the game, and he needed an answer.

"Which? Dead or hurt? Answer me!"

Forcing her to make a choice, to choose the pain he would inflict, was like honey to him. Her torment was his sweet. His tongue moved over his lips as if he could taste the sweetness thrown out by her raging emotions. Fear. Confusion. Hopelessness.

Lyn saw the contortion of pleasure on his face. She didn't understand it, but she knew she must answer.

"Please. Just hurt me...don't kill me...please."

Lylee smiled happily. "All right then. Hurt it is. You know I'll give you what you want, honey. Now you give me what I want."

Lylee's mind and body were awash with surging arousal. Lyn trembled at the realization that she had taken a step, a long stride, towards the end.

She was losing, and soon he would have all that he wanted from her. When that was done, it would be over. He would feed on her living remains until her corpse ceased twitching and she was no longer alive. She wondered whether not being alive would be better.

She was oblivious to the knock at the door, but the moment of surprise and indecision she saw in the gray animal eyes caused her brow to furrow in confusion. Something had happened. What, she wondered.

Pushing her hard into the chair, he moved quickly and lightly to the window where he peered out between curtains. His thumb rotated the large knife in his hand as he contemplated the source of the knock at the door.

Then a voice from some faraway place drifted into the room, pulling Lyn ever so slightly from the reality of the cabin.

"Rye County sheriff!" the voice called. "Need to speak with you for a minute. Open the door please."

324

83. Silence in the Woods

Standing on the porch to the side of the door and away from the window, Deputy Grover Parsons saw the curtains part slightly as someone peered out.

"Open the door please," he repeated. "I need to speak with you for a minute."

"Just a minute, deputy," a male voice with a definite Texas twang called out from behind the door. "My wife and I been sleeping and, you know, well, we're not dressed. Let me grab my pants!"

"Right, sir. Just hurry up and open the door!" Grover called back. His hand was on the pistol at his side.

Inside the cabin, Leyland Torkman, felt the pressure of being the hunted, and although it was a new sensation, he did not panic. Lyn watched motionless from the chair as he pulled on his blue jeans and tee shirt and slid his feet into his shoes.

Looking at Lyn, he said in a hissing whisper, "Any sound and I will slit your throat and gut you before I kill him. You understand? He cannot save you, but I can hurt you. And I will hurt you...bad."

He stared at her, waiting, and was about to speak again when she finally nodded her comprehension. Lyn watched from the chair in helpless torment as he moved to the door, desperate to call out, to make some sound, but frozen instead. It was as if she were watching the drama play out on a screen, and she could only sit, breathlessly waiting for the next terrible scene.

Partially opening the door with his left hand, he peered out, the hand holding the edge of the door as if to slam it shut at any second. From behind, Lyn could see the hunting knife in the waistband of his jeans over his right hip. She could not see the deputy, who was so close, but still an invisible voice to her.

As the door opened, she became aware of the rushing of the creek outside. It seemed to rush into the room, the sound pulling her a little further into the reality of the here and now.

"Hey, deputy. What can we do for you?" Lylee's voice was light and friendly, and non-menacing. He could see that the deputy's hand rested lightly on the butt of his sidearm.

"Need to come in and talk to you…and your wife."

"My wife, too?"

"Your wife, too," Grover replied, pausing and then adding a formal, "sir".

Parsons watched as the man at the door turned his head and called over his shoulder, "Honey, cover yourself up! We got company."

And with that, the man at the door opened it slightly farther to allow the deputy to enter the cabin. The deputy started into the room, tensed and alert, eyes searching for the girl somewhere in the dim interior of the cabin.

Something glittered in the afternoon sunlight shining through the door. Parsons' eyes flicked to the right. The reflected light sparkled from the Texas longhorn ring on the finger of the man's hand, holding the door, just at Parsons' eye level.

It was an awkward way to hold the door, the deputy thought. At the same moment, he knew that it was the ring described and noted carefully on the small pad in the breast pocket of his shirt, along with the description of a medium built man with a Texas twang and driving an old Chevy with Texas plates. He knew it instantly, but it was an instant too late.

As the deputy's hand began to lift the pistol from its holster, the man's left hand jerked the door fully open and then came across the back of the deputy's shoulders until the forearm was across the front of Parsons' throat.

Simultaneously, the knife moved with practiced precision and uncanny speed from the waistband of his jeans into Lylee's right hand and then to the opening between the front and rear panels of the protective vest the deputy wore. The deputy's pistol had not fully cleared its holster when the heavy blade was pushed deep into his side.

A gasp, followed by a deep-throated grunt of pain escaped through the deputy's quivering lips. He clutched at the man who had just taken his life. They stood in an intimate embrace in the doorway. The deputy struggled to turn and put his arms around the man that

326

had killed him while the other tried to extricate himself from the grasp of his dying victim.

As light and life faded from young Deputy Parsons' eyes, he saw the girl, seated on the chair across the room. Their eyes met, and he struggled to hold more tightly to the man in his grasp. The girl's eyes were wide and staring into the deputy's face.

"Run."

The girl stared back. He had said something, and somehow, dimly she knew he had spoken to her.

"Run!" The deputy's voice was a hoarse grunt.

Grover Parsons sank to his knees as the girl's eyes cleared with understanding. She sprang from the chair and through the cabin's back door as the deputy's eyes clouded and his life bled out onto the cabin floor. Yet still, in death, he clutched at the man who had killed him.

It only took seconds for Lylee to pull himself from the deputy's death grip. But those seconds were enough for Lyn to make her attempt at escape, and as she moved, her mind came crashing back into the real world of the present.

Clay knelt in the foliage at the edge of the tree line behind the cabin, resting the shotgun on his bent knee. Deputy Parsons had disappeared around the front of the cabin not more than three minutes earlier, when Clay heard the noises. They were indistinguishable, muffled sounds, barely audible over the creek's rushing. For a moment, he thought to go to the front and help Deputy Parsons with whatever was happening, but then the rear door of the cabin slammed open.

Startled, he raised the shotgun to his shoulder, fearing what might happen next. Kneeling in the brush contemplating taking a man's life was far different from sitting in a tree stand stalking white tail deer.

An instant later, he lowered the shotgun to his side and stood up. The girl, completely nude and covered in bleeding cuts, ran across the cabin's small backyard. He stood still in the shock of the moment.

327

It was Lyn. It was the girl they had dropped at the truck stop just yesterday morning; the girl that had become his obsession. The object of his pursuit and search was before him, and yet seeing her so suddenly and in that condition immobilized him. He watched her run, directly at him, her eyes unrecognizing. He tried to speak and move, and think what to do next.

But what to do next took care of itself. The cabin's rear door banged again. A man in tee shirt and jeans sprinted from the back door and into the yard, clearly in pursuit of the girl.

Lifting the shotgun to his shoulder, Clay shouted, "Drop! Lyn, drop!"

For the first time in her panicked flight, Lyn became aware of the young man in work clothes standing in front of her. He shouted something. He looked familiar. Why was he shouting? What was he shouting?

She saw him raise a big gun to his shoulder, pointing it at her. Why would he do that? Why would he point a gun at her? He was shouting again.

Fearing the shotgun's blast, one more in a long series of fears she had faced in the last two days, Lyn dropped to the ground. Behind her, Lylee slowed as he became aware of the young man at the edge of the woods pointing the shotgun at him.

"Whoa! Hold on, don't shoot, son. I'm one of the good guys."

"Stop right there!" Clay gripped the shotgun tightly. "Who are you? Where's Deputy Parsons?"

"I'm Tommy Sims," Lylee said, the lie tripping off his tongue as if it were a truth he had learned from his mama. "Maintenance man here. I was down by the creek, and I heard the commotion so I came to check it out. Found the deputy and some other fella inside on the floor and saw the girl running out the back door." He smiled and put his hands out, showing the young man that they were empty. "Just trying to help. Please take it easy with that shotgun, buddy."

The young man was still wary and cautious, but Lylee saw the small signs as the boy relaxed, just slightly. A small change in his posture. A slight variation in his breathing.

Lying in the cool, damp grass between the two men, Lyn became

328

aware of talking above her. Why were they talking? She recognized one of the voices. It was the boy, Clay. He had given her a ride. She closed her eyes and smelled the fragrant grass.

The other voice spoke again and she recognized it too. It was...the man. Her throat struggled to form words. Her breath came in pants, and she tried to push herself up to flee once more, but could barely come to her knees.

"No," the sound came from her in a whisper. "No, no." She struggled to form other words, to warn the young man. None came.

Hearing the whispers, Clay looked down at the girl. That brief second was all that the Lylee required.

Reaching in his rear pocket, he pulled the small .38 Smith and Wesson taken from old Harold Sims in his moment of death two nights earlier. An instant later, as the young man with the shotgun just barely became aware of his movement, he pulled the trigger of the small revolver, and then pulled it two more times.

Thunder cracked over her head, and Lyn tried to claw her way into the ground. And then after the last thunderous crack, a deeper louder roar that seemed to shake the ground and grass around her, pounded down on her, taking her breath away.

The three bullets slammed Clay in the chest and abdomen plunging him into stunned and breathless shock. He fell with the realization that he had failed. He had found Lyn only to know that she would be murdered.

The ground came up and slammed him in the back. The shotgun rose slightly from the impact. He became aware that he still held the gun and that his finger was still locked on the trigger as he fell. With one last conscious thought, Clay put the slight amount of pressure required on the trigger, and the shotgun roared as it bucked from his hand. It was the last thing he knew.

Leyland, "Lylee", Torkman, predator, howled and snarled his curse in pain. The shotgun blast had not been a direct hit, but three .00 buck pellets had struck him in the left leg, one piercing his kneecap.

The voice of caution screeched in his ear, End it! I told you! END IT!

The agonizing throbbing in his leg and the screech inside his head forced him up to stand on his remaining good leg. The girl lay trembling in the grass before him, face buried in the dirt.

He would have preferred the knife. Even in the disappointment of not having all that he wanted from the girl, the knife would have made the end better...sweeter.

But the knife was lodged in the side of the deputy lying on the cabin floor. He had left it there in his pursuit of the girl. The small revolver would have to do.

There were three rounds left. It would only take one. He raised his arm and pointed the pistol at the back of the girl's head. The muzzle of the pistol was barely two feet from its target. He smiled at the thought that the medical examiner would find powder residue in the wound.

The Pickham County pickup came fishtailing off the highway and down the drive of the Creek Side Cabins. Roaring past the office, George and Sharon ignored the couple still standing there arm-in-arm and pointing down the drive. They knew from the alert given by the Rye County deputy where they were going.

At the turn along the creek, they saw no one by the Rye County car. The deputy had advised dispatch that he was going to check the situation and then explained tersely to his sheriff over the open radio waves that if the girl was there, she was in danger, imminent or not. Every minute of delay constituted an increase in the threat to the girl. He was going to check it out, despite the sheriff's objections.

After that, no one had come on the radio to argue with him. Any one of the units responding might have made the same decision, probably would have.

Correct procedure in law enforcement is often a very subjective thing. This was not accounting or engineering. Answers were not defined by mathematics and science.

The right or wrong thing to do usually depended largely on an officer's interpretation of the facts, the perceived threat, and a million other subjective bits of information. Often, there was no absolute 'right' answer, and the right or wrong of it was determined by the outcome, or the press, or the courts years later.

Gunning the engine as they made the turn along the creek, George brought the pickup to a sliding halt just short of the last cabin. From the angle, he could see that the front door was open. There was no movement inside.

The crack and roar of Sharon Price's pistol reverberated through the cab of the truck as George started to climb out, scaring the shit out of him in the process. Price stood just outside the truck with the door open, surrounded by the dust of the pickup's braking. Her pistol was pointed towards the backyard, visible from their angle on the road.

The pop of a small caliber weapon and the whiz of a round overhead caused George to crouch by the car as Sharon's weapon discharged again. Peering over the hood of the pickup, George saw a man limp into the woods carrying something that looked like a rifle or shotgun. Clearly, it was not the weapon he had fired at George and Sharon.

Two bodies were visible on the ground where the man had stood a moment before.

"Did you hit him…or anything at that range?" George asked, judging the distance to the backyard at about seventy-five yards, a long distance for an accurate shot from Price's nine-millimeter pistol.

"No, pretty sure I didn't, but he was about to put a round into one of those bodies. Had to get his attention." Still holding the pistol, Sharon Price had jogged half way up the side yard towards the back before George made it around the pickup and started after her. "Come on," she called over her shoulder.

Approaching the bodies on the ground, they slowed. George could barely bring himself to examine them. They were bloody. The girl was nude. The young man was… "Shit," he said. "That's the kid from last night, isn't it?" George stood with his Glock at the ready, in a two-handed stance, watching the woods where the man who had fired at them had disappeared.

Price knelt to check the bodies as George stood watch. "Yeah. It's him, Clay was his name." Three spreading red spots covered his work shirt, the same shirt he had been wearing the night before as

331

they sat talking in the state patrol office.

She turned towards the nude girl. "This would be the girl they left at the truck stop, the one on the voice mail." She knelt beside the girl and placed her hand on her head as if trying to take away the terror and fear she had felt in the last day, in her last moments.

The tear that ran down George's face dropped silently into the grass beside the girl. Late. Again.

Frustration and desperate anger rose in him, and something else. George Mackey was the hunter now. He knew how to hunt, and he would hunt down this animal.

The blood trail on the ground showed the way. Young Clay must have given a good account of himself before he went down. George moved towards the woods but stopped at Price's next words.

"She's alive."

"What?" George spoke the word softly as a prayer and looked at Sharon who was now kneeling beside the girl.

Sharon placed her hand on the girl's bare, bloody back. There was an unmistakable shudder, followed by a low, soft sob and then a whispered question, too low to be understood.

"What's that, baby? What did you say?" Sharon Price knelt with her mouth near the girl's ear, hand still softly resting on her back.

"Is – he – gone?" The words were spoken so softly and with evident terror of the possible response that they were barely audible, even with Sharon so close.

"He's gone baby. He's gone. He won't hurt you now. We won't let him." Price whispered the words into the girl's ear, putting an arm around her on the ground and stroking her hair as if she were a child having a bad dream.

"He came for me."

"Who baby. Who came for you?"

"The boy. His name is Clay. I left him a message, and he came for me."

"I know. I know." Sharon's words were whispered softly as she looked at the young man in the bloody shirt and brushed away her own tears.

"He came for me. He saved me. Where is he?"

Sharon had already shifted on her knees to the young man's body. Gently, she felt for the carotid artery, and then more firmly pressed into his neck with two fingers, a look of surprise and urgency on her face. Pulling the portable radio from her belt, Price looked up at George Mackey and nodded. Her eyes burned into his taking only a second to say, "Go! Do what you have to do. Find him. End this." And then she raised the radio and spoke.

As he disappeared into the tree line, George heard Price's call for EMT's. "...person shot...vital signs weak..."

The blood trail was clear at first. In the low foliage and brush at the edge of the woods, it was easily visible. It did not appear to be arterial bleeding. Not enough blood and not spread far enough to be from a spurting artery. It was likely that he would not bleed out before George found him. That was good, George thought. Very good.

As he moved deeper into the gloom of the woods, the trail became harder to follow. The blood blended in with the leaves and pine straw on the ground and was not as visible as when spattered across the green foliage in the daylight.

George lifted his head from his inspection of the ground to peer into the thick foliage around him. He was keenly aware that the danger here was watching the blood trail on the ground too closely and not his surroundings, becoming an easy, unaware target.

There was a loud popping bang not fifty yards away, followed by the sounds of rustling leaves and snapping twigs, and ending with an almost simultaneous dull thud as the bullet plowed into a tree to his right. Okay. I'm in the general vicinity, at least.

George moved around a tree to his front, advanced a few yards, staying low, and then found cover behind a large hickory. His efforts drew a quick bang followed by the buzz of the round flying by into the ground.

Closer, but still no immediate threat. The shooter was not much of a shot, he thought. Still he had a gun, and it only took one round to make him a great shot, and George a very dead deputy.

George took stock and thought. Looked like three rounds into the boy, Clay. One fired at them as they pulled up in the pickup. Two here in the woods. That made six. Unless he had reloads, he was out of ammo, for the revolver at least. And George doubted that he had any reloads. He knew that the pistol must be the one he took from Harold Sims, and it was not likely that Sims was carrying any extra rounds.

That left the long weapon, rifle or shotgun. George suspected it was the deputy's shotgun loaned to the boy to watch the back door while he checked things out. It was just a guess, but it made sense. He had no idea how young Clay had found them and showed up at the Creek Side Cabins, but having done so, he was clearly not the kind to let the deputy go to the door of the cabin without some backup. As George pondered it, he was sure the weapon must be the deputy's shotgun.

His thoughts were confirmed a second later when a loud roar slammed through the woods sending numerous pellets ricocheting through the trees. Shotgun it was.

So, the shooter had taken one round from Clay and was bleeding. He had fired one wild round into the trees, either to draw George out or to see what he might hit. That left three to five rounds or so, depending on the shotgun's magazine, the make of the shotgun, whether there was a round in the chamber with a full magazine or whether Clay had had to pump a round in before firing. In short, George had no way of knowing exactly how many rounds the shooter had left.

He took a breath and decided he wasn't going to wait to find out. Slowly, he moved his head to the side of the hickory and studied the woods ahead, showing just enough of his face to allow his right eye to see forward.

The light in the woods was dim and dusky in the waning autumn afternoon. The sun set early in the mountain valleys where the horizon was a thousand feet above your head.

It occurred to George that he did not want to be out here in the dark, looking for a wounded man with a shotgun. He studied the woods ahead, hunting and searching one small area at a time, eliminating an area with his eyes and then moving to the next, looking for any movement. There was none, except for the rustling of squirrels in the trees overhead.

George wanted very much to pull his head back behind the safety of the large tree trunk, but he knew that he couldn't. He had to spot the shooter before he was spotted.

So far, the shooting had been erratic and not aimed. It was suppression fire, hoping to discourage the pursuer. At other times, it might have suppressed the hell out of George. But not this time. George Mackey would see this through. He may have been too late to prevent much of anything, but he would not be late for the ending.

Staring through the dim light, George's eyes were drawn to something that didn't look right. A large tree lay on the ground not fifty feet away, probably knocked over by one of the springtime thunderstorms. Protruding up from the fallen trunk was something not quite...normal. It was straight...too straight to be a natural limb or branch.

Peering intently, George saw that it looked to be long and cylindrical. And then it moved.

It didn't move greatly. The end just waivered and swung slightly, making a small arc in the air as if someone was holding it and was moving. George waited.

When the crown of a head slowly pulled itself above the fallen tree trunk, it was all George could do to keep from pulling his head back behind the hickory. But he remained motionless, knowing that the man holding the shotgun would have a hard time spotting him.

Hurt, bleeding, and in pain, the man with the shotgun would want to hide behind the fallen tree and lick his wounds, like any animal. George knew that as long as he remained immobile, it was unlikely that the man would spot him. In the dim light, he would just appear to be a lump on the side of a tree.

George watched, still and quiet. After two long minutes of searching, the man slowly withdrew his head down and out of sight. The barrel of the shotgun, still visible above the tree, wavered and then settled into a position pointing off to George's left. The Glock in George's hand felt light and insubstantial up against the shotgun, but considering the situation, it was the right weapon.

Distant sounds of sirens filtered into the woods, muffled and dispersed by the trees and foliage, but audible. The EMT's and backup units from Rye County and the state patrol would be arriving at any minute.

It took roughly ten seconds for George to consider the odds. The man was injured, hurt, and bleeding. He was armed with a shotgun but did not know where George was.

On the other hand, George knew exactly where he was and knew that he was a killer, and that he enjoyed killing in painful, terrible ways. He would kill again if given the chance because that was what he loved doing. It was what he needed to do.

During those ten seconds taking stock of the situation and considering the odds, the images floated in front of him. Old Mr. Sims lying in a pool of blood in the church parking lot, his kidneys and liver turned to jelly by the savage thrusts of the knife. The girl thrown into the weeds on the side of Ridley Road, a hundred cuts on her body and then strangled to death. The girl, Lyn, nude on the ground, covered in the same tortuous cuts and alive by the grace of...who? Young Clay with three bullets in his chest, turning his shirt bright red. The deputy from Rye County, not yet found and status unknown, who had decided to check things out, saving the life of a girl he did not know.

As the last of those ten seconds ticked away, the images moved away and George sprang from behind the hickory. Moving to the right, he stayed out of the direct line of the shotgun barrel.

Crashing through the foliage and fallen limbs covering the ground under the trees, he was heard instantly by the man with the shotgun. A roaring burst went crashing through the woods to his left. The killer's head popped above the tree trunk searching for his target. It took him several seconds to acquire the man crouching and running towards him through the trees. George stumbled, then steadied himself and leapt the fallen tree trunk as the man was trying to bring the barrel of the shotgun around to bear.

George slid in the leaves and debris as he landed, twisting his knee painfully. It didn't matter.

Looking into the barrel of the Glock from a distance of five feet, the man's hand froze. The eyes staring back at him over the sights of

336

the handgun were focused and hard. There would be no hesitation with this man. No moment of uncertainty. Slowly and deliberately, he laid the shotgun on the ground beside him.

After the shotgun's roar and the sounds of George's rushing assault on the fallen tree trunk, an eerie silence had enveloped the woods. George looked into the eyes of his quarry and saw...nothing. They were empty.

The animal spoke.

"You got me, deputy." Lylee lifted one hand in surrender while gingerly touching the bloody mess that was his left knee and leg with the other. "That was a hell of a thing, charging at me like that...hell of a thing."

He smiled boyishly up at the big deputy holding the pistol pointed at his face. It was the friendly grin of a boy bested by his friend in a wrestling match and giving up good-naturedly. It was disarming. It was one of Lylee's best performances. Considering the pain in his leg and the pistol in his face, it was a great performance...and it was of no use.

Looking into the deputy's eyes, the uselessness of his masterful act dawned on him. Slowly, like the sun rising over the swamp chasing away the dark shadows, he understood. The realization filled his eyes, glaring back at the deputy.

George waited, allowing the awareness to settle in until...the man...the animal...snarled.

There were no words, just bared teeth between which the guttural, primal growl hissed and grunted out.

The Glock bucked in his hand, filling the silent woods with a single sharp explosion. The echo faded slowly until there was silence again.

Doubled over on his side, the man clutched his chest, snarling and thrashing in the dirt. The gray eyes flashed up at the deputy who had killed him until the light slowly faded from them. Narrowing to slits, they stared vacantly into the dirt as the man's head slumped to the side. Then he was dead.

84. Done

Covered in a metallic looking thermal blanket Sharon Price had retrieved from the Pickham County pickup's emergency kit, Lyn heard the final roar of thunder. It came distantly, filtering its way through the woods and out into the open yard of the cabin.

Price, kneeling beside the young man with three holes in his body, looked up, and her hand moved to the pistol on her belt. Then all was quiet again, and she went back to her work trying to stop the blood that oozed from the boy into the red, Georgia clay.

The roar and scream of racing engines and sirens filled the air. Vehicles began pulling into the drive along the creek, and as they came to a stop, one by one they cut their sirens until the air around the cabin was quiet again and hushed except for the rushing of the creek.

The sound of tumbling water seemed to wash over everything, cleansing away what had happened there. It was reassuring. The creek would be there after the people had departed, gurgling and washing the evil memories away, until all that would remain were the trees and the hills and the water.

An ambulance came roaring up the rise from the drive into the backyard of the cabin. The doors flung open, and two paramedics raced towards them.

Sharon stood up and saw two troopers and a Ryc County deputy run across the yard on foot towards the woods to be met by George Mackey making his way out of the tree line. He spoke to them briefly and then pointed into the woods. The deputy and troopers nodded and then fanned out, moving deliberately and carefully into the trees.

One of the paramedics looked up from Clay. She and her partner were working quickly and efficiently to stop the bleeding and start an IV. She nodded at the girl huddled and shivering under the thin thermal blanket.

"Injuries?" she queried Sharon.

"A lot of cuts and bruises. Not lethal, but she bled out a bit. Bleeding seems pretty much stopped. Mostly shock and mental trauma."

The paramedic nodded, turning back to her work on Clay. "There's a heavier blanket in the back of the ambulance in the equipment locker. Get it and wrap it around her. Warm her up good and put her on the cot in the back of the ambulance."

Rye County Sheriff, John Siler, walked carefully up the steps of the cabin to the open front door. There was no movement from inside. Being from the old school, he carried a revolver, not an automatic, and the Smith and Wesson Model 60, .357 magnum was gripped snugly in his right hand.

All of the activity was happening at the back of the cabin and in the woods to the rear. But his deputy was not in the backyard and had not been seen. He stepped to the side so as not to approach the doorway head on. Easing along the wall he called out softly, "Grover, you in there?"

Hearing no response, the sheriff moved to the door and turned into it, the .357 extended in front of him in a two handed grip, pointed slightly down.

"Grover, you in..." Sheriff Siler stopped mid-sentence as his worst fears were realized.

Stepping over the young deputy's feet, he squatted by his side trying to avoid the pooling blood on the floor and felt his neck for a carotid pulse. The quantity of blood on the floor told the experienced law enforcement officer that there was no point in checking, but he did so anyway, mostly because there was nothing else to do.

A large hunting knife protruded in an ugly way from the boy's side. Siler almost reached out to remove the offending blade, but refrained. Removing the knife could worsen the deputy's injuries, but Grover was dead. His injuries could be no worse. The sheriff left the knife in place because it was evidence. It would be retrieved during the crime scene investigation or after the autopsy.

Reaching for his portable radio, he started to call for the paramedics, but then put the radio back in its holder on his belt. Grover Parsons was gone. The others might make it. Grover would not. It was a matter of logic, reason, and best use of available

339

resources, and it broke Siler's heart.

The sheriff stepped out onto the front porch, sat down on the top step, put his head in his hands, and cried for the boy, who less than an hour ago, he had tried to convince over the radio to wait for backup. Grover Parsons had done what he had to do. He did his duty, and the young girl would survive because of it.

Sheriff Siler would now do his duty and try to explain to Gerald Parsons that his son, who just happened to be on duty, and who just happened to stop for lunch in Crichton, had had a friendly conversation with Gannet Carlson. And during that friendly chat, he discovered that a murderer and his next victim were holed up in a cabin at the Carlson's. He would explain that the son, who was the pride and joy of his daddy, was gone, never to return, a hunting knife protruding obscenely from his side while blood pooled thickly around his cold body.

He would do his duty and tell Gerald Parsons all of this, but first Sheriff Siler sat on the top step while his tears dripped softly onto the boards of the porch steps, soaking into the weathered wood.

More sirens and more units arrived on the drive beside the creek. The ambulance backed rapidly across the cabin's yard guided by deputies and volunteer firefighters who had arrived at the scene. Sharon watched it bump down onto the drive and accelerate rapidly up the hill towards the highway.

In the rear, the young girl, Lyn, lay on one side, wrapped in blankets, traumatized and nearly comatose from her ordeal. Clay lay across from her, carefully attended to by the paramedic and fighting for his life.

On the winding roads, the ambulance would take twenty minutes at high-speed, to make the journey to the little league field in Crichton where there was space enough for the life flight helicopter to land and take the two patients aboard. From there they would be transported to the emergency trauma center in Athens.

The girl would survive her physical injuries. The mental and emotional traumas were a different matter. Undoubtedly, those scars would leave far deeper marks on her, and their effect would be far more devastating in the coming years.

The young man was a different story. His hold on life was tenuous. The bullets had managed to miss his heart and aorta. A hit to either would have surely resulted in his immediate death, and the round from the shotgun that slowed the killer and his execution of the girl might never have been fired.

Fortunately for Clay, the rounds from the short-barreled .38 were underpowered, hardball ammunition. Had Harold Sims loaded the weapon with high-powered hollow points, Clay would not be unconscious in the rear of the ambulance. He would be lying in the cabin's backyard waiting for the crime scene techs to take their pictures and gather evidence from around his corpse.

Still, the outcome for Clay was very much in doubt. Knowing this, the medic driver pushed the unwieldy ambulance to its limits around the curves while those in the back hung on.

George Mackey limped over to the spot where the young man had lain. The ground was stained with his blood. A few feet away, a smaller stain marked the spot where the shotgun pellets had torn into the killer's leg.

Footsteps approached from behind and George turned. Sharon Price looked him squarely in the eye from a distance of three feet. No words were spoken. After a few seconds, George nodded and Sharon returned the nod. Words were unnecessary. It was done.

85. Epilogue

Three days later, Chief Deputy Ronnie Kupman sat across from Sheriff Klineman's desk while the latter studied the papers clipped neatly into a manila file. After several minutes, the sheriff straightened the papers and closed the file, placing it precisely in the center of his desk. He pushed it with two fingers towards his chief deputy as if its continued presence might be infectious.

"So, George got him," the sheriff said. It was not a question. It was a statement, tinged with distaste and disappointment, which he was unable to control.

"Yes, he did. He and the GBI and the Rye County deputy who found the car and the killer."

"But Mackey was the one who got him in the end, alone." Again the distaste with undertones of incredulity.

"Yes. George got him. Killed him if that's what you mean."

"Yes, about that," the sheriff said pausing before continuing. "The report states the subject was shot at close range."

"Right."

"It also says that the trajectory of the round that killed him came from about three feet above and five feet away." Klineman regarded Kupman carefully, seeking any sign of concern or deception. The chief deputy, however, was completely unconcerned and unperturbed.

"Also correct, Sheriff."

"And the shotgun was on the ground beside the subject...on the left side. He was right-handed?"

"Yes. From the thrusts of the knife that killed the Rye County deputy and Mr. Sims, it does appear that the subject was right-handed." Ronnie nodded, smiling at the sheriff's query as he crossed his legs comfortably.

Klineman had had enough. "Cut the bullshit, Kupman!"

"I'm not sure what you mean Sheriff." But Ronnie Kupman knew exactly what the sheriff of Pickham County meant.

"The shooting should be investigated! You know as well as I do

342

that this was not a legal shooting." He stopped to control the anger rising inside, and the heartburn that accompanied it, and then continued through gritted teeth. "George Mackey executed the killer, Leyland Torkman."

"He did?" Kupman raised his eyebrows in mock surprise. "And you know this because...?"

"Because my common sense tells me so, and the evidence in the report points in that direction."

"Well, the report from Rye County doesn't..."

"Don't talk to me about Rye County. I know Sheriff Siler. He loves his deputies as if they were his own kids. He would accept any report that justified the elimination of the killer of one of 'his boys', legalities be damned."

"Is that so?" Kupman returned the sheriff's angry gaze calmly. "Hmm. Well, there's also the GBI's report. I believe it says 'no evidence that the shooting was not legal and justifiable, performed in the due course of attempting to arrest a violent felon who had already committed two known murders and two attempted murders at the time of the shooting'. I'm just paraphrasing, of course, but that seemed to be the gist of the report...as I recall it." He smiled serenely at the man the voters of Pickham County had made his boss.

Sheriff Klineman swallowed hard in an attempt to remain calm, or at least as calm as possible. "Well, then we will conduct our own investigation into the shooting."

"We will?"

"Yes. We will, and as I apparently can't trust anyone else to handle it honestly, I will conduct it myself."

"Really? Do you think that is wise, Sheriff?" The question's tone carried the undercurrent of a threat. Ronnie let that sink in for a moment before continuing in a conciliatory tone. "I mean that George Mackey is a hero in Pickham County. The people love him, the press loves him, and the GBI is standing behind him." Kupman gave a sighing shrug. "If you try to hang George out to dry on this, it might backfire on you." And then Ronnie Kupman looked his boss squarely in the eye and said with finality. "I guarantee you that it will backfire on you."

"What? What, did you just say?" The sheriff seemed about to come out of his chair. "Did you just threaten me? Speak up! Say that again."

Ronnie shook his head in disgust as he leaned forward and spoke, raising his voice for the first time. "Sheriff, I know that you record the conversations that take place in this office. Hell, it's no secret, everyone knows. So, I'll say it again. If you try to bring charges against a deputy who has been exonerated by the GBI and who did this county a valuable service, and who is a hero by all accounts, it will backfire on you. I'll be even more clear…you will regret it." He leaned back in his seat, continuing. "If you want to take that as a threat, so be it. As far as I'm concerned," and Kupman raised his voice for the recorder again, "I am offering advice to the Sheriff of Pickham County. As the chief deputy, that is my duty."

Chief Deputy Ronnie Kupman took the shooting file off the sheriff's desk and walked out of the office, allowing the door to thump closed behind him.

The secret video camera, which everyone knew about, recorded Sheriff Richard Klineman sitting motionless and staring at the desktop for a long while. After a few minutes, his hand reached under the desk and the video went black.

****

Bob Shaklee leaned against the doorframe of the office in a building in Savannah. Located in a quiet office park filled with trees and manicured grass, the building was leased by the state for the GBI. Inside the building, investigators considered the terrible things contained in the case files on their desks and searched for answers. Outside, landscapers mowed the grass and planted flowers, and lunchtime joggers wandered the paths of the park.

"Forensics are in."

Sharon Price looked up from the follow-up report she was writing. Leyland 'Lylee' Torkman it turns out was not missed. After tracing the vehicle identification number on the Chevy, she had started the interviews. Work – he did his job, kept his nose clean, and people did not interfere with him. Neighbors – he was an unknown, no interaction with anyone, kept quietly to himself, although Mrs. Abbot across the street always knew there was something 'strange' about him. Friends – none. Relatives – none. Criminal history – none, at least none ever recorded, until now.

"That's good. Anything?" Her eyes met his, conveying her unspoken concern about what the report might contain.

"No. Not really." He smiled back and gave just the slightest shake of his head acknowledging her concern and removing it at the same time. "The rounds that hit the boy were plain enough. We were able to find one of your rounds fired from the truck in a tree trunk at the tree line, but we dug .00 buck shot out of the trees in the woods for three days trying to recreate the scene for the follow-up on the shooting report."

Sharon placed the papers in her hand on the desk and looked up and directly into Bob Shaklee's eyes.

"And? What's the follow up?"

"Nothing much, I guess." Shaklee broke away from her gaze and looked out the window behind her where beds of geraniums and petunias showed off their colors in the sunlight. "Pretty much like you and George said. Working your search pattern in the area when the call comes out. The deputy from Rye County advises over the radio that he is going to check things out and then you arrive on the scene..."

"Grover."

"What?"

"Grover Parsons. That was his name, the Rye County deputy. Just a boy really, barely old enough to be a deputy."

"Oh, right. Sorry, I don't have much on that. Rye County is working that part of the case. He was a brave boy. He did his duty." Shaklee waited for a moment. It was clear that the death of the young deputy along with everything else was a painful memory. "He did his duty, just as you and George did."

"Did we?"

"Yes. You did." He waited until Sharon's moist eyes looked up. "You did your duty, Sharon. Saved the girl's life and the boy who

345

followed her. Parsons did his duty. He did what any of us would have done, and yes, he paid the price for it. I don't have an answer for that." Shrugging as if to ward off the inevitable, he added, "Sometimes bad things happen to good people, no matter what you do."

"Yes, sometimes," Sharon agreed. "And the shooting?"

"That. Yes, well that seems to be pretty straightforward, doesn't it? You were in hot pursuit of a killer. He exchanged fire with you. George tracked him into the woods. Another exchange of gunfire. George ended it using the force necessary to take the suspect out before he hurt someone else. One round fired at fairly close rang. Forensics confirms it was from George's Glock."

"That's it?"

"Shouldn't it be?" He was looking out of the window behind Price. "I can't think of anything else, Sharon. Can you?" His eyes shifted to her face.

"No," she said firmly. "But I've heard that that asshole sheriff down in Pickham is making a stir. That we didn't look at all of the evidence. That the shooting was more than just self-defense. He's calling it an execution, but he doesn't want to do the investigation himself. Too much political liability."

"Really. So, what do you think?"

"I think George did what he had to do." The statement and the look on her face indicated the finality of her opinion in the matter.

"Yes, well I look at it this way. There was a firefight that started when the killer fired on you and continued when George followed him into the woods. There were a number of gunshots, and the bad guy ended up dead. Anything else is pure speculation, and we don't deal in speculation." Now the look of finality was on Shaklee's face. "Like you said, George did what he had to do."

He looked out to the landscaped flower beds again. The matter was closed from the GBI's point of view.

"So, partner," he continued. "Have a new case for us. Series of convenience store robberies between here and Macon. Locals, a police chief and a sheriff, are requesting assistance with the investigation. You up for it?"

"Chief and a sheriff? Geez, how could I refuse."

"Good, meet me for lunch, and we'll go over the case file."

Bob Shaklee turned and walked down the corridor with a final wave of his hand. Sharon Price picked up the pages of the report and dropped them in the out basket at the edge of her desk. Case closed.

****

The small group on the porch was quiet. The glasses of sweet iced tea in their hands dripped condensation onto the bare planks where the water soaked in and disappeared.

The parents of Paula Jean Glover looked across the yard to the trees and the path leading through the woods to the old church and tried to understand the events that had connected their pretty, petite daughter to Mrs. Sims and her dead husband, Harold. There were no satisfactory answers.

Angel Sims sat quietly, her son's hand resting on top of hers on the arm of the rocking chair. Other than greetings and small talk about the weather, there had not been much conversation.

Finally, Paula Glover's mother pulled her eyes away from the trees and faced them.

"I...we can't tell you how sorry we are for the loss of your husband, Mrs. Sims."

"There's nothing to say," Mrs. Sims replied in a small voice that was almost a whisper. "What's done, is done."

"I know, but somehow, it feels...it feels wrong that you were dragged into this situation."

The old woman studied the younger woman for a moment before speaking. "Honey, there is no need for guilt. You lost a daughter. I lost my Harold. A bad man did it, not you. He did bad things to Harold and to your girl, and now he's gone."

There was finality to her words. Nothing would change what had happened. Bad things happened to people sometimes. Too many times, Angel Sims thought, but they happened anyway. She had lived long enough to accept the inevitability of that fact.

"Your husband tried to save our little girl." Paula Glover's father turned his tear stained face towards Mrs. Sims and her son. "I thank you for that."

There was nothing more to say. The losses of both families were equally tragic and equally inexplicable. A terrible, bad thing had happened, and the lives of the old man and young girl had meandered through the world until they met in the dark in the church parking lot. There was no meaning, only pain.

A few minutes later, the dripping glasses were placed gently on the porch, and the Glovers drove away.

****

The out-of-focus form over him slowly took shape. His eyes felt glued together.

"Cy," was all Clay could manage to say at the sight of his brother. He felt Cy's strong grip on his hand.

"'Bout time you woke up." Clay perceived that the smile on Cy's face was more one of relief than any other emotion.

"Mama?"

"She's fine. Been by your side for a week now. I sent her back to the motel to get some rest. I'll let her know you're awake. She'll want to be here."

Clay nodded.

"The girl. Last I remember…" His voice faded. It was an effort to force the air up from his lungs, over the vocal chords and out of his mouth to speak.

"She's alive. Not good though. The things that he did to her. They don't tell us much, but it was bad. They have her in a room. She'll be okay physically, lot of cuts and scars, but she'll heal. They have her in some kind of counseling for emotional and mental trauma. I've been checking on her. I knew you'd want to know. I guess it'll be a while before things get back to normal for her, if they ever do."

The look of guilt and pain that flashed across the young man's face was unmistakable.

"It's not your fault brother," Cy said. "If anyone is to blame, it's

348

me. I'm the one who wanted her gone so we could get back to work. She was just a distraction." He paused and then continued, "I'm the guilty one. Not you. You saved her life they say. You and that deputy in Rye County. That buckshot you put in his leg slowed him down, and the deputy from Pickham killed him. Been in all the papers, not just the Everett Gazette, but the Atlanta Journal-Constitution, too. You're a pretty big deal."

"Don't feel too much like a big deal," he managed to whisper.

"Well, you are." Cy's grip on his brothers hand tightened. "I'm proud of you. And something else, I wish I had been...I wish I *was* more like you."

The brothers sat hand in hand until Clay drifted off to sleep again, and Cy could wipe the tears off of his face.

****

In another room, on another floor, Lyn sat in a chair staring out into the hospital courtyard. Ruby Stinson sat beside her daughter, their arms entwined. They spent much of the time like that.

Lyn seemed to drift off to another place, a place her mother could not go, and it made the burden of guilt heavy for the older woman. She had sent her young daughter out into a world she knew nothing about. It was an act of desperation, but in doing so, she had almost lost her daughter. Still, she did not know what else she could have done. Her father would have beaten her, probably to death.

She reached up, touched the swollen side of her own face, and then withdrew her hand at the pain. As it was, the old man had beaten her badly after regaining consciousness the night Lyn left. So badly, that she had called the law on him, for the first time. Oh, there had been plenty of other times she could have called, should have called, she knew. But fearing for her daughter's life and sending her away and then the beating...it was too much, the final pain and degradation.

The old man was in the Pickham County Jail on domestic violence charges where he would probably stay until trial. Word around Judges Creek was that no one would be bailing the mean, son of a bitch out of jail, so they were safe, for a while. It seemed that Carl Stinson's relationship with the world was no better than with his family.

Ruby wondered if it had always been that way. There must have been some happy times early on. If so, the memories had faded in the swirl of physical and mental abuse that had become her life.

The sheriff's department had put her in touch with a women's advocacy group. Lyn's ordeal had received a good deal of coverage in the press, and the group was going to great lengths to assist the mother and daughter.

The case's notoriety had put a spotlight on the abuse of women and children. And while the group would have assisted in any event, they were sparing no effort or expense to help the two. She had a hotel room in Athens for as long as Lyn was recovering in the hospital.

They were helping with something else too. For the first time, Ruby was talking to someone who could help her understand the patterns of domestic violence, and her own self-worth so that the pattern in this case would be broken permanently.

The counseling for the mother would continue for months. For the daughter, it might be necessary for the rest of her life. Lyn's counselor had assured her mother that the emotional scars her daughter bore would heal slowly. They might possibly be healed completely, one day, but there were no guarantees.

The guilt for what had happened to Lyn was overwhelming. She could have acted to stop the abuse years ago. She should have, she knew it. Somehow, she couldn't. She had been trapped.

But now, maybe the puzzle could be unraveled. Maybe, with the counseling, she would end the cycle. She was coming to understand that what had happened to her daughter was the result of a long chain of events. Break that chain, and you could change your life. Ruby Stinson's heart ached for not having broken the chain earlier.

Wrapping her arm more tightly around Lyn's, she pulled the girl as close to her as she could. There was no response, but the warmth of the contact with her daughter brought her some small comfort.

Lyn's eyes focused intently on the tops of the swaying pine trees in the courtyard. They pulled her in, and she felt herself leaving the hospital room again, even as her mother struggled to hold her close. It was to no avail. Lyn drifted to a faraway place where her mother could not go.

****

Gerald Parsons sat quietly on the porch of his small house nestled among the trees at the base of one of the foothills of the Appalachian Mountains. The southern end of the Appalachian Trail was only a few miles from that spot. From there you could hike all the way to Maine if you had a mind to, and good, strong set of legs. He and Grover had hiked parts of it all through north Georgia when Grover was still a boy.

"Good night, Gerald." Sheriff Bill Siler had been coming by to visit Grover's father as much as possible since the young deputy's murder. They rarely spoke. There wasn't anything to say.

Mostly, Siler just sat on the porch with him hoping in some way that his company might dull the knifing pain in the father's heart. It seemed to have no effect, but he would not abandon the man whose boy did not abandon his duty.

Parsons pulled his empty gaze away from the darkness that surrounded the small house and nodded his good night back to the sheriff. An instant later, he was lost again in the darkness. There was no other world for him, only the dark loss of the boy that had been his life

Things moved in the dark, in the trees. Mostly harmless, some not. Gerald Parsons ignored them all and listened, straining to hear. But the husky, happy voice of his son was gone. So many things were gone.

****

Some small creature moved in the high grass in the ditch alongside the dirt road. Tom Ridley took no notice. He stood quietly at the edge of his property looking down the dirt road. The place where he had found the young girl's body was visible. The grass and weeds had been trampled down by the deputies and GBI people. Remnants of yellow crime scene tape fluttered in the breeze. It was still dark, but in the dim, misty light of the oncoming day, he could just make out the silhouette of a vehicle.

Behind him in the little frame house, he could hear his wife busying herself with breakfast. It was a comforting sound. One he took pleasure in most mornings as he stood for a few minutes in the yard looking at the sky, watching the stars fade. After a few minutes, he would smell coffee and sometimes bacon frying. But this morning, he paid no attention to the homey sounds and smells. Turning, he walked briskly into the house.

"Breakfast be ready in a few minutes, Tom," Margaret said from the kitchen.

Reaching up over the front door, he took the shotgun from the two pegs that served as a gun rack and then reached into a box on a shelf under the pegs, pulling out four .00 buckshot shells.

"Tom?" Margaret said from the doorway. "What are you doing?"

Without looking he said, "Nothing. Just gonna go check something."

"Tom! What is it? You stop right there and tell me what's going on."

He turned and looked at her. "Nothing...probably nothing. Looks like a car or truck down the road. Down there where..."

Margaret Ridley nodded her head. "All right then. Be careful."

Tom nodded, turned, and walked out the door. As he crossed the little dirt yard, he heard the screen door open behind him. He knew that Margaret would be watching from the driveway.

Holding the shotgun in both hands, the barrel pointing to the side but at the ready, he walked quickly and quietly down the road. His boots made no sound in the dirt.

As he got within fifty feet of the vehicle, the door opened and the interior light came on. Tom relaxed and let the barrel of the shotgun lower, resting it under one arm.

George Mackey stepped out of the truck.

"Morning, Tom."

"Mornin', George." Ridley came closer until they could see each other clearly in the dim light from the truck's interior.

"You're not going to shoot me with that are you?"

"Naw, George, not gonna shoot you. Didn't know who it was down here. Just checking."

"Yea. I know. Me too."

The two men stood there, looking into the weeds and grass on the side of the road. The yellow crime scene tape was still there, wrapped around trees and brush, marking off the area where the girl's body had been found.

Tom reached into his shirt pocket, pulled a cigarette from a beat up pack, and lit up. He looked at George and held the pack out. George just shook his head. The two men leaned against the sheriff's truck not saying anything for a few minutes.

Finally, Tom broke the silence.

"I thought it was you."

"What?"

"That morning. I was standing in the yard and heard the car tires moving. I thought it was you. Figured you'd been napping."

"I know. You told me. I wish to God it had been me, Tom."

"Yea, me too. I reckon that fella would have had a surprise when he pulled down my road if you'd been there."

"Yea, Tom. I reckon...who knows...maybe I'd have had the surprise."

"Oh, you'd have got him, George. You're a good deputy."

George felt the guilt well up inside him. He looked over at Tom.

"Not that good, Tom. Not very good at all."

Tom let the words fade away for a moment before speaking. "George, you didn't kill that girl. She was already dead." They were almost the same words George had spoken to him the day Tom found the girl's body.

George looked down at the dust around his feet. "You know, I *was* napping that night. Just not on your road, Tom."

Tom said nothing. Taking a long drag on his cigarette, the glow of the butt cast an orange hue over his face.

George went on, "I saw the car go by...I didn't stop it. I didn't do anything. Just went back to napping. I could have, but I didn't." His words faded off.

Tom thought this over, considering what George had said and weighing what it meant. Then he spoke.

"No, George. You're a good deputy. Everyone does things they wish they didn't do. That don't make them bad. That's just mistakes. The fella that did what he did to that little girl was just bad. Bad as I've ever seen. But he did it, not you. Maybe you could have caught him that night if you weren't napping. That would have been a good thing. Maybe you wouldn't have caught him. Maybe he would have killed you too. That's a lot of maybe's. No way to know. But you did get him, George. Remember that. You got him."

George made no response, and the silence grew up around them again.

After a few more minutes, Tom said, "Well, I gotta go get to work. I'll be seeing you, George."

"Yeah," George replied, as Tom turned and walked back up the dirt road, shotgun under his arm. The sky was slowly changing from deep black to charcoal gray. The day was coming on now, and George could make out the form of a woman up the road by the Ridley's drive. It was Margaret, watching and waiting for Tom to return.

George knew that Tom would be shoveling chicken shit out of the barns most of the day. Even so, life for the Ridleys in the little frame house was good enough. Maybe not special. It didn't have to be anything special. Just life was good enough. He wasn't sure that it would ever be good enough for him again.

Deputy George Mackey's head turned at the sound of a breeze rustling through the weeds on the side of the road where the girl's body had lain. Climbing into the pickup, he drove slowly down Ridley Road. His eyes avoided the rearview mirror.

End

Hi and thanks for reading. As an independent author, a Review is always appreciated. Also, be the first to know when my next book is available! Follow me on Book Bub at <ins>https://www.bookbub.com/authors/glenn-trust</ins> to get an alert whenever there is a new release, preorder, or discount!

Grab Your Next Suspense Thriller

What would they do for power? Everything.

Ready for a political conspiracy thriller that will keep you on the edge of your seat? When prominent leaders of both political parties begin turning up dead The Hunters are called in to track down the killers. Book 2 in The Hunters Series will have you wondering who the good and bad guys are. Check out Sanctioned Murder, a taut political conspiracy thriller. Find it at this link online: <ins>https://www.bookbub.com/books/sanctioned-murder-the-term-limits-conspiracy-the-hunters-book-2-by-glenn-trust</ins> to get your copy now or click the book cover below.

FREE Book Here!

The lightning waits for us all. When it calls, we will go.

Join us at Glenn Trust Books and receive a free download of

Lightning in the Clouds

Download your Free copy today by Clicking Here or follow this
link>>> https://dl.bookfunnel.com/7046vhk5f9

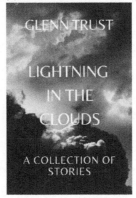

In addition to your Free copy of Lightning in the Clouds, you'll
receive:

- Exclusive previews, insights and samples of New
  Releases

- Book Launch Giveaways and Promotions

- Advance Notice of Member Discounts and Sales

**No Spam – No More than one email per Week – We never share
your address... Ever.**

Contact Glenn Trust

I love hearing from readers, so feel free to email me at
gtrust@glenntrust.com. I respond to all emails personally, so be
patient, I promise to get to yours.

You can also contact me at my Facebook Page at
https://www.facebook.com/GlennTrustBooks/ and leave a
message.

About the Author

Glenn Trust is a native of the south but has lived in most regions
of the country at one time or another. Varied experiences from
construction worker to police officer, corporate executive to city

manager, color and provide insight into the characters he creates. His stories are known for detailed plots, solid research, and realism.

There are no superheroes or knights in shining armor in his stories. According to Trust, knights are for fairy tales. His books are gritty and based in the real world with characters who face their frailties while dealing with their roles in the story. The heroes are average people doing the best they can.

Also missing from his stories are any references to vampires, zombies, super villains, or other assorted monsters. Trust's monsters hide behind the smiling faces that pass us on the street. They look like us, and this makes them more frightening.

He is the author of the bestselling Hunters, Blue Eyes-The Journey, and Sole Justice Series of mystery/suspense/thrillers as well as stand-alone novels and short stories.

Today, he writes full-time and lives quietly with his wife and two dogs, Gunner and Charlie. You can find all of his work on his Book Bub author page, or check out his Facebook Page - Glenn Trust Books where you can sign up for his email group to receive updates on new releases and upcoming book promotions.

More Books by Glenn Trust

Click Here > Glenn Trust Books to find all of his work, including:

The Hunters Series:
Eyes of the Predator
Sanctioned Murder
Black Water Murder
Blood Reckoning
Redemption
The Killing Ground
Walk into Darkness
Lost

Blue Eyes Series:
An Eye for Death
A Desert View
Blue Water Horizon
Nowhere Land
Fruits of Evil
Color of Death

Sole Justice Series:
Sole Survivor
Road to Justice
Target Down
The Ghost (October 2021)

Other Novels:
Dying Embers
Mojave Sun

Lightning in the Clouds - A collection of Short Stories

Made in United States
Orlando, FL
28 January 2022